Praise for Spencer Wise's *The E[mperor of Shoes]*

"Evocative... *The Emperor of Shoes* underscor[es]
promise of economic opportunity still moves people across great distances
on our planet... [A novel] of our times..."

—*New York Times Book Review*

"[Wise's] illuminating debut novel, with its dark subplot, is an eye-opener
on China's poor laborers and their often perilous attempts to seek justice.
The Emperor of Shoes is a story that will stay with you."

—*NJ.com*

"East meets West in this accomplished debut novel about globalization,
capitalist exploitation of workers, and father/son relationships....
Recommended for readers interested in globalization, diversity, and social
justice."

—*Library Journal*

"Vividly rendered... A fascinating look at China's race for economic growth."

—*Kirkus Reviews*

"Alex is a fine disciple of the anxious and articulate narrators in whose
footsteps he follows. Many readers will be taken in by him and the well-
constructed plot of the book."

—*Jewish Book Council*

"There is a looking glass through which we'd usually rather not peer, one
whose vista reveals the human, social and political costs paid overseas
so that we can enjoy our low-cost lifestyle at home. When Spencer Wise,
in his debut novel, *The Emperor of Shoes*, directs our gaze, however, we
see not only the dangers and exploitations of such a system, but also the
hopes, dreams and delicate relationships that make it work and that must
be risked if change is possible. Part love story, part father-son fable, part
dark initiation, this powerful debut novel wonderfully brings into focus the
ways we are all interconnected in a complex and global world."

—**Adam Johnson, Pulitzer Prize–winning author of**
The Orphan Master's Son

"Wise has written a funny, illuminating page turner of a novel about an American father and son and a shoe factory in China. *The Emperor of Shoes* is heartbreakingly personal, timely and political, written with plenty of Yiddish and humor. 'Made in China' the label says, but few of us have any idea what that means. Through unforgettable characters and dire circumstances, Wise shows us factory life and politics, ultimately pointing us in the direction of the possibility for a better future."

—Bethany Ball, author of *What to Do About the Solomons*

"Spencer Wise's *The Emperor of Shoes* is the most complex, nuanced, character-rich first novel I have ever read. It is utterly original in portraying a twenty-first-century Jewish diaspora with an accompanying empathy for China's grassroots aspirations. Wise comes to us fully flighted as a master stylist and a compelling storyteller."

—Robert Olen Butler, Pulitzer Prize–winning author of *A Good Scent from a Strange Mountain*

"What Wise brings to a story of hot-button issues is a light hand, a mix of sensitive characters, a propulsive plot, and humor."

—Louisa Ermelino, *Publishers Weekly*

"Brimming with comedic genius, *The Emperor of Shoes* is a commentary on American naivete and willfully blind greed that speaks to our collective human history of oppression and inhumanity. Wise opens us up with humor then refuses to pull his punches. He remains hopeful—against diminishing odds—about love and the sacrifices we make in its name."

—Julianna Baggott, author of *Pure* and *The Seventh Book of Wonders*

"Fresh and innovative, Spencer Wise's *The Emperor of Shoes* is the latest addition to the tradition of young-man fiction that starts with Bellow and Roth... I've taught for more than forty years; this is the best first novel I've ever read."

—David Kirby, National Book Award–nominated author of *The House on Boulevard St.*

"A boisterous debut, Spencer Wise's *The Emperor of Shoes* keenly evokes the contradictions of a rapidly evolving China: the ugliness and the beauty; the cynicism and the passion; the absurdity and the tragedy. With his energetic characterization and winning dialogue, Wise turns a sharp yet compassionate eye on the foibles of a not-so-innocent abroad. This is an accomplished, engaging novel."

—Molly Patterson, author of *Rebellion*

THE
EMPEROR
OF
SHOES

—————— A NOVEL ——————

SPENCER WISE

HANOVER
SQUARE
PRESS

HANOVER
SQUARE
PRESS

Recycling programs
for this product may
not exist in your area.

ISBN-13: 978-1-335-00548-9

The Emperor of Shoes

A hardcover edition of this book was published in 2018 by Hanover Square Press.

First Hanover Square Press trade paperback edition published May 2019.

Library of Congress Cataloging-in-Publication Data has been applied for.

HanoverSqPress.com
BookClubbish.com

Printed in U.S.A.

for my dad

THE
EMPEROR
OF
SHOES

IT'S A BRIGHT MOON OUTSIDE, AND FROM THE window of my house I can see the skeletal gray of the factory, the banners draped like sashes and the deep arterial red of Mandarin characters demanding change, and I'm wondering how the fuck this Jewish kid from Boston could somehow wind up a YouTube hero in the Chinese Revolution.

I'm standing by the window thinking about Jews and shoes and this beautiful Chinese woman asleep behind me.

Ivy.

I should go to her now. Crawl into bed and wrap her in my arms.

But I don't move.

I see my face half-dissolved in the glass. My own eyes reflected back.

So this is the place I came to first for my father. Guangdong, where Dad has made shoes for what feels like forever. South China. This country that my father embraced. In his own demented way, of course. He wanted me here. But not *here* here, as in this moment, on the night of the protests.

Something else must've brought me to this country. Because I ended up someplace I never would've expected. Nor my father. Nor any of us.

It's quiet in the house, but I can still hear the workers chanting. What a sound. They listened to us, didn't they? The workers. And tomorrow more people will listen and see on YouTube.

I brace myself against the window frame and turn back to Ivy on the bed. I can see her clearly, bluing in the moonlight behind me, twisted in the white sheet. She's knitting her brow the way she does when she calls me on my bullshit—of which there's plenty—and her lips are moving silently as if she's still shouting into the megaphone, dreaming of what we've been through.

But I never could have anticipated her being here in my bed.

I know her, don't I? I've been to her village, to Beijing—places sacred to her.

But there's always something out of reach. Some feeling that even as well as I know her now, I'm not sure I know her at all.

I turn back to the window.

Palm trees in the yard, trunks white with lime. Rain dripping off the broad leaves. A scrungy cat hiding in the hollow of a banyan tree.

I can't sleep.

Dad's over at the hotel in Nanhai and maybe he's in the tub and the water's rushing up, the faucet steams, the water rises, lapping at the sides, spilling over onto the white tiles. The water keeps rising until it's right under his nose, even with the lip of the tub, and he says to Karri, "Shut it off."

But you're kidding yourself, Pops. There's no shutting it off now.

There are decisions to make by sunrise. My father. Ivy.

This world is opening. Has opened. It's not the closed little plant that my father built. It's a different world, the one I'm going to be living in, and I don't understand my place in it.

A Jew. Is that what I am? I don't know. Maybe I'm the schmuck who lost China. Who ruined everything.

What does that even mean here in China? To be a Jew. I'm now a citizen of the world? We've always been citizens of the world. No, that's not true. We've always been outsiders. On the run.

But where to?

I turn away from the window and I walk over to the bed and sit on the edge of the mattress with my back to Ivy.

And I think: it was just her and me and whatever passed between us on her grandmother's houseboat. The beginning, for us, for everything. That much I know, even if the rest is not very clear. It was Ivy and me sitting back-to-back on a tin-roofed houseboat on the Pearl River with a nuclear power plant vanishing in the dusk along the far bank, while her grandmother cleaned a chicken and threw the feathers overboard.

One

IVY WAS A STITCHER FROM THE SAMPLE ROOM and a former organizer at Tiananmen. Her name of course is not Ivy but Hanjia Liu, a name I was always botching, my up-tones down, or down up, and even though I very badly wanted to say it correctly, it wound up being this terrible mystery in my mouth.

I felt her damp back against mine, a heat spreading along her spine—this was more than we'd ever touched. I wanted to reach back and take her hand, but I knew this wasn't a date. It was very hot. Sitting there quietly was enough. *Dayenu.* That drippy Passover song triggered on reflex. *It would have been enough.* The lie of gratitude. Everyone wants more.

Suddenly I felt the weight of Ivy's hair lifted off my shoulders, a coolness on my neck, and without turning around I knew she had put up her hair in a hastily swirled bun without any sort of tie as she always did before she ate. She handed me a piece of dragon fruit, and I bit it, crisp and light, crunched on the tiny black seeds. Before the sweetness on my lips evaporated, her hand was beside my ear again, another pearly white slice pinched between her index and middle fingers. Already she had sewing knuckles, bony red swelling in the joints below her nails. I took the fruit. We ate in silence. I had the urge to fill it with any old nonsense, just to hear noise, terrified by the calmness like a boot on my chest. If only there was a way to stay in that moment. Of course I couldn't. I had to face my father. Ivy said she didn't want to make me choose between them, between a father and a *dagongmei*, a migrant, working girl.

I had to get back; I was going to be late to meet him for dinner at the hotel. A whole afternoon had quietly slipped past since I got on the back of Ivy's motorbike at the shoe factory *like a lunatic who wants to get kidnapped*, as my father would say, and she took me here to her grandmother's riverboat on the eve of the Tomb Sweeping holiday when it's expected that all children come home.

The way out was climbing onto one of the Styrofoam block rafts and ferrying myself to shore and taking Ivy's motorbike back to the hotel where my father was likely tying an Izod pullover around his waist, slipping into boat shoes and dabbing a swale of Neosporin under each nostril so he didn't catch a cold because *China is the last place to fuck around*. And unbeknownst to my father but very beknownst to Ivy, his own security guards, for an extra fifty yuan, had slid Ivy's leaflets for a new workers' union under the doors at the dormitories. But as long as I sat there in the old tin-roofed houseboat, as long as I stayed put and focused on what was in front of me, I was fine. The moment I moved I became a traitor.

Enough already. I rose to my feet, my legs numb from sitting so long, and as I was punching my thighs to get the blood flowing, Ivy bickered with her grandmother in Chinese. I swung my leg over the gunwale and my foot touched the Styrofoam block, this makeshift raft in the water that would take me the fifty yards to shore. Ivy handed me the ferry pole, warning that it wasn't as easy as it looked, balancing on this block not much wider than my shoulders. Now I had both feet down, wobbling badly, and I paddled in long strokes like a ferryman. I felt the whole village's eyes on me, the weight of expectation. My father had probably left for dinner without me, and he was already at the *churrascaria* in the hotel yelling *fish*! at the waiters carrying swords of lamb. The Emperor demanded fish, not *treif*. Dad had as much religion as you'd find in a pork bun, but that wouldn't stop him from invoking God if that fish didn't come snappy.

The raft teetered to the left, dipped below the waterline, and I was squatting flat-footed and spread-kneed as I'd seen the fishermen do; it was a position you had to learn in China to survive. There was no reason I couldn't. On the top of my thighs I felt a good burn and an ache building in my knees, but you couldn't stand up, no one did. I made twenty yards without too much problem when my knees began to quake. I felt eyes on me. But I couldn't go back, couldn't lose face even in front of strangers.

So I kept dipping the pole into the water and pulling it along the length of my body, but the burn in my knees turned to a violent tremble, and I stood. One moment, my shoulders squared to the shore, the next I'd fallen off the raft, straight into my father's poison. Our poison. This river roiling with chrome and lime, sulfur and soda ash. *It's nasty business, boy.* For a moment I saw it coming right up to my face like black syrup, a hard sheen, and then I hit on my right side. Under. The water singeing my nostrils. Lye. I tucked my chin to my chest and blew out through my nose. Eyes sealed tight, lips too, but a taste of rust bled through, a drop of silver on the tip of my tongue. Blackness and terror. The knock of the tip of my sneaker against something hard. Drag of my heavy clothes, as if the river was going to swallow me, draw me deeper. One arm was quick to fly up while the other scraped to the side, my legs, too, out of sync, lost in my own body thrashing for the surface. A burn in my lungs. My blood screamed.

My head broke free. I took a huge breath and I heard the village laughing and yelling, *gweilo*! Ghost man in Cantonese. In the factory everyone was known by their job: heel puller, freight girl, fecalist, glue mixer, and I was the Head of Development, but as soon as I stepped outside the factory I was *gweilo* and had been from the start a year ago. A heavy ammoniac smell wafted off the water as I swam, lifting my chin high, to the cement landing on the shore, not ten feet from a yawning corrugated metal sewage pipe.

A Chinese man in a white pressed shirt and slacks stood on the landing with his kid and wife who was lifting her long skirt slightly off the wet slab. The husband waved RMB bills in the air, shouting to the boats for fresh carp, and I tried not to think about that fish coming out of the same river. But I was glad he was there, because the houseboats tacked over to business mode and forgot me. Reaching into their pails, the fishermen hooked a finger into the gills of the carp, and held them high above their heads, tails flapping, for the customer to choose.

I hauled myself out of the water onto the landing right beside the city man who took one glance and said, Ah, ah, ah, then went right back to haggling, as if nothing unusual happened: another fully clothed *gweilo* crawling out of the river. On top of the steep bank, Ivy's motorbike, an old Honda CG125 with a bright orange fuel tank, leaned up against the skeleton of a Russian Tupolev plane, crash-landed and abandoned in a bramble of bamboo and vine, and stripped clean as a scalded pig, a steel carcass with the iron beams curved like whale bones. Most of the roofs on the houseboats were scrabbled together with aluminum paneling from the plane. These were China's first commercial planes, the ones my father rode from Beijing to Guangzhou, bucking and diving under inexperienced hands, falling from the sky all over the country.

One of the men on the bank loading his flatbed with crates of lychee stopped to throw me a fishy towel from the cab of his truck. A coarse rag with deep crimson stains, sparkle of scales and a heavy scent. But he was watching me closely, so I wiped myself down, leaving my face alone, and tossed it back. Reeking of fish guts and dehairing chemicals was not how I wanted to show up late to dinner with my father. But if I got right on the bike and hurried then maybe I'd have time to change, though, by now, he was probably done with his meal and reaching his hand over the glass sneeze-guard of the Häagen-Dazs cart with the sign on top that reads Ice Cream: Messiah of Happiness and scooping himself a big bowl of French vanilla while one of the waitresses rushed across the room, waving her hands over her head and apologizing for neglecting him. *Oh, now you come running?*

I pulled my cell phone out of my pocket but of course it was dead. The last text message from my father received a few hours ago had read: "ERA?," and I'd sent back, "In Little League? About 7.25. 10 if I was crying." He'd meant ETA of course, but I'd silenced the phone after that, so whatever he wrote back was a mystery.

Turning to Ivy's motorbike, I lifted the choke, pulled the clutch and slammed my foot down on the kick start, all in the order that she'd taught me. I waved one last time to Ivy, who was standing on the bow of the boat. Aside from her, I think the whole village was ready for me to leave.

Ivy had lied to her grandmother and pretended I was her boyfriend. "A white boyfriend is better than nothing," she'd said to me. Her family called her *sheng nu,* a leftover woman, she'd told me, while we were eating at the BBQ street stalls outside the market in Li Shui, not far from the factory. That's where we first started talking, over oysters with garlic, chicken feet, pork sausage.

"Unwanted," she whispered, and I thought, That's crazy, you're not unwanted by me. I bet a hell of a lot of people want you.

I'd figured she wasn't more than twenty-four, but who knew. I didn't pretend to understand Chinese culture. Maybe twenty-four was late. Or maybe she was much older and I couldn't tell.

"Is your family originally from down here?" I asked.

"Yes. But I have business in Beijing."

"Business."

"Yes."

She left it vague. Maybe she meant an ex-husband. Or maybe she *was* married. I didn't want to push.

"It's nice?" I asked. "Beijing. I haven't been yet."

"It's changed."

"Since?"

Ivy tightened up. She stared at me. Didn't blink or look away.

"Tiananmen," she said.

"You mean—" And then I stopped myself because it was obvious that's what she meant. I straightened up in my chair. Thinking about 1989, trying to do the math in my head. Was she forty? She could be. Even with me figuring she was twenty-four she could be forty. I looked harder and there was a puckering around the eyes, a wrinkle—no, I was making all that up. There were no signs. You wouldn't know. Maybe if you were Chinese and you knew where to look. But not me.

"So you were young," I said. "When everything—"

She nodded. "I am thirty-six."

She wasn't shy about it.

"I'm sorry," I said. Then I tapped myself on the forehead. "Not about thirty-six. About the other—"

"It's okay," she said, smiling.

I turned away from her.

A few tables down, a girl was taking the extensions out of her friend's hair. It was like she was reaching into the roots and peeling off these wide wefts of stiff black hair, and I suddenly had this flash of one of my mother's wigs—one of these *sheitels* she wore once she'd gone full-blown Orthodox—hanging on the bedpost, its bald owner smoking by the window.

I looked back at Ivy.

Her hair was her own. Real. I was thinking about what had happened in that decade, that black hole between us, whatever it was she'd seen. She knew things, more than me, and I wanted to know everything, and suddenly I was think-ing about her hair falling forward into my face and her lips hovering above mine and somehow I ended up saying, "I'm younger."

She laughed. "I know."

"I'm twenty-six," I said. I should've lied. Tried thirty-one on her.

"You wouldn't remember—you're too young."

Tiananmen she meant. It took me a second because I was thinking about what she called me. "I do a little," I lied. "Some things. I remember my father talking."

She drew back, but she didn't answer. She wound up chang-ing topics. I read that as her way of saying there was too much between us.

But on the riverboat, I knew Ivy had used me to give her grandmother hope, and the truth was I didn't mind being used as long as I was useful to her. Since her grandmother disliked Americans and the British for political reasons, I'd played, at Ivy's suggestion, an inspired Australian language teacher, faultlessly rendered, every stereotype I could recall, until the grandmother told me I sounded nothing like the Australian missionary stationed at her house when she was ten. Ivy had translated this to me and finished by saying, "She spent a lot of time with him, and she doesn't think you sound Australian."

"What happened to *'She'll buy anything'*?" I asked.

"I forgot about Australia," Ivy said. "Sorry. But don't make frowns or she'll know she caught us. Can you do a Switzerland accent? I promise she does not know about Switzerland."

So I became Swiss, though mostly it sounded as if I'd had a sudden stroke that left the right side of my face paralyzed. Ivy's grandmother smiled politely and let me get through a few sentences before saying something in Cantonese, which Ivy translated as, "You can't put a swan back in its egg."

I'd brought Ivy's grandmother the hopelessly lame present of espadrille heels from the factory. She blushed when she tried them on, somehow squeezing her foot—like splintered driftwood, knobby and crooked—inside the shoes. Better I should have given her a head of cabbage. Still, she wore them for the rest of the afternoon while mending one of her fishing nets and prepping dinner. A few times I caught her wincing when she had to walk, possibly bleeding on the back of the heel, but when we told her to take them off and relax, she crossed her legs at the knee, arched her back and lifted her chin. "I feel like a woman you see out in the world," she said. "This is how city girls sit, isn't it?" Ivy giggled through the translation. Then her grandmother put her legs wide apart, and leaned forward, elbows on thick knees. "This is how we sit in the country. Always something between our legs." She grabbed her fishing net, dropped it between her feet and began sewing.

I remembered this botched plan as I went wheeling on the motorbike down the narrow dirt paths between rice paddies.

My skin tingled, a dull itchy burn, and the cold wind pasted my wet jeans to my legs. I passed women walking back from the fields, slow and determined, wooden yokes across their shoulders carrying bamboo bundles lashed with string. The rice fields ran up to a village, and I was weaving through snug alleys with the smell of wood smoke and there was a family stir-frying *shahe fen* for the holiday by a fire pit and I could see just a part of their faces, each one lit in the quiet flame, but one face jumped out, that of a young woman, and just for a brief second her round face rose to mine and just as quickly it vanished.

Foshan in the distance: spotlights on top of the skyscrapers scanned the river as if they were looking for someone down below where the first fireworks came sizzling off the barges, exploding red and gold against the tarred sky. I couldn't walk into the hotel restaurant like this: shivering, clothes rumpled and half-wet, smelling like old fish and factory sludge. One step in and Dad would size me right up: *Oh, you've decided to come dressed like our old super, Chaim Pupik, from the cellar.* I turned onto Haiwu Road, the Intercontinental Hotel rose before me like a black column. A fog had rolled in, sitting high up on the building, which looked like an upside-down reflection of itself in the water: the bottom half-smooth and slate, the top all wiggly and distorted and smoky, as if the hotel grew through a misty lake. The building was brand-spanking new, in the last four years, same with the canal and the lake; nothing here, not even the blacktop beneath my tires, was more than five years old. Every pavilion and park and shrub, balanced and harmonized, five elements in perfect accord, clean and tidy, and on the street-side of the Interconti, standing on the manicured grass, a taxi driver was pissing on a red azalea bush.

I parked Ivy's bike beside a fleet of Rolls Royces and Bentleys. The head doorman, Li Jun—hair oiled back—came bombing down the steps and asked, "Good evening, Mr. Younger Cohen? And how is the respected one above, Mr. Cohen?"

"Just fine."

Li Jun has known my father for as long as he's lived in this hotel. But I bet my dad doesn't even know his name.

I palmed Li Jun two ten-yuan coins to park the bike under the hotel. He shook them like dice in his fist—that was the sound of the hotel—coins jangling. If you didn't tip, you might as well have been a ghost, no one would serve you.

Past the revolving lobby doors, the first blast of air-conditioning swam up to my chin. I shivered, my shirt like wet cardboard. Coming straight toward me was Karri, the Chinese hotel manager in her cardinal-red pencil skirt, matching blazer, hair tied back in a solemn bun, and her hands folded in front. Her heels conked on the marble then silently sank into the crimson rug with golden arabesques that looked like hundreds of flirty eyes winking. She was in my father's shoes. One of his designs: faux snake, a pink plug on the vamp.

I was betting she was going to say something related to my attire: "Perhaps you aren't aware of our rear door?" She'd studied hospitality in Sweden. *Imagine the house she keeps.* But instead Karri said, "Pursue me," pivoted sharply on one heel, a military vestige of her middle-school PLA training, and walked briskly toward the elevator.

"Follow you?" I asked.

She was already ten steps ahead when she wheeled around with her eyes closed in frustration. "Yes. Yes. Follow. In present."

"Now?"

"YES!" She tapped the glass face of her watch with her nail. "Fedor—Mr. Cohen—is forecasting you upstairs. He does not like waiting. Therefore, more speedy." She was off again toward the elevator banks, and all of a sudden there was a rush of heat to my face and I knew. It was her. Karri was Dad's mistress. *A woman like that is her own dowry!* The old dog. Of course—was it a month ago? Two?—in this same lobby, Pop and I had been waiting for a factory car and I was telling him about a late shipment while he was staring over at Karri in her red uniform, like a burning phoenix flower, smiling and chatting away with a rakish older Brit, and Dad tilted his head in the man's direction. "That old-timer thinks he's going to put the wood to her."

"Pop," I said. "Did you hear anything? We'll lose the whole margin."

Now it was obvious. He was really saying, *I'm the one schtupping this broad.* As I was sure he'd *schtupped* for twenty years. Up and down the coast.

Karri pressed the button for the sixteenth floor and, once the elevator doors closed, she took out a white handkerchief from her breast pocket and wiped away her fingerprints from the gold-plated panel, as though we were running a jewel heist. Same fingers that had gripped my father's jug-handle ears and poured him out; those polished French tips scribbling down his hairy back toward the one sneaky mole down by his ass that he swore would kill him in the end. Karri started wiping down the brass railing inside the elevator, the wood beads of her Mala bracelet rustling. She was Buddhist and *potching* my dad. Sort of added up actually: if life was suffering she wasn't taking any shortcuts.

But if that was the Buddhist part of her, there was another part too, which I saw by looking over her shoulder down the narrow lapel of her blazer, down the shirred V-neckline of her blouse to a glimpse of scalloped lace on her lime-green bra peeking out, which quickly disappeared with a scoop of her finger. Karri gave me a weak smile and reflexively folded her arms across her chest, bracelet against breast like a twofer of secrets.

Looking me up and down, she frowned at my filthy outfit said, "Next time use my rear entrance."

"That's definitely not what you mean," I said.

The sixteenth floor opened to the Brazilian restaurant. Karri led me past the salad bar and the pasta station. Usually my father was at one of these buffets, never ordering anything, just leaning way too close to the food, saying, *What's this, what's this, what's this* and abruptly shaking his head like he was calling off a catcher. At the back of the restaurant a Filipino woman sang Tracy Chapman's "Fast Car" in a short sequined dress. We whisked past waiters carrying charred flanks and squeezed through tables—six inches of space—and where a sideways Karri slipped easily through, I was dragging my belly and groin against the shoulders of women in backless gowns, apologizing to everyone I touched.

Behind the band stage we reached a door that opened to a private room. There was my dad at a round table talking with the top management of the factory. I felt a sudden sharp shift in the air, a rush of cold that knifed the words off my father's lips midsentence. I could not move from the weight of his look across the room, could scarcely draw a breath, but then his mouth broke into a faint, slow smile where only the right side of his lip curled up.

The special room was a circle of onyx walls polished to a high gloss so I could see my own face in a murky reflection above Dad's head, staved together on a totem pole.

"The VIP graces us," Dad said.

I said a cursory hello to the table and went to sit down, forgetting all my *guanxi*—no, it wasn't that I forgot, it was Karri pushing me, her warm hand in the small of my back, toward the armless white leather chair, which my father was stroking like a cat. I sat down while Karri leaned toward him. They began discussing the dinner menu. I needed to stand up, bow formally and shake hands, but right as I moved to stand, the head waitress buzzed into the room talking in Chinese. For such an intimate room, there were people rushing back and forth, conversations in all these languages, and Dad had his big gut pressed against the table. All the muscle was in his shoulders, wide and stout, regular suits never fit, so he was wearing one of his custom-made getups. Most of the other men wore simple tailored black jackets with gold ties and khakis, but Dad was sitting there in a bright velvet suit like a giant purple berry. Holdover pimp from the '80s. *It's style, kid, you wouldn't understand.*

There was a famous tailor in Hong Kong who made custom suits off a mannequin replica of my father. On your first visit, he slathered you up in this gummy silicone and mummy-wrapped you in plaster bandages. The tailor stored the mannequin in an underground warehouse; all these body doubles in perfect neat rows like the terra-cotta warriors at Xi'an. "Say you want a new suit," Dad said to anyone who'd listen, "you just call up. Never have to waste a trip—ach, wasted trips!—never again. That's Chinese efficiency. Tailors, you got to understand, are like the early primates of Jewish business. Sure we invented off-the-rack, but the Chinese hang you by it." Dad's little setup took real discipline though. Don't dare gain a pound, otherwise the tailor has to start all over. For it to work, you are who you are forever.

"…and very well, sir," Karri said. "The duck prepared how? Szechuan, the entire head, breast, thigh, or you like Peking, sliced skin rolled up with scallion?"

"Oh, no," Dad said, looking her dead in the eye. "I want the whole bird." His jaw twitched. She touched the gold butterfly at the base of her throat. Those were thin soles on her shoes, and I knew she felt the cold tile on the bottom of her feet, and she was knuckling her toes. Were they painted pink or red? It was a rule in this hotel that all employees wear closed shoes. Five-star but not a single toe.

"Of course, sir," Karri said politely and walked off, leaving a zip of some sweet scent like Ivory soap behind.

"Stand up now," Dad said to me. "I want you to meet Gang Xiaodan."

I stood. "I thought this was a dinner for just us two?" I whispered to Dad. "Shouldn't I change?"

"No, no, we waited long enough," Dad said, grinning, and I didn't know how to read that smile or why the hell they were all here, Yong, the co-owner with my dad, and Shen, the plant manager, one Taiwanese, the other Chinese, but especially Gang, the mayor of Foshan. Gang was probably in his early sixties, wearing an old-school button-down tunic. One of these guys from whose face all expression had been sandblasted away by decades of loony Mao slogans piped in through a red squawk box mounted high in the corner of his courtyard.

Dad said, "Gang, this is my boy I was telling you about," like I was twelve years old again. Gang didn't respond right away. You could tell by the way he circled a burl on the table with his finger that he enjoyed an obvious and prolonged show of deference. One of his eyes was brown and the other was dead. It was this milky fog, the right eye, the slightest hint of a colored iris, dull green, beneath a cloud. I was in Gang's blind spot, wondering if he could see me at all. It was a bit strange that no one had mentioned I was late or that I smelled like raw sewage. You'd think that would come up right away, but they were letting it all slide and there had to be a reason. I felt my future getting sorted out in this black fishbowl with a smooth gold ceiling, not in any understandable way of course, just a crinkling around the edges of my consciousness.

"Eldest son," Gang said to me, familiarly, but not smiling,

"why do you look nervous? Relax around me." Somehow I got the hunch he could see me through his dead eye. Also that no one had ever relaxed around him. "I have a son too," he continued. "In Manchester right now studying for exams, or so he tells me. His credit cards tell me something else." He smiled now, too perfectly; his teeth must have been veneers. "I am only here to wish you congratulations. Also I never turn down a free meal. That is my secret—no filling me up. I am always hungry. It is a curse. I can eat and eat and never gain weight. Still I weigh a hundred sixty pounds. Never feel full. Well, tonight I try again. I want to welcome you officially to Foshan and ask you to think of her as your new hometown. Tell me that. Repeat it now for me with conviction."

This struck me as a very odd thing to do, to have me repeat this, as though it was boot camp, but he was a decorated party member and I was just a guest, a temporary resident. So I said it. "Foshan is my hometown."

"I don't believe you," he said, "still too nervous."

Just then Dad nodded to a waitress waiting by the bar below an enormous flat-screen TV, who whispered something into the microphone pinned to her vest, and then the doors blew open and two other waitresses, wearing sleeveless red-and-gold *qipao* with stand-up collars and double slits up the legs marched into the room—one holding a tray with a fountain pen and ink pot, the other carrying a stack of documents on a red velvet pillow cushion.

The girls set the pillow and ink tray down in front of Dad, who nodded, the head waitress nodded, Yong and Shen nodded— some secret communiqué passing between them all—and the young waitress in a short *qipao* lifted a bottle of red wine off the bar. It had all been planned out in advance, rehearsed; my only surprise was that I didn't notice it sooner. Everything in Dad's world order made sense.

Dad handed me the pillow with the documents on top, and before it was even in my hands I knew it was infinitely heavy. He stood up and raised his glass. "I'm not one to make speeches," he began, the typical opening of someone who loves nothing more. "So I'll keep this short. It was only a year ago that I brought Alex up to Dongguan to the Avon business, which you remember we were doing out there with Winston and Jerry. So we're all around the conference table finishing our tea and Winston, you know how he works. He was doing twenty-hour days in the factory, don't ask me how this is even possible, but he's designing samples one day and he passes out right in the cutting room. He is out cold. Goes into a coma. This is true. He's in a coma for about a month when he comes out. He tells me he's fine, no problem. 'Oh, we're so sorry,' I say, 'that's awful, horrible, da-te-da-te-da,' because it really is, so I say. And Alex, do you know his words to Winston? He says, 'What was it like?' To the poor man he says this. You have to admit you said that, Alex. What were you expecting? 'Oh, I caught up on my reading.' Did you think he'd recommend a coma? It's not a day spa, Alex. 'How was it?' You have to admit this was not your finest moment. Gang, Yong, Shen, I said to myself, we've got trouble, major tsuris. Point is, that's long in the past and we've seen much better days since. Alex, I want you to take over the business for me. I'll shadow you, but I want to officially sign it over. There's legal reasons and financial ones too. I can't do this forever, everyone here agrees. It's 2015. We're tired. We don't look it but we are, and you're ready, at least we hope to God you are, I'm kidding, you're ready. It's time."

This whole while I'd been holding the pillow, heavier and heavier in my hands, my palm sweat seeping into the velvet. They all turned to look at me, impatient for the reaction—the *correct* reaction, which I knew I wasn't capable of giving.

No, it wasn't that I couldn't, I just wouldn't. I was conscious of the fact that I stunk, my clothes still damp and acrid from the river, and somehow that rickety houseboat with the heat crackling over yellow snakeweed, a surge of camphor when the wind picked up—somehow that seemed much safer than this place now.

My hand went to the pen and held it. It was shaking, and I worried that they would see my shaking hand. This was planned too, I was sure, since the day Dad first held me, wet and bleating, smoothed the blond down on my head like he was testing top grain. So this had always been my fate, ever since the cattle carrier huffed out of Belgium with my grandfather. Okay, Dad, I thought, I'll be you, and do it just as well.

"Sign, Alex," Yong said, smiling, "or we drown you in the Pearl."

He was joking, I hoped, but they were all a little afraid inside. I saw that. The pen was in my hand, my fingers flared, and they were staring at me, at my power to fill up the room. No, I could do this better than Dad. He'd been at it too long; he was dried up. A new approach. Fresh ideas. I'd nudge Dad aside, push if I had to. First I'd ditch the midtier department stores and go after the boutiques and higher-level brands. Get out of knockoffs. I wanted to do something my father never could because, smart as he was, he was a knockoff himself, a duplicate of duplicators. I wanted to design originals. Artisan leathers—kid and calfskin—those delicate, soft, supple leathers Dad wouldn't touch anymore. My own brand I wanted. Stop screwing around with table runs of 60 percent C-grade hides. No more private label. I saw my own designer brand on the floor at Nordstrom or even Neiman Marcus, under my name. Or some name. I'd find a name. I would try at least. And I figured if it got to be too much, if Dad wouldn't let me breathe, well, I could pull the rip cord, escape if I needed to. I could always get the hell out.

There was a silence in the room and I could see my father fidgeting, crossing one leg then the other. I saw his hands too were trembling. The cool air moved across my neck. And there was a drop of ink quivering on the end of the fountain pen. Yong raised his wineglass to me. "Good luck, Alex. You can't forget what the Pirkei Avot says, 'Love work. Don't get friendly with the government.'"

"That's a Chinese favorite," Dad said. "They think he's the Jewish Confucius."

Here's the part where you pledge devotion until death, I told myself. And I saw my name bloom in wet ink.

Two

I COULDN'T SLEEP THAT NIGHT. I LAY IN BED trying to make sense of it. What the hell had Dad been thinking? Why would he start this transition now? To train me, sure. Hawk over me as I learned on the job. Okay. But he clearly didn't trust me. So why now? For himself, of course. Always. Because it was his immortality on the line. So he needed to pass the company over to me. It was his way of saying, *You're the heir to my empire. You're locked in. You're not going to leave in two years. You're on the line. On the hook.*

You're on the hook to be me.

There it is. That's what it meant. I pulled a pillow over my head. It was obvious now. Still, I didn't think he had any confidence in me and that was why he was always throwing little tests at me. This morning had been one. Over breakfast downstairs. Dad had been eating a grapefruit as I slurped away at the house congee. "You're going native on me," he said. Usually he watched CNN on the TV behind my head, but this morning he'd studied me closely. He wagged his spoon a few inches from my face. "Alex," he said—I tried to ignore him and continue eating my congee, this watery rice gruel with dried pork flakes that look like hair from our cowhides—I didn't even like it, but I kept ordering it every morning. Stubborn. As if one morning I'd love it. "Alex," Dad said, tapping my hand with the back of his spoon. "Alex. Tell me how, if you had to, you'd manufacture this spoon."

"That spoon?" I said, looking up.

He waved it slowly back and forth, close to my nose, like he was trying to mesmerize me. "Grapefruit spoon," he corrected me. He ran the tip of his finger along the serrated edge. "Come on, who's your buyer?"

"No one's buying grapefruit spoons, Dad. Hotels. F&B managers at the hotels…"

"There you go," Dad cut me off. "These hotels are a business. Say a guy comes in right off his flight from Chicago, he's all *ishkabibbled*, comes to this restaurant, last thing he wants is that watery shit you're eating."

"Congee."

"Congo," Dad said. "No, he wants a good old-fashioned pink ruby."

I had an idea. "You know what's in these days—broiled grapefruit."

"Oh, Jesus," Dad said, leaning forward in his seat. "This happens?"

"Fancy dinners," I said. "First course. You're with the boss talking around a promotion and the waitress sets a broiled grapefruit on your plate. But you got a common spoon like this." I held mine up.

Dad held his right beside it, pensive for a second, before saying, "I like that—'common spoon.' Puffs mine up. Puts it up there with the lobster cracker or oyster fork in the rank of elite utensils. The Cohain of spoons. So fine, you got your customer. Now what do you do?"

He wasn't going to let up. Right then I knew it was a test.

"Okay," I said. "Selling's the easy part. Making is another story. We're not hand-forging spoons here. The goal is to mass-produce. Not sixty. We need six hundred thousand."

He nodded.

"Now if we can make it for pennies on the dollar then we can sell it. Materials are our number one cost. You know the shoe-dog saying—leather's worth more than labor. Same with spoons. We got to maximize materials. Vertically integrate. And never stop the line, not even to shit."

I thought at the time: I'm fucking with him, parroting his own slogans back to him, and there he was enchanted with the sound of his own voice, but Jesus, now, lying in bed, I understood that was the moment that put the pen in my hand.

That convinced him.

"Wow," he said, smiling. "That's damn good. You surprise me sometimes."

"The real question is why you eat so many grapefruits. Are you trying to give yourself an ulcer?"

"Lately it hurts on my side, is this an ulcer?"

"You know," I said, "if we were really going into spoons, the way things are changing here, I'd have to move the factory to Cambodia or Vietnam."

He crossed his arms and leaned back in his chair. Then he hit me with that broad inviting smile, the one that made my chest swell, the one I wanted so badly and that somehow always left me feeling bruised on the inside.

Now I pulled the pillow tighter around my head, but I kept seeing that smile. Replaying it all in my head. Finally, sometime in the middle of the night, I dozed off.

In the morning, down in the lobby, there was no sign of Dad in his usual spots, either over by the shoe-dogs or hovering by Karri's terminal. He no-showed for breakfast too, and a thought flashed that maybe I'd tuned him out when he delivered some important information like the fact he was leaving China forever, goodbye and good luck. Had he said that? Did he leave me alone? For a moment I stood in the lobby with this uncertainty swelling in my chest.

Foshan's four main manufacturers were sitting in separate areas like a high school cafeteria: bras, shoes, ceramics and electronics. At the main desk, Karri was checking in a new guest in a red tapered fez and gray suit. She looked exactly as she did yesterday, as she always looked. I'd never seen her change.

The lobby was crowded with loudmouth foreigners waiting for their drivers. We were all one thin pane of glass away from being totally lost. I didn't even know how to get to the factory from here. I'd never driven myself there. Forced outside, I imagined us all walking aimlessly down the street in a herd, scrutinizing signage we couldn't understand, ignoring the plosive tongue-clack of cabdrivers, a slow barn-animal procession down the highway; cud-chewers ready to walk off Shusheng Bridge into our own reflections.

The two bellhops, boys in red caps and jackets with gold buttons, stared at me as if to say, "Go sit with your division. Hovering makes us nervous." I couldn't bring myself to go sit because of Don Bauer, a Hasidic Jew, an old shoe-dog from back in Lynn. Dad had brought Bauer over here to head our leather purchasing department a few years back. I heard his high voice lecturing to some new kid I'd never seen before about China while I pretended to study the gold metal statue in the middle of the lobby that either depicted the local karst mountains or an epileptic stock chart, impossible to say which.

I saw my old friend Bernie enter the lobby in a gabardine suit. It was tolerable with Bernie here. I didn't see him every day, but we grew up together. Both our families in the footwear business. As kids we used to get baked and play pickup basketball in the basement of the synagogue, this infernally hot little court, sliding off the sweaty, hairy backs of paunchy old shirtless Jews wearing rec specs and rainbowing hook shots. Jews only. Bernie *levitated* because he could jump three inches off the ground. Everyone took a *schvitz* afterward. Splayed out on wood benches. Everything hanging out. The shamelessness of those men. Me and Bernie in our tighty-whities giggling.

I walked over to the purple couches by the tall sunny windows where Bauer, reeking of the canned tuna fish he carried in his suitcase, was telling the new kid which red-light streets in Hong Kong to visit on the weekends.

"Actually," Don said, answering his own question, "I prefer a lineup of girls. What can I tell from a book of pictures? Do I have chemistry with a photo? One *mamasan*, get this, asked *me* for a photo. To show her girls. Even the hookers are getting picky. Everyone in China's asking for more."

Don's new employee had hair that was blond and straight as Midwest corn, and a round scar between his eyes like maybe a vestigial horn had been removed at birth. When Don ran out of air, I said hi to Bernie and I stuck out my hand and said hello to the new kid. Kid's name was Todd. I was about to say, It goes with your face, which wasn't my instinct, but something Dad would say. Christ, Dad was probably halfway to Boston by now and engaged to a Chinese stewardess from Cathay Pacific. *It's those red scarves, Alex. They hurt my insides, is this my liver? That knot—double-French, Boho loop?—so fluffy and delicate like a red butterfly exploding from her neck.* These slip-ups, mistaking Dad's words for mine, kept happening more and more. I put his voice out of my head, and told Todd that if he wanted to see something local, a temple or something, I'd show him. The kid's face lit up at this and he said, "Geez," and I felt bad for him. I had a hunch he wouldn't last. Maybe his dad sent him. Maybe Perdue did. We got a lot of our hides from their Dallas headquarters, and they always sent over these barrel-chested suppliers in ten-gallon hats who slapped the Chinese hard on the shoulder and called everyone Buddy. Maybe Todd was Perdue's apology to China. How else would a kid like that end up here?

Don said, "Nah, once you've seen one temple you've seen them all."

The four other old-timers agreed.

"And I'm a religious man," Don said humbly.

"You were a Sunday school teacher," Bernie said. "That's the scary thing."

Dad had helped Bernie get his first job over here and now he was a major accounts sales manager at Blakes. We'd grown up in the same town outside Boston, going to the same temple, listening to Rabbi Gelman drone on that Moses was the JFK of the Torah and we should all strive to reach those higher offices of kingdom.

But Bernie had always been a little weird. One time he came to our place for Passover and he was in the kitchen talking to my mother and pulling a sweatshirt from his book bag when out flew a pair of handcuffs. The look on my mother's face as she spread butter and jam on a latke. Who brings handcuffs to Passover?

Right then I saw Dad stagger off the elevator, frazzled, his fly wide open.

"I overslept," Dad announced to us all. "It's official—I'm out of control."

"Don't hang yourself," Don said. "We're getting old."

Dad looked at the ceiling. "What's next?"

"What's next is you start using the hotel pool," Bernie said, and the guys laughed.

"You mean I become a *tourist*?"

"We evolve," Bernie said.

"Not me. I'm no common tourist. I've been here. I smelled Nixon's greasy Brylcreem in the Beijing airport. That's how long I've been here."

If we were alone, I'd call him out. Dad was fifteen years behind Nixon. Soon he'll claim he was on Air Force One arguing over the window seat. Dad looked past Don's head at Karri, who was behind the front desk checking in two Japanese businesswomen. She looked up from her screen and smiled. All the hems and edges and folds of her garnet blouse were ironed sharp enough to cut your finger. I wanted to confront Dad about her but I knew this wasn't the time.

"She called my room. Thank God for Karri," Dad said, short of breath, as if she'd saved him from stepping off the curb into the path of a bus. "Alex would have let me sleep all day."

Outside, the blue Chrysler factory van was just pulling up to the door.

"Zip your fly," I said to Dad, and he did so with one quick flash, telling the shoe-dogs goodbye. I told Bernie I'd call him soon. Dad clipped his fanny pack loaded with emergency pharmaceuticals around his waist.

"This way, Mr. Cohen," the bellhop said, and he set our bags in the trunk. Dad reflexively reached into his pocket and palmed the bellboy a few bills.

"Thank you, Mr. Cohen," the bellboy said. "Your children will be famous."

Dad stopped abruptly and pointed at me, "This is my son. Does he look famous to you?"

I apologized to the puzzled bellboy as Dad climbed into the van. As usual, he sat in the row of seats facing backward. Facing me. Even though we were the only ones in the van, he loved riding backward. It made me sick as hell. Plus it bothered me that he was looking at me the whole way with our knees touching.

"Face forward, why don't you," I said.

"I like it," he said and gazed out the window.

Ten minutes into the ride, he announced that he wanted me to run the presentation that afternoon with Abelson's, our main customer. We were showing our new spring line—seven styles I helped Dad design, and out of instinct to please I said brusquely, "Got it," before realizing what I'd agreed to. "Wait, what am I supposed to do?"

He unzipped his fanny pack, took out ChapStick and rubbed it over his lips. "Give 'em the whole works. Bring in the foot model. Sing about these shoes like they're stitched with gold. Close the deal. Hard, soft, who cares. Just make the deal. But stay relaxed. I'll save you before you crash and burn."

As he was putting away the ChapStick, I said, "No one's crashing, Mr. Fannypack."

"This is called a waist belt," he said. "For emergencies."

He kept Cipro, Imodium, amoxicillin, Sudafed. A whole pharmacy hidden in there.

"Made in China from 75 percent hypochondria and 50 percent *mishegas*," I said, realizing my mistake a second too late.

"You can't even add," he said. "How can you run a business?"

"Where's your faith? Where's the man from last night making speeches, bring him back, I like him better. He thought I could do this."

"That was all for show. What I say in front of the Chinese has almost no basis in reality."

"So you were lying?"

"Saying what they need to hear. Look, if you want me to lie to you too, I will."

"Why do we have to lie to anyone?"

"Alex," he said with a theatrical sigh, "you have a way of making everyday life sound like a crime."

So we both turned awkwardly to opposite windows. We were up on the highway driving past the Nanguo Peach Garden. Without turning back, I said, "You had me fooled. For a second there last night, I thought you actually trusted me. Ridiculous."

"I'm only kidding, Mr. Serious. It's not just you. Everything I worked for, built up, is on the edge. This place is a ticking time bomb."

"Okay, Mr. Despair," I said, "all I can tell you is that we won't be short on orders after today."

"There you go. Good man. But we're still short on labor."

"We'll recruit more," I said.

"I'm trying. Greed has this country by the throat. We used to have to beat them off with a stick. Literally. We'd fill all the jobs and the leftovers we'd chase out of the gate with sticks. But they don't need us anymore."

We drove past rows of chop shops and ma-and-pa factory-garages, and roadside fruit stands, and the sky was gray as a tombstone; we hadn't seen the sun in a month, Yong blamed fog, I said pollution, Dad said who the hell cares, we weren't here to sunbathe.

"I want you to promise me something," Dad said. "Keep clear from Gang. When he comes by, let me handle him. There's procedures. That's who we're serving. We're married to him. You understand? Everyone is."

"Why?"

"Don't ask why. Just do like I say. Okay? Promise me that."

"Okay," I said, "I heard you."

"Whatever he does, that's his choice. We do things the right way. Look, my point is you don't fuck over your own people. You understand? That's all I'm saying. There's ethics to this, it may not look like it most of the time, but that's not us. We do things different. Honest. Just because you're in another country doesn't mean you change. We're Cohains, the priestly tribe. Cohains first before anything else. From my mouth to your ear."

Once he got all that out I could tell he wasn't done thinking on it because he removed his watch and started rubbing the back of his wrist against his lips, which meant he was thinking hard, though I think he also liked the way his wrist smelled after wearing a leather band all day. The Cohain business was my grandmother Nana's obsession. One of the original twelve tribes of Israel. High priests. Direct descendants of Aaron, brother of Moses. Jewish, she'd said, but with a little something extra.

When we lived for those couple of years in the Brickyard in Lynn, Nana kept putting cloth napkins down wherever she sat so she wouldn't be infected by poverty. Kennedy had killed the domestic factories with the Trade Expansion Act, docking tariffs by 50 percent. Factories were shutting down in Lynn and Beverly and Haverhill, guys snowed under. The work moved offshore and these guys couldn't or refused to move with it. Men like my grandfather who bought their wives fur coats and Cadillacs slumped off to the Brickyard or threw themselves off Haverhill Bridge like my uncle Max, who the sheriff scooped out of a sluice gate at the end of a mill run. Fish had nibbled off his eyelids and fingertips.

My Zayde held on. Tight on cash flow, he started pocketing the federal withholding tax to run the business. He swore that when it turned around he'd pay back the government. The feds got him on fraud and tax liability for ninety thousand, and we were sunk. The agents in slick suits walked right into the factory, and Zayde asked, "Do you have to do this here?" My dad was sweeping the floor with a broom. "Not in front of the kid," Zayde said, even though Dad was already thirty and married.

In the Brickyard, Lynn turned seemingly overnight into a wasteland of looted factories. Hard to come by a single loaf of challah on the Sabbath. Nana said, as always, "We're Cohains, a priestly tribe, and we find a way." Zayde mumbled, "Vera, we don't have two dollars savings. Give it a rest."

We'd always succeed, she believed, and Zayde's failure was just further evidence that she'd been snookered into a bad marriage, that he was, as she'd accuse him long after his death, never a *true* Cohain. A Levite maybe, Galitzianer or Yisrael, but no Cohain. The Jewish elite. The magic of that word, *elite*, mangled our blood. Everything was for Cohain, this legacy of grief.

All was lost until Dad saved the business. Nana fell to her knees and pulled at her hair in gratitude. She could finally ditch her Oldsmobile, go back to eating off Royal Doulton sterling silver. All of life's necessities returned. By then she'd already sworn off Zayde as a lousy good-for-nothing, a New York shit, and she kissed the tops of my father's shoes and called him the *Moschiach*, which is Hebrew for Messiah.

The deep, rich smell of shit and cow skin, mixed with notes of mango from the trees planted along the sidewalk wafted through the open window of the van as we turned off Qifeng Gongye into the factory. Dad asked if it was just him or did everything in China smell either like shit or flowers. I told him it was because he only goes to the shoe factory and the overspritzed hotel. If he went someplace else he might enjoy a third smell.

"Where else would I go?" he said.

Even though we were only an hour from Guangzhou, no taxi driver had ever heard of these roads. On Google Maps we were a blank gray stretch intersected by a few highways. You had to be led here.

A Chinese worker in loose trousers and white shirt pulled a metal rickshaw full of yellow-and-blue lasts, the plastic models shaped like a foot around which you build a shoe. My skin bumped when I saw them stacked all around the factory, in rusty drums or giant baskets, hundreds of lasts of mismatched colors and sizes, like feet without shoes or shoes without feet, a weird double nothingness. Today though I took an odd sort of pleasure in imagining them bringing to life my own designs, assuming I didn't fuck things up at the presentation with Abelson's later.

Tiger Step factory was just five cement buildings clad with shiny peach-and-white tiles stained from acid rain, leather dust and the blue clay blown over from the brick factory next door. I could smell the factory, that sickly sweet adhesive cement glue burning my nostrils. The administrative building sat right across from the dormitories, adjacent to the two production plants.

I got out of the van and scanned the bank of steel sash windows, hoping to see Ivy in the sample room, not wanting to see her hands at work, just her face in profile, but the disc of sun glinted off the windows, and even when shielding my eyes I could make out only the silhouettes of workers' heads. Maybe she was in her dormitory, tired from visiting her grandmother over the holiday. It was still early.

I turned around to her dorm. Up on a fourth-floor balcony a young woman was snipping a spring onion from a flower-pot with a pair of scissors. The moment she felt my eyes on her, she lowered her head, without finishing, and disappeared. Only I still saw her eyes behind a beaded curtain waiting for me to leave. Another woman I'd never know, and I wondered what had been moving through her as she trimmed the green stalks. I often wondered that, riding the subway alone into Guangzhou as I was squished right up against a woman in a silk chemise with a tortoise shell hairclip at her temple, who turned and looked at me with all the enthusiasm of a pall-bearer, that dour inert glare as she brushed right past me at her stop, her body sliding over mine, knowing with each passing moment that it was my last chance to speak to her, knowing better still that I'd sound like an idiot if I tried.

Dad shoved my messenger bag into my chest. "Come on," he said. "I'm *schvitzing*." It was eighty-five degrees but inside the plant it was probably ninety-five under the heat setter boxes. I heard the hiss of hydraulic machines, the musky and wonderful smell of treated leather. Right outside our office, the same state employees were digging up the street—sparks flew as their mattocks glanced off limestone rocks, five feet down in the ground. They were fixing nothing. Nothing was broken. A year in China and I understood the importance of imaginary jobs, they were practically indispensable, but there was a third man in the crew who didn't even pretend to dig. He sat on a stool outside the trench staring as I passed, his eyes bloodshot, muzzle like an angry electric socket, and I was relieved to get inside the vestibule where I quickly called the elevator.

"The smoke tickles my throat," Dad said. In the corner stood a small shrine with the enameled figurine of Guan Gong, the God of Business, with bamboo shoots and burning sticks of sandalwood. "You think Yong minds if I—" Dad licked his finger and reached to pinch the red ember right as the bell chimed and I yanked him inside the elevator.

On the way up I could tell the incense had set off some obsessive part of his brain because for five flights he was just listing foods that bothered his throat and mouth. Potato chips, toasted bread, frisée. As soon as the doors opened I almost jogged to my office and set my bag down on my desk. I wasn't in there long before there was a knock on my door, and Hongjin, a tall, scrawny Chinese man attempting to grow a goatee, came into the room. Hongjin was thirty-one years old and our account manager for Abelson's, the Midwestern department store we'd worked with for the past five years.

He knuckled his black frame glasses back up to the bridge of his nose. "Is it true Fedor has made a partner out of you?"

"Yes. Partners."

At twenty-seven, Hongjin had a heart attack from over-working at the Bureau of Municipal Economy. He'd been doing sixteen- or seventeen-hour days and right as he was thinking about cutting back, his heart just gave out. When Hongjin interviewed for the job here at Tiger Step, Dad asked to see the scars on his chest, not because Dad didn't believe him, but because he had almost a holy reverence for scars. Dad kept saying, "Poor thing," as he traced with his forefinger the crooked scar tissue on Hongjin's chest, not actually touching him but just a few inches away. Dad hired him on the spot. The thing that really got to him was that Hongjin never told his parents about his heart attack. He said he didn't want to worry them. Dad talked about that for days.

"Congratulations." Hongjin came over and hugged me, and I could smell the smoke on his clothes. He chain-smoked Yangcheng cigarettes, Kings unfiltered, except he was respect-ful enough not to do it in front of my father, saying it was bad for Dad's allergies, but I knew it was because Dad gave him a second chance and he almost touched his scar.

Hongjin was examining the blue last on the folding table.

The presentation was only a few hours away and I realized I had this idea in the back of my head.

"Hongjin, why do we use Die Jo as a foot model?"

"She's not a football," he said over his shoulder.

"Foot *model*."

"Oh," he said, turning around. "Sorry. To be the foot model, you have to be most beautiful girl in the factory."

"She's almost sixty years old."

"She speaks a little English, and she's a size six. They call her Butterfly Queen."

"That doesn't make her one," I said, and I realized that I was pushing him only to justify in my own mind a decision I'd already made.

"Can you get her for me, please?"

Ten minutes later Hongjin brought Die Jo into the office. She had a short bob haircut, heavy crow's-feet, and she wore a black dress like she was in mourning. It was quiet now, just the gurgling of the air conditioner. "Welcome," I said, and already my throat felt dry.

"Thank you, Mr. Cohen, dollface," she said, and her face changed, now she was looking at me with great pity and tenderness, as a mother would. "Do you like China? Wouldn't you rather be back at the Tropicana dancing Charleston with a swell dame?"

I smiled politely. She talked in a language learned from her father's contraband noir and detective films; it was all the English she knew. The buyers loved it when she said, "Sure, pal, I'd buy these heels, I'm no dumb Dora." Some customers thought we taught her this language as some kind of sales shtick. I could see she was frustrated. No choice but to get to the point. I told her I had to relocate her.

"Who's the new gal?" she said.

"Let's not worry about that. The point is we need to relocate you."

In desperation she turned and spoke to Hongjin in Cantonese. His eyes were wide and serious. She nodded. For what felt like a long time he spoke and I didn't know what was happening, other than the fact he wasn't supposed to say anything at all. When he was done, she sat taller, almost like she was straining to reach something high with her chin. "Baloney!" she said, a bird's wing of red lipstick trembling across her lips. "You've seen my gams. It's what I was built for. I'm a star. Who's better?"

She stood slowly. She wouldn't look at me. "You ain't so tough," she said, barely audible.

I looked to Hongjin. "What the fuck did you tell her?"

Hongjin told me about her *hukou,* her household registration pass. She held a village pass so if we fired her, she had to go back. I'd never heard anything about it before, my face prickled with embarrassment, and I suddenly felt like a fraud. How had I never heard of this? Flashing across the front of my brain was that Dad knew all about the *hukou* system and never spoke a word of it to me.

"I didn't say anything about firing," I said.

"You said relocate."

Die Jo was walking in slow motion toward the door.

I called her back to the chair. "You aren't fired, okay. Nobody has to go anywhere. Let's make this work. Is there anything else you can do here? Can you work the line maybe, stitch, pattern in the sample room?"

A little color came back into her cheeks. "I play poker. I'm a big cheese. A four-flusher like Black Cocoa in Honolulu."

"I have no idea what she's saying," I told Hongjin, "but good enough." I invented a position for Die Jo: Chairwoman of the Workers' Recreation Poker Committee. That sounded sufficiently bureaucratic. Hongjin asked if I could do that and I told him I didn't see why not. Who was stopping me? Die Jo smiled, came over to the other side of the table and bowed very formally. I bowed back and Hongjin escorted the

Butterfly Queen out of my office. I waited until I couldn't hear their footsteps to go find Ivy.

I headed down the back stairwell where no one would see me. It wouldn't have looked good if Dad or Yong or Shen or any of the managers saw me bring Ivy, a stitcher, up the front stairs. I paused right before the green steel door, because I could hear the girls' voices on the other side. The door's metal arm was cool in the heat of the building. I knew what would happen when I opened the door, all the sounds would stop, the women would look down as though they worked twelve-hour days without uttering a word. Badly, I wanted them to look at me, and then, in the exact opposite way, I wished they'd forget about me and act the way Ivy said they did when I wasn't around, talking and laughing and fighting, making fun of me and Dad. But there was no place I could stand without them seeing me. Not over by the hand-lasters with their metal beaked claws, or the women burnishing leather on a horsehair wheel, or the ones hunched over open ceramic bowls of latex cement, their noses constantly running as they glued suede kiltie tassels to a pair of oxfords—so many operations to make a pair of fucking shoes, hundreds of steps, and I couldn't find a place to stand and watch and listen without ruining everything.

When I pushed open the door, a cold hopeless silence fell over the room. Dad always mistook this for a sign of respect. Ivy was at a rectangular wood table with five other girls, tracing a design pattern on a full grain hide with a silver pen. The whole trick of making a shoe is turning a two-dimensional object into a three-dimensional object. How to take something flat, a drawing, an animal hide, and give it body, shape, form; breathe some life into it like a golem. I called to Ivy. She came over, everyone watching without watching, and we walked out of the sample room in silence save for the squeak of sewing machine pedals, the slug of the needle and the clack of the bobbin.

Up in my office, I asked Ivy to have a seat. She was wearing dark blue jeans and a white T-shirt. We had never been in my office together before and though we flirted there was nothing beyond that. Not even a discussion of beyond.

"How's it going down there?" I asked from my chair behind my desk. Her eyes went to the curtains I'd closed so that no one from the plant could see us. I winced a little in shame.

"Going as you expect," she said, looking at her fingernails. "We're making your shoes."

"Right." She seemed much darker here, unreadable, and I pulled my chair out from behind my desk and sat closer to her.

"Ivy, I've let Die Jo go as our foot model and—"

"I know," she interrupted. "I saw Die Jo in the sample room crying."

"We need a younger girl."

"There's millions of them in China."

My problem with women was always thinking that I was as clever as they were. Earlier on, I had somehow got it stuck in my head that seduction was like sales, if you said enough of the right things, you closed the deal. That the world went to the best liars. Even now, when I wanted to be honest with Ivy, I heard myself lying. It was not that I needed younger. It was her.

"I want you to be the new girl. You're perfect for this."

She laughed, but at least the darkness lifted from her face. "I suspect this is what you want. The girls are talking. Your father made you a partner? I thought you did not know if you wanted this business."

"Well, I lost that fight."

"We all lost, this is why we are here. Let me ask something. Why are you messing around with me?" She gave me a sly smile. "I'm just a factory girl."

That didn't sit with me. The way she spoke English so well. Her smarts. None of it ever added up. Most of the girls in the factory hadn't gotten out of grade school.

"Are you really?" I asked.

"I have a history with shoes," she said, crossing her legs. "Before the revolution, my grandfather worked for the Foot Emancipation Society. He went town to town educating women about liberating their feet."

She hadn't answered my question, but now wasn't the time to push. "See?" I said. "It's fate that we're together." Right when I said that I felt a heat on my ears and face, reddening for having suggested something between us. Something more. I've never had sense enough to keep my mouth shut.

"How do you know I am the right size?"

"I saw your flip-flop on your grandmother's boat. Size six."

"Is that sweet or weird?"

"Both? Look, Ivy, you're born for this." That was the wrong thing to say.

"For foot modeling? Sort of the way you are born for this factory."

"Should I have turned it down?" I asked.

"I bet you thought about it. I don't blame you. You don't see other options yet. Well, look, I am sure you can capitalize on my feet. Put them to good use."

"We can spend more time together."

"Oh," she said, smiling. "Is that what I want? I love when men tell me what to want. How else can I know?"

"Come on. I didn't mean it like that."

"There is an old tradition. When born, the mother puts a jug of wine under your bed. Supposed to save this for marriage day.

But me and my girlfriend drank it one time, maybe we were thirteen, and got drunk. I wanted the jug gone. It was under my head my whole life. Very bad taste. Bad vinegar. We go see fortune-teller, old lady no one seeks anymore, but she reads the coins, Book of Changes—says in big voice that I am born to raise geese, chicken, in a field. We laugh at her. Rude girls. But she was so wrong. So maybe you take birth too serious?"

I started fiddling with the measuring tape on my desk. A pang in my stomach, that twisted ache when you want someone very badly. I couldn't think of an answer. I didn't know what to say. It seemed like a chance to say something honest but I heard myself slide right into business mode.

"This brings a bump in your pay."

"This is your answer?" she said. "After what I tell you? You are ridiculous. What are you so scared of?"

"Nothing," I said. "Who said anything about scared? It's what's best for the company."

There was a loud banging on the wall behind me and I heard Dad's voice on the other side of the wall. "Young man. Young man, a glass of water. Drying up over here. So parched!"

Ivy gave a little bit of a smirk, one side of her lip curled. "You better hurry."

"Don't worry," I said. "He's not dying."

"Dying!" Dad yelled.

I turned to the wall as if I was going to be able to see through it and glare him silent, but when I turned back, Ivy was already slipping out the door. "Hurry with water, young man," she said.

"Will you do it?"

"Oh," she said, with a knowing smile. "Yes. I do it. Whatever is best for the company."

Then her face vanished behind the door and the dark diagonal slice of the hallway was gone.

After lunch at the canteen, I was wearing my suit and sitting in the wood-paneled conference room with Dad, Hongjin, Yong and the two women from Abelson's, Marie and Esme from Chicago. There was no telling how Dad would react when he saw Ivy walk in. He hated change that he didn't initiate. His ethos of total control and supervision matched China's rather nicely. Growing up he refused to squirt WD-40 on the door hinges; the unique door squeaks told him who moved where. A terrifying omnipotence like a ghost following you through the house.

A soft knock at the door and Ivy walked in wearing a floral dress that tied at the waist and fell softly on her body and flared just above her knee. Dad's mouth fell open, Yong's as well, not because it wasn't Die Jo, but because she looked beautiful. She didn't look like a stitcher at the factory, not a typical inland girl who left her village. She looked modern, like she was born in Guangzhou and had always belonged there. Yong whispered something to my dad and I saw them both shrug. I'd assumed correctly that they wouldn't jeopardize the presentation by making a scene. Dad didn't shout, *Where's the normal girl, ignoramus!* He said, "Hello, Ivy," barely opening his mouth.

"Mr. Cohen," she said, bowing her head ever so slightly before taking a seat with us around the oval table. On the table, I'd arranged the collection from heels to flats, and I found myself unconsciously knocking each shoe against the table as I gave a brief overview of the line to the ladies, just like Dad did, using each shoe almost as a gavel to emphasize the point.

I asked Ivy to try on the first pair of heels. Behind us was a little wooden stage with three steps and a narrow red carpet across the top. I offered her my hand as she went up the steps but she shook her head and seemed to float up there on her own in these black strappy sandals with a cork wedge, little tortoise discs on the vamp glimmering, and she rose above us all in a loose-fitting cotton dress, which caused the men in the room to involuntarily smooth their hair and rub their kneecaps as if there'd been another factory fire and everyone was checking to make sure they were still alive.

I wanted to show the ladies something special about this shoe. I asked her to turn around so they could see the profile of the heel from the back and I climbed up onstage with Ivy, got down on my knees, and I touched her ankle, the hollow right below the bone, and I lifted her foot up to straighten it out because I wanted to show the buyers how we sculpted and tapered the wedge to look like a true heel from the back; how up close you also could see little gold flakes sparkle in the cork, but the moment I touched her ankle everything vanished from my head. Because her ankle had turned inward, turned *toward* my touch, and there was a thump of hope in my chest and that was when I forgot everything.

I heard Dad say, "Pick up her foot."

Yong said, "Ach, ach, ach."

Her feet were so soft and white they reminded me of the picture Mom had hung behind the toilet growing up—the Lux soap girl perched on a wood Thatcher chair.

Ivy had long, slender toes, elegant and tapered, that never quite lay flat but angled upward, flaring, nothing like the folded and withered toes her grandparents must have seen under the binding bandages.

Dad was beside me whispering in my ear, "Your tie."

I looked down.

My tie was under her shoe. She was stepping on my tie.

Dad said, "Give me," and he tapped Ivy's calf, and she said,

"Oops, sorry," and Dad flipped my tie over my shoulder so it rested behind my back, then he returned to his seat and apologized to the ladies. "This is his first time."

And now I was talking about the things I was supposed to talk about, but my mind wasn't really there. I was thinking about her toenails, unpainted, but smooth and shiny, lacquered—she didn't wear makeup either, did she? No color at all. I'd always preferred heavy makeup, but seeing this now, some new kind of nakedness, I couldn't remember why I'd liked all those done-up faces. And there was an honesty to Ivy's foot, like the shop women on Changshou Lu with all their merchandise spread on the sidewalk: statues of Michael Jackson, Playboy Bunny socks, bootleg cigarettes, clothing with way too much lace; their lives right out on the street for you to step on and walk over.

"The fit is perfect," I said to the Abelson's ladies, my finger jangling along her hollow arch where I could see pale blue veins, all the inner workings, like the underside of a leaf. "This kind of fit comes from the precision of our lasts and our patterns. You can't get a fit half this good anywhere else, even Dongguan, not at this price point." The swelled joint at the base of Ivy's big toe nestled perfectly between the crisscross straps. "Not a millimeter to spare," I said, talking the way I was supposed to. The creak of wood under her wobbling foot, the thickened white froth of a callus on the back of her heel.

I was thinking how marvelous it would be to see one of these designs on Ivy's foot—it was on her foot, of course, but I mean out in the world, on the subway, and maybe I would gift her a pair of these sandals, which looked like they were made for her anyway, and it dawned on me that maybe I designed them, this whole line, with her in mind and it was always her foot I'd been imagining. The next sandals I showed—the ones done in woven raffia with a hand-crocheted peony flower that sat right on the cone of the foot—those were for her. I would leave them for her at her dormitory—and I was talking this whole time, surprised that I could do both at once, but every time I touched her skin, or the leather that was almost softer to my fingertips than her skin, my mind emptied again.

On the surface they were asking: "Are the top-lines too high? Could we do this taupe or bone? What's the duty on that shoe?" And I was even answering: "Yes, to me they're three millimeters off. Of course, we can do any color you want. Ten percent duty, buckle or zipper." But beneath that, I was noticing that Ivy's hair was the same color as the tea leaves drying on rattan mats beside the old man asleep in a chair out on the sidewalk. We went through eight or nine pairs of sandals and flats. With each new pair, she changed little but appeared to be a brand-new woman each time. And because my hands had touched her foot, because I'd made this shoe for her, it was almost like hearing her speak in her own language, knowing the shape of her foot down to the milli-meter, its swells and soft curves, its movement, the fall of its line—its *voice*—and for a second I felt like I knew her more intimately than if I'd ever kissed her lips or breasts. For a mo-ment, my fingertips nibbling along the soft white skin of her foot to show them the feather-line, I felt like I understood the aching and lovely mysteries inside her. For an absurd moment I felt like I knew her.

The Abelson's ladies said, "Does she speak English?" and I felt my stomach turn, the reverie gone, and I found myself saying defensively, "Of course she speaks," and I told them that in fact *only* the fit model's opinion matters, which was true, but I said it like I'd just discovered it now. "Nothing is precise here," I said, "we're not making electronics, which is all to spec. Black or white. Making shoes is about a feel. We must ask her."

"First show them the hand," Dad said breathlessly. And I

started explaining to them the touch of the leather, how soft it was because we used lamb-cow and they laughed at this, and Marie said, "You crossbred a cow and lamb?", and Dad said, "No, no, he's not explaining it right, this is his first time, it's just an in-house name, soft like a lamb but it's cow." They reached out to touch Ivy's foot. Then I asked Ivy to lift up high as if she were picking a persimmon off a high branch so the ladies could see how flexible the wood grain bottom was and Ivy's feet came off the foot beds and the heel of her foot was like a slice of white chestnut. I heard Yong sigh and Hongjin touched his chest.

Marie said to Ivy, "Would you buy them?"

"Yes."

"Would you purge them from your closet if you owned them?" Yong asked.

"No."

Dad said, "Are you sure you'd buy them?"

"Yes," she said, "but personally I like to wear two different shoes on each foot."

"Why?" Dad asked. "That's nuts."

"I think all shoes should be scrambled," Ivy said.

"What does that mean?" my father said. "That is crazy talk."

Ivy said, "It is something Trotsky said about wealth."

"Trotsky?" Dad asked, his voice pitched high. "The communist? I mean, we're all for communists here, but the Russian? Is this the League of Nations? When I want your political opinions I'll ask. Let's stick to shoes. Do they feel good on your feet?"

"Yes."

"Are you sure? There's nineteen muscles in there, half a mile of blood vessels, all crossing and mixing, a miracle of engineering—"

"It is very comfortable," she said.

"Okay, good. You don't want a shoe too large for your foot," he said, with a real edge, and now I knew what he was doing, because that was something Nana used to say about women trying to marry men above their class. He was being a prick to her.

"No," Ivy said, still polite but her voice flat and without emotion.

I could tell Ivy was getting under Dad's skin, but he pulled it together and asked Marie a dozen times if she liked the bling, and he wiggled his eyebrows at me each time he said it because it wasn't his generation's word. There was a strip of sequins and beads that looked like a garter belt and it sparkled and shone.

"Do you like that?" he asked. "Every collection needs bling." And then he noticed the sequins were moving in two different directions on the shoe, someone had applied them incorrectly. He apologized to Marie and Esme, who both said it was fine and they hadn't noticed. "No," Dad said, and he shook his head violently. It would not stand. Back down on his knees he got to work straightening the sequins to flow in the same direction, all the time chastising himself for the oversight.

Yong apologized to the ladies for my father's behavior. "He is an artist."

"I see that," Marie said, and Esme harrumphed because she went to design school in Chicago for four years to call herself an artist while my father was almost illiterate, at least emotionally.

"I fix, I fix," Dad said, dragging himself across the stage on his belly and the Abelson's ladies widened their eyes at the sight of this large man sprawled out with very delicate hands gently touching these sequins. Later I wouldn't be surprised if he told me it was perfect all along. Nothing whatsoever for him to fix, but he just had to find a way down there because that was who he was, he was too far from the action and he only knew the world by touch.

The Abelson's ladies placed orders for twenty thousand pairs of one of the casuals, a hundred thousand for each of the cork-bottom sandals, and they passed on the rest. Dad hugged me and hugged the ladies and everyone hugged like we were all new parents. Dad said, "On his deathbed, Rabbi Akiba told his son, 'Wear a decent pair of shoes.' Those were his last words."

"Very nice," Esme said, rolling her eyes. Marie elbowed her.

"This rabbi is your friend?" asked Yong.

"He is two thousand years old."

"Big reputation," Yong said. "Then these shoes we make are worthy of Rabbi Akimbo."

Marie said she needed to get back to the hotel and she thanked everyone except Ivy, who was the one who tried them on in the first place and made them beautiful. The Abelson's ladies went over some of the corrections. They'd like the shoes on the floor if possible by January.

"Of course possible," Dad said. "The Chinese are dogs. I mean they work like dogs. Naturally. They live for work. I happen to respect this."

"Please, don't hesitate to inform on us if there are any problems," Yong said.

They left me in the room with Ivy to take down the corrections and mark them on the shoes. I took out the tape measure and the little awl for making notches in the leather and my notebook where I'd written down the notes.

"Congratulations," Ivy said. "Now you can die of happiness."

"Better than getting hit by a bus," I said. "You read about that? A Chinese banker run over while texting his mistress on his iPhone. The phone survived. His last words were some nonsense about chrysanthemums."

She laughed. "You are losing a lot in translation. He's talking about anal sex."

"Is that the chrysanthemum? Wow. I really missed that one."

"I read about it," she said. "That's modern Chinese death. Warm spring, texting your mistress on the way from work, and a bus driver worried about his son's *gaokao* exam drives an orange bus into your chest. And your last words are about anal sex."

I got back down on the floor with the tape measure, silver pen and wood-handled awl. "Maybe this guy had a good death."

"For me," Ivy said, "good death is in the struggle. That's how we used to die. For true socialism. Die so we aren't footstools for capitalists and colonialists and foreigners to rest their feet on. Smash all divisions. Die for this *thing* hidden inside everyone. This thing that can make someone like my grandmother bite through someone's jugular."

The tape measure I was wrapping around her instep slackened. I sat back on my heels and looked up. "Jesus, your grandmother did that?"

"She was a girl. But, yes. A Japanese soldier. When he dragged her off to the camps during occupation."

"Did she kill him?"

"I don't know. They beat her almost blind."

"And now you get hit by a bus while sexting."

She giggled. "This is what Hegel calls irony of history."

I finished the instep and moved on to the lift of the heel. "You did a real good job today. Thanks for helping."

"Will you declare me a model female worker?"

"You're very sarcastic today," I said, marking the leather with a silver pen.

"I think I look beautiful in this dress," she said in a sad and plaintive tone that made me stop working. I was about to agree but she kept talking.

"There is a girl in my room, Alex, I haven't mentioned her to you, I don't think. Named Ruxi, and for two weeks she cries and cries. She try to quit and go back to her home, she is from a north province, small village, but Tiger Step has her *hukou* papers and says she owes them money for permits. The foreman says work until the end of season, and so she does this. He still won't let her go. Ruxi goes to Yong, never dreamed of talking to a rich man before but she does, and he says six more months. Can you help this girl? She has a brother who must go off to school and she needs to care for her parents."

"I'm sure it's just a misunderstanding," I said, but I felt stirred by Ruxi's story, stirred maybe because what if it was true?

"No, they have denied her request to quit. They keep her money."

"I doubt it," I said, though what if they really were withholding her wages and making it impossible for her to leave? What if they weren't going to give her the money she earned?

"You must do something. Bad enough what our own government does to us. Bullshit talk of equality and shared prosperity. Now we have to deal with you foreigners fucking us over too. Everyone thinks the foreigners will save us but there's just more."

"I'm not fucking anyone, Ivy. Why don't we let the labor union handle it?"

"Daigao's union? Are you kidding with me? Puppet union. You must know. Daigao is appointed by central labor bureau. Who is committee chair? Yong. You think he hires someone to cut down his own money? Help her. Be like a Trotsky."

"Trotsky only helped himself," I said. I didn't really know

what I was talking about, but my grandfather had actually met Trotsky. Zayde always told this story of meeting him at the Triangle Diner in the Bronx eating cabbage rolls in exile.

"He was a Jew. Like you."

"Not really," I said. "He changed his name." I pictured him alone at this New York diner stuffing his face with blintzes and brisket and kugel, dreaming of killing the czar. I had far more in common with fat New York Trotsky than the lean wolf storming the Winter Palace in his greatcoat and breeches. Was that what she wanted?

"Ruxi thinks Yong will let her go but she's crazy. Says she has faith. It is a spell. This whole country is like a spell. People like Ruxi have faith in this country that only lets them down."

Again I said there must have been a misunderstanding, and I got back to work with the awl marking the notches on the leather strap around her ankle, but inside I was afraid of the way Ivy was talking. I felt my hands starting to sweat, because I was also embarrassed, an idiot for not knowing. How much didn't I know? Ivy was saying, "Well, Alex, what do I say to her?" and I told her to hold still, stop moving, and she said, "Alex, it is cruel, it is slavery, what it is, human bondage," and that was when my hand slipped and the point of the awl pierced her foot.

She screamed. Not in pain, I don't think, but frustration. A speck of blood emerged on the side of her foot, and as I was apologizing, unconsciously, I swiped the blood away with my thumb.

"Can you do this for her?" Ivy said. "Help."

"Well, I don't know. My father would—"

And she balled her fists tight by her ears, furious now, not about the foot, but her face was red, and she said, "Are you always going to be your father's puppet? A war is coming."

She turned and ran out of the conference room and suddenly

I remembered where I'd heard that before. Fireworks, petit fours and afternoon tea at the Peninsula Hotel in Hong Kong. The anniversary of Handover Day, marking the end of British rule. I had just flown in, dizzy with jet lag and homesick, and Dad, in his peculiarly Dad way, said out of nowhere, "Do you have to pee? Let me show you something." We rode the elevator to the Felix restaurant on the thirtieth floor. In the bathroom, the urinals faced an enormous glass wall overlooking all of Hong Kong. We stood next to each other peeing and looking out over the parade of ships flying Chinese flags in the harbor, holding our dicks in our hands as firework ash sifted down like salt over the water. I felt like God taking a leak on the greatest city in the world. The street thronged with people who, if they only looked up, could see my circumcised cock. "It's Handover Day," Dad said, and I didn't understand it then, but I do now, and then he said the same thing Ivy said, I heard them at the same time in my head. *There's war coming.* And I was alone now in the conference room looking down at my hand where the rich red drop clung stubbornly to my thumb, quivering, and I lifted it to my mouth.

Three

LATER THAT EVENING, IN THE GOLD-FILIGREED restaurant of the Hotel Fontainebleau, Dad and I were moving in two directions. He was scooting his chair to his left, and I was going right, both of us hiding from the smoky eyes of the Indonesian woman singing Rod Stewart songs as if she'd written them for us. Around the table we went until eventually we came together, our shoulders nearly touching and our backs to the band.

"We can go someplace else," Dad said. "Papa treated me after my first sale, and you'll do it for your own son." He leaned in, smiling, looking at the empty chair beside me as if he saw my imaginary son drinking a Shirley Temple.

I told him this place was fine.

"You think the food's lousy?" A desperation in his voice. "Do you? I want you to be happy. This is your night." His shoulders banked at the mention of bad food. "We could go back to our hotel and do the buffet on the first floor. But it's too much. We're not buffet people. Here we can have a little noodles, some mustard greens, and that's enough. I'm not a balloon. But if you want, we can gorge at the buffet. It's chaos in there. Maybe you like that? A zillion kids running around like their pants are on fire, Chinese families, the kids, you know, since One Child, anything goes. You want to eat the chef's hat—'Chef, put your hat in the wok for my daughter.' The parents don't even pretend to control them. One child hit me in the penis with her nose."

"Keep your voice down, will you?" I said and then in an exaggerated whisper he said, "She was running full speed away from her brother, pigtails flapping, and smashed into my crotch. Never saw her coming. I dropped my tray, won-ton soup in her hair, all over my nice chinos. Parents yelling in Chinese. Little girls flying at your crotch. Is this what you want?"

"Enough of that story," I said. "It's great here. Couldn't be happier."

He shouted for the waitress and then, under his breath, "Make sure you wear an athletic cup is the last thing I'll say."

Dad asked our waitress, Wong, for a wine list. She shook off this request and said, "You try 47201."

"You heard of this?" Dad asked me, but before I could answer, Wong snapped, "You try," and disappeared.

"Always an adventure," said Dad.

Wong came back with a bottle of Italian pinot grigio. "47201," she said, nestling the bottle like a baby along her forearm.

"How much?" Dad asked.

"Doesn't matter," she said. "Excellent good."

She poured the wine and took our order. When she was gone, Dad pointed to the little pink sticker below the Italian label.

"She's reading the serial number off the wine. That's where

she got that number from. I was going to say something but why embarrass her? Two Wongs don't make a right."

I rolled my eyes. This surprised me. Not the corny, semi-racist pun, but the fact he refrained from correcting her. He never hesitated to embarrass me. I was prepared to lay into him about Ivy's friend, but since he was in this gracious mood, I decided I'd come at him soft. Lowball him.

Wong brought beef and dumpling soup in sterling silver tureens, essentially street food marked up 200 percent. But Dad's basic philosophy was that quality was directly propor-tionate to price. This was Nana's credo too: *always buy the best*. She never had a reason; never needed one. Expensive things were better. Wong brought bamboo baskets of pork dumplings with a vinegar dipping sauce; mustard greens; oyster mush-rooms; string beans and pork; a stir-fry noodle; some dish called "chicken without a sex life" wrapped in lettuce; roast pigeon, its body butterflied, head on the plate, beak pointed in the air, half-open.

Dad made a face after tasting the string beans. "They're squeakers," he said, putting it back on his plate half-bitten. I told him to send it back, but he refused.

"Why make trouble?"

I saw what was happening. He was doing this gracious act because he anticipated something coming. Or maybe that was paranoia on my part. I didn't know. With someone like Dad, so good at manipulating, it was hard to know what was sincere. We dipped our chopsticks in the dish of *lajiao*, diced green and red chili oil, and scarfed down the food, comment-ing on every dish, chatting around the big sale. I timed it up so that I was pouring Dad a second glass of 47201 when I said, "I hear we're holding a worker's *hukou* papers because she owes us money. You know anything about this?" I was careful to leave Ivy's name out of it.

"I don't know nothing," he said, but I noticed that for a split second he'd stopped chewing his food. "What's the word?" he asked.

"*Hukou.* Identification papers that tell you where you can legally live."

Dad looked contemplatively at the chandelier. "Nah, never heard of that. Who's talking to you? This Ivy telling you?"

"No," I said. "People talk. I hear things."

"Mmm," he said, sawing into the breast of roast pigeon. "What's going on with you two? You and Ivy. First it's off to Grandmother's house, now she's the foot model, which, I got to hand it to you, was a good idea. Better than old Methuselah. So what's the story? You're not thinking about dating her, are you?"

"No," I said, and I absentmindedly swirled the noodles and ginger around on my plate. "Absolutely not. We're friends." I doubt he bought that line of bullshit, so I went on the defensive. "I can't have any friends in China? Just because you don't? Well, you have one friend I know about. You have Karri."

I sat back and took a sip of wine. The Indonesian woman had taken her microphone off the stand and was walking up to the tables and crooning to the guests.

"Okay," Dad said, "so you know about me and Karri. It's no big secret. Would have told you sooner or later. I don't have to share every detail of my life with you. We're not the Manson Family."

"I have no idea what that means," I said.

"Look, I've been at this a long time."

"At what?" I said, arching my eyebrow.

"Work. Work is my only friend. You think I don't have friends by choice? You think I'm living it up over here in China, don't you? I used to stay at the Hotel National—only hotel that accepted foreigners. Pillows hard as stones. I mean they were actual rocks—weapons in case the Japs invaded again. I'm kidding, Mr. Serious, they weren't weapons, but I *slept* on rocks. Brushed my teeth with beer. Because the water would kill you. That part is true. I've been sentenced here a quarter of my life. For what? For my health? No, for you, your sister, your mother. It's all for you."

That was the Triple-A ball of Jewish guilt. He'd have to do a lot better. So I was under his skin and that could be a good thing. I couldn't tell yet.

"Let's go over the process," I said, in a soft voice. "You know it better than me, you know it inside out." That was a classic pitch he'd taught me. Talk the other guy up. Let him feel valued, in charge, let him feel like an expert and you're just some clueless schmuck, and then, once he loosens up, you slit his throat. "So say a new girl comes in wanting work. I'm talking about a specific worker named Ruxi. Okay, so, first Ruxi needed work permits from the town and permits from the factory."

"No, first she shows the *hukou*—"

"I thought you didn't know what that was? A moment ago."

"Oh, okay," Dad said. "The *hukou*. Sure. It's basically like an ID. It was the way you pronounced it."

I pronounced it the same way he did, but I let that slide. "And what happens if the worker doesn't have all the money up front?"

"We loan them the money, Alex. We want the workers. God knows we need the help. We want all we can get."

"Sure, I understand. But what if this girl needs to leave? She can't leave without the *hukou*. Without the *hukou* she's living illegally here in the city. Now, do you give her the money we owe her? Do you give her the *hukou* back? It's a simple question."

Dad laid his chopsticks sideways across his plate to signal to

Wong that he was done—ever the gentleman—and pushed his chair back, dabbed at the corners of his mouth with the pink cloth napkin and crossed his legs.

"Let's finish this conversation outside," he said. "We over-ordered again. I'm a balloon. This is what happens at the buffet. Why'd you let me order so much? Next time stop me."

Outside, the air was warm and carried the scent of jasmine. We walked the grounds, a French Renaissance–style garden shaped in perfect symmetry and order, every shrub obedient, every unkempt branch snipped, every flower pruned. We walked along the flagstones, hedgerows up to our waists, long as the conveyor belts at the factory.

"It's complicated," Dad said. "What you're asking. More variables than you think. But I trust Yong. If Yong says she owes six months, she owes. But we'd never hold someone against her will."

Then Dad washed his hands clean.

"Listen, Yong handles the floor and all the workers. He speaks the language. You only worry about product develop-ment. Head down, okay? That's our way. You land in a place, find a way to blend in and keep your business to yourself, and that's that."

"Right," I said, "but you brought me in to take over the factory after you, and to do that I need the whole picture. I need to know how it all works. So it doesn't really matter if I'm development or the janitor. I'm responsible. It's on me if we sink."

"This is a question I need to ask Yong," Dad said.

"No, I'll ask him."

"Look, it's not summer camp," Dad said, throwing his hands up. "Sure, some of these girls have a raw deal. Imagine doing the same repetitive motion, day in and day out. I'm sure some go crazy. But I also know a lot of them are grateful. They're not farming anymore. They're out of the village and moving up. They're where we were seventy years ago. That's the free market."

I said, "I get the sense there are things going on at this factory I don't know about. Things I don't agree with. If we can make a few little changes to improve things without hurting our margins, why wouldn't we do that?"

"Is this Ivy giving you these ideas? She is, isn't she? She's the one talking Trotsky in your ear. You didn't talk like this before. This is new. You don't know from trouble. If she's here to start trouble, I'll have Yong get rid of her."

That was the ultimate power play and he knew it. He'd fire her. Simple as that. We turned off onto a side path that led to a small pond and a not-so-French octagonal pavilion with flying eaves and red hanging paper lanterns. We could smell the lotus blooming on top of the water, the red light rippled over the pond, and I could see my father's weary face in the glow. He leaned forward on the railing and sighed.

I was staring straight ahead, but I could feel Dad side-eyeing me. I knew he was thinking: *I created you.* Like how the old rabbis would mold a mystical golem to follow orders—I honestly think that's how Dad saw fatherhood. And now he was worried that his divine creation was beginning to turn against him. I felt him out of the corner of my eye. Weighing the question so intensely I could almost hear the deep drive of his voice asking: *Hey, schmekel, are you about to turn?*

"She's not a problem," I said. For some reason I felt the need to reassure him. "She's looking out for a friend, that's all, okay. No one's causing problems. I feel for her friend. If it's true. It's hard enough working on the line. You know that. Hell, you barely even go on the line anymore."

"That's because of my allergies."

"Still. As you said. It's not summer camp."

I could make out the silhouettes of night cranes standing on one leg around the bank of the pond. Dad's arm snaked around my shoulders. I felt it heavy on the back of my neck, the prickly bristles of hair on his forearm.

He said, "We need to think long-term, you and me. This is how I beat everyone to China. Everyone else liquidated or quit or drowned. I thought ahead. Not a week out, not a month. Five, ten years down the line. Where do you want to be? I can get you there, but you got to stop being an idiot. I know it's hard for you, but try. Stop with these girls. Are you lonely, is that it? Am I not enough company?"

"No, no." He was under my skin now. "It's not that."

"Alex, we're doing a quarter million pairs this season—sure we're way down from last year and the year before—but we need the line running full steam. We need girls like Ruxi. It takes five Americans to do the work of a single Chinese girl. Their values are in the right place. Like ours. We need them. Give me workers. Communists, fascists, tramps—I don't care who they belong to. I need bodies on the line."

He was talking big now. Pushing further and further away from my questions.

"Just answer me. Did you already know about Ruxi and her situation?"

"Not at all," he said. "If I knew, I'd tell. To be honest, thousands of workers have passed through and I've never talked to a single one."

"You don't think it's odd you've never talked to one of your workers?"

"What's to say? They don't speak English. They aren't educated. I have enough worries. I have to place orders and deliver. What do I care how their lives are?"

"You damn well should care. I care. Let's start there. So if you don't know anything, let me bring it to Yong."

"Stay out of it, Alex. Don't be a hero. You know who's a hero? The rabbi who snipped your dick. Who snipped all those dicks. One tiny slip and you ruin a man's life forever. Ha! That's a hero. Don't be something you're not."

"Come off it with the jokes," I said, my voice rising. "Let's be straight."

"Okay, let's be straight. I think you're only interested in this for Ivy. That's what I think. You want to get in her panties."

"Watch it."

"Don't poke," he said, and only then did I realize my index finger was in the center of his chest and my feet, unbidden, had carried me close enough to see the spool-shaped scar beside his eye where Nana almost blinded him with her high-heeled shoe for proposing to a shiksa.

"This isn't Camp Wekeela, Alex." He pushed the barrel of my finger aside. "No more Friday night latkes and applesauce, every *pish* in the pool wins a trophy for not drowning."

"You're an asshole."

"This isn't your fight. This Ruxi girl. It's got nothing to do with you. You know your problem? Your mother made you her way. Center of the world. That's my fault for leaving you alone with her. A sickness to be smothered. Like Nana did to me. I had to save you. I brought you in. I saved you. Did you want to carry an umbrella for the rest of your life?"

My face flushed, fingers curled into a fist. Mom had me carry an open white umbrella everywhere I went to hide me from the Angel of Death. Religion had scrambled her brains. But Dad was every bit as smothering as my mother, ten times more, painting her to sound like a psychopath, left to raise two kids on her own while her husband traipsed through the Far East. Of course she turned to religion. And the fact Dad cast himself in this role of Messiah was pure delusion. There was no use talking to him. I turned and started back to the hotel, back through the diamond hedges and the tunnel of trees, but now they took on a whole different shape—the canopy of cypresses and firs packed tight and tall, closing in on me.

I heard his voice. "Where you going? The van won't leave without me. Jianguo's a loyal driver. He's my guy. They're *all* my guys. I built this empire."

Squawks from a pyramid of geese flying overhead, migrating back north, calling to each other, but it sounded like they were laughing at me.

Dad's gravelly voice behind me. The clap of his soles on the flagstone. Louder. "This is a shoe factory in the asshole of the world, princess. You're here now. It's all yours, babes, and fucking a Chinese peasant isn't going to change a thing."

Before he could react, I swiveled around and grabbed him by the shoulders. I tried to twist him down, but he widened his base, planted his feet apart and gripped my tie in his fist, shaking, dead black eyes, his breath crackled in his nose.

"Come off it," he said. "Cohains aren't animals." I took a vine step across his body and staked my left foot behind his calf and tried to whip him down. This noise, a growl, mine or his, our chests too close to tell. His knee gave, waist buckled, and he rolled a little but didn't go down. His left arm still clutched my tie but his right was free. A boxer in the reserves in Shelby, Mississippi, undefeated only because the goys wouldn't fight him. I knew my jaw was open if he wanted it, one jab was all it'd take. He saw it too, but didn't throw. It must have looked like I was holding him in a dip. He was going to crack some lame joke. *How did the Chinese judge score us?* I wouldn't let him. I smoothed off the wrinkled fabric at his shoulders and set him right. What was the use? Even if I knocked his ass out, he'd keep getting up, keep coming at me.

"What were you going to do exactly?" he asked, hands on his knees, taking short breaths. "Out of curiosity."

"Kill you."

"That's great. The instinct, I mean. You can't teach that. Now aim it at the business instead of old farts like me." He reached for my tie and began wriggling the knot back into place. "Look how I almost destroyed it. I'm sorry. I love this tie. You remember Levenstein's?"

Levenstein's was the top men's store in Lynn. He once took me to get a suit for my bar mitzvah and this red tie with the smallest blue corn silk flowers, way too long for me then, hung down past my dick, but he wouldn't buy me a kid's tie. *The necktie makes the man.* What a piece of work. He thought I'd fall for it. Get a little schmaltzy and all was forgiven.

"You were almost feral when I took you to that shop. You used to blow your nose in the bottom of your shirt, remember that? And now look at you. A true Cohain. The Chinese see it. Why do you think they like us so much? They know we aren't ordinary. You laugh, but it's true. I'm sorry I laid hands on you."

He was holding my chin. "I'm not going to let you piss this all away like my father did." He slapped me real soft on the cheek twice and held his palm there the third time.

"Now let's go home and get a drink at the Amazonia," he said. "I still owe you a goddamn drink. Two hundred thousand pairs this afternoon. That's nothing to be ashamed of. And remember you put that line together mostly. That's your baby."

He took a quick swipe at his eye with the back of his wrist.

"Jesus, Pop, are you crying?" Could be out of pride for what I sold, or maybe he was hurt that I tried to knock him down. Either way, I felt a prickle of shame and couldn't bear to look at him.

"No," Dad said, seizing up. "You nuts? Eh, maybe a little. I only saw Papa cry once. Well, twice. A little when I graduated high school, but then for sure when I got the house in

Swampscott with a swimming pool. He wouldn't budge from it. Covered his face with his hands. Can't forget it. He said, 'I never thought a son of mine would have something like this.'"

Back at the hotel, I rode the elevator up to the forty-ninth floor. In my room, I was met by a spiteful cloud of cinnamon freshener. Everything was back to its starting point: my toiletries hidden away, my books back in my suitcase, everything, even the brochures fanned evenly on the desk, the room immaculately clean, any hint that someone lived here scoured away. It was always my first night.

There was a silver tray on my desk with a bottle of wine, a long-stem rose in a champagne flute, a box of Godiva chocolates. Even the gifts were a kind of mockery: *here, enjoy a long sensual evening by yourself.* These came courtesy of the hotel, once a week, for Ambassador-level guests. You reached Ambassador when you'd spent a good three-quarters of your life on the road sleeping in their hotels. It got passed down too, an inheritance you didn't earn. Death by luxury.

I slowly undressed and got into the shower. Growing up we had an endless stockpile of these mini-soaps and mini-shampoos that Dad had plundered from hotels around the world. Do Not Disturb signs, too, hung from the knob of every door in our house. *Busy come back later. Can't you read the sign?*

There were mirrors on all sides of the bathroom. No one needed to look at themselves this much. I tried to let my thoughts go, but for some reason I thought of the time I worked a summer as a chicken-gutter for Boston Rotisserie wearing a hairnet—even this was in line with my fate. Written across my forehead like the Hebrew word for *truth* that brought the golem to life. I was born into this, right? Cows, chickens. Why did we kill so much? My family. Were we butchers? We must have been. We were.

I let the water beat down on my shoulders, let the water fill up my mouth—*don't swallow!*—and let it dribble out. I thought about taking a shower as a kid with my mother right outside the bathroom door, braced for a sudden, calamitous thud. And for a perverse moment I wished to hear her voice, something calming in her craziness. "I don't want a slip and spill, Alex! They're not just brains, Alex. Private school brains! I'm protecting my investment."

Elsa and Fedor. Mom and Dad. Everything missed with them.

When did Mom finally snap? Maybe it was when she took us to the Chagall exhibit at the Boston MFA. I was young. A kid. It was the happiest I'd ever seen her. Her knees buckled in front of *I and the Village*. This was a painting my mother spoke about in hushed tones reserved for UFO sightings. "This is the pomegranate, soft like mortal men, and this is the ram's horn Elijah blows to raise the dead"—and suddenly Dad interrupted to say: "What's with the stupid goat?" My mother let out a groan she'd been saving forever and stormed off. That one goat cost me years of therapy where a very nice lady told me, in brief, *Forgive*, but it was too late to supplant the original Sunday school message: *never forget*. The therapists and the rabbis had their signals crossed. But my mother. Jesus. She didn't talk for the rest of the day.

It wasn't long after that she joined the ladies auxiliary club at the synagogue and they were restoring this gorgeous mural they'd discovered. The mural was almost a hundred years old, and no one knew it was hiding back there until the cruddy paint started peeling off the wall.

Then she got in deep. Orthodox deep. But my mother had also taught me how to say fuck off in Russian. How to pinch

an orange from the fruit carts on Boylston Street beside the
T station when the vendor wasn't looking. I mean she was
fun too. If you got a putty knife and scraped off the topcoat,
there was something hiding behind all that.

I got out and dried off. I was standing naked now at the window looking out over Qiangling Lake and I could see the dark
silhouette of the dragon boats moving like silk over the water,
their oars stroking in unison, and the sound of the coxswain
keeping time with a leather drum, a deep bass pounding in my
ears. Could they see me, stark naked and afraid, hanging here
by the window on the forty-ninth floor? I wanted to call Ivy on
her cell phone and ask the name of the tree blossoming white
under the lantern by the lake. How would I know anything if
I couldn't name that tree? What was a dragon boat anyway? In
Mandarin, Cantonese, English, Pinyin, who cares, tell me all
the names because all that I don't know makes my head dizzy,
makes me deeply afraid. Did we really hold workers hostage?
Was Ruxi not free to go? I could see in the window the lake
but also my own naked body, a hairy chest, flabby midsection,
flat feet—she probably wanted a man like Trotsky, lean, sinewy,
great arches, someone slick enough to scale a Palace wall. Not
a pudgy Jew. The dragon boat rowed toward me now, spear-
ing my chest, moving through me, superimposed on the window, and it sifted through me like a ghost ship or I through
it. What was I so afraid of? That I'd always need someone to
translate the world for me.

Four

IN THE FACTORY'S FREIGHT ELEVATOR THERE
were two signs written in English:

Do Not Carry Explosives.

Trapped? Stay Calm and Wait for Help.

Below them, carved with an edging knife, were the initials
of two lovers. I'd come in the morning to the third floor to
find Shen, the production manager, to ask about Ruxi. If I
went straight to Yong it would only get back to Dad, and he
could get pissed enough to fire Ivy.

The elevator opened onto a room the size of an airplane
hangar, and the dank warm air from the heat setter boxes
slipped over my face like a pillow. A boy with a Mohawk
scowled at me: a stump for a right arm, severed at the elbow
by the steel embossing plate on the leather grain press. A girl,
eyes jaundiced, punch-drunk, the first flush of benzene poi-
soning from cement glue vapors, scratched at her arm. Everywhere, people and machines. The sandpaper wheel kicked up
dust, and these yellow orbs floated past the sallow face of a girl
shouldering a steel leather horse down the line. Iron shavings

glittered on the floor. The constant tinny plink of hammers, each little tack driving deeper in my skull, the whirring of the roughing belt, the sweet, sickly smell of cement glue curled my toes. Signs around the factory: Don't Spit—50¥ Fine. The crouching, slavering, overheated machines, and the utter sincerity of levers, wheels, sprockets, buttons.

This was why I tried to avoid coming to the line. Shocking more people didn't faint in here. Dad had already come up with his own excuses for avoiding the floor, allergies, bad for his lungs, too loud, and maybe that was as honest as he could get.

A red paper Fu bat hung from the wall above Shen's desk at the head of the first line, but he wasn't there. I turned to walk to the other end of the plant when a line manager, showing off for me, slapped his hand down hard on the table between two stitchers giggling, and so I didn't consciously notice Dad walking toward me until he handed me a spec form for a riding boot. I looked down at the paper and saw the words *Lt Peanut* on top.

"Who's Lieutenant Peanut?" I asked.

"It's a color, moron. Light peanut. Where's your head?"

I didn't know. He walked back to his office. It was hard to concentrate in here. Everyone on their way to becoming something else. Everyone telling themselves this was their last day. It was the only way into tomorrow. You didn't care what they took out of your check. What *we* took. It was we, not they. If nothing else, I had to get my pronouns right. This was why I hated walking the line, because everything I knew loosened, broke off and got hauled away like granite rocks. Outside it was spring, but really it was always the dead of July, your clothes hard and rough, stiff from sweat, a constant awareness of them pressing you, like a second skin.

Shen was on the fifth production line standing beside Xiafei, the head of Industrial Engineering. Xiafei, a frail young man with khaki pants hiked up to his belly button, held a clipboard in one hand and a stopwatch connected to a lanyard around his neck. Both men hovered behind a young woman's shoulder as she operated the cutting machine. She was probably in her early twenties, a low bridge to her nose, a touch of auburn in her hair, wearing a loose yellow tunic and jean shorts. They were timing how fast she could cut patterns out of a hide of leather. Every time she pressed the triggers, the hydraulics hissed and the giant steel plate lowered over the die, a deep satisfying thunk as it bit into the leather.

After a curt hello, they continued scrutinizing the girl's movements. "Faster," Shen shouted at her. Her hands trembled. Cutting the upper for this boot, said Xiafei, who saw the world in milliseconds, should take 13.57 seconds, but she was at 14.16 without changing the die. The girl reached across her body for the next quarter hide of finished leather, the muscles bubbling in her shoulders.

"Wasted movement!" Shen yelled. He deplored waste with every fiber of his being. "Why doesn't she reach with her left hand? She wasted 1.16 seconds."

"So lazy," Xiafei said.

"She needs to maximize her productivity," Shen said. "Xiafei!" he shouted to the man standing right beside him. "How much is this costing us?"

Xiafei touched the tip of his tongue with the pencil eraser and announced in a flinty voice that she wasted seventy yuan over the course of the day. Shen rubbed both hands over his face very fast like he was just waking up, and, leaning toward me, asked, "Is it true in your country you can hit a person smaller than yourself? Is this law?"

"You can't hit anyone in either of our countries," I said.

The girl knew something was terribly wrong. Her eyes

jittered back and forth. She worked faster. A drop of sweat clung to an incisor of peach fuzz on the side of her face. By Xiafei's calculations, she wasted eight and a half minutes a week, putting her in the bottom 10 percent of workers.

"Remember to breathe," Xiafei said, consoling Shen.

"Breathing is for monks," Shen said, turning purple. He stamped his foot. "Counter-efficiency is the one thing I cannot tolerate. Eight and a half minutes! One could make a child with his wife in that time. Xiafei! Is it true?"

"I have never timed *that*," Xiafei said, blushing, and lowering his stopwatch.

"Shen," I said, interrupting them. "I need to speak to a worker."

"Of course, Alex. But please let me first finish. Then we talk all you want." He turned to Xiafei. "I am afraid there is only one thing to do with this worker."

"You cannot fire her," I told him. "You don't have permission."

"Fire? No, I was going to kill her."

Xiafei said, "Why don't we put her in dog cage?"

"There's a dog cage?" I asked, my voice thin. I grabbed the edge of the table so I wouldn't fall over.

Shen laughed. "No, of course not. Xiafei exaggerates everything."

But Xiafei's face betrayed him, and I was starting to realize there were two factories: the one I thought I saw, and the one that existed once I turned my back.

"This woman is capable," I said. "Look at how nervous you make her. No one can work under these conditions. Train her so her numbers improve. Now please, apologize on my behalf to her."

She blushed deeply when they apologized to her and bowed.

"Shen," I said, "I need to speak to a worker named Ruxi. In private."

"Ruxi?" Shen said, and stared up at the metal trusses on the ceiling. "We have a few Ruxi."

Xiafei said, "He must mean to see worker 329017."

"Oh, 329017! Of course," Shen said, scowling. "She is a tapeworm in my belly. Finally she reached your attention. It is time we fire her. This is a good day. She is not a diligent and keen one. Xiafei! Her numbers."

"Bottom 5 percent. Insole press. Line three."

"Take me to her," I said.

As we walked over to line three, Shen almost jogged ahead of me, saying he needed someone from the top to smash her. "I told her you would come for her. She is Nakhi tribe from the north, this is why she is so lazy. My recommendation is we stop hiring this minority. Also they eat their children. This is fact."

He was giving me a headache. "Let me handle it," I said. Now was not the time to set him straight about the reason for the meeting. I needed to get her alone. I needed her to trust me. Shen stopped in front of a girl whose hair was pulled back in a ponytail.

"This is the deplorable worker," he said.

At the sound of Shen's voice, the girl snapped out of whatever deep trance she was in and spun around to face us, head lowered.

In my awful Mandarin I asked her name. She recited in a soft voice her ID number, and I felt a surge of heat along my neck.

"No, your real name."

"Ruxi," she said.

I held out my hand. She wiped the sweat off her face with her protective forearm sleeve hand sewn from cotton scraps, and reached out her hand, but stopped herself short, holding up her palms to show me they were filthy, stained in grease and oil from the machine, black along her skinny fingers.

"It's okay," I said, wagging my hand, and hesitantly she reached out. Her palms were heavily callused. She barely gripped my hand.

For some reason I thought she'd be much older, but she was quite young with long lashes that stood apart and high cheekbones. She wore a T-shirt that said Baby Love, jeans that ended at her calves and scrungy, once-white Keds.

"I fine her on repeat," Shen said. "I try every means of torture, but nothing communicates to her. Look at her pile compared to better girls."

There were four insole press machines in a row, the metal jaws molding the thin fiberboard to the last. The girls stacked them in plastic bins. At a glance, Ruxi had maybe a third of what the other girls produced.

"I need to speak with both of you in private," I said to Shen. "In my office."

They said this to her and her eyes widened. Right as she picked up her ID card off the table and clipped it to her belt, the first rumble of thunder shook the building. The late-morning thunderstorm was starting early. The three of us walked across the floor and up the green stairs to the administrative offices, but in the hallway I was cut off by Dad, flustered, bug-eyed, holding two huge shopping bags. He needed me to go down to the tannery in Tai-San and give these gifts to Peng, the village chief.

"That's not my job," I said. He was crazy if he thought I was running deliveries. And I tried to go around him but he cut me off.

"It *is* your job."

Out of respect, Shen and Ruxi turned at the same time and

pretended to take great interest in the antique wood rickshaw in the corner with a bleached cow's skull on the bench seat, half its jawbone missing, wide-eyed, watching us in hatred.

I saw Dad wasn't going anywhere, so I told Shen and Ruxi that we'd have to meet that evening. Then I pulled Dad into my office. He set the heavy bags down on the table.

"I'm a partner now," I said. "Not an errand boy."

"Hey, I did it coming up. Now it's your turn. The driver's waiting downstairs." He crossed his arms.

I peeked inside the bags. Cartons of cigarettes, bottles of expensive *baijiu* and a tin box that looked like it held Christmas cookies. I opened it and inside there were stacks of hundred dollar bills fixed with rubber bands.

"Fuck," I said, "how much is in here?"

"Enough."

"I'm not carrying this. What if I get spot-checked by the police?"

"There's plenty in there."

Now it came back to me all the times Don Bauer went down to the tannery carrying these bags, which, like a moron, I'd always thought were full of leather swatches. Dad had gone down there too.

"Have Don do it," I said. "I'm not moving it."

"He's up north looking at a new supplier."

"It doesn't have to be like this."

"Just deliver the fucking bags to Peng, will you? I'm not asking you to sleep with the guy. Peng speaks English, so you'll be fine, but I don't go anywhere without a translator. Take Taishu from the outsole plant if you want. I'm sure he could use the air."

The minute he mentioned a translator I saw my chance. "Okay, I'll do it this once."

"That's more like it. Good boy. Car's waiting. I'll see you tonight for dinner," he said and left the office.

Ignoring Dad's request to take Taishu, I sent a text to Ivy and waited about ten minutes for the reply, then I lifted the bags off the table and carried them down the stairs to the street.

Ivy was standing inside the security guard's boot, holding her palm out in the rain falling in long gray sheets, already filling the irrigation ditches and bubbling up out of the sewer holes and then, without warning, the rain stopped. She stepped toward me, and I noticed she was wearing different-colored sandals: one black, the other dark green.

She looked very beautiful, and I wanted to tell her this but I was sure she knew, I was sure she'd been told that many times and was tired of hearing it, and maybe it was a terrible thing to be that beautiful. So instead, I said, "Sorry for stabbing you yesterday."

She laughed and shrugged her shoulders. "I am sorry too."

The heat returned. Mist steamed off the asphalt and the fishtail palms shimmered in the sunlight, and the breeze carried the sweet fragrance of frangipani blossoms in the direction of the river.

"So," she said, looking at the bags in my hands with a knowing smile, "we go down to Tai-San to cultivate friendship?"

"Yes, unfortunately. It's my first time running this errand." I explained to her that we were in a joint venture with this local official down there named Peng, who was the majority owner and set all the prices. I was also going to text Shen to make sure he knew that I needed her as a translator.

"Thank you," she said.

"So you're coming?"

She smiled. "No offense, but anything is better than working here."

"It's on the beach," I said, climbing into the back of the van, and she was already making that face, knitted tight, before I realized how stupid that had sounded. She went to get into the front seat next to the driver, but I asked her to sit in the back with me. I'd never sat up front.

"I can't," she said. "It will make Jianguo feel like a chauffeur."

My shoulders arched. "He kind of is the chauffeur. Right? He's our driver."

"Maybe on the return," she said and climbed into the front seat as Jianguo scrambled to clear his newspaper and smokes and cell phone off the seat. He glanced back to confirm this was okay with me. I shrugged. Now that she was riding up there with Jianguo, I felt a pinch of shame for always riding in the back, for knowing him a whole year and only communicating through shrugs and nods and hand gestures.

Ivy said over her shoulder, "So, do you feel like your father's delivery boy?"

"No, I'm more like a service dog."

"China does not recognize service animals."

"But you do," I said, grinning at her, and she smiled back at me, then faced the front.

Jianguo drove us out of town up onto the highway an hour south into Tai-San. We drove along the narrow river, past a marina of docked squid fishing boats. Ivy said it was mating season, so the fishermen couldn't go out. They were sitting around tables playing liar's dice and chess with their shirts off, out in front of their handshake houses. We wove past them onto a narrow dirt road toward the South China Sea. The tannery sat on a marsh that we filled in and leveled with dirt from the last drumlin swarm before the ground turned to mud. One of these knolls was cut in half as if someone dropped a guillotine blade on its neck. One side of the knoll had a blunt face of dirt and clay, but the other side was dotted with rows of young green trees, no underbrush anywhere.

"Those trees," I asked. "What are they?"

"I don't know how you call them in English. Koala bears eat."

"Eucalyptus?"

"Yes. From Australia. Our government plants them everywhere. They grow fast and tall, but they drink all the nutrition in the soil and kill off other plants. Very bad. In English I think you call it invader species. I don't know. Someone makes a lot of money off them."

I felt like she was talking about me. I know she was, but I didn't want to call her on it and come off sounding paranoid, though maybe I was getting paranoid.

We pulled into the tannery and parked between a large hangar and a huge in-ground rainwater tank. There were a few workers inside the open garage door of the tannery wearing straw hats, rubber gloves and boots, broom-pushing puddles of cow blood across the floor into narrow gutters.

"Nice beach," Ivy said, once we were out of the car. We hid our noses in our shirts. The smell was crippling: rotten eggs and meat and feces, a smell that made my stomach muscles clench and triggered a surge of adrenaline screaming at me to flee.

After ten minutes of waiting, Peng, the village chief, pulled up in a black Audi and got out wearing a red Scottie Pippen Bulls jersey, acid-washed blue jeans and black leather sandals. In addition to handing off the bribe, I wanted to check that he installed the equipment to get the recycling program started. The mayor of Foshan, his uncle, said we needed to recycle 25 percent of the waste material by 2016 or he'd kick us out.

"Who's this?" Peng said, first thing out of his car, smiling with yellow crooked teeth. Instead of the usual brush cut, he wore a toupee, at least I thought it was one, combed over sharply to the right. I'd met him a few times before when he came to the factory. Now he gave me a quick shake. Ivy also stuck out her hand, introducing herself, but Peng leaned over, bowed and daintily kissed the backside of her hand. He made a real show out of it, and while he was down there he lifted his eyes and they flashed wickedly. Ivy pulled her hand away.

"She's my translator," I said.

"Alex, you know I speak English good. So something else going on. Fine. None of my business."

Out of the corner of her eye, Ivy glanced at me. Peng straightened up and said to Ivy in a syrupy voice, *"Enchanté."* There was a pause. "That's French," he added. Ivy laughed and said it was clear that she was in the presence of a man of great importance.

Missing the sarcasm, Peng commended her on her taste and said he knew the minute he saw her that she was a splendid flower, a rare flower, not the typical country girl.

"You have no idea," she said.

He looked down at the bags in my hand. "Why don't we go up to my office?"

We walked up the terrazzo staircase to his office on the second floor with a high ceiling and a long oak desk. His secretary brought in a tray of green tea and poured the steaming water into our small cups. When she was done pouring, Ivy put two knuckles down on the table as a way of saying thank you, the symbol of someone prostrate on her knees, and Peng observed all this, eyebrows arched, and said, "You don't have to show Ms. Li such respect. She's a secretary."

"Then she deserves even more," Ivy said.

Peng clapped his hands together. "Ah, beauty and good

health, impeccable manners, but a soft heart too? You have it all. I should leave my wife and marry you."

"I am not available," she said, "and you're too old for me."

"Age," he snuffled. "What's age? With age comes wisdom. Wisdom and *experience*." His eyes flashed again and I felt like punching him.

He said he wasn't stung by this rejection, however, because he already had a girlfriend, much too young, who fancied herself an actress. "If I want to see her, I must pay for everything. She says she loves me but of course they all say that. Prove it. She could buy dinner once, just once, couldn't she? Contribute a little. Show me you care."

"This shouldn't happen to men of your importance," Ivy said.

"Exactly," he shouted and slapped his forehead with his palm. "See, you understand me."

She rolled her eyes at me subtly. The idea crept up on me to stand up and say, We aren't doing business like this anymore, and walk out with Ivy, but I pushed it aside. Just give him the bags and get out. "From my father," I said, this lame attempt to cut myself out of it, and reached the bags across the table. I didn't know if there was bribe etiquette to follow. If it was like Christmas where we were supposed to watch him unwrap the gifts. He took the bags, peered inside, set them down by his feet and with a self-satisfied smirk said, "Good." He didn't even bother to take any of it out of the bag.

"Tell your father thank you," he said, "and the prices of course stay the same."

And now I knew I had to show some gratitude. Ivy looked away. I muttered a thank you under my breath.

"Also tell him the audit will go fine this quarter," Peng said.

"How do you know that?" I asked, but I knew damn well

why we never ran into problems. I just wanted to see if he'd cop to it.

He reached for a pack of toothpicks on his desk and started to clean his teeth, but he didn't have the class to cover his mouth with one hand. He picked away, smacking his lips, running his tongue over his teeth.

"I am on the auditing board. It is a private company."

Ivy laughed out loud and then stifled it with her palm.

Peng glared at her. "What is so funny?"

"She's laughing at me, Peng," I said, and I half believed it. Why call out the obvious? Of course he was making money off his own fake audits.

"Oh," Peng said, his face softening. "In that case laugh all you want."

I stood up. I couldn't take being in his office a second more. "Can we see the recycling program?" I asked.

Back outside, the air was thick and humid. Peng threw a handful of pebbles at a scraggly dog with red skin sores. It barked once and scurried away. We walked across the uneven pavement to the first hangar, the smell more pronounced, fetid meat mixed with a salt breeze.

They were all men, the workers, young too, staring at us as we walked past the glistening pink-and-brown rawhides packed in salt and stacked on wood pallets. The workers wore butcher aprons, jeans and rubber boots, steel mesh gloves and T-shirts, their forearms covered in jerry-rigged rubber sleeves. They were hanging the hides by two corners on meat hooks connected to an overhead track, while another group beat the hides with shovels to remove the salt and sand, and a last group swept the dirt and salt and hair that fell off into tall piles with a few cow tails sticking out.

Peng leaned in and said, "No place for a pretty girl, Miss Ivy."

She waved him off and walked in. No ventilation here aside from the open shipping door and a few standing fans. Dozens of rawhides hanging from meat hooks moved like tattered sails along the ceiling, giant torn flags of skin, loose and heavy.

In front of us, the workers slipped rawhides into the loud fleshing machines where rolling knives and grinding bricks stripped the fat and muscle.

Everything had a green patina of rust so all the machinery looked like it had been salvaged from a deepwater shipwreck. The irrigation gutters in the floor carried the hair and the chrome and lime past our feet, chopped up bits of fat in soapy water, trailed by some bluish-green sludge flowing to the open-air cement recycling tanks dug into the ground.

"See," Peng said, "I held up my end of the deal. We are recycling." His cell phone went off. "Excuse me," he said.

Alone, Ivy and I walked past the splitting machines, where four men dragged the lime-swollen hides through a thin band saw. The bottom was suede, the top was full grain. It was difficult to see, but no one wore a mask. Suede was so dusty some tanneries sold it off because they didn't want to deal with it, but we did well with suede. We passed the workers simulating grain on the cheap leather, the stuff with nicks and scratches. Plating machines exerted tons of pressure to give it an ostrich grain or snake or alligator. Around us, elevated on a metal scaffold were giant wooden tumble drums—the hides pickling in brine, sulfuric acid and ammonium salts.

Then we came to the last room where a steep staircase led to a giant silo for recycling the cow hair. The manager here wore a teddy bear rhinestone shirt and wedge platform sandals, a streak of her hair dyed pink and held back by a barrette. She greeted us in Chinese. It was clear that each morning she spent time on her looks despite being the only female in the plant beside the secretary, despite working here at the end of the continent, in shit and mud and blood. We walked four flights of stairs up to the top of the silo. She kept doing this bashful outward roll of her foot as she talked, explaining that the hair recycling separated protein from water and waste. By adding hot air they made a powder, which fell down like snow. This powder was used for pillows and sofa fillers, fertilizer, even animal feed. Peng had caught up with us by now and he was making a big show to the girl about there not being safety ropes or a railing up there, and while they were arguing, Ivy slipped away. I followed her down the stairs and she opened the door to the silo with a grin. We ducked inside and sure enough it was snowing.

"I never saw snow before," she said, holding out her hands. It fell softly on her hair and shoulders. Fat flakes, twizzling, like flies at the canteen.

"Is this what it feels like?" she asked. "Real snow."

I told her yes, except colder. "Come on. I don't think it's good to have this stuff on us."

"It is beautiful." She held out her tongue and let the snow or cow hair or whatever the fuck it was fall on the tip.

"Don't do that," I said.

She closed her eyes.

"What are you doing?" I asked.

"Trying to picture cold," she said. "Being stuck alone in snow and thinking you are going to freeze to death like Trotsky in Siberia. He was saved, you know, by a Jewish farmer driving a horse cart. This farmer was on his way home to bring his wife a duck to cook for the special day of week. What do you call this?"

"The Sabbath."

"That's it. The farmer had gone far for this duck to make

his wife happy. This was the first thing I learned about Jews, they want to make their wives happy, is that true?"

Her shoulders were covered in snow, her hair too. I could see the side of her face by the small square of light from the isinglass on the hatch door. "Not all the time. We don't have a policy."

"Trotsky," she said, "hid under blankets holding the duck, and the Jew farmer drove by the last guard station along the river, praying. Then they hear the duck. The duck is going real crazy, barking. No, ducks don't bark. I can't say in English."

"Quack." The snow beating down. Light and soft. Thickening in her hair. I couldn't see my breath.

"Yes, quack. Doing this and Trotsky says I have to, I am so sorry, my friend. Then he snaps its neck. And then they drive all night and smuggle Trotsky free. So there's no revolution without a Jewish duck farmer. But I feel very bad for his wife who probably yelled at him. She didn't know how much her husband risked. He was also the father of the revolution even if he was just a farmer. Do you think of this, Alex? Both of us are small people. You are very rich, but still small. Do you wonder maybe if there is someone greater inside? Someone like a duck farmer?"

"I like you," I said moronically. I couldn't think of anything else.

Ivy smiled at me in the darkness, one panel on her cheek illuminated, and I wanted to aim for that square and kiss her.

"I like you too," she said.

"Why?"

"At university, there was one rule—never ask why."

She was right up against me, I could feel her breath. I felt cold now, after hearing this story. She leaned closer. Lifted her head and the panel of light was on her white throat. She traced my lips with her finger and then her head tilted forward and her lips covered mine. Her tongue turned in my mouth and then curled as if she was trying to hook me. Her hands floated up my back; her skin smelled a little like the sweet cement glue at the factory and a little like talcum powder, in the whirling whiteness, and then she drew her head back slightly. Then it was silent except for our faint quick breaths.

"You just said that you went to college," I said.

"I did," she said.

"Why are you really working at a shoe factory? No one who's gone to college works at a factory."

"So much questions." She put her hand on my chest. "Can you put your arms here?" She raised my hands to her hips.

"Tell me something. Tell me what happened in Tiananmen."

We heard banging on the outside of the silo, a deep hollow reverberation and Peng's voice: "Hullo? You two in there? Where did they go?"

"I was there." Her voice a rustle.

"What happened?"

"Hullo?" Peng shouted. "I lost them. In my own tannery, where are they hiding? Hullo? Mr. Younger Cohen and beautiful Ivy?"

"What happened?" I asked.

"I got my sister killed."

The hatch door opened and we were flooded in light and I saw that her face was anguished and twisted.

"Look what I found," said Peng. "Two sparrows in a nest. Ivy, you cheat on me already and we just met. I could take you to more romancing place than tannery."

My hands dropped. Hers too. "I'm sorry," I said, but she was already walking out, and the snow sloughed off her hair and back, trailing her feet.

"Give me a minute," I told Peng, and I followed Ivy, who

had crossed the lot and was now standing on the foundation wall overlooking the green sea.

For a second I felt like I was back on the beach in Lynn. The small granite hills, the smell of the salt marsh, the tall cordgrass curved like scythes.

"Don't mind him," I said, "he's an asshole." She didn't answer. "Are you upset I kissed you?"

"I want to be honest with you," she said. "But there's so much you don't know."

No beach here: just a deserted coastline, the wind banging the door of a ramshackle fisherman's hut.

"You don't have to tell me," I said. That was a lie.

"No," she said, "I do. I am going to need you."

Ivy sat in the back of the van with me. I didn't make a big deal out of it, I was just glad she was there. We watched the girl in the teddy bear shirt waving goodbye as we drove off. Then Ivy asked if we could make a stop in the Wuling valley. There was something she wanted to show me.

"I don't know. I told Dad I'd be back right away. He needs me for confirmation samples on the Abelson's line. Sorry."

She drew back. "Your father will never know. Jianguo won't tell. Come on. The factory does not walk away. It will stay waiting for you."

"Sorry."

I said it ten times in my head to try to purge it from my brain. I felt like it was all I said anymore. How was mea culpa not Yiddish? This stunned me in middle school Latin class.

"Have you ever tried not listening to him?" Ivy asked. "Even to see what happens?"

I'd always held at third base. Back on Duggar's field in Lynn, and I'd just lofted a fastball over the right fielder who was chasing it all the way to the fence, and I rounded second when the third base coach flashed the sign—palms flat, away from his body—hold. Stop. Don't run up the score on the sucky Andover Pirates. Never once did I blow through his sign. I trotted into third and stayed, and my father wasn't there, he was probably in a German hostel in Taichung the first time it happened and sat bolt upright in his bed as God spoke unto him, "The boy obeys the signs," and Dad rubbed his eyes and said, *The boy listens? He's a good boy? Not the worst? Thank you, amen or whatever*—

We rumbled over a wooden bridge crossing the Bei River, and down below, a fisherman slipped by in his sampan, an oily cormorant perched in the bow with a noose around its neck, the rope ending in the owner's clenched fist.

"Okay," I said. "You know what? Fuck it, let's go."

Five

AFTER IVY GAVE JIANGUO DIRECTIONS, WE turned off the highway, riding now past watercress and goose farms, the rustle of rice stalks, wending between the karst mountains. The sound of the tires changed with the terrain: pocked asphalt to gravel to dirt, and we stopped at a village called Yingde in front of a house with a crescent pond. All the houses had wok-handle roofs, curved like a bell in front, with scrollwork of crabs and cranes and roosters. We got out of the van right as a few boys zipped past on scooters and waved to Ivy.

"Do they know you?" I asked.

"Of course," she said, pointing to the cottage in front of us. "I grew up here."

The whitewash plaster of her house had mostly peeled away from the gable wall and you could see every generation of infill—mud brick, tamped earth, daub and, most recently, cement, as if you were using tree rings to see into the past. We walked through double-leaf doors, and lizards skittered across the mud walls of a tight square room with no furniture. She led me into another bare room.

"This was my room growing up. No one has lived here for a long time." I stepped inside and it was a bare cement room. There was no one around. I touched the walls, moist and cool. Aside from the frogs lowing in the pond and the crackling cicadas, it was eerily quiet.

"Where is everyone?" I asked.

"Only old people and babies live here anymore. Everyone left for cities," she said plainly, as though everyone would agree that working in a factory and staying in a dorm the size of a coffee can was preferable to living here.

The house had three square bays and a narrow sky-well in the middle. She held out her hand as she'd done that morning at the factory as if she suspected rain to come dribbling down the ridge tiles.

She showed me a bullet bite in the sky-well. "My grandfather," she said. "He owned a lot of land here. During the Anti-Rightist Movement they blindfolded him and shot him against his own house, right here."

"Who's they?"

"Neighbors. His own people. They dumped him into the river where you met my grandmother. She moved there after. She's not Tanka like the rest of the fishermen there. She is just watching over my grandfather."

"That's awful," I said, like an idiot. She traced her index finger around the outline of the bullet hole in the brick.

"I told you when he was young he worked for the Foot Emancipation Society. This all seems very long ago, but then, when I look around, I think China is still an old woman with golden lotus feet."

"Is that true? You guys are in hyper-speed. You did the West's twentieth century in about fifteen years."

"No," she said, "I don't mean industry and development. I mean the revolution did not succeed. People are afraid. Since Tiananmen people are scared of being radical. But that's what it will take. Did you talk to your father about Ruxi?"

Right then I remembered that I was supposed to meet Ruxi and Shen that evening. I'd completely forgotten. I looked down at my watch. If I left now I could probably make it back in time.

"I talked to my father and I got a meeting set up with Ruxi."

"Thank you," she said, touching my arm.

"We can make a new policy."

"Why don't you do what is right?"

"We'll make a policy to do what's right."

She shook her head and frowned.

"Tomorrow," I said. "I already set it up." I shuddered with guilt and looked away.

"That is good. Ruxi's desperate. She is saying crazy things."

Ivy led me back outside. The air was much lighter. I took a deep breath as a few elderly women came out of the warren of alleys, faces like blueing leather, and they started talking with Ivy. A bone-thin tabby scratched his ear against a pillar, and when I moved forward he darted away.

I followed Ivy through a moon gate into a courtyard to a small ceremonial room. A red light swam down the walls from a swaying paper lantern hanging from the ridgepole. Wrappers of spent fireworks scattered the ground. Lizards warmed themselves in pools of sunlight. Along the back wall there was a long table holding ancestral tablets. Coiling smoke of sandalwood incense rose. This was the direction we faced, the two stone tablets with the names of the village families written in beautiful calligraphy, and one small framed photo of a woman. Young. She had that old Shanghai glam. Fox shawl and pearls. Her hair in pinned-back finger waves. Beautiful. Like Ivy. I wondered who she was. I tried to picture my mother in that kind of portrait. She must have looked just as beautiful once, and suddenly all I wanted was a photo of my mother like that. Because owning one said something about you. Said you knew certain things, and you weren't foolishly young anymore.

We removed our shoes, knelt on two red plump cushions and I watched Ivy kowtow, lips murmuring, her feet tucked beneath her rear end, as she leaned all the way forward and almost touched her forehead against the ground. I did this two or three times. I didn't say anything in my head at first, and then, because I felt like I should out of respect, I told my mother sorry for wishing she'd hurry up and die just so I could get a memorial photo of her.

Then I told Ivy's ancestors I was sorry. I didn't even know what I was sorry about. Maybe that their village would have a Starbucks in a few years, maybe that all the people between sixteen and forty-five were away in the cities and never coming back. I wasn't really sure. It was hot and sweaty and I wanted air-conditioning and I apologized to the ancestors for that too.

I snuck a peek at Ivy. She was still praying, her eyes closed. A natural wave to her hair. My mother's wigs looked real. None of the cheap synthetic ones with cowlicks or mesh caps. Once, as a kid, I'd seen through the crack of the bedroom door my mother putting on her wig before dinner. I knew I shouldn't have looked, but I stood there frozen as she carefully flipped the wig inside out and stretched the lace cap over her head, pink and flaking and wrinkled: her true self. Inside me something stirred. It was ugly and I hated myself for thinking so. Then I watched her pull the wig into place, touch her temples to make sure it wasn't crooked. She bobby-pinned the hair behind her ears, checked the mirror for flyaways, and before she could turn around I was running down the hall.

Now Ivy lifted her hand and tucked her hair behind her ear, and this struck me somehow, the sudden view of her ear up close, the whorls and folds of this delicate pink-and-brown ear. When I was little I was always in and out of the doctor with ear infections and they put tubes in my ears. I almost went deaf. Once I'd tried to look at my eardrum in the mirror using a flashlight and a pair of needle-nose pliers and a magnifying glass when my mother walked by and screamed, "Fedor, the moron's trying to kill himself again!"—*again* being the time I walked barefoot to the baseball diamond, and Mom shouted from the stoop, "There's such a thing as tetanus, you know! How do you think Thoreau died?" I was eight. It scared the shit out of me. Years passed before I dared walk across a rug without slippers. But now I was barefoot in a temple, asking Ivy's ancestors for an otoscope to peer into her ear, down the dogleg of tissue delicate as organza, to the drum softly pulsing, milky and nacreous as a saltwater pearl. Maybe the desire curling in me now like the incense smoke around the tablet was to hear with Ivy's ears, to understand what the fuck was happening to me.

All was quiet until Ivy asked, "Can you ride a bike?"

"A bicycle? Yeah, sure."

"Okay, it is just that you are large."

"You're calling me fat."

"No, not for your country," she said.

Back outside, an old shirtless man shook an empty cigarette pack and walked right past without seeing us. Ivy went into a little shed and wheeled out two bikes, one was an old girl's bike with a basket on front and pink decals on the frame. "Here, try this. My cousin Jin San was the fattest girl in our village." Then she bent down and picked up a large stick and handed it to me.

"What's this for?"

"Rabid dogs. In case it gets late. At night the rabid ones go crazy."

"Great." I took a few practice swings while riding in circles on the bike.

"Where are we going?" I called out. Ivy was already ahead of me.

"To the peach blossom spring."

My tires skidded on the little dirt trails between the rice shoots. Ivy led us through the banana plantation trails, cool wells of air beneath the leafy trees, and the farmers in the fields looked up from under their conical hats. I saw a water buffalo's leg stuck in the teeth of a harrow, blood ribboning down, its bald owner down on his knees in mud pulling for their lives, and then they were gone. Geese lunged out of the way of my front tire. We climbed, pedaling hard, I felt the burn in my calves, the bike wheel squeaking with every turn.

We came to a fork in the trail. Two steep switchbacks up the side of the mountain.

"Which way?" I asked.

"I always take the small road," she said, leaning into the turn, bunch grasses whipping at our legs.

After a long steep ride, we stopped at a little cottage beside a small pond on a plateau. "It's beautiful here," I said, looking out to the small pond and the valley beyond it.

I got off the bike and leaned it up against the trunk of a bright red crepe myrtle. And instead of putting her bike on the other side of the tree, Ivy leaned hers right up against mine, I noticed that, the handlebars entangled, the seats touching.

We walked toward a little cottage. A sweet and generous

scent of orange jasmine around us. She said they call this the seven-mile smell.

There was no roof to the cottage, just four walls, very odd-looking, like it was put up overnight. No glass in the windows either, but I saw a stocked kitchen and a sink.

"This is my house," she said. "I bought it last year and built it myself." She was laughing for some reason. "Do you want to see?" We walked in through the door into the one room and I realized the kitchen was actually a design printed on wallpaper, it was a picture of a French homey cottage kitchen with a stove and sink and teakettle.

"Want some bread?" she asked, laughing and positioning her hands beneath the steaming baguette on the counter as if she were holding it.

"I don't get it," I said. "It's all fake."

"I bought this land, but at some point the building codes changed and this was considered residential instead of farm-land. They had plans to develop here. We are not too far outside Foshan and as the city grows, people will need to live. To get a residential permit for the land I had to prove I lived here. They sent local officials out to verify. So I built a cottage with four walls and the officials came with cameras and said, 'These are just four walls, no one lives here, permit denied.' I said, 'Give me a week.' They gave me two days. So I dragged in this sofa from a junkyard and an old straw mattress and found this broken chair on the road and I put up this fake wallpaper of a kitchen. A week later the same officials come out and say, 'Very nice kitchen. Cozy. We love your place. But you need running water.' So I point at the sink faucet on the wallpaper with water coming out, and they all nod and take pictures. Then they submit their photos to the government who look them over and agree this is nice house. And I get the permit. It is insane."

"I love China," I said.

"I did not bribe them or anything. So now this is my house and I have protected the graves of my grandparents. My grandmother and great-aunt both want to be buried here. If the graves were destroyed or removed then their souls would wander in suffering. Eventually the place you saw will be destroyed. The fishing village you saw too. They have only a few years left. And since my sister is dead, and the other grandchildren moved away, one to England, one to America, I am the only grandchild left, so this is my duty."

"You must be buried here too," I said, and I realized I'd asked for a selfish reason.

"Yes. The dead hold on to the living. I dreamed of leaving and going away, London, New York. To visit these places. Or live. The world is so big. I can have a hundred imaginations about my new life. I know people who can get me out of China for good. Many times I pack my suitcase. But in the end I cannot."

Then she knelt in front of an old PLA munitions box in the kitchen, snapped open the rusty latches and pulled out a parchment scroll with two gold handles. It was the only art she owned, she said, a forgery of course, but her grandfather had given it to her. She unwound the scroll using the two gold handles. The scroll was silk painted with black ink. It was called *A Dream Journey to the Peach Blossom Spring.* The left side of the painting was reality: dramatic mountain peaks surrounded in bands of mist and gnarled trees with clawed branches. A stream in the middle of the scroll led to the mouth of a cave where a fisherman crouched, poised to enter this paradise of red peach blossoms and people working, eating, playing.

"Beautiful," I said.

"The people are too small," she said. "Compared to the

trees and mountains. Like nothing. But maybe I don't understand art."

"What is the story?"

Every Chinese schoolkid knew it, she said. A nobody fisherman who worked his ass off to scrape out a living for his family got lost one day in his sampan when he smelled peach blossoms. He followed a little stream that led to a cave. He squeezed through the cave and found, on the other side, a village. It was utopia. A garden. The people were happy and well fed and lived in peace. But soon he started missing his wife and kids, and he left the place, promising to keep it a secret. But back home he couldn't resist telling his wife. So together they went back. They followed the stream but there was no grove, no paradise. He searched all night but never found the place again.

It must have killed him not to be able to show his wife, but then again he went back for her. He could have stayed. I would have stayed. Wouldn't I? What a decision to make. And then the rest of this dude's life was yearning to get back to this place he couldn't find again.

I told Ivy the story from the Talmud that my mother believed. Before we are born an angel teaches us everything we need to know in our lives, takes us to the end of our life and back, we meet everyone, see everything, we learn the Torah in the womb by the light of a pale yellow lamp—and right before we are born the angel slaps us on the mouth and we forget everything. And so your whole life you're just trying to remember what you've already forgotten. But in the World to Come, which is sort of like Heaven, you remember everything.

"That is pretty," she said. We were silent for a moment then she added, "You never drank Old Lady Meng's soup."

"What's that?"

"If you drink Lady Meng's soup you lose your memory. An old expression. Silly. But I think I understand your meaning. I am someone who cannot forget."

"It's not such a blessing."

"No."

She wanted to know if everyone had their own angel, but I honestly didn't know. "Maybe I am your angel," she said, half-joking. "Does the angel hit hard?"

"Yeah, I mean it doesn't say if the angel works out or anything, but she hits you on the mouth, right here. That's why we have a cleft beneath our noses." I raised my finger, slow to make sure she wasn't going to push me away. I touched the cleft on her upper lip, a little valley. She smiled and pulled my hand down.

"But we're not in the womb or the peach garden. That's the whole problem. Except you are rich. Maybe you and your father are in the peach garden and your question is the same as the fisherman's. Will you leave?"

"For you," I said.

"Men always promise to return."

"But I mean it."

"Have we kissed now? Before, I mean," she asked. "Did we? And have forgotten?"

She leaned forward and covered my mouth with her lips. She grabbed my hand and pulled me toward the bed and we were kissing while walking backward. My hands were on her face and our faces were thrust forward, nibbling on each other's lips, and then her tongue curled inside my mouth again, warm and insistent, we fell onto the straw bed, she tugged at my belt. I dropped the straps from her dress and there was a coolness on the tops of her shoulders, and I kissed her neck, I kissed down to her breasts, goose bumped, her skin smooth, the nipple the same color as her tongue, and I closed my mouth around it, as she grabbed me there and I jumped in her hand, and pulled my pants down in one motion, as she hooked her legs around my waist and pulled me into her, she was wet there, and we both moaned as I slid into her, farther still, and her head dropped back, she put a hand on my ass and pulled me deeper, said something in Chinese in a half-choked breath, and my knees trembled, and she arched her back saying look at me right as I come. After, when I went to move, she held me inside, folding her arms behind my neck, her muscles faintly twitched, then she turned her head and let out a soft moan as we parted. I fell beside her, both of us perfectly still and quiet.

We lay there looking into each other's eyes.

Then we heard a soft rustling noise outside that seemed to distract her. Her mind moving away. She smiled at me. A last connectedness and it was over.

She sat up. Turned to the window.

It was quiet except for the quick trill of the yellow buntings we'd seen everywhere, and I was thinking how we'd just had sex on this giant ancient tomb. Her people below us. In the ground. Generations back. And I was wondering if she was thinking about that too.

Still facing the window, she said softly, "We used to go bird hunting."

Then she lay back down facing me. Her hand under her cheek, flat on the pillow.

"My father," she clarified.

I don't think I'd ever heard her say anything about him before then.

"Partridges. He carry a big shotgun. And he always wants to bring me. So I go and try to be a dutiful daughter. I am a good daughter, I believe. I watch for birds. Partridge is quiet bird. You hear more than see. Hard to find. We walk low.

'Look and listen, only,' he says. Hours like this. This is my torture. I want to talk. Joke. Anything. But always, 'Shush.'"

Ivy was quiet for a moment.

"He learned as a boy. Mao said kill all sparrows. So he listens. He rush out and shoot anything in the sky. This is how he learned. This is how my father thinks. You listen. All trouble starts in your big mouth. *Noticed* is a bad thing. This makes me angry. I do not agree. He does. We fight.

"Sometimes we find the partridge, and we squat and crawl closer. You must sneak forward and surprise them. But right before Father is ready, I make a noise—I cough, step on branch, ask a loud question—and the birds fly off. And he yells at me, 'Stupid girl. Why can't you listen? Just like your sister. You deserve a thousand slaps.' I say it was an accident, but I think he knew.

"Then he shouts how he misses Mao, how he wishes for order and structure, a country with values and morals. This is what he misses. My generation is too wild. No honor. Selfish and greed. Not true Chinese.

"It make me so angry. So this one time, the last time, we go into the woods, I try and tell him my opinion. Big fight. He will not listen. Everything I say, he answers, 'I don't accept.'"

She stopped talking for a moment. She swallowed. I didn't speak. I didn't move a muscle.

"I think he wished he had a son. I know he did.

"So we go home. That same day. With just one bird. I hold by its little feet. Father walks into house very tall. Proud. I hand it to Mother. She cuts off its head. Hangs the bird. Cooks. We sit at the table, she brings the food and I say I won't eat. My father sits across the table. He stares at me. Hating me. *Eat*, he says. And I shake my head. Mother looks down at her bowl. My father says, *Eat*. Again I shake my head, no.

"He stares at me and maybe he remembers sparrows. Duty.

Honor. He is back in the Cultural Revolution. You never allowed to say those words in my house. His face doesn't move.
Shooting this stare at me, like 'You say no to *me*?' Big man
with big gun? Former Red Army officer. *Eat now.*"

"So he forced you?" I asked.

"No. I cross my arms. I refuse."

Ivy smiled, remembering it.

"Did he lose his mind?"

"No one speaks. He didn't speak. Not for a long time. We
never go into woods again. Never the same. No one said 'the
end' but this is the end. We go different ways."

"But you came back," I said. "Here. To his land."

"He abandoned it. When the black cars came, we left for
the city. In China, always best to disappear. This is how he
thinks. Now he works as government librarian in a basement."

"I see," I said.

She furrowed her brow. I knew she wanted to say more.

I started thinking about my own father. I needed to get back
to the factory. I felt him glaring at me from across the desk.
That was the worst. Worse than yelling. The glare. It made my
skin go cold. But when he had to, he could listen. He really
could, I think. Because I was more than my father's spotter.
We had a closeness. But Dad was the last person I wanted to
be thinking about after sex. Or her father. Any fathers. Still,
I was honored that she'd talk to me about it, about him.

"Kind of sucks you don't get along," I said. "I mean, what
does he want from you?"

"I think he fantasize about me marrying local boy and pregnant and baking. Two or three grandchildren. This is optimal,
he said. Like I am one of his chickens."

I laughed. "I'm sorry for laughing. It's just funny how you
said it."

"No, Alex. It's good. This is why I tell you. It's how I got here. Today. Away from my father, from the ghost of Mao, from the Red Army. From everything. I think I am trying to say I was like this when I was young."

"Like what?"

"This way." She laughed at herself. Her voice had strained, gone up a few octaves. "I'm trying but can't say it."

"I think you say it perfect. It makes sense. Every word."

Her eyes dipped.

"Ivy?" I said.

She nodded. And then she looked up at me, smiling.

"It's okay," she said. "I try another time."

She got up and went to wash herself in the pond and I stood too and watched her cup the water in her hand and lap it up onto her arms and between her legs. I was standing on the grass in just my boxer shorts. I was barefoot, Mother, fuck Thoreau. I stretched my arms over my head and my back crackled.

We rode peacefully down the mountain into the village where Ivy leaned the bikes against an old banyan tree, the sunlight streaming down through the broad leaves and sparkling off the chrome frames. Jianguo was beside the van eating an ear of steamed yellow corn. I felt bad that we'd kept him waiting all this time.

He smiled as we approached, enough distance between us not to be obvious, but it seemed like he knew. Why else would he smile like that? Maybe my hair gave us away. I reached up and smoothed it out. Out of the corner of my eye I saw Ivy doing the same. She talked to Jianguo in Cantonese and he said, "Ah, ah, ah," then climbed in and started the van.

Ivy got in back with me. I saw Jianguo's eyes on me in the rearview mirror. A hard late-afternoon rain came down, chattering against the van. Outside, pigs huddled under banana trees, and I moved my hand quietly to the space on the seat between us, but I stopped there, afraid to touch her. Felt like Jianguo was watching. What if he reported back to Dad? It made me feel like I was in grade school again, but I couldn't take the chance. We could talk. Since Jianguo didn't speak English, that would have to be enough.

"You are my first," she said, but then her lips pursed like she was fighting off a grin.

"Not the way you're doing it," I said.

She let herself laugh. "I lied. I thought this is something men like to hear. Are you upset that you are not first?"

"Not at all. First times are pretty awful. I was way too young. I thought you were supposed to test the condoms—Dad said watch out for bad quality—so right before sex I filled the condom up like a water balloon. No holes. Perfect. Ran back to bed and tried to tug it on unrolled. Impossible. Like putting a wet suit on a baby."

She laughed. "I cannot picture this."

"Then why are you laughing?"

"The way you speak it," she said.

"Anyway, I tested all three condoms. A nightmare by the time we finally did it."

"True," she said. "That was also my case. A French boy at my university. During sex he looked like he was posing for movie. In bed with him I spoke French. With the British boy, English. All these languages. I never know what will come out. What language—with you—did I use?"

"Chinese," I said, my hand starting to sweat on the vinyl seat, close to her.

"That is very good. I am glad it was not English," she said. "With you I felt different. They were only stones in a river of men."

"A whole river?" I asked.

"Wait, no. I did not fuck the whole river. Our proverbs do not make sense in English."

Outside, the karst mountains sloped into loose red clay and the light grew weaker.

"In America," I said, "we have Born Again virgins. Have you heard of this? It's a religion. All you do is join and everything bad is in the past. A clean start."

"Like the reincarnated. They are Buddhist?"

"No, almost the opposite."

"I don't think Borning Again should be so easy. Also, all those bad times trained me for now. How do I know *this* if I forget the others? Even the ones who made me ashamed of myself. I do not want to get rid of."

The road curved like a bow and we sank into a tunnel boring through a limestone mountain and the sound of the rain flattened with a pop. In the darkness, she snaked her fingers through mine.

Six

I GOT TO WORK LATE IN THE MORNING RIGHT as Gang was coming out of Dad's office. He was wearing an olive two-button wool-and-cashmere suit with a silk tie and leather shoes. I stopped right in front of him.

"Alex," he said, shaking my hand. "Good to see you. Your father said you had important morning business meeting."

I swallowed hard. He'd covered for me.

"Yes," I said. "At the hotel. It was just a few people. Some friends. I don't know."

"You must know who your friends are."

"I do. I mean, yes, of course I know who they are. I didn't think you wanted *names*—but it was a very successful meeting."

"Excellent," he said. His feet were wide apart, and I found myself imitating his stance. "Low export volume at the other plants. But Fedor says no problem for you here."

I nodded. Another lie.

"Good. Work, work. Always. To get rich is glorious."

"Deng Xiaoping," I said.

He clapped. "See. You are almost Chinese now. I can trust

you. You know how much the commissars in Beijing view us as the model city. Our numbers lead the country. We have responsibility."

He looked at his watch. "I must go. I need to be downtown. Officer at the housing management bureau had an accident. She fell and died."

"That's terrible," I said.

"Very sad. Best and most promising internal compliance officer. Young. Only starting her career."

A hard shiver ferreted its way down my back.

"Very sad, these accidents," he continued, shaking his head. "So I go there right now but later I go to lunch at my favorite seafood restaurant in Long Yuan Xi. Pick my own fish out of tank. This is my advice," he said, leaning forward. "You look at the eyes. Should be clear. Foggy eyes, no good. Old fish. Sick fish. Something wrong. Need bright clear eyes."

Right then I heard Dad bark my name.

Gang stepped aside.

I gave him a quick bow before stepping into Dad's office. I sank into the chair opposite him and let out a deep breath.

Dad closed the finance report on his desk. "You don't need to talk to him."

"He talked to me. What was I going to do? Ignore him? Be rude?"

"That's never stopped you before. Now listen. Hold on." He reached into his top drawer and spritzed Afrin up his nose. Two good pumps. *So my sinuses can finally find peace.* "You look well rested," he said. "Is it the shirt? Something's different."

Okay, I'd let him change the subject. Dad was only trying to protect me from Gang, after all. Fine. But he was right before. We were all serving him. Everyone in the city.

The shirt I was wearing was old, I told him. A black

cowboy-style collared shirt with metal snaps. Came from the Salvation Army.

He rolled his eyes. "My son shops with the homeless."

There was a sharp knock on the door, and Yong poked in his head to tell Dad that a January ex-factory date was too late for resort season. He'd have to airfreight. Dad nodded at him. Yong said, "Alex, I love that shirt," as he slipped out the door.

Dad flung his reading glasses down on his desk. "What's wrong with people? I wouldn't dry dishes with that *schmatte*."

"It's hip," I said.

"Oh, so you're hip and cool now. I guess I missed that."

For a few minutes he seemed discombobulated by all the papers on his desk, as if they'd just suddenly materialized. He was muttering to himself, moving stacks around, and I made it worse by softly tapping my knuckles against the chair arm.

"Knock that off," he said, and he dropped all the papers and looked up at me. "You look too happy."

"I'll try to be more miserable," I said.

"It's Ivy, isn't it? Did you *schtup* her?"

I kept still. Didn't even blink. Dad had no evidence, nothing, he just jumped to that assumption.

He said, "Jianguo told me you took her along as your translator. I asked you to bring Taishu."

"He was busy," I said, "and you rushed me."

"This is the wrong country to be such a terrible liar. Float down from that mushroom cloud and listen to me. You're going to lose your focus if you go down this road, trust me. She's not worth it."

There he went. Off and running with that premise. How the hell did he know everything? He didn't know. I didn't have to cop to anything. "We took care of business," I said. Probably the wrong choice of words.

"Harmless fun, is that what you think?" Dad said. "Wrong.

There is no fun here. You need to struggle. You need to eat bitterness like the Chinese always say. Is your snot black? When your snot's black, you've worked hard."

"You're overreacting," I said. I found myself slouching in the chair like I was a teenager again getting scolded. "I know where my focus is."

"You're getting too close to her. For what? I hope you realize you aren't Chinese. They already have a God of Pigsties so you're disqualified."

"I'm not pretending to be Chinese."

"Have you ever seen one of the Chinese Jews from Kaifeng? Wearing a Mao suit and a *kippah*. They don't know their asses from their emperors. All mixed up."

I straightened up in my chair and said, "I'm sorry I came back late yesterday. We delivered the bags and then we went kayaking out on the river." It was the first innocuous-sounding lie that came to mind, but I realized immediately it made me sound like a fuckup.

"On the disgusting Pearl river? Why aren't you at work? A man lives with his work, remember that. P.S., this is a good way to get yourself really sick. Do you think this is Venice? Let me tell you the difference between the Pearl and the Po—from someone who has seen both. Minus the gondoliers, violins, vineyards, all that shit—let me tell you the difference—*polio*. Polio's back. You'd know this if you'd bookmarked the CDC webpage like I asked. Measles is up. Dengue's hot. Avian flu. H1N1. They're all back. You're crazy to go anywhere."

He was just ranting now. I tried to change the subject. "Peng appreciated the gifts and says we'll be fine on the next audit. Leather prices are steady. He hopes you'll visit him soon."

"Impossible," Dad said, waving his hands. "I can't use the bathrooms there. I should squat? In a tannery. At my age. In filth and germs and disease? Alongside those, those butchers?"

"If they're butchers what does that make you?" I asked.

"*Vey iz mir!* We're shoe men, Alex, artists! Have I slaughtered a bull lately? Have you? Get out," he said, flicking his wrist. "I have work to do."

I walked down to my own office and closed the door and sat behind my desk. My window looked out to the top floor of Plant B, maybe twenty yards away, a bank of windows with dirty gauzy curtains through which I saw the shaggy outline of workers, the whirl of hands over machines as the shoes assumed their shape, flowing down the line to the girls who nestled them delicately in tissue paper like two ducks with folded necks into the Abelson's boxes. Above the windows: just the stubble of PVC ventilation pipes, a swath of gray sky and a silhouette moving along the roof. I leaned forward.

It was a woman. She stepped closer. To the parapet. She was wearing a loose white dress, a paisley design, bow on the waist of the dress, her hair was long and held back with a headband. Beautiful. Very pale and white. And I rubbed my eyes because this couldn't be true. It must be a ghost. No reason for anyone to be up there. My chest seized. I lurched out of my seat, straining to see, sure that I'd gone mad, because it looked like Ruxi. Before I could even bang on the window, she glided to the ledge. Never looking down. She took a step that wasn't there. It was her.

Her face pitched forward, arms spread out as if they were wings, she dove out into the air, and for a split second she lifted her chin, her eyes raised to my window, where my nose was pressed against glass, and she saw me, she must have, her face utterly placid, no sense of fear or panic. Then her body crimped and knifed down, her legs pale and straight, and she hit the pavement with a heavy thump. I'd never heard that sound before. I'd never seen anyone die.

I looked to the roof where she'd been a moment ago, but

I didn't look down yet. I was hoping that when I did she wouldn't be there. She would have just kept sailing, through pavement, through dirt, past the water table and molten lava, landing on a rattan mat back home in her village. She just fell home. I looked. She was on the pavement, facedown, her cheek smashed against the cement, a ring of blood edging around her head.

For a moment it was perfectly silent. No one outside to witness, and the thought raced through my mind that I must get down there first and move her body before anyone sees. And I was telling my legs to move, but the ground felt liquid, like I'd fall over if I budged from the spot, but I knew I must go.

I went running through the hall, down the stairwell and out into the muggy stubborn heat. I approached her body. Still no one around. I crept up slowly, half-afraid that she would sit up. I knelt down. It was as if she were sleeping with her legs twisted. A thin pool of blood by her ear.

My hands on my knees. I could smell the boiling roots and herbs from the Chinese pharmacist's little shop. I felt nauseous. Her death was my fault. Forgive me. I was the one who had delayed the meeting, skipped it altogether. If I'd skipped the village with Ivy and come straight back, this never would have happened. Everything my father predicted had come true. I'd lost focus. He'd warned me.

The three canteen cooks came out into the road. The last maker's son with plastic shavings in his hair like garlands, no more than sixteen, timidly approached.

"Alex." Ivy's voice. I raised my eyes. She covered her mouth with her hand.

"She was here a moment ago," I said. I lifted my head, but no one was on the roof, just the dull aching sky.

Kneeling beside me, Ivy slowly turned Ruxi over onto her

back. She pressed two fingers against Ruxi's neck, feeling for life under the skin.

"Nothing," Ivy said.

I looked at Ruxi. A livid, deep purple contusion ran from her cheek up to the corner of her eye. Caved in. Her forearms skinned, pavement grit sparkled inside her palms. Abrasions along her legs. Knees grated. I heard myself groan.

One of Ruxi's sandals had blown off on impact. I saw it a few feet away and rushed to retrieve it. One of ours. Soft Atanado. I'd hated this sandal, but Dad wouldn't listen. I said let's do all-over black. This color blocking, a garish Moroccan blue and fuchsia, I told Dad, it was screaming.

Now I took Ruxi's foot in my hand.

"What are you doing?" Ivy asked. She shook my shoulders. I needed her hands back the instant they were gone.

Carefully, I slipped Ruxi's big toe into the toe-loop and nestled her foot on the midsole, pulled the strap up over her ankle.

"They are coming," Ivy said. The workers. I heard their footsteps before I saw them, streaming out of every door, hundreds, gathering, pressing, in a circle around us, ten deep, in tattered trousers, jeans, overalls, high on shoe cement. Crying, shouting, fanning themselves.

The head of security, Longwei, prim and buttoned, pushed his way to the middle. Thin as a sliver of soap. He released the catch on his polished pistol, aimed it at the sky and fired one round, its leaden echo rolling.

"What the hell are you doing?" I said, leaping up from the ground.

"I don't want a riot," he said in English.

"Don't shoot again," I said, struggling to get a full breath. "You can't."

Over his shoulder, I saw Dad standing a few yards off, his hands up by his ears, like a kid at a horror movie, and I waved him over. He squeezed through the crowd and when he saw Ruxi, he put a chilled hand on my elbow and squeezed.

"My God," he said. He was sweating.

I told Longwei to order the crowd to give us room. Longwei holstered his pistol and yelled at the workers in Chinese. But no one left. The workers closed in. They were pushing.

"Longwei," I said, "tell them to go back to the dorms."

"They do not listen, Mr. Younger Cohen. I use the tear gas now."

He pulled out a gray metal canister and curled his trigger finger around the pin.

"No," I said. "God, no. You'll start a riot."

I saw Hongjin holding the workers back with his arms spread. They were trying to get to Ruxi's body. To see. I knelt back down beside Ivy.

"I better call the police," I said to her.

"No," she said. "They will cremate her. The police will. Her body needs to go home. Or she wanders forever."

Ruxi's hair was fanned out like duckweed, slick with blood. Long shadows over her body. I kept staring at her like she'd quit being dead, sit up straight and talk.

"Alex," Ivy whispered. "I can help. I can calm them down. But you need to help me too."

"Anything," I said.

She dragged her fingers over Ruxi's eyes, then stood up and holding her arms over her head yelled in Chinese and the crowd slowly backed off.

"We have to move her," I said.

"Are you sure?" Dad asked. Eyes wide and spooked. "Let's call the police."

"No police. They'll shut us down for a week," I said, and that could've been true, but I wasn't really thinking about the factory. I needed to make this right. And the only chance that Ruxi got back to her parents was if we sent her. But we couldn't just carry her body upstairs. Or we could, but I didn't want anyone else to see her this way. She needed to be covered.

I told Dad to stay put and ran to the finishing plant. The bay door opened to a scrim of leather dust and mold stench. I was looking for something: a stretcher, a cart, folding table, even a tarp. Nothing. Only cut sides. My eye fell on a pallet of full hides in the corner. I carried one out as Longwei and Hongjin were leading the workers back to the dorms.

"What are you doing?" Dad asked when he saw the hide. I knew he was about to say, *That's a fifty-dollar hide you'll ruin.* His lips parted. I glared at him and he made a husky cough deep in his throat.

"Help," I said to Ivy. We unrolled the dark brown hide across the pavement, the corners curled stiff. I could see the scars along the neck where the spooked steer had cut himself on barbed wire trying to escape the pen.

The guards were preoccupied and Dad was still nailed to the spot. I turned to Ivy.

"Grab her legs."

She reached for Ruxi's ankles. I was up by her head, but her hands were too limp for me to get a firm hold, so I squatted down and grabbed her forearms. I paused for a second. "Will the workers talk to the police?" I asked Ivy.

She shook her head. "Never. They are terrified of police. They don't trust."

The moment we lifted Ruxi off the ground, her head flopped back and she was staring at me upside down, her face as calm as a child, but then her mouth opened, baring her teeth, and now all I saw in her face was agony, this silent scream.

We set her down on the leather and started rolling her into the hide. It was hideous how easily she turned over. I half closed my eyes until she was enveloped, only her feet poking out the bottom and a fist of black hair that crept out the top.

"We'll carry her to the office," I said, and I saw Hongjin running back from the dorms. I shouted to him to clear the way. Dad was standing still, rooted to the spot. Ivy and I lifted Ruxi. We brought her slowly, in short choppy steps, to the elevator, then up to the third floor. I walked backward, looking over my shoulder. Ivy staggered forward telling me to slow down, but my wrists were burning. Hers too, I was sure. The hide loosened with every step, just needed it to hold a little longer, down this hall a bit farther.

"Where?" Ivy said. She was breathing hard.

"Conference room," I panted. It was the only table big enough. "Don't drop her." Hongjin pushed open the door, and we laid her down.

"Jesus," I said.

"Go check on the workers," I told Hongjin, who was clearly in shock. He left without responding.

Ivy wiped her forehead with her sleeve. Then she lightly touched the bolt of Ruxi's hair dangling out of the end of the rolled leather hide. "Do you think she knows she's dead?" Ivy said.

I told her I didn't know. When I saw Ruxi's face, it seemed that she was aware of it all. That she kept on feeling. From the hallway came the scuff of footsteps on linoleum. Maybe it was Dad. Or more guards. Ivy lifted her eyes to mine and I felt the darkness of her look run right through me. "Hide her," she said. "If the police find her, they will cremate her. Make up a story in the news. Cover this up. We can't trust them to send her home to her family and admit the truth. You understand?"

I nodded.

Ivy squeezed my hand and in a low voice said, "I have to see you tonight."

Seven

I PEEKED OUT THE DOOR. HALLWAY TO MY left—a clear shot down to the makeshift *churrascaria* kitchen that Yong had installed last year. Time to make a move before anyone showed up. Not daring to take her out of the leather shroud, I edged Ruxi off the table into my arms, her body already stiff from rigor mortis, so it was like carrying lumber.

I ferried her to the low chest freezer in the kitchen. With my pinky outstretched, I lifted open the cover. A rush of cold water vapor chuffed up around my face, this thick milky fog, and suddenly I couldn't see my own arms in front of my face, like I was the one who was dead and there was no peach garden, no World to Come, only this gray miasma, ringlets of smoke, but when the murk cleared there were forearms, mine, emerging sharply, and Ruxi's shroud, and the plastic baggies of beef ribs, chicken hearts, wings, shoulders, rumps, livers, tongues, all sparkling with ice crystals—everything finding its shape again.

I took a deep breath and set her down on top of the bags. I was about to close the lid and beat it out of there when I tripped over this thought. The Buddhists say consciousness stays with the body for three days, so even though Ruxi's eyes were closed and she was all wrapped up, maybe she saw me. Maybe she was in there watching.

Out loud I told her I was sorry. It was my fault after all. If I'd been a little bit smarter or luckier, I could've prevented it.

Still, that was pretty weak comfort coming from someone who was about to hide you in an ice chest. All I knew was that I wasn't feeling right anymore. Not with the factory or my job or the heat. Not anything. I slammed the lid over her and it cut off the steam to my head and everything was almost back to normal.

I headed back down the hall and sat at my desk, my back to the view of the roof where Ruxi jumped, wondering why? For what? What did that accomplish, her jumping? I told myself not to waste another minute thinking about the past or what could've been. What's done was done. It wasn't my fault.

That's what Trotsky basically told my grandfather at the Triangle Diner in the Bronx when Zayde kept calling him Lev Bronstein, his real name, and Trotsky flicked the peak of his wool Budenovka hat, saying, "It's Trotsky now," no anger in his voice, like the revolution burned the Jew right out of him. Zayde didn't let up; he was probably eating his stewed prunes like he did every morning and kept pushing. The Talmud says there are three kinds of tears, those caused by smoke, grief and constipation. We're a family of pushers. So Zayde pressed him on which Russians he'd save in the end: the workers or the Jews, and Trotsky took off his steel pince-nez, his eyes real blue, like the flame of a gas range burner, a wolfish diamond face, and he said real calmly, "Comrade, I am a Marxist. This skin isn't my fault."

"What's the matter with you?" Zayde asked. "What about Kishinev? The Black Hundreds?"

"The final triumph of communism will solve that," said Trotsky.

Zayde spluttered, "Here in America, hotshot, if you haven't noticed, here we have the vote!"

"Who's we?" Trotsky said and he reached for the check under his coffee mug, but Zayde grabbed it saying he wouldn't let Trotsky demean the laboring class by paying for a hot meal.

I was thinking all this through as I took the stairs down to the canteen. Thinking like Trotsky. This skin wasn't my fault. Which made me feel better. The fact was that some shoes failed inspection, some hands got chewed up by the fleshing machines, and some Chinese girls in summer dresses fell from the sky on a clear bright day. You couldn't know why. Trotsky would tell me that the sooner you accept who you are, the sooner you'd get your shit together.

I pushed open the steel door, and the warm air from the street hit my face like a wet mop and seared my lungs.

But a little doubt rolled into me. What did I have to do with anything if some invisible hand was moving us around? If Ruxi's death wasn't connected to me, that left what? This mystery crouching in the center of our lives. I just didn't want to be a shitbum, a nothing—that's what I feared more than anything, the torment of being ordinary.

I smelled the brick kiln behind our factory, the air redolent of sweet burned blue clay. It was a good smell. Sitting on the bench outside of Plant B was Die Jo of all people, the former foot model, smacking a pack of King's against the heel of her wrist. She smiled at me politely and I could see her lips moving, her eyes lifted on the diagonal, like she was rehearsing a line, and she said, "Hello, sugar. Hello, trouble." The words came out slow like she was reading off a teleprompter.

I said hello.

"Big Sleep," she said.

I thought she was talking about Ruxi, but maybe she meant the movie.

"No police. I shut the clam door for you, doll," she said and winked, making it clear which one she meant.

Then she took off her black cloth shoes and pushed them under the bench and put her bare feet down on the pavement that was wet and cool. Before lunch I always saw the janitor out here watering the flagstones. I thought he was crazy for that, an old man in a blue jumper who watered the pavement. But now I saw that he did it for Die Jo. A kindness. So she could enjoy a post-lunch smoke with her shoes off, feet firm on the ground, smooth and slender, the nails painted maroon. She cared for them. And she had the janitor keeping them cool on these blistering days when you wanted to step in a gallon of ice cream to stop your skin from boiling.

I gave her a curt wave and she held her arm up elegantly like she was waving goodbye with a handkerchief, and it seemed smug, like she was really saying, "You're in over your head. You don't know shit about us."

That evening, Dad and I drove in silence back to the hotel. From his fanny pack, he found by touch a tube of some lotion and squeezed a dollop in his palm and rubbed it on his face meticulously, in small circles with his fingers. I figured it was sunscreen, one last application to cover his ass all ten feet from the van into the hotel lobby.

It was 7:00 p.m. by the time we got back, and he said he was going to sack out early, get room service, something he only did when he was real sick.

"Bad day," he said. "Twenty years in China. Right after Nixon, and that was my first jumper."

That made my eye twitch. *A jumper.* I thought he was going to say something else, but he sighed, took a hesitant step in the direction of Karri's empty desk and then pivoted back, like all of a sudden he wanted a hug.

But he stopped just short of my reach. He cleared his throat. Okay, I thought, here it comes. Something weighty. Finally some honesty.

"How's my T-zone?" he asked.

"Your what?"

"My face." He pulled the sunscreen tube out of his fanny pack. "This crap Karri gave me. Antiaging cream." He stared at me impatiently. "It's technically a serum," he clarified, like I'd challenged him.

"The ginseng tightens you up. Depuffs. Do I look depuffed?"

I was about ready to pick him up and throw him into the elevator. I wanted to say: I give a fuck about your T-zone?

Turning the tube over, he read from the back. "Summer glow my ass. Am I glowing?"

I took a good hard look. Usually I tried not to look at him too long or too directly, like he was some kind of gorgon. I mean, every father is his son's creation—that's our only revenge. But this time I forced myself to look—his skin sagging around his face and neck, red and flaky, hair gone gray.

He took a step closer, right up on me now. He was not a close talker, so I was thinking it was awkward hug time, and right then it hit me that all his controlling and bossiness were meant to hide the simple fact he was terrified of the storm just outside his door.

This memory swept over me of going with him as a kid to Yugoslavia to liquidate his factories. My first get-your-shit-together trip, back when I thought I'd make a living selling my Bo Jackson posterboard collages or live on a mountain breeding angora rabbits, anything so long as it didn't involve shoes. Back before I realized you had to choose a path or risk becoming nothing.

We'd left Bugojno driving east through farmland toward the airport in Belgrade when we'd hit a checkpoint. A bearded soldier in black fatigues and a beret tapped the car window with the muzzle of his AK-47 and, pressing the gun to my father's temple, ordered us to get out of the car and lie down in the road.

I remember lying with my cheek in the dirt, my eyes facing a grove of pear trees sparkling with green glass bottles. It was bright out, the sun singed my neck, and I saw all those glinting bottles roosting in the trees like grackles, and I realized suddenly how they got the pears inside the bottles of Kruska, the strong-ass brandy that made me throw up my lamb the night before. I'd thought for sure they blew the glass around the pear, I mean I spent all night thinking about how they got the goddamn pear into the bottle, but now it was very obvious that they slid the glass over the tiny bud and the pear grew inside the bottle's chest like an embryo, cell by cell, until it ripened.

I don't remember the bearded soldier stabbing the car seats or Dad forking over the bribe money that finally got us out of there. Only the glass pear tree and reaching over to take Dad's hand. He always said too much touching and I wouldn't turn out right, like raising a kid was the same as making Baked Alaska—the last thing you want to have to do is chuck it and start over. On the ground, he whispered, "You okay, Bagel?" That's what he called me at home. Bagel-boy. I hated the name. I was doing my best—everything short of wearing a gold chain crucifix—to pretend I wasn't Jewish. But the moment Dad said *Bagel-boy* outside Bugojno, I knew it was less of a name than a wish. He needed me. I inched my arm over and squeezed his hand to let him know I was there and at least we'd be shot and thrown into the Sava river together.

And I couldn't shake that feeling again, here in the hotel

lobby—that I was supposed to be *his* father, that God got it all flipped around. So I placed my hand on his shoulder and squeezed, and there was a lot of muscle packed in those shoulders, like my own.

The moment I touched him, Dad's chin dropped to his chest and he exhaled, a puff of prune juice on my face, like the jammy Slivovitz on the mouth of the bearded soldier lifting me off the ground by my armpits as the piss dribbled out of my pant leg and made a puddle in the dirt.

I thought Dad was about to start crying. He swiped at his nose with the back of his wrist, and I let my arm fall from his shoulder.

Screw it; let him feel something he couldn't control for once. Only Dad could turn an employee's suicide into his own maudlin pity party.

"Get some rest," I said. My voice sounded heavy. Strained. I wanted to say: Here's the truth, old man. This is on us. Don't pretend China's got you by the balls. You got it all backward. Everything's out of your control *but* this. This we could have done something about and we didn't. If you want to own anything, own that.

"Sure, sure," he said, real distant. "Same for you."

Then he slumped off to the elevator banks, and I was surprised to feel a little sad when he was gone.

Upstairs, I lay down on my bed waiting for Ivy. Focusing on the popcorn ceiling, I heard in my head, *You think Ruxi's got it bad, have you seen my goddamn T-Zone lately? The heat's doing a number on me.* I thought I was rid of that. Slipping into his voice to avoid the hard stuff. As soon as Ivy arrived I was going to tell her the truth—the new Abelson's CEO was driving their business into the ground, fewer orders every season. We were going to have to lay people off if it didn't pick up. So how about me and you just haul it out of town and go live on some aboriginal island off Taiwan and spear fish and grow pears. Brew our own Kruska. What did you need to grow pears, anyway? Bees? And you probably needed other pear trees too. Lots of them. That was the hell of it. You always needed your own kind to survive.

At 8:00 p.m. I rode the employee elevator down to the garage where they kept the Bentleys and Rollses. I slipped out the side door right as a blue taxi pulled up to the curb. The door opened and one of our pewter gladiator sandals planted itself on the ground. Ivy got out of the car and came toward me, wearing a jean skirt and a black tank top, her hair thick and dark and long, a soft wave at the ends.

The cab reversed and the yellow beams lit her up from behind so I saw only her silhouette, this fuzzy penumbra around her body, a white hum that looked kind of sinister, like one of those famished, wandering ghosts coming to reach inside me, but then the light slipped away, the cab was gone and she was wrapping her arms around my neck.

I led her to the elevator. She was smart to have suggested the back entrance. I felt lousy about smuggling her into the hotel, but there was no way of getting in through the front, not with Karri snooping around, the bellboys, the maids. There was a tight network of surveillance, and they knew right away when someone didn't belong, like they could read your net worth from a glance.

We walked through a narrow halogen-lit hallway up a staircase to the mezzanine and past the hotel library with ceiling-high oak bookcases full of leather-bound faux books, and then past the frosted green doors of the hotel salon onto another set of elevator banks.

A fresh stack of towels sat outside my hotel room door wrapped in sheaves of tissue paper with a note on top that I picked up and read:

Dear Alex,
A fresh set of towels. You should always use fresh. I believe this was the cause of your jock itch.
Love, Dad.

"What is it?" Ivy asked, her breath warm on my shoulder.

"Nothing," I tell her, crumpling the note and shoving it deep in my pocket. It was heat rash anyway. In the hotel sauna a few days ago, I'd shown Dad a rash on my thigh. "Jungle rot," he said, whistling low. *"Buhao."* No good. After the sauna, he insisted on showing me the correct way to towel off, swabbing every nook and cranny. "Don't forget your ass," he said dead serious, like Moses ran out of room on the tablets for that nugget on Mount Zion. *Tell your sons. Tell everyone. Dry thoroughly and don't forget the ass.*

Ivy crossed the room and stood by the window under the big double pouf valance, rubbing her bare shoulders. The floor boy had the air conditioner turned down to sixty-four degrees. I gave her one of my sweatshirts, which she pulled over her head, and it hung down to her knees.

Her eyes slid around the room and settled on the complimentary wine and fruit basket on a silver tray, sitting in the middle of the fluffy king-size bed, and I worried that she thought I put it there as a romantic gesture. I wanted to tell her I wasn't one of those guys. I could've told her that it came every night for everyone at the Ambassador level, but that somehow sounded even worse.

"Do you want to shower?" I said, and Ivy's arms were still crossed. Maybe that offended her. Made her feel like a charity case. At the dorms they had to wait in a long line to shower and there was only hot water at 8:00 a.m. or 8:00 p.m. and even then they were timed at five minutes.

She said, "With you?" which stopped me cold.

"It's a nice shower," I told her. "The soap's flown in from Italy or someplace."

What the hell was I talking about? I'd already slept with her. The whole point of sleeping with someone was so you could finally reveal that you're a real person.

"Yes," I said. "Together."

She smiled now. I hadn't fucked the whole thing up. And I was glad for that. Glad that around her I could blurt out the first thought from my gut without dreying over everything.

"You're fine?" I said. In my head I was thinking, Stop dreying.

"I will tell you if not," she said, and she laid the towel on the desk chair and pulled off the sweatshirt. "I can take care of myself," she said, tossing it to me. Her skirt rasped down her legs.

"Damn right," I said.

I followed her to the bathroom. And that thump was back once we were inside the shower with all the mirrors. Mirrors were forbidden in the dorms, because Yong said vanity alone can bring a factory to its knees. The girls, he said, must think of the factory as having one body, one face, one voice. *You are all the arms and legs; we are the head and voice. Together we are the body.*

Here though, it was all mirrors, and I turned on the water pretty hot and she was pressed right up against me. Her lips crushed against mine and there was a quickening in me as I got down on the tile floor on my knees and washed her feet with the bar of soap. The contrast between the black tiles and her white feet. My hand a washcloth gliding along the curve of her ankle joint down to the negative space of her arch, where these tributaries of sole creases—some strong, some weak—flowed side by side until a sudden confluence, one deep line flowing toward the ball of her foot. And then up over her instep, the washcloth traveling over the forked vein, a pale denim blue.

I stood back up, and she reached between my legs and squeezed me, firm in her hand, clutching me, and then she was down on her knees washing me with soap and taking me into her mouth and when I closed my eyes there was a bright bloom of color, I was gone and something else came in, God, or I didn't know what, and I ceased to exist, and then the wanting badly to see her face, opening my eyes, but behind her long hair her face was hidden, which made everything ache, even my metal fillings. I leaped at the sight of Ivy's tongue, pink and long, running slow along the length of me, and she looked up at me, the last inhibition steamed off, and I pulled her up to her feet, pressed her chest against the wall, and she arched her back, and she reached down and slid me inside of her and I groaned, the water breaking over her back in foamy streams and I was inside her and we were alone there.

No Dad on the toilet with the door wide-open, shouting, "Elsa, where'd you hide my goddamned reading glasses?"

No mother pounding on the bathroom door yelling at me that Lilith will steal my seed and bear me demon sons if I masturbate; that God always sees me even if she can't.

I clenched my eyes and Ivy pushed back against me, moaning against my ear, she ground hard against me, my knees trembled and everything went black and crushed as she said something in Chinese in a half-choked breath, craning her neck back with her mouth open.

Afterward, I watched Ivy drying herself off in front of the sink. Dad would have been pleased at her thoroughness. She didn't forget the ass. Her skin was all goose-bumped and red. She knotted a bath towel at her chest, and we lay down in the bed on top of the sheets and everything felt sedate and good. She was pressed up against me, along my left side. She'd brought a peach to bed. As she was paring it with a knife, I thought, That's how you cut a peach? That's not how I'd cut a peach.

I wondered how I was supposed to go through life with Dad's nonsense in my head. But it wasn't just nonsense. There was also an edge to it.

I remembered my mother at the kitchen table once reading an old mystical text for the sages called the Zohar, and my father whisked through the room saying, sarcastically, "Elsa, you're so smart you should be reading this?" A lifetime of these little jabs.

"I'm a Cohain, aren't I?" she snapped. Everyone fell back on that.

"Relax, Elsa. Read your fancy book."

She ignored him.

When he was gone, I went up to her and said, "Hey, Ma," but she didn't look up. Her lips kept moving. Reading the words. In the second century these rabbis went into a cave, took their clothes off, buried themselves in sand and twelve years later came out with the Zohar.

Finally, she realized I was there and her head snapped up.

"You want ginger ale?" she asked. That line came out whenever she wasn't listening to me. Like whatever the problem was, ginger ale would solve it.

I shook my head. I didn't even know what I was going to say. There was a look on her face. Like she wouldn't mind burying herself in a cave for a few years. She was off on an island where Dad couldn't reach her. But that meant I couldn't either.

Then she reached out and stroked my hair, and said, "You're okay, darling."

Sometimes I'd volunteer to practice reading Hebrew just because I liked her standing close behind me: her hand on my shoulder squeezing when I flubbed a word, softening when I found my groove.

I wanted to tell Ivy all of this, but right as I was thinking about how to begin, she asked me a question.

"Who was your first girlfriend?"

"Danielle Feeley," I said. "She was an all-state swimmer and always had a fever blister on her lower lip. I don't know if those two things are related."

Ivy made a face.

"I wasn't in a position to get picky."

I told Ivy about how Danielle and I had snuck off into Harold King Forest and lay down on some shiny green ground cover to fool around, which led to my first blow job. But that night I felt an itch at dinner, which grew into this horrible burn by nighttime as I lay in bed convinced I'd gotten gonorrhea and everything my mother warned me about the goyem—non-Jewish girls—was true.

"I am goyem?" Ivy asked.

"Big time. Anyway, it turns out you don't all have gonorrhea. By 10:00 p.m. I knew it was poison ivy. This isn't a joke on your name by the way. This is true. Do you have it in China? Poison ivy."

She rolled her eyes. "Yes, of course."

"I didn't know. Well, it was on my penis and the itch was absolutely horrible. Sure that I needed to go to the hospital, I woke up my parents. Dad started yelling in the hall, 'On your *schmekel*? The hell were you doing?' Then my sister came running out in her nightgown—'That's why I call you dickweed!'—

and Mom was cursing and Dad said, 'Everyone just hold on a second, let me get my reading glasses.'"

Ivy's forehead wrinkled up and she leaned back. "Why did he want to see?"

"I don't know. He's fucking nuts. To diagnose it, I guess. But that's my father. I mean, I couldn't even have *that* to myself. My first blow job. Even that turned into a disaster. Standing in the bathroom. Dad doing his real low whistle."

I did the whistle and Ivy laughed. "This is a terrible story," she said. She'd throw herself down a well before showing herself like that to her parents.

Then she blushed a little and said, "Mine was better?"

"Much better," I said and smiled.

We were quiet for a while and I was about to ask about her first, but something on her face told me she'd moved on from that.

"Are you thinking about Ruxi?" I asked, my hand folded behind my head.

"No," she said. She turned on her side and faced me with her elbow on the pillow. She drew a sharp breath.

"Alex, I have to go to Beijing this weekend and I want you to come with me."

"Beijing? Why? Did you tell your work-team leader?"

A darkness came over her face. Or maybe it was pity, I couldn't tell, some distance, even though she was still pressed right against me.

"Did ever something bad happen to you? A tragedy?" she said.

I was quiet for too long. I could hear her swallow.

"Mmm," she said, her question lingering. There was Ruxi of course. But before that there was Bernie and me at nine years old sitting in his mother's room and she was spluttering into a napkin while stroking Bernie's arm and I found that odd and beautiful, that she'd stroke his arm when she was the one dying from cancer, and he had his head on her chest, her breath coming short and labored, and I was standing by the foot of the bed, imagining her feet swollen and purple under the covers, and she whispered something to him and then it was like she left her smell behind in him, because from then on he smelled like her always. Kind of like the glossy pages of an old magazine. In gym class for weeks, months, he'd suddenly drop the floor-hockey stick or basketball and walk off into the corner and start talking, all animated, to the cement wall, gesturing and pleading and arguing and then he'd come back and say he had a fight with his mother and point to the wall saying, *Don't you see her?* And it threw this chill over my skin like I'd jumped in a cold lake, mostly because his eyes were intense and alive, black as fresh tar, and I knew he wasn't fucking with me. I knew he was talking to a real ghost.

So I was about to tell Ivy about that when I had this terrible thought—my life has been too easy, suspiciously so, and what if there's been someone at the reins, someone out of sight, greasing the wheels, getting a mild-grade screwup like me into a good college like Brandeis. Getting me third and fourth chances. Getting me from intern to staff at *Traveler* magazine in a few months. I'd never asked. I hadn't asked the hardest questions of myself. Or maybe I'd always known it was Dad. It was him pulling the strings. Not God.

"Tell me about your sister," I said. "I want to know everything about you."

"Walk it with me," she said.

"Walk what?"

"Tiananmen. Come with me to Beijing if you want to know."

She was talking softly but her voice was firm and insistent.

"I can't explain in words," she continued. "When I try, it

is like leaving the kettle boiling too long and all the water disappears."

"Evaporates," I said, before I could stop myself.

She started picking at a loose thread on the pillowcase. I knew I'd said the wrong thing. I was scared, that's all, and a little embarrassed because I'd never had my face pushed down in it, not like Ivy, so I flexed some muscle by correcting her vocabulary. Scared she'd think I was soft. And she'd be right. The only real grief I'd had was those four months in New York alone working at The Plaza Hotel as a shoe-shine boy—Bernie's dad got me the job. He knew the front office manager, Anthony. Old black guy. "Use your bare hands," Anthony told me when he saw me applying polish with a rag. He used to hover over my shoulder. "The warmth melts the polish into the leather. Go on. It won't hurt. There's nothing to be afraid of." That man was a saint. I worked hard for him. Kneeling before that mahogany throne with brass stirrups and pearl knobs. Buffing and polishing three coats, all dizzy from the heavy naphtha smell, until I could see my own face in the guy's shoe. But I can't explain it. Why it felt so desolate. I know you can get a story out with all the words in the right order, but it doesn't put you in control of the thing. Ivy didn't want me to understand, she wanted me to feel it. She was asking for something, so I needed to stop being a selfish prick. She wanted to show me. Shut up and say yes.

I remember how sometimes, if the customer was a friend of his, Anthony would let me put a nice gob of polish on the toe box and set it on fire with a lighter. A bright blue flame. I wanted him for a father. Feels like I could've done something with my life if Anthony was around every day to tell me there was nothing to be afraid of.

"Okay, I'll go," I said to Ivy, suddenly, almost surprising

myself, and I expected her to be real happy about this but her mouth drew a hard line.

"Alex," she said, "it is not just my sister. I have a meeting in Beijing. Let me say all this at once. I try to tell you before. I belong to a political party called the DRP. The Democratic Revolutionary Party. That is who I am."

"Is it legal? This party."

"No. We remain a secret. Others registered with the government officially. The LCCP and the DCP. But they all disappeared or got arrested or fled."

"Is this why you came here tonight?"

Her face flattened.

"No, I needed to see you. Just you. But also this I needed to tell you in person. The phones and the computers are not safe."

Did Gang, the mayor, set it all up—wiretaps, surveillance—to see anything he wanted? Hadn't he told me at the restaurant to watch myself; people disappeared in Foshan all the time.

"It is worse for me," she said. "My cell phone and my email is monitored because of my sister's part in '89. Same with my parents. My role in the DRP is a secret. For now. But they want to meet you."

I sat up in bed. "Me? You told them about me? Are you fucking crazy? They could shut me down. Close the factory. I could get thrown in jail."

"It is secret," she said, shushing me with her hands. "I promise. Believe me. No one finds out."

It was quiet for a moment while I tried to sort out my thoughts but they were coming fast and muddy.

"Is this what you were trying to tell me back at your village?"

She nodded.

"Why do you need to get mixed up in this? I don't want you getting caught. What about all the reformers these days?"

I didn't know what the hell I meant by that. Only that I'd read in the news about reformers like Bo Xilai in Chongqing. With capitalism everywhere, the Communist Party of China saw what was happening. Democracy couldn't be far off.

"The reformers are more corrupt than CCP. No one will surrender power. No autocrats do. Not in time. This is the male ego. You hold on for life."

"What do you do in this party? Are you terrorists?"

"No. We are for a New Society. Chinese but freethinking individuals. Without individuality there is no State. No government can serve the people through corruption and repression and censorship. No one my age believes in the party anymore but since '89 everyone is too scared or passive to do anything about it. The party thinks we are pacified with China's rising wealth and power, but this is small part of China. Almost nobody. We want representation, not fear. This starts with workers. The head of the DRP, Zhang, I met in college. He is a good man. He sends me to your factory to organize—"

Her voice trailed off as she read the doubt on my face. The blankets felt very hot and oppressive, and I stood up.

"They think you can help," she said. I started pacing the room. "I think you can help. When I met you I know there is more. You don't even like making your father's shoes. Once I know you I feel this is someone who maybe can understand our side. Someone who wants to make things better. We never had anyone from your side."

"My side?"

"The private sector. A foreigner. Capitalist. Someone inside. If you want you can actually change things. Others will copycat."

When she said that, *inside*, this current of fear jolted through me and kept pulsing slowly like one of those overhead factory lights on the fritz.

I realized I was still pacing. I picked up her tank top on the chair and without even thinking I threw it to her. And this anguished look came over her face. She put it on, her head lowered, and the room got quiet again.

"So is that why you're with me?" I said. "Using me because I'm on the *inside*? That's what this is?"

"Don't give words I never said."

"Because I'm young. I'm a dumb kid to you. Twenty-six."

"Do you think this all along? What the fuck? I don't care numbers. Do you? What if we switched? Who cares? I don't have online dating account saying I want this size and shape and hair. I want a person. You."

She shook her head. Took a deep breath.

"I like your age," she continued, softer. "Okay? I like it. You are exotic."

"I'm exotic?"

"Strong arms. Hands. Wide chest, shoulders. I like this. Good?" She threw her hands up. "Why do I have to explain what I like?"

"Because," I said. "Look. I haven't seen as much as you. You've done a lot of shit. You know a lot. And then there's me. I feel sometimes like some fucking naive kid."

"Because your father," she said.

"Sure. Maybe. But you drop all of *this* and I worry. I can worry, you know. That this is some long con. You're using me to help your cause. That's what this all is."

It was all fucking muddled in my head. Ivy whipped off the comforter and stretched her legs, long and smooth, varnished by the syrupy sodium lights off the street and this tripped my brain, the sudden flash of how she'd sit on a beach, whether she'd dig her feet into the sand or lock her insteps together, and it was such a dumb and irrelevant thought, like any of that mattered. Her eyes were watery now and I couldn't read her next move. Maybe she was going to just get up and walk out. Or say something. Explain. I didn't know. You can't ever know what's going on inside a person.

"Alex," she said, her voice bubbling. "That is not why. Not how I feel about you. If anything this, us, got in the way of everything. My goal is the same if I never met you. But I did. This is never a plan. You have to believe that. It kills me if you think bad of me. Come to Beijing, please. I want you to know everything about me. I never said that to someone before. No secrets. If you don't want to attend the party meeting, you don't have to. You don't. Really."

She shooed me away with both hands, like I was supposed to leave my own hotel room.

I was going around fast in circles in the room and Ivy said, "Are you okay?" holding the sheets in a fist by her chest. A slight tremble in her voice. When I didn't answer she dropped her chin.

I believed her that this wasn't some furtive plan all along. That was way too speculative. And maybe Ivy was right, that I could help. Maybe she was right when she said there was a little Trotsky in my blood. You can't fight blood.

So maybe I wasn't going to storm The Great Hall of the People on horseback with a gold saber and a garrison's cap, but what if I could help just a little? Get everything aboveboard. No more withholding *hukous* or IDs. Small pay raises. Little things without sacrificing profit.

Without realizing it, I was already moving to the bed without any articulate thought formed, the only sure thing I knew was that I didn't want to be Dad's flunky, the eternal Bagel-boy.

I sat beside Ivy on the bed. "When's the train leave?"

She smiled and lowered her forehead to my shoulder. I put my arm around her.

"Only sixteen hours from here on the T98."

"First we have to bring Ruxi home," I said. "Hongjin will help. I know he will. He'll do anything for a day off. Then we can keep going to Beijing."

A fitful night of sleep. Ivy burrowed into me and I burrowed into her and it was like we couldn't get close enough and I only hoped it was really me Ivy desired from someplace deep in herself and not just an idea in her head.

In the midst of these thoughts, it hit me that Ivy wasn't even the name her family called her. It was a made-up name. If I was smarter I would've put it together earlier, the fact that she was using a fake ID, because the Party watched her. No way she would roll into our factory with her real ID. The Party knew everything. So she was working on forged or stolen papers and this should've pissed me off but for some reason it didn't.

It was just a name. Trotsky was Bronstein. So what? Didn't actually matter any more than if water disappeared or evaporated. I squeezed Ivy close. She turned her back to me and rubbed her cold feet against my shins. She pulled my arm over her chest and I cupped her right breast and then it struck me that I might actually love the girl.

Eight

TWO DAYS LATER, ON FRIDAY MORNING, I WAS in the back of Hongjin's Jetta with Ivy riding shotgun and Ruxi thawing in the trunk. Hongjin was telling me about how he souped up the car with suspensions and hydraulics, shit I didn't know anything about but I feigned comprehension. I was right thinking he'd jump at a day off.

As we drove north, Ivy started telling this story about how back in the day when someone died far from home, people used to walk the body back to his village. This was a real job, shitty but real, walking the dead. Corpse walkers they were called.

"You remember," she said, "the roads were no good and there weren't cars I don't think. Were there cars?"

"How the fuck would I know?" Hongjin said.

Ivy ignored this and said that if the body never came home it was a serious dishonor and failure. The ghost of the dead person would haunt them. It would wander forever. So the family paid guys to walk the corpse covered in a blanket for hundreds of miles sometimes but only certain places would let corpse walkers actually sleep in town. She didn't know why.

Hongjin said, "Because they were carrying around a dead

body. By the way, Alex, no one believes this shit anymore. This is *old* thinking."

Every now and then when the car hit a stitch in the highway we heard Ruxi knocking around in the trunk and Hongjin turned the music up.

Then they started arguing about all the dying Chinese traditions and that made me think of home, which always made me sleepy and I couldn't fight it anymore.

But I didn't have a dream really. What settled in me was a memory of me and my sister sneaking to the front door with a screwdriver and taking off the mezuzah, the little scroll that every Jew has nailed to the doorpost to let the world know they're special. We wanted, or at least I wanted, a closer look. Everyone had one but no one ever opened it. It was all a big secret. So I carried it, warm in my fist—it was heavy bronze with a glass face—down into the basement and I put it down on the cement floor and gave my sister a socket wrench off the workbench.

She insisted she put a handkerchief under it.

"It's not alive," I told her but I wasn't so sure. Anyway, I got the handkerchief and folded it nice under the mezuzah for her, and I said now do it.

"You sure we won't go to hell?" she asked.

"We don't even believe in hell. Go."

She lifted the wrench over her head and I held my breath, half fearing a swarm of locusts to burst through the hopper window. The glass smashed but that's all. No locusts. No hail.

"Now what, dickweed?" my sister said. And I didn't know the now what.

I think I vaguely knew it was my grandfather's and that he probably smuggled it across the Atlantic in his underwear, at least that's how my mother acted when she found out we broke it, but I just wanted to know the secret. What treasure lay hiding in the sacred case that we all hung on our doorposts?

My sister and I unrolled the scroll inside—very old, yellow vellum, and it was just miniature Hebrew cursive, the same stuff Mom was trying to write. I don't know what words could be so important, but they were written in a beautiful hand, black ink, almost microscopically, like you picture a guy in prison writes his life story on a single sheet of toilet paper. Like you needed one of the secret decoder rings from my cereal box to read this thing.

All I remember next was sitting in that tall yellow corduroy chair in the corner of their bedroom and watching her cry. My mother. Holding the busted case and the scroll, saying faintly, "Shema," which means "hear" in Hebrew. That's what was written on the scroll I realized after she'd said it a dozen times. It's a long prayer. Probably a million books have been written on it, and I'm sure it's about God or witnessing or whatever, but all I knew was the first word. *Hear.*

And right before my mother slapped me I woke up with this upswell in my chest, all unsettled, and we were rushing alongside a stand of pine trees and old broken-down watchtowers, way out in the country, and Hongjin said, "You sleep very good. We are almost there. Probably one kilometer—"

"Stop the car," I said suddenly, startling Hongjin, who swerved the wheel hard to the right and skittered in a cloud of dust.

"Fuck, man," he said.

"What's wrong?" Ivy said.

"We'll walk her," I said, almost hushed. This feeling had come over me with something like religious purpose. I trusted the impulse only because it came out of my throat before I knew what happened. Like I'd woken up with this weight pressing down on me, pressing on my face and chest, and the only way to get it off was to do this.

"We're going to walk Ruxi," I said to Ivy. "Me and you.

Like you said before. The walkers. They did that, right? You weren't making it up."

"Oh fuck, man," Hongjin said. "I told you, no one believes anymore."

I told him to follow us in the car and then I opened the door and got out. Before me in the evening light were settlements of low cheap houses with red dragon scale roofs. The trunk was wet where Ruxi had defrosted during the ride. I bent my knees and hoisted her out of the car and Ivy helped me stand her up between us. I lifted her arm but she was real stiff.

"I could just carry her over my shoulder," I said.

"No, it has to look like she's walking," Ivy said.

So I pulled her arm up around my shoulder and I snaked my hand around her waist.

"We need a blanket over her," Ivy said, "to do it right."

I draped the leather hide over Ruxi's head and it still had that rich earthy tanning smell. You couldn't see anything but her sandaled feet and ankles. I reached back around her waist and we started to walk. It was hard to get the timing. We had to sort of sway from side to side to simulate her feet moving.

We wound past a row of houses with brick walls, lurching along. And maybe I was doing all this for Ivy. Or to prove something to myself. I knew I had my reasons even if I couldn't fully make sense of them.

When we were about a half mile away, the kids from the edge of the village came running out. Some of them ran straight to Hongjin's souped-up car but others, two or three, fell in step with me and Ivy, asking questions, tugging on Ivy's arm.

"They ask what we are doing," Ivy said. "Bringing her home, I say."

The kids were talking fast.

Ivy said, "They ask why a blanket over her? Does she have a face? I say, 'Ask your mothers.'"

We drew a little group. Maybe five or six children walking with us. A boy dribbling a basketball through his legs. Another pushing along his bike. Two girls hand in hand.

We passed by a crumbling shadow wall out in front of a broken-down stone and brick house on the outskirts of the village. Big banyan trees grew wild with tendrils dangling down all over the place. The air smelled like burning firewood.

An older woman hooked her finger into one of the boys' collars and pulled him back. She spoke in a cold, croaky voice to Ivy and threw me a look that made me shrivel.

"She wants to know who you are," Ivy said.

"Tell her it was my fault," I said.

"No," Ivy said. "They won't forgive you."

She spoke to the woman in Chinese and the woman nodded and smiled at me.

Ivy said, "I tell her you are a friend. You know Ruxi belongs here."

The old woman's face softened up.

As we kept walking, more people came out, word going around about what was happening.

Ruxi started slipping down, and we stopped to readjust. I dug my left hip into her side to help prop her up. As we began moving again I started to think about who she was. I remembered her Baby Love T-shirt. I wondered if a boyfriend had given it to her. If she'd ever been in love.

In the half-light off to the elbow of the road, I saw a woman sitting on a lashed bundle of bamboo and smoking. She nodded at me. Not a smile or anything but enough to say I wasn't a stranger any longer. With each step we took together as a group I felt more sure of it. Because I helped bring their daughter home to the place she belonged.

And when I focused on each step I wound up getting our feet mixed, the kids' next to me, and the ones in front of me, all the thong sandals and sneakers; you couldn't tell what belonged to whom. It all got mixed up in my head, where you started or ended.

We wove through the alleys of the village, and I kept seeing the same graffiti—a Chinese character circled and slashed—spray-painted on every house.

And then a kid came running up and he froze when he saw Ruxi's white braided sandals, and that was how I knew he was her little brother, because he recognized right away his big sister's shoes, like shoes somehow have a way of making themselves heard.

He knew these sandals in his bones. His nose started trickling, then he started scratching at this one spot on his bare arm, anguish on his face, the kind of pain that I hadn't seen on too many faces.

Out of one of the houses came her mother, you could just tell because of how achingly slow she walked toward us, how everyone else watched her. The mother's face was creased like C-grade leather, where the cows have all scratched themselves on barbed wire. Ivy spoke to her in Mandarin and I had no idea what was going on but it was pretty clear that Ivy was explaining things, and then the mother hugged Ivy and before I knew it her arms were around me too, and she smelled like copper and rice vinegar and she looked me in the eye and said something in Chinese that I didn't know, and just as suddenly we were surrounded by people from the village pushing me through the latticed doors of Ruxi's house.

A large paddle fan spun above an old woman at the center table with gray-and-silver hair. I looked down at her red shoes with embroidered peonies done in gold silk thread. The toe came to an odd sharp point, and I saw the binding cloth peeking out over the vamp. She had bound feet. Golden lotuses. Must be almost a hundred years old. One of the last of her kind. The wooden soles were flat, concealing her steep cracked arches, her toes folded down, squeezed and pointed like a spade head. She caught me staring so I turned away.

The family filed into the house followed by Ivy and Hongjin. The mother brought us soup—with soybean, sweet potato, carrots, in a pork broth. We ate sitting on low benches and drank hot tea. For a long time everyone talked in Chinese and I had no idea what was going on except the ancient grandmother kept nudging a bowl of fuzzy, yellow-skinned wampees toward me until I popped one in my mouth. An old man in the corner shaving palm fronds with a dull fishing knife, silent this whole time, finally finished his work, rose slowly with tears in his eyes, and before walking out of the house, he said, according to Hongjin, he was going outside to hang himself.

The young brother stared at me curious and wide-eyed from behind the door. There was an old framed poster of Mao on the mud wall. A statue of Guanyin, goddess of mercy. I wanted out of there badly. The air was stagnant, no breeze. And for some reason it all made me angry. I thought there'd be something romantic about villages like this, like if you didn't have a flat-screen TV you were living some pure ascetic life, but no, it was just miserably poor and forgotten and despairing. There was no mercy here. Everyone was over sixty or under ten and the rest had deserted. It wouldn't do anymore to be farmers. You had to be a giant onstage.

Ivy told me they were thanking us, but I almost didn't care anymore. I wanted to punch someone, Xi Jinping, the portrait of Mao, my father, myself. I wanted to destroy something. It was balled up in my shoulders. All the romantic country bullshit was dreamed up by people like me who breezed through these places and thought there was something ennobling about sticking seeds in mud all day or hacking bamboo with a machete in a hundred degrees even though I'd never do it myself for a second, and even if I did I'd start bitching after ten minutes for a break.

Hongjin wanted a smoke. He slapped me on the shoulder and we went outside.

"You saw how they look at me, right? Why are you so fucking rich? Your money must be dirty. It must be corrupted. You must do bad things. That is the attitude."

"I didn't see it, man," I said.

He shook his head. "Oh, man, these people are poor. The fucked-up part is they were probably rich landlords a hundred years ago. I can tell from the old Amah's bound feet. Fuck, man."

I could only think of one thing to say back. "Fuck, man."

"There is a new saying in China—life is like being raped, if you can't stop it, just enjoy it."

"That's a terrible saying."

"It means life is shit and you can't change it. Nothing you can do."

"I know what it means. It's still terrible."

He smiled at that and put his hands on his hips. "Be careful in Beijing, okay? Secret police everywhere. You're eye candy, you know? Serious. My friend's door was kicked down by police for posting shit on Weibo. And no jury in China. Lawyers give judges juicy fat bribes. It is a rotten apple from the root. Lin Yutang was right. 'Every man past forty is a crook.'"

Hongjin dropped us off nearby at the Chenzou West Railway Station. He was going to listen to thrash metal the whole way back to the factory. This was his favorite music, but he'd spared us on the ride up. We thanked him for that. Said our goodbyes. Then we got on the train heading north for Beijing. I fell asleep almost immediately, and when I woke up we were crossing the Yellow River basin outside Zhengzhou, the powdery yellow dust of the loess plains chattering against the train's sides. The river was all muddy and yellow with silt. They called it the river of sorrow from all the floods and famine. It did seem

very romantic, and even though I'd never seen this place before, I started feeling real fucking nostalgic as if I had. What
was that? This overrefined, overindulgent sense of nostalgia.

We rumbled across the Henan oil fields, and on the hori-
zon, the silhouettes of thousands of horsehead pumps sawing
up and down in unison like the whole earth was sighing. Then
it was the great delta plains, with the green-and-blue mountains way off to the west. Closer were the sandstone foothills
of the coal mines outside Taiyuan.

"Tell me a story," Ivy said. "About your family."

I told her about my uncle Mo sweeping the factory floor
while a mile away a boy fresh out of the war rubbed Tung oil
on the blond stock of his Ruger .22, enjoying the strong nutty
smell when a bullet suddenly discharged from his rifle, broke
through the window and spun a whole fucking mile straight
into Uncle Mo's right temple, who calmly released his broom
and dropped dead on the floor. I told her how his wife, Ethel,
the artist, went mad and started painting the same portrait of
him thousands of times. I told her about me and Bernie lay-
ing jump ropes end to end in the grass in a ring and beating
the shit out of each other with boxing gloves. Or how my
mother used to set a pot of matzo ball soup steaming on the
stove and lock herself in the room for days.

I told her about Mom sewing my name onto everything.
My hats, my belt, my underwear.

"That's crazy," Ivy said.

"I know. Why would I take my underwear off at school?"
Ivy giggled.

"I asked my mother the same question. She said, 'Who knows
why you do anything?' I said, 'Ma, it's not a Roman bathhouse.
The other boys wouldn't put on the wrong underwear.' And
she said, 'I'm not worried about other boys.'"

"She sounds funny," Ivy said.

"She is," I said. "I think she is. Hard to say. I think she'd like you."

You could see Ivy's top front teeth when she smiled. One was turned in a little, but otherwise they were real straight and white. Dad would like that if he could get past everything else. Like most things, he found the current state of dental hygiene sickening.

As I was talking, we ran past a range of karst peaks, steep escarpments and ridges of craggy limestone sloping into loose red clay, and we started to see roads and tall housing complexes on the city outskirts, and then with a pop the train dipped underground and the cabin lights came on, and I talked us all the way into the Beijing station in Dongcheng.

The conductors blew their whistles and flared their hands to keep order, but the passengers were already climbing through the open windows and clogging the vestibules, trying to get off the train. We pushed through the thick crowd to the subway and rode only a few stops before getting off at Tiananmen station in the underpass beneath the Forbidden City.

In the distance, over by the stairs, a man on kneepads with no arms begged for change and I felt a horrible drop in my gut, because I recognized those suppurate blisters and scars as benzene burns. In any shoe factory when the cement glue gets too close to the heat setters, it goes up like kindling, causing those types of burns.

It wasn't my factory though. It was someplace else. Nothing to do with me.

Ivy told me the placard around his neck said that his factory had locked the doors from the outside and no one could get out. He also claimed that he was a descendant of Empress Cixi, and I saw people laughing as they hustled past him. His legs were white as corn silk where the charred flesh had fallen off in patches. Again and again he rolled forward trying to stand up. Out of all the people streaming through the corridor it was me he stared at, like he knew me from somewhere, eyes bloodshot and gums black, he rolled forward and lunged at me, calling me *batgwai*, white devil, and Ivy hooked my elbow with her arm and quickly pulled me away.

When we came out of the ground, I could see on the northwest corner the modular police security hut that admitted us into the square, but first we were funneled into a tight cordon of fences, a single winding chute with the bright sun shining off the metal railings.

Suddenly the crowd dropped into a single file.

"None of this was here," Ivy said.

We inched forward. A woman in a white crocheted shift was reapplying her lipstick in the reflection of her husband's sunglasses.

"Take out your passport," Ivy said, once we were close to the security check.

She swung her canvas messenger bag off her shoulder and set it down on the conveyor belt that ran through an X-ray machine. She handed the guard her ID.

Before us stood a Chinese policeman in a starched short-sleeved white military shirt, peaked cap and white cloth gloves. Beside him were soldiers in dark green fatigues and army boots, machine guns crossing their chests.

The policeman ran my passport through the machine, then he did the same with Ivy's. He spent twice as long with her ID, flipped it around, scanned it under some blue light, spoke to her in Chinese. He had a chiseled face. If she was nervous, she didn't show it. He flicked his chin toward the metal detector and we passed through into the square.

The space was gray, dour, wide as six soccer fields. And the two massive buildings—the National Museum and the Great Hall of the People—loomed over the square. We were on the west side, close to the Great Hall where two Chinese men dressed as Santa Claus were performing choreographed kung fu for a crowd.

Ivy had her hand out in front of her like she was feeling for a bannister that wasn't there. Her head turned back over her shoulder to the giant portrait of Mao—a smug shit-eating grin on his face—hanging down off the rostrum of Tiananmen Gate.

It was him she was looking at, not the glittering gold roofs of the Forbidden City behind him, all the while walking forward, and at the last second I pulled her away from a marble lion.

Ivy led me south toward the Monument to the People's Heroes, a tall granite obelisk at the center of the square. Flanking the monument on both sides sat two enormous video screens flashing white characters against a red background. They were surrounded by a horseshoe of Chinese tourists.

Ivy translated the words in this robotic voice as they scrolled across the screen. "Prosperity, Democracy, Harmony, Justice, Rule of Law, Patriotism, Integrity, Bullshit."

"I like that last one," I said, and she smiled.

When we reached the terrace on the northwest side of the monument, Ivy stopped and touched the marble balustrade, traced it slowly with her finger and I did the same thing.

"This is where I found her," Ivy said.

She then pointed to the Great Hall and then north to Tiananmen Gate.

"This was all covered in tents. Many many. Here I find Hu Dan. Hawthorns around her neck. So skinny. Could barely smile. She was part of the hunger strike and I knew it. It said in *The Monkey King*, our favorite book, that if you wear hawthorns, you won't starve."

Ivy slumped against the balustrade.

"She used to read me that old, old book. We shared a bed. She was beautiful. They said when she walked by even the river stopped to watch. Back home they said that."

Her eyes welled and her voice quavered as she spoke. "I can't believe I was here."

She pointed to the area around the flagpole. "We built a bonfire and burned the *People's Daily* for calling us criminals. Then it rained. It made this sound, when it hit the fire. And it made smoke. Smelled like a ferret. I spit pumpkin seed shells into the fire."

A group of soldiers marched past us in starched white uniforms and long shiny boots. The tourists all ran over to get their picture as they kicked their legs up high in perfect unison.

Locked legs. Their legs shot up almost parallel to the ground and then the foot came down perfectly flat, no heel strike or push off, nothing of a human gait. Their boots aimed straight and fell even. Arms too, only from the elbow, firing off at a precise forty-five degrees. Palms flat. Heads still. No shoulder drop. Everything sparkling and shining, buttons and brims and trouser stripes. Men pretending not to have knees. Pretending not to love a single thing in the world.

It stunned me, really. This zombie ballet.

This is how the Great Hall would march if it came loose from its slab and grew legs. No, this is how the Nazis marched. That's what stunned me. I'd seen it before. If only in those grainy black-and-white videos of the Wehrmacht goose-stepping across the terrace in Nuremberg, and yet I knew that walk as intimately as if they'd marched straight through my bedroom. Field-gray gabardine. Thousands of them. Stone-faced machines, their legs flying out like switchblades, the glinting bayonet blades up by their shoulders and their legs locked like there were iron rods in them, nothing else, no sap, no human, just iron. And I was afraid. Deeply afraid of them.

Ivy's voice suddenly ripped past me.

"I wanted her to leave the protest. Before the trouble. Everyone knew. All day and night. Loudspeakers warning us. Evacuate immediately."

Two beefy-looking soldiers in short-sleeved fatigues and peaked black caps and fingerless black gloves passed by us walking German shepherds.

"Helicopters," she said, a little too loudly. "Yellow jackets. White paper falling. Thousands of leaflets. Get out. Before too late."

The soldiers glared at her briefly and continued their patrol.

"So hot," she said. "And we had no fresh water. And the square smelled like piss."

She turned. The two JumboTrons flashed video of Tibetans in cowboy hats prancing through a field of barley then a cut to Chinese Turks in tasseled fezzes dancing with red ribbons.

Ivy tugged on my sleeve, her eyes wide and alert.

I wished I could see what she was seeing. I needed to if I was ever going to understand her.

I followed her up to the third terrace of the monument. There was a round discoloration in the marble carving. A spackle job covering a hole that was perfectly round. About the size of a bullet.

"That's when it happened," she said.

"What happened?"

She walked down the steps of the monument and a few paces toward the Great Hall and stopped. "The army. Over there under Tiananmen Gate. And over there through the museum and here from the Great Hall. Shiny steel helmets. Many. With machine guns. Metal toeplates on their boots made this terrible sound."

She tapped the gray paving stone with her sandals.

"Coming from there too," Ivy said, pointing to the portico of the Great Hall, when the bronze doors suddenly opened and out walked a throng of schoolkids who started swinging on the granite columns.

"I had gone into the square to keep the bonfire alive. The rain was cold. And then I heard shots way off. I ran back for

Hu Dan. She was standing at the bottom of the monument holding an umbrella. I grab her wrist and I say run. She doesn't move. Refuses. Then I see a young man running at us in a white shirt covered in blood, the whole chest, and he says they're shooting. They're shooting everyone."

Right then a kid rode up to us with a satchel full of Little Red Mao books.

"Five yuan," he said to me. I shook my head. Then he seemed to notice Ivy. He leaned his forearms against the bike handle and listened.

"Machine guns. Tanks. Trucks. The army facing us. An officer lean out of the army truck with bullhorn. He's got on this cap with a gold emblem. A lieutenant. And us. Students. But mostly ordinary people. Bicycles stacked high as a blockade. The front row holding hands. Human chain. Singing 'Internationale.'"

She bowed out her elbows as if on either side the students were looping their arms through hers, and then she clasped her hands by her waist to lock them all together. She staked her feet wide apart and puffed out her chest. Then she began singing "Internationale" in a low, scratchy voice.

A crowd was starting to gather. Tourists with shopping bags. Teens in school uniforms. A vendor with knockoff handbags. They stopped to listen. Plenty of them understood English. Knew what Ivy was saying.

And then she was doing the lieutenant. Moving in quick steps back and forth. She was talking louder now. Holding up an invisible bullhorn, saying, "Evacuate immediately. Clear the way or we shoot."

She said that right in Tiananmen Square. Not loudly, but saying it at all is loud enough. I felt a tightening along my shoulders. I should get her out of here. You weren't supposed to mention the day much less go to the square and fucking act it out.

I looked around. Past the crowd, over by the security hut,

I saw the policemen with AK-47s strapped across their backs. They were looking in our direction, interested in what was going on. The commotion. But they were far enough away where they couldn't hear.

"Hey, we should get going," I said to Ivy.

She ignored me. "You can't shoot the revolution," Ivy said. Her fists balled. She wasn't herself anymore. An angry student now. She was there. In the moment so deeply that I'm not sure she realized how risky it was.

Her eyes drew a hard line. Her chin dropped. She was the lieutenant.

"Get out," she said.

Then she was that same student stepping forward. A boy.

"Fuck your ancestors," she said. The boy's words.

The crowd gasped.

Ivy ducked down, on the balls of her feet. Cowering. The terrified students.

Then she shouted an order in Chinese in the lieutenant's deep voice. She imitated the soldiers lifting their guns to their shoulders and aiming at the people.

"I pulled Hu Dan's arm," Ivy said. "Come, come. Run. She pushed me off. I said, 'Are you crazy? You are about to die.'"

The crowd pushed forward, bunching tighter. I narrowed my shoulders.

"We were trapped," Ivy continued. "The tanks, trucks—everything closing in. People started throwing bricks and glass bottles at the army. Then a horrible cracking sound. Bullets. Flashing. I can't describe. And smoke. Before I could blink, the whole front row of students dropped. There were people and then they were gone. Innocent boys and girls." She searched the faces of the crowd. "You understand?"

Then she wasn't acting anymore. She wasn't anyone but herself. "Hu Dan," she said, kneeling down and slapping the gray paving stones. "This spot. The end of my family."

The crowd murmured, growing restless. A guy next to me holding a boom box flicked his wrist saying, "I wipe my ass with this country."

I looked to the security hut. The officers were on their walkie-talkies looking over at us. "We need to go," I said to Ivy. "Now. There are police everywhere."

She didn't respond. I had to get her out of there.

So I reached for Ivy's elbow, but she brushed me off. She sat down on the ground and then she proceeded to lie flat on her back on the smooth stones with her arms and legs splayed out.

"What are you doing?" I asked. "I need you to get up. Before they see you."

It was too late. The officers started walking toward us. They were still a distance off.

Some people stopped and pointed at Ivy. They laughed. The ones passing by or the ones who didn't speak English thought it was some kind of modern play. They stopped and took pictures of her lying there on the granite flagstones with her arms spread in this impromptu demonstration they were all mistaking for some strange performance art piece.

Her eyes were fixed straight ahead. "Water," she murmured. "So hard to get. Fresh water. We were all so fucking thirsty."

"Hey, you got to get up," I said. "I'm not kidding around."

Ivy still didn't move.

She was dead. She was Hu Dan dead on the ground and the police were drawing closer. Three policemen in white uniforms and peaked black caps were coming toward us with their German shepherds. The one out front swelled his chest and shouted, "What is happening?"

The officers were nearing the outer perimeter of the crowd. The onlookers began to part.

Suddenly Ivy jumped to her feet.

Snarling at Ivy, the officer's dog lunged forward, but right before it reached her, the officer snapped the leash taut and the dog heeled.

The officer shouted at Ivy, "Hey! What is this? What's going on here?"

"I was resting," Ivy said. "Very dehydrated. And no benches to sit in the square. So I lie down. If I have committed a crime against the country by sitting down, I apologize. Forgive me." She held up her ID and she took a slow step backward. "I am a good proper citizen. I bleed nationalism!"

The main officer frowned. His eyes flashed from Ivy to the noisy crowd. Eyebrow cocked. I could tell he was trying to make a quick decision: Am I going to arrest them all, or am I going to arrest her?

He didn't know what the hell to do. He barked an order to his subordinates and one of the officers went up to a lady in a neon visor and oversize shades and started dumping the contents of her purse on the ground. I could hear the other officer shouting for IDs.

I turned my head. Out of the corner of my eye, I saw Ivy inching away toward the edge of the crowd. For a second our eyes met. A look. I wasn't sure what she meant by it—if I was supposed to follow or stay.

To follow, wouldn't that just draw attention to her? And if she's seen with a Westerner maybe that would make things worse for her. When the officers first came up, it wasn't clear that I was with her. But if they now see that I'm attached to her they're going to think that something really bad was happening back there.

Just then, in the middle of these thoughts, a young performer in a full clown suit with a red button nose rode past with a bouquet of roses in the basket of his bike and he honked his nose-horn twice.

The dog began barking its head off. The crowd laughed

and jostled. The head officer yelled and shook his fist as the clown quickly pedaled off with another few honks.

I glanced over my shoulder to see Ivy edging away. She'd almost made it out. Almost reached the West Side Road where she could slip into the flow of tourists. I could go after her. I had an opening with the officers distracted. I wanted to follow. No, I shouldn't. Hang back a little. Play it safe. Let her get out ahead. That's it. I made up my mind.

The head officer blew a shrill note on his whistle. He'd heard enough laughing. He drew an imaginary line with his gloved hand and started waving people behind it. The officers pulled people apart, trying to organize them, shouting, "You, over there. One line. No, no, no. Get over here. Don't object!"

Over my shoulder I saw Ivy fall in step with the tourists burdened with shopping bags marching toward Chang'an Avenue. Her head was down. I made the right choice. She'd wanted me to stay.

I waited a few minutes to show my passport to one of the officers, who, upon seeing that I was American, grunted and waved me off.

Then I started up the West Side Road after Ivy. For a moment, I turned back. I saw that the officers had the crowd lined up now, shoulder to shoulder, heads bowed, and I felt my skin prickle because it was as I always imagined the soldiers in Lithuania with the Jews lined up on the riverbank. The kind of soldiers who never waste bullets. Who even make you take off your shoes at the Vilija riverbank before tying up everyone's hands and feet in a human chain. Then they shoot one Jew in the back, who falls dead into the icy river, dragging the others in to drown, and all that's left of them are shoes lined up along the snowbank.

I dashed after Ivy. I was moving north on Renda Huitang road, past the I Heart Beijing T-shirt vendors, and I was thinking about the stones it took for the Chinese to come out into the street and take on the CCP and the Red Army. Was that smart or insane? Have we Jews ever done anything like that? I mean, did we ever gather in the shadow of the Sphinx singing *V'shamru* and protesting? Or have we always played it safe? No, I remembered my grandparents telling me about Vilna. Their hero, Hirsh Lekert. Twenty-two-year-old boot maker who had the balls to shoot the governor in the back of the head at the playhouse, middle of the second act, shot him for whipping Jews—Bundists—on May Day. They hanged Lekert and threw his ass in the river. After that my grandparents helped close up the shul and they set up in the brick cellar beneath the Vilnius Opera House. They waited for the pit orchestra to lift their instruments and start playing before praying. Have we always known that? That you were a Jew in the cellar but a good honest Litvak in the street.

Ivy was just up ahead waiting at a stoplight at a big intersection on Chang'an.

"You scared me back there," I said, once I caught up to her.

She didn't answer. Ivy kept looking straight ahead. I let it go at that.

"I ran," she said after a moment. Her eyes were bloodshot. Face pale. "I ran away. It happened so fast I ran."

She was talking about back then. It took me a second to get that.

"You had to," I said. I wanted to do or say something more but I didn't know what.

Then there was the tingle of a bell and she pulled me back from the edge of the sidewalk right as a bicycle swiped across my face, and the rider, a lady carrying a baby on her back and a suitcase in her free hand, shot me a foul look.

"Careful," Ivy said.

She led us down into the Zhongsheng *hutong* crisscrossed with overhead power lines. Above us, roosting in the branches of the poplars, jackdaws cawed loudly but I kept hearing those goose-stepping boots thundering, the ones that could well have trampled Hu Dan or my grandparents' cousins crouched in a basement sump pit.

"Back home," Ivy said, "the police came to our door and make us sign papers apologizing for Hu Dan's crimes. But no burying. No. If you died in Tiananmen, your body does not go home. I only wish I do for her what we do for Ruxi. Something like this. You don't leave a body out in the world alone. To turn into a famished ghost. A lonely soul. We slept in a bed together for years and kept warm. She was my other half. But I made a choice. You understand?"

I nodded. I felt nauseous by the whole thing.

It was a sunny day and there was the smell of real strong coffee wafting out of the UBC café we passed and if I wanted to be honest with myself, me, my family, we got rich off Tiananmen. What was Tiananmen to me? To any American when it happened: a story on the news for ten fucking minutes before flipping to *Cheers*. Then I got this flash of Dad at the Vegas shoe show with his old partner Alan Berkowitz after they'd closed the booth and Tiananmen's on every TV and Dad's saying to him: "Now there's a government that doesn't jerk you off. Not like our yellow gutless George. The balls to act—that's what counts. Making tough decisions. You know what this is, Alan, do you? This isn't censorship. It's a free TV spot saying, 'We don't give a shit about our people and neither should you. You want to manufacture? Here's the place. You won't hear a peep out of our workers. Why? Because business comes first.' You see that, Alan? See how it's wonderful news. An opportunity. Is it still a *shanda*? Yes, a sin. Terrible what happened. But it's also our chance."

That hurt to think about. After everything we'd been through, Dad would see Tiananmen on TV and think jackpot. Playing right into that *goyische* stereotype of the greedy Jew. Usurer. Loan shark.

Worse is that he went through with it. Willing to turn around and do the same things to others that had been done to us for hundreds of years. Sure, he didn't shoot anyone, it's true. But pogroms and shooting kids in public streets weren't the only ways to persecute people. He'd lost something. Dad had. Reciting kiddush and breaking some matzo didn't cut it. Something deeper. His deepest Jewishness.

Maybe, when it came to Dad, this was right in front of my face the whole time. Who he really was. Or also was. I just didn't want to look. A man who would run through a brick wall for his family but everyone else could go to hell.

It wasn't going to happen to me. I wouldn't let it.

It was making my palms sweat to think about.

I wanted to say to him: How did you miss it? How many Tiananmen Squares have we been through? That's me and you out there running from tanks and goose-stepping troops. We've been persecuted and poor, and now you've just turned around and done it to other people. Exploiting, abusing—how do you call yourself Jewish?

We walked past little outdoor food stalls, *suan fen* and chicken wings, and the smell of chili and vinegar wafting out of the iron wok. And we stopped at one of them and ordered two beers.

We took our beers over to a plastic picnic table up against the *hutong* wall. The beer was real cold. I drank half of it in a gulp and held the sweating bottle against my cheek.

I watched this tree sparrow dive in and out of a hole in the rotted roof beam of the restaurant. She had a little crab apple in her mouth. She hopped and screeched and then flew away, refusing to feed it to her babies who ventured closer to the edge of the hole, and maybe she was trying to lure them out because they'd outgrown their place, outgrown her, and she was saying, *Get the hell out. Come on. Fly off. Go.*

"One of the Four Pests," Ivy said, tracking my eyes.

"Sparrows?"

"Like I told you with my father. Mao accused them of eating the people's grain, so they had to be killed. Greedy, bourgeois birds."

Shaping her hand like a gun, she aimed at the bird, squinted one eye closed and triggered her thumb.

I thought of her father. I thought of Mao ordering the peasants to exterminate all the sparrows. Chased with rakes and hoes and wood spoons, chased until they dropped from the sky exhausted because you can only run for so long.

"This might sound weird," I said, "but I used to be afraid of my parents' shower. Closed on all four sides. No curtain. A door—frosted glass. Floor to ceiling. Tight box. When it got all steamed up, I thought it was gas. I know. I was little— four or five. Before I even knew the words *Zyklon B prussic acid*. You get what I'm saying?"

She nodded.

"From Hebrew school I knew the gas was colorless—like steam—and smelled like almonds, like the shampoo my mom bought. So—"

"You were a boy."

"It's not rational, I know. Doesn't need to be. I mean, I saw the steam and smelled the almond and felt terrified. Obviously my parents wouldn't gas me. I wasn't that bad. But for a split second, I believed."

She lifted an eyebrow, took a swig of her beer and set the bottle down hard on the table. She was studying me. Trying to read my face. I was only trying to comfort her, trying to say that we were together, or made the same way, or some greater reason brought us together, something, when all that just floated out, like flakes of charcoal ash off the barbecue grill beside us roasting oysters on the half shell.

It was stupid what I said. In light of everything here. Which I couldn't pretend to understand. But I understood what she was acting out in the square. I knew the anger. The fear. That you were always an outsider and the moment they found out who you really were, they'd hunt you dead. That the world was just one big crawling cattle car where everyone slept on the edge of a train whistle and you only opened your mouth to scream.

Ivy stared at me. The oysters hissed and a long silence stretched out.

"Maybe I am a traitor," she said.

"No, don't say that. You were smart. Brave. Really fucking brave."

I was almost jealous of her. To survive this there had to be something in you—not just some Cohain bullshit, but something truly rare.

"What could I do?" she said. "I saw arms and legs. People. Blood—" Her voice trailed off. Then she covered her mouth with her hand, but I still heard her say, "How do I know she was dead?"

"No, you couldn't go back. Go back out there you're shot. You did everything you could," I said.

"I don't know," Ivy said, lowering her eyes to the ground. "Worst is not knowing what happened. Maybe she was trampled by soldiers, stepped on."

She took a swig of her beer.

"Sometimes," Ivy said, "I wish I did more. Do you understand how I said this?"

"I know. We've been through this too. So many times. It keeps happening."

"And what did you do?" she said, leaning in closer. "Your people."

"We ran. We moved. Exactly what you did. Go on. That's the only revenge."

I wasn't sure she understood what I was saying, but she nodded her head just once, firmly, sat back in her chair and gave me a sad little smile.

★ ★ ★

In the middle of the night, I woke suddenly in our hotel room in Wangfujing. On the far wall, bathed in moonlight, I saw the silhouette of Ivy's hands crossed and flattened, and I rubbed my eyes and focused, saw she was making a kite, her fingers the wings, gliding, running over a field, and it sent this chill down my back.

I said her name.

"I didn't know you are up," she said.

"I'm up," I said, propping myself up and facing her. "What are you doing?"

"Bad dream," she said. The glider vanished. "They come to our village with paint. Mark the walls *chai*. Paint the big character. White with big circle around. Dripping. They go house to house, painting it on the doors. Then the big yellow bulldozers come."

"Chai?" I asked. "What does that mean? In Hebrew it's life."

She shook her head. "Demolition. Remember Ruxi's village."

I remembered graffiti, but I thought it was the same kind you'd find anywhere. A kid's tag-name. Or a fuck you to anyone who'd listen.

"This is how they mark the buildings. In my dream, they paint on the people. My mother, grandmother. Their chest. White. To be destroyed."

"Jesus," I said. "Where were you?"

"I ran away," she said.

Then she rolled over, her palm under her cheek, facing the wall, and she drew her knees up, and then I thought I heard her say, quietly, "I won't allow," and that gave me a chill too, not what she said, but this eerie feeling that she wasn't speaking to me.

Nine

THE NEXT DAY WE WERE WALKING UP TEN flights of stairs at an apartment complex outside the south gate of Tsinghua University in Wudaokou.

The face that answered the door was hard and flat, and I knew right away it was Zhang, the leader of the Democratic Revolutionary Party, and it took only a split second for him to recognize me too. His face softened and he bowed slightly, smiling, and said, "Come in please," in English. Behind my shoulder, Ivy greeted him in Chinese. I stepped into his flat and it was too quiet. There was no one else in the apartment.

"To the left," Zhang called out, and I moved through an open door into a small living room with a writing desk and bookcase on the left wall and a two-seat red chenille couch on the right, where we sat down. Zhang took the matching love seat beside it. We were facing a little tea table with a bowl of apples. In front of me was a pass-through window into the kitchen.

Most of the stuff in the flat looked like standard IKEA crap, except a small, tapered shrine table flanked by round-back chairs with characters carved on the splats. Probably belonged to his parents. On top of the table was a frosted glass figurine of Guanyin, an enameled offering plate in front of her with some coins, orphaned keys, a bike tire air cap.

"I never introduced myself," Zhang said all of a sudden, slapping his knees and standing.

Shaking hands, we exchanged our full names. Bowed at the shoulders. He was scrawny. Thin wrists. When he lifted his head I noticed a touch of gray in his hair. He was older than Ivy by a few years. Or it was his eyes. Dark and sad. Heavy lids. A stitch of wrinkles at the corners. Acne scars on his face. He must have had pretty shitty skin as a kid, and that couldn't have been an easy way to go through life.

"You speak perfect English," I told him. "I didn't expect that."

"My father. A professor, before he was blacklisted. I also studied at university for many years with the others."

"Where are the others?" I asked. There were other things I wanted to ask but couldn't. It was a delicate balance. You couldn't just come right out and say, Okay dude, what kind of revolution are you running from this sleepy flat? Does one of these walls open up? Secret door? Where are the guns? The arsenal?

"The others are coming," he said, but his eyes skittered just enough to give him away. My hunch was he wanted to test me out first on his own. See if he trusted me. He struck me as a good leader. Maybe it was his eyes. The strong jaw.

He saw me taking in his outfit: a pointed waiter's vest and black trousers.

"Work later," he said. "Beijing Hotel. I work as a waiter."

"I see."

"The son pays for the father. They are one. His crimes are mine."

I nodded my head. He meant he was blacklisted too. From better jobs. The last trace of filial piety left in the system.

"It's not the Intercontinental," he added with a little bite.

How much had Ivy told him? I wondered. But then Zhang's gaze slid toward the foyer and when I followed his eyes a breath popped out of my chest. A three-foot lizard was squatting by the door, his tongue flickering, bright green, a crest of black horns along his back down to a long tapered tail.

I waited a beat or two for Zhang to explain the reptile situation, but then I realized he was waiting for me to say something about my hotel.

"Actually I'm pretty tired of it," I said.

He arched an eyebrow.

"The staff," I explained, "are too nice. It's fake."

He snickered, which made me self-conscious, like he was laughing at me and not my observation.

In my periphery, the lizard wobbled toward me. I heard the click of its yellow craggily nails on the wood floor. Same color as my grandfather's fingernails.

The lizard stopped a few feet away and looked up at me with his bright orange eyes and cocked his head to the side like he was saying, *Zhang, bub, what's with the Jew?*

Zhang didn't even glance over. Seemed to make a point of *not* looking. He just clapped his hands and, searching our faces, said, "Tea?"

"Please," Ivy said.

He stepped right over the lizard, and went to the kitchen, returning with a glazed porcelain *gaiwan* and three small *pinming* cups.

"From Hangzhou," he said, and poured the tea into our small drinking cups. The color was light green. A feathery smoke lifted off the surface.

"Drink," he said.

I held the cup between my palms and the tea was light and clean and warming. A nice floral smell. Chrysanthemum.

Zhang took a sip.

"Too strong?" he asked.

"No, I like strong."

"Americans do?"

"It depends. Everyone's a little different."

He smiled at this. He struck me as very shrewd.

I set my empty cup down on the table and placed two knuckles down on the table.

He laughed, reaching for the *gaiwan,* and refilled my cup. "An old tradition. How do you know?"

"Like a servant kneeling," I said, which was how my knuckles looked forked down on the table. "Shows humility. Obedience."

His eyes widened. "Some traditions wear out," he said.

Out of the corner of my eye, I kept watch on the lizard. He had his eyes closed, head bobbing like the headphone kids on the subway.

"My grandmother drank her tea through a sugar cube," I told Zhang. "Held in her front teeth. That's how the old Russian Jews did it."

"Russian, Jewish, American. How can you be all? Or do you pick one?"

"I've never been to Russia. And the Jewish part is just stories, traditions handed down. For me."

"That's a lot," he said. "You're loyal to them. Nothing wrong with that." Zhang dragged out the word *loyal*. He was playing with me. It felt as though he was implying something about Ruxi and the factory, but there was no conspiratorial grin on his face. Nothing to give him away. But everything about him felt calculated, cautious.

"It is easier for us," he said. "No choice. We're one thing. Chinese."

"I doubt it's that simple," I pushed back. "Say someone opposes the Chinese government, can he still call himself Chinese?"

Zhang smiled, and I knew I'd passed whatever test he laid out for me. The first one at least.

The lizard waddled close to me. His orange throat flared. Zhang's hand shot out flat like he was commanding the lizard to be still.

"Don't look him in the eye," he said to me. "He hates strangers."

"What is it?"

"A Chinese water dragon. His colors change. He came to me in Beihai Park. Out of the lake. I'm born in Water Dragon Year. It was a sign."

Zhang saw I was pretty squirmy with the lizard and he left and returned with a Tupperware container full of what looked like loose dirt, but when he sat back down I saw movement inside.

"Crickets," he said.

They were crawling around on an upturned egg carton in the tub. Zhang took off the top. In his right hand he held a pair of plastic chopsticks. Reaching in, slow and deliberate, he snagged a cricket.

I thought crickets were pretty good luck, so I was surprised to see one on the end of Zhang's chopsticks. Its antennae flickered; little legs struggling.

The water dragon flicked his meaty purple tongue. Jaws snapped.

It was a hard world. Tooth and claw, and someone always got eaten. I guess I'd grown up thinking this way. The way Dad thought. At war with everyone. Someone had to lose and it wasn't going to be us.

Maybe that was why Dad never reused a towel or refilled a water bottle. If he couldn't outlive everyone, the least he could do was use up all their shit before he went.

I was arguing this out with myself while Zhang fed a couple more crickets to his lizard, and I got this sudden chill that what I'd said to Ivy back in Tiananmen wasn't right. Going on wasn't enough. There had to be something beyond that. Where did you look for it? Was that really why I was here? In Zhang's flat.

"Full?" Zhang asked the lizard. He closed up the cricket box and the lizard wandered off to the other side of the apartment.

"He is going to nap," Zhang said.

"That's good," I said, like we were talking about putting our child to bed. It seemed important to Zhang that I cared. He rubbed his hands together and leaned forward.

"So. Tell me. What did you think of Tiananmen? After what you heard." He stressed the last word to make it clear that Ivy had already spoken to him about it.

"When we left," I said, "a huge crowd was coming in to watch the flag-lowering ceremony. The nationalism is strange. Given what happened." I paused to take a sip of tea. "Can I ask you a personal question?"

"Of course," he said, "we are talking."

"Were you in Tiananmen?"

He was silent for a moment. Exchanged a glance with Ivy and seemed to blink away some private thought.

"I was," he said, looking at his hands.

"The government didn't—arrest you?"

"Not all of us. No."

I'd caught him off guard it seemed, though he must have known I'd ask. Maybe he wasn't as prepared as he thought.

"Growing up," he said, "in my Little Red Book—you know we all had, I remember a famous quote, 'If we do not speak, who will speak? If we do not act, who will act?' Something like this."

I was midsip when he said this, and it was so familiar that it startled me and the tea slid down the wrong tube. I started coughing. Dad was one of the great mealtime coughers himself—in fact I couldn't remember a single family meal without a dramatic hacking fit and him wheezing, *What kind of God puts two tubes so close together?* But what set off my coughing jag was this clear memory of my mother spending one deranged year trying to write in perfect Hebrew calligraphy the old lines of Rabbi Hillel, *If I am not for myself, who will be for me? But if I am only for myself, who am I? If not now, when?*

Now Zhang was telling me Mao said the same thing. Couldn't be a coincidence. I swore he was fucking with me. No other possible explanation, unless this guy could read my mind.

I turned to the window and for a second the gray crumpled clouds mixed with the wadded-up drafts my mother tossed behind her shoulder, littering the kitchen floor. Over a hundred and fifty laws concerning how to write the Hebrew alphabet and she'd violated a dozen of them. The angles of her letters were wrong, the faces shouldn't touch, the left leg couldn't meet the roof, there must be room for a single strand of hair between them. This was the essence of Judea, she'd said.

Ivy was patting me on the back.

"I'm fine," I said.

"Let me get you water," Zhang said and he jogged into the kitchen.

She wasn't right—my mother about Judaism—was she? All the rules were just *mishegas*. It was the same as any religion—a way of explaining the mystery, the fucking blizzard right outside your door. The thing we were all terrified of and turned away from.

Maybe the essence was democracy. Maybe that's what Hillel meant. You *must* get involved.

Zhang returned with a glass of cold water, and I drank half of it down and it cooled my throat.

"Thank you," I said, wondering if Zhang hadn't intentionally kicked this all up inside me.

"So," he said, stretching into a long pause, "your father owns it."

He left out the noun, factory, like he'd been thinking about it so intently that it was obvious what he meant.

And honestly it sort of pissed me off that he asked a question he no doubt knew the answer to already. Ivy had surely told him.

"Yes," I said. "A joint venture with a Chinese owner and a local party member. And me. I'm a part owner now."

Zhang wasn't really listening to my answer. Something in his soft expression felt patronizing. Then I realized why I was actually pissed off—he was insinuating that I didn't *earn* it. Like I was just one of those new China *princelings*—the bratty kids of party officials who never worked a day in their lives. Though by that logic my father hadn't earned it and neither had my grandfather. I needed to make something clear to Zhang.

"It goes back generations in our family," I said. "Back to the old country."

"Factories?"

"Shoes."

"Ah," he said. "Inheritance. Dragons beget dragons. It should be the case. And I work as a waiter because of my father. The son pays for the father. They are one. True? His crimes are mine."

"The difference," I said, a bit sharper than intended, "is that my father hasn't been accused of committing crimes."

Zhang's head tilted to the side. For a second I thought he

was going to ask why I was here. Which is what I'd feared since the moment I sat down. I didn't know my answer. My reasons—one big slurry in my head, like the floating bits of fat and fur skating across the surface of the dehairing vats. But Zhang didn't ask this. He seemed to read something else into my defensiveness.

"He doesn't know you're here in Beijing," said Zhang. "Your father." Then he grinned, taking obvious pleasure in his discovery.

I didn't respond. Tried to remain mysterious. But my silence probably told Zhang more than he needed to know.

"It's okay," Zhang continued. "There are many things my father doesn't know about me. Which only cause pain. In China," he said with a sad smile, "you expect suffering."

That sort of crawled under my skin, though it probably shouldn't. I wanted to say, Look, Zhang, you can't just jump to the head of the pain queue; wait your turn.

"In Vilnius," I said, "during the roundups, my great-aunt hanged herself by her own hair."

Before I finished saying it, I could already feel a flush rising up from my neck and under my chin. Was I twelve years old showing off? The persecuted's version of my dad can beat up your dad. What did saying that prove?

Zhang replied calmly, "In the famine, we ate mud. It was white and sweet."

"*We* ate?" I asked.

He lifted an eyebrow, before catching my meaning.

"My family," he said. "I wasn't alive."

I could've been less of a dick about it, but his digs about inheritance got to me. He was calling me a fake. Or maybe that was my weakness, maybe Zhang didn't mean it that way. Trying to ease off, I said, "Sorry, I just wanted to understand."

"I can speak more plain for you," he said.

We stared at each other. It was conversations like this where I wished I smoked. Something to do with my hands. He didn't either. What kind of half-assed revolutionary didn't smoke?

"Tell me," Zhang said, "what do you police at the factory?"

An odd choice of words. I explained that I didn't really police anything. He frowned.

"What is your role then?" Zhang asked.

"Footwear design. In charge of development. Putting the seasonal lines together."

"You must have contact with the workers, no?" Zhang asked. "Do you supervise?"

"Each plant has its own supervisor and team leaders, and they all answer to different managers."

"A little city," he said. "With its own bureaucracy."

"Exactly. It's huge. Outsole plant, sample room, leather finishing plant."

"Who supervises workers after hours?" Zhang asked.

"No one. There's a curfew. Gates lock at 10:00 p.m. and there's an 11:00 p.m. curfew where everyone's in their dorms. There's guards on duty too."

"I see," he said, drawing his fingertip over the herringbone pattern of the sofa's arm.

"Do the different plants see each other?" he continued. "Do the workers ever communicate?"

"Mealtimes or in the dorms," I said.

"Do you eat with them?"

"There's a separate canteen for management."

"So you never bring all the employees together for training or to enforce rules?"

"All together? Only a few times."

"Where?" he asked, leaning forward.

The top floor of Plant C was empty. Not enough orders to make it worth a line. Sure it was big enough to hold everyone, but I wasn't coughing that up to Zhang. Let me see where he was going first, what his angle was.

"There's room," I said.

"Do you allow cell phones inside the plants?"

His mind kept skipping around.

"We have to. No one would work for us."

"I see," he said. Quiet for a moment. "Do you know the mayor?"

"Gang. Yes. My father does. I've met him a few times."

"But no one reports to you directly."

"Everyone reports to my father."

"It sounds like a difficult job. A lot of responsibility. Answering to your father."

"I don't answer to him," I said, maybe a little too quickly. Zhang arched an eyebrow. "No?"

"We see things different," I explained.

"This means?"

"He wants to stay the course. I'm not sure that works anymore. Labor isn't there. People don't want the factories. There's other jobs. Better pay. This is hot, long, dangerous work."

"I know."

"Picture doing the same thing over and over again."

To show him what I meant, I lifted up the teacup and moved it half a foot to my right and set it back down.

"That's it. One operation. Over and over. Four thousand times a day. You'd go crazy."

"According to reason," Zhang said, in what must have been some clunky translation of a Chinese term of agreement.

"It bothers me," I said. "To see. After a while. At first maybe I didn't notice too much. But at the end of the day, everyone's going back to the dorms. Gray faces. Shoes in hand from swollen feet. The stench. Decay. Who can breathe it all day? It's like the march of the dead and it—"

"Bothers you," he said, completing my sentence, before I even realized that I'd trailed off.

"Yes," I said. "It's the job though. Footwear's one of those industries where the machines can't do everything. Think of a tie. Simple. A machine makes a necktie. Snip, fold, stitch, done. Like a bris."

I paused for a moment.

"That's a joke—never mind. But you can't program a machine to make a shoe—even dumb sandals, simple you'd think, easy, but maybe a hundred and fifty different people handle it start to finish."

"Is it so?"

"Yes," I said, slapping my hands together. "You need people in my business. They aren't replaceable. That's what I'm saying."

Actually I was saying it for the first time, which occurred to me right as I finished and Zhang nodded his head.

"Machines you can trust," Zhang said, no sarcasm in his tone. "Not people."

I was taken aback. This from Zhang. Like he was arguing from my side of things. Or what my side should be. Like *he* owned the factory.

"If you can't get labor," Zhang asked, "you go where? Vietnam? India?"

"I don't want to. I want to make it work where we are."

His eyes widened. It was as much a surprise to me as it was to him. All my life running. Whenever it got tough. That was Dad's creed too—Yugo, Brazil, Taiwan, China—keep moving. Always. China was the first place he'd really settled down for any length of time.

Out of my periphery, I saw Ivy looking over at me—probably because I'd never said that out loud before—but I didn't turn to her because I didn't want Zhang thinking she was controlling me or that I was doing all this just to get laid.

My reasons, the real ones, were surfacing slowly. Fleeing didn't seem possible anymore. Before Ivy I was what? What was before? It was hard to even remember. Everything before was only preparing me for her. For this. It didn't seem possible to go on the same way. With Dad. With the factory. With anything. And all this coming from inside me surprised me too.

"There's money and then there's people," I said to Zhang, my voice a little wobbly. "That's the problem, isn't it?"

"Not harmonious."

"Never. Too bad you can't keep them separate. In my business it should work for all parties."

"You're talking about loyalty."

"Sure."

"At my last hotel," Zhang said, "a coworker cut his finger with a knife. Very bad. I take him to the hospital and all night I stay. When I come back to the hotel, my boss said I have no more job. Fired."

"For loyalty," I said. "For doing something *compassionate*. Impossible to know who to trust."

"This is humanity today. The daughter of our premier drives a Ferrari, bought with my tax money of course. I valet her at the hotel sometimes and she covers—it is true—the seat with napkins. Kleenex. So my poor working ass doesn't touch her premier leather."

"Bitch," I said. "Nice car though?"

"It has wings," Zhang said, smiling. Then he took a deep breath and rolled his wrists again.

"May I be honest with you?" Zhang asked. "For a moment."

"Of course."

"What brings you to me? To us? Why are you here?"

There. He said it. Finally. And what was the answer? Ivy partly. For sure, Ivy. But that wasn't all of it. What did we, me, my family, my ancestors—what did we make all these shoes for? To lift ourselves out of poverty and only to say to hell with the rest of you? To persecute others the same way we were persecuted?

"I'm a believer," I said.

"In what?"

"Democracy."

"A straight foot is not afraid of a crooked shoe?" he asked.

I was not even sure what I was prepared to do at the factory. The system was fucked—but turning the factory into some kind of socialist collective wasn't going to solve anything.

Plus it had been all over the news recently. Factories crippled by strikes. Factories burned to the ground by workers, terrorists. For all I knew, Zhang had a hand in some of it. Was that what he was planning for my factory? Somehow I had to get the answers out of him without seeming too obvious.

"Why factories?" I asked.

"Instead of what? Students? Like Tiananmen. No, this new generation is cold. They know what the world is, but they think, 'What can we do to change it? We are powerless. So I will do my things well and try to get successful. Why should I sacrifice my goals for bettering China?' You understand, Alex?"

"Sure. But why *my* factory?"

"*You* found us," he said.

"I did?"

"Yes. Because you know we're right."

His eyes didn't move off me, dark and hypnotic, and for a moment I thought he might be speaking the truth but I couldn't tell if I trusted him.

"Let me ask you something," I said, trying another angle. "You ever feed your lizard anything big? Or you always give him crickets?"

"Little food," he answered.

"Ever give him a rat or mouse to go after?" I asked.

"A mouse?" He shook his head, lips pursed. "He is only juvenile. When he is adult, strong, maybe he eats bigger."

"Okay, why not give him a little mouse. He could easily take down a mouse."

"Mouse bites back. Defends itself. Too dangerous. No, no. And he would eat it. Even if it killed him. Eyes bigger than mouth or however this saying goes."

He drew his head back suddenly.

"Why are you asking?" he said.

"We're talking," I said.

"Talk?" he asked doubtfully.

"Just talk. Freedom of thought. That's what you want, isn't it? Freedom to talk. Listen, say I go out of my way to help you. Let's say I want to do that for you. Where do we start?"

He was silent for a moment. Blinking his thoughts into focus.

"Start small and build up slow. Same as with the water dragon. Start small. Feed crickets."

"Okay," I said. "Because it's one thing to talk compassion, it's another to talk revolution—"

"No, no," he said, waving his hands in protest. "Alex, the democratic revolution is a long road. I misled you, if you thought revolution means military—no, my goals are small-small. I am not rash. I don't fear going slow. If China is a great country, it is only thanks to slow patience. This was the problem in Tiananmen. We were too idealistic and not willing to compromise. Had we just met with Premier Peng—then maybe a different outcome—who knows? Alex, let us not use the word *revolution* anymore, it is so far from my mind. I wouldn't insult you. To say this to you, I would lose face."

"That's good," I said. "Because if you go in representing

the Democratic Revolutionary Party my father will bite back. He'll shut you right down."

"*Small*, Alex," he said, showing me with the end of his thumb and index finger, a sliver of space. "This small."

"What's the move?"

"A union," he said, slapping his knees. "See? What did I say? Small. That's all. A little union. These are everywhere now in China. Like fruit stand. It will be very familiar to you and your father. Hardly notice. Same as in the States. Bargain, compromise."

"And this is what you've done at other factories?"

"Yes. Absolutely. It is delicate like cooking a small fish. We don't want to eat misfortune."

"What about strikes?" I asked. "Do you support them?"

"Of course. The workers must be allowed to strike. Without losing their jobs."

"See that's the problem. That's agitating. That's aggressive. A strike would cripple the business. If that happens we'll have a catastrophe."

It was true I wanted change, but I didn't know if I could trust Zhang. He seemed a little nuts, frankly. Ivy had vouched for him. Called him intense. Maybe I should walk out—I kept thinking I should get up and leave, but something was keeping me there. Listening.

"*Méi shì, méi shì,*" Zhang said. "No problem. This is not going to happen. It is only the extreme. This is what I thought you were asking. In the organizing I have done, we never strike. The right diplomacy and it never comes to this. I understand you. That is why I say small. Workers striking your factory is like a praying mantis trying to block a tank with his little arms. It is futile. No, you would just bring in new workers. This is not the way to solve problems."

"What is the way?"

"Little meetings. You give Ivy a position. Let her educate workers. She can talk free and get them to consider joining the union. We see if it happens. Maybe a few meetings. Maybe they get bigger. Still nothing you can't recognize. Talking. That's all. Working together. Me and you. See, it's smart thinking."

I looked at Ivy. Her face was drawn and anxious but her eyes were gentle even as they widened.

I turned slowly back to face Zhang.

"My great-grandfather wasn't one of them but his brother was a member of the Bund, underground socialists, like you, and they got more recruits and grew bold. So they went to the Russian Rittmeister and said the leather workers want to unionize."

"This is when you had the arm tattoos of numbers?"

"That came later. So the guy says, of course, only fair. What you need to do is go down to this town, fifteen miles away, and get your union cards. Great. They all go off like it's a parade walking down the road, but when they reach the town it's empty. All that's left is the brick factory in the hands of the Cossacks. My great-granduncle says, 'Where's the union office, we come for our cards.' And the commander leads them over to a clay pit in the ground."

"What happens?"

"They made them strip down and shot them into the pit and covered it with clay. That was the end of the union. Finished after that."

"It is a horrible story," Zhang said, "Almost same happened when my father spoke out against the party."

"Sometimes," I said, improvising, speaking in a voice that I didn't even fully recognize, "by wanting to do right, you only make it worse, I'm telling you. But my great-grandfather— he was Jewish too of course but pretended to be Polish. So he could go to school and so his own classmates wouldn't throw rocks through his windows or break his ribs. A lot of Jews did that. Not that they were ashamed or anything, but it's easier. Sometimes it's better off to hide what you are. That's how you survive."

Maybe it was the voice of my great-grandfather, who I'd only ever seen in one photo: seated at a workbench in Vilnius, pulling twine with his teeth, hog bristle and wax, welting an army boot. I didn't see it, but people always said I looked like him.

Zhang arched his eyebrows like he was impressed. "We stand in the same shoes," he said. Then he suddenly stood up and, drawing his hand over his face, started pacing across the room.

"*Aiya,*" he said. "Well, let me think over this. Because you introduce good points. I see. I need to think it out. I may even need the night to consider what you say and give you answer."

I sort of surprised myself, saying all that. Coming out of my own mouth just on instinct, no thinking. Same way I could see that the quarterlines on a pair of booties were off by a few millimeters without picking up a tape measure.

Zhang continued pacing, stroking the side of his cheek.

But what I told Zhang was right: everything had to stay quiet. The most minor change sent Dad into a tailspin—one time on the plane he looked over and I was using blue pen on the immigration form instead of black *and that's the kind of horseshit that gets your ass thrown on the blacklist*—so I couldn't imagine what he'd do with a factory strike.

Zhang sat right back down and looked at me.

"*Nèige,*" he said, "maybe you are correct. Black cat, white cat—as long as we catch mice, this is what is important. Yes? The color of the cat doesn't need to be *unions*. You see, Alex," he said tapping his head. "You think like I think. We are of one mind. Harmonious. Maybe we are separated brothers?"

That made me feel better. Like we were the same—me and him. One guy. Not a world apart. Not all that different. I was doing the right thing. Maybe Zhang was all right. He wasn't some quacked-out vigilante.

I reclined into the couch and my shoulders sank into the back pillow, warm and snug, and to myself I was going, This is where you are. You've arrived. This place. A nice firm grip on me. Maybe it was because after a while I started to notice the way the Chinese kind of folded in their shoulders right as I passed on the street, like they didn't want a hair follicle of mine grazing them, not so much as a skin cell rubbing off on them, and maybe Zhang, because of his past, knew that feeling.

He was nodding his head and I found myself nodding back, and even though our mouths weren't moving, we were agreeing on a lot of stuff.

"Fate," he continued, "brings people together no matter how far apart they are. Now there's certain…responsibilities. You have to be careful what you say. Who you talk to. Because life can get difficult."

"For me?" I asked.

"For you. If you speak to the wrong person. I wouldn't be able to prevent consequences."

I turned to Ivy and her eyes narrowed at me, and her look confirmed what I thought. Zhang was warning me. Or, in his own polite way, he was actually threatening me. Meaning, if I made the wrong decisions, *he* would cause the consequences. Give the orders himself.

I turned back to face him.

"Don't worry about me," I said.

"Good," he said. "Good good."

Then we shook hands, his grip strong and cold. I shivered at this. Maybe his handshake. Maybe the word, *fate*, he'd said, like he knew something about me. I felt cold, even after he released my hand, the cold mixing with this image that came to me of two thousand *dagongmei* dragging me out of Plant C and toward the outdoor pavilion and one of them pushing the cold snout of a Walther PK to my temple and I smelled the cement glue on her hands, heard the hammer softly cock, felt her wrist shaking, and I fell into the brick-walled cellar of the synagogue beneath the Vilnius Opera house where my great-grandparents danced one last *Freylekhs* while Victor von Wahl split the backs of the Jewish Bund out in the palace courtyard with a bullwhip, and I crumbled into my grandmother's lap as she tickled my feet and buried my face in her dark vinegar-scented neck, saying, *Who's a good boy.*

I pushed the thought away. Zhang's eyes weren't telling me this. About fate. I was just drawing on old movies. Walther's the old James Bond gun. Probably didn't even cock. Why would factory girls even have British secret agent guns? My mind was much better at paranoia than period details.

Zhang's dark eyes were on me.

"I'm loyal," I said.

"We can trust you," Zhang said, but it was hard to tell by his inflection if it was a question or a fact. A simple nod wouldn't reassure him.

"Yes," I answered. "You can trust me. I'm your friend."

Ten

A MAN IN A BLUE CLOTH JACKET IN THE TRAIN berth beside us was eating ginger and pig's feet, and our cabin filled with the scent of sweet vinegar. I swung my feet off the bed, climbed down the little ladder—Ivy asleep in the cot under mine—and I walked down to the food car squishing on longan shells thrown in the aisles.

At the food car, I ordered fried peanuts and stood by the window, feeling my lips tingle from the salt, and I watched the maize fields slip past the window.

I saw old crumbling watchtowers, and suddenly a red-and-yellow circus tent, the pink neon of a tall spoked Ferris wheel, the loopy parabola of roller coaster tracks—right out in the clearing of the maize field—and then that was all gone too.

The train brakes squealed around a bend and it sounded like the pitched cry of the roller coaster grinding metal back at Revere Beach. Summer, and Dad had been protesting fun by wearing a wool suit on the beach in the dead of July. He was sitting stiff on a folding chair, sweating like a pig, and my mother was saying, "Can't you pretend to enjoy it?" His oxfords touched the corner of my beach towel, right by my face. I could see the unsanded tips of his tassels—I knew them the way Ruxi's little brother knew her sandals, and I could smell the fried clams from Kelly's nearby and I saw the salt barnacles on the dock pilings, and the black girls braiding each other's hair in the sash windows behind the boardwalk, and the street kids tagging the metal struts of the roller coaster, and the easels along the boardwalk where they'd airbrush your face on a T-shirt and I wanted one bad but worried I'd come out looking like some German wartime caricature.

Enough. I was willing memories again. I didn't feel the tug of them; no flip in my gut. It was all real distant and abstract, like that part of me was gone, missing like the sawed-off noses on the Buddhist busts at the Guangzhou Museum where Ivy had once taken me and we lagged behind the tour group, laughing as the security guards herded us along, saying, "Catch up! No sleepywalk!"

I was in the right place. I was sure of it. What was here now? Grim-faced, half-asleep Chinese slumped at booth tables, mouths agape. The same position my workers would be in if the managers didn't blow a whistle the moment a girl yawned.

Forty people packed in this dining car. We had a rule at the factory that no more than twenty people could meet together recreationally. A Yong rule. But I was going to abolish that first thing when I got back to Foshan.

I turned back to the window, to the jagged silhouette of karst mountains far off, and I let myself slip into this little fantasy of a packed meeting at my factory up on the third floor of Plant C. Nighttime. Everyone had brought makeshift lamps and hung them on the back of chairs and they were shushing each other to be quiet. Smelled of sweat and sweet cement glue. Everyone took off their hats out of respect for Ivy, who

was standing up on a workbench in a white work shirt, stiff
and crisp, and a thin red belt, talking to the workers. The
meeting was packed, not a seat left, people had to climb up
on the leather horses just to listen. Ivy was punching the air
with her fist, talking about real doctors, not the sham ones
on our payroll. Talking about training courses. Accounting.
Business admin. English lessons. OSHA seminars.

And maybe I got up there to speak at the meeting and I told
them what? Told them how my grandfather made a pair of shoes
for FDR. Black wing tip brogues. Crepe soles. Size twelve.
The highlight of Zayde's whole life. Back before OSHA. Back
when safety training meant watching the machinist with the
fewest scars on his forearms. Now things needed to be different. Go forward, not back. We weren't in darkness anymore.
And they were applauding. The whole crowd was.

Still I was on this train staring out the window and the
world seemed fast and trackless, seemed to peel itself away
layer by layer without the slightest feeling of flight.

I was daydreaming away, feeling real good, when I suddenly felt a shift in the current of air, and I knew someone
was standing right behind me. I turned around. An old Chinese woman with lips stained bloodred and teeth black, like
she'd just bitten the head off a rooster, was standing there
with a fistful of betel nuts in her hand. She was right up in
my face, talking fast and crazy. I couldn't understand. And
as everyone in the canteen started laughing, my good feeling
drained away fast, and I wasn't part of some revolutionary factory meeting, I was just a white guy sweating his balls off on
a train. I backed away from the old woman, away from the
window, hustling back to my little berth, the woman's voice
echoing in my head, *gweilo*, ghost man, she'd said, looking at
me like I had a sawed-off nose, like she knew I was always
going to be incomplete.

★ ★ ★

By the time the train pulled into the Guangzhou Railway Station it was getting late. Ivy was talking about riding the subway down to Foshan, then catching a bus to the factory, but I finally convinced her to take some money for a taxi ride. We were at the curb stand where the taxis lined up. I held open the door for her but she suddenly froze.

"It's okay?" she said.

I told her don't be ridiculous, I wasn't going to let her take the subway alone at night, but the way she squeezed her eyebrows together made me realize she wasn't talking about the stupid subway. She meant *it*. Everything in Beijing. And everything to come.

I nodded. She gave me a kiss on the lips and ducked into the cab. Words still didn't come to me in the cab, but it wasn't a bad feeling, just a quiet one.

In the lobby of my hotel, the employees came running up for the welcoming ritual, and I just flipped my chin at everyone, even Karri over at her desk. I didn't play along like usual. Something was off. I felt like I wasn't in my body.

Upstairs I stood in the center of my room and the fresh fruit, champagne and chocolate were arranged on the tray on the bed and everything was back in its proper location, and this instinct surged up—not quite even an articulate feeling—but I found myself opening the closet door and taking out my suitcase. I started throwing in my underwear and shirts from the drawers. There was a manager's house at the factory, next to the dorms. Yong sometimes stayed there. That was where I should be. Move to the factory. Out of the hotel. Get out of here. There was a clear thought, the first in a while, and it scared the shit out of me.

I left my suitcase open and half-packed. Everything seemed to be rushing forward in me at once. I found the edge of the bed, sat down, and my chest got all tight. I could see myself rocking back and forth in the reflection of the window and I heard the drums of the dragon boats down in the lake, like their oars reached all the way down my throat into the center of me. Don't, I told myself. Think about windows. How did they get the windows so fucking clean on the outside? Pull it together. But then I started crying. A part of me said, Alex, you're overtired, and that voice also told me that the hotel must have guys belay down off the roof, dangling on ropes, to wash the windows, and then this other part of me said simply, Don't listen to him. Let go.

The next day at the factory, I was only settled at my desk for ten minutes when the phone rang. "Fedor," said the voice, a Chinese man, and I told him no, sorry, it was Alex, and I was about to transfer the call, but I recognized the voice from somewhere.

"This is Gang," he said.

It took a moment to settle in me. Gang. The mayor. Party secretary of Foshan.

I raised my voice a few octaves to sound gracious and asked him a few bullshitty questions about how things were going and then I told him I'd send him over to Dad.

But he said, "It's you."

And this surprised me.

"What's me?" I said.

I heard him laugh on the other line. "I want to talk with you," he said. "Not your father. I want to invite you for tea."

My throat went dry when he said this. Even a *gweilo* knew that a tea invitation from a party member was never good.

Gang was one of the princelings. The inner circle. His father, chummy with Jiang Zemin, had risen to minister of finance and handed Gang a plum job. Inside track to deputy

county party boss in Foshan. Then mayor. Then party secretary. This was the kind of guy who made people disappear.

"Of course," I said.

"Excellent," he said. "At my office. Today you can? Now?"

"Should I invite Dad?"

"Unnecessary."

He gave me a curt goodbye, and I was left wondering what
just happened. Why did Gang want to see me? It couldn't be
about the factory. He was a part owner, sure, but he didn't
have any input on the business. We paid him a cut for oper-
ating on his turf. He was a Brooklyn mob boss in Mao jacket
and togs. But no, he was more than that. The CCP loved him.
For turning 13 percent annual growth. For turning a back-
water industrial shithole into a thriving megalopolis. He was
on his way up.

So was it about Ivy? If he knew about that, I was fucked,
but it couldn't be that. If he knew about Ivy she'd be long
gone. This guy made people disappear with a nod of the head.
Maybe he was keeping her around on purpose. And he wanted
me to get names out of her. All the names of the Democratic
Revolutionary Party. He knew I'd been up to Beijing, maybe,
and he wanted me to turn them in. What was I going to say?
It was simple. I was fucked. Going up to Beijing seemed like
a big mistake right now.

I walked down the hall to Dad's office to let him know,
but he was tied up on the phone, yelling at customs for holding one of our shipments in dry dock, so I left without telling him anything.

A taxi brought me to the seat of government over in
Chancheng District. I stepped out into the humid air and
found myself standing for the first time in front of the gate
to the Foshan People's Government, a boxy gray eight-floor

building with a flat roof and two long wings. From the out-side, it wasn't all that ornate, nothing like what I'd seen in Tiananmen.

Over by the Chinese national flag, a female guard was sit-ting under an umbrella. As I approached her, she rose. She led me into her security office and called the main building. Then she hung up the phone and drew a chunky, heavy-looking Magnum from her belt holster and turned on the red laser sight and nonchalantly, as if she were folding clothes, whistling a tune to herself, lifted the gun with two hands and aimed it at my forehead.

My hand groped back for the doorknob and I took a small step back, catching it right on top of my ass bone, and I winced.

She said, "Stop. Can't shoot if moving."

She squeezed the trigger and I closed my eyes.

No sound. Nothing. I slowly opened my eyes. She was reading a number on the digital screen on the back of the gun. Thirty-seven.

"No fever," she said. It was a temperature gun. If such a thing really existed. I nodded and wiped my mouth with my hand.

"Move," she said and flicked the snout of the gun toward the door.

We trooped through the parking lot of unmarked black Audis and up a flight of terrazzo stairs under a columned por-tico, through a set of sliding doors. At the elevator she said, "Roof." I assumed she meant the top floor, so I pressed the number eight as the doors closed.

While riding up, I remembered how a friend of Dad's, this American guy, tried to move his joint-venture cement fac-tory up north and Gang accused him of embezzlement, sent underage hookers to his hotel. Ruined him. Gang then nationalized the company, which meant he owned it all. That happened here. If you stepped out of line.

At Gang's office a secretary rose from her seat, nodded to me and made a big show out of flinging open the quartered oak doors.

I stepped inside. In deep shit again. Always.

From the other side of the room, behind a long wood desk flanked by potted ginkgo trees, Gang rose. He still wore that old military-style cloth Mao suit, stooped like he was coming back from the Long March.

We walked toward each other. Gang pulled at the hem of his tunic and stuck out his hand.

I gave him a faint smile and wiped my palms on the side of my pants. Gang scared me shitless.

We shook. His hand was rough as the wool brush we used to burnish cheap leather.

Then, as if he read what I was thinking, he released his tight grip and held up his calloused palms.

"Tea picking," he said. "As a boy. During the Cultural Revolution. I was a sent-down youth. Ruined my hands. My wife soak them in hibiscus, ginseng, fish eggs—to soften me. You know women."

I shrugged.

He nodded at the cane-back chair in front of his desk. I sat down. While he walked around to his side of the desk, I quickly took note of the exits in the room—a habit inherited from Dad—the oak doors I'd come through and a servant's access door between two inlaid bookcases, floor to ceiling.

I'd heard Gang had a switch at his desk that controlled the color of the water fountains all over the city, and another one that piped different music into the streets. But all I saw was his laptop, stapler, printer, little tubs of miscellaneous office supplies. No switches that I could see.

"Trouble finding me?" he asked.

"No trouble," I said.

A waitress brisked in from the servant's door with a tray of tea. Gang nodded thank you and she scurried away.

"Oolong," he said, and half smiled, like he wasn't all that accustomed to smiling. It was almost a wince.

"This is what I picked in the country. I only drink oolong. Helps me remember where I am from."

Gang took a sip and leaned back in his chair. His face was stoic and weary, but when he held it a certain way he looked almost young.

"I pick slow," he said. "With two hands. Bad technique. My heart in another place. A lazy bastard I was. Five yuan a day. For the ignorant and poor. But everyone has his place. Right?"

"Right," I said in a reedy voice. It was obvious that he knew. Everything about me. Ivy. Zhang. My right leg started jittering.

He leaned forward in his chair and reached for the top drawer of his desk, this terror clawing in my chest—my mind reeling off gangster movie clichés: he was going to pull Ivy's decapitated head out of his drawer, or draw a knife to cut off my fingers one by one until I confessed.

But Gang pulled out a bottle of Maotai and set it down hard on the desk.

"Too early?" he asked, taking out two small *pinming* cups as well.

I took a deep breath. "Never too early," I said.

He poured the liquor into the cups, and without a ceremonial *gambei*, a bad sign, he shot it down. Then he pointed with his chin to my cup. I drank. The liquor burned down my throat.

"Helps loosen your tongue," he said, and then suddenly

he pushed his chair back, the legs scraping against the tiles, a noise that straightened my back.

"I am interested in you," he said.

"That's good," I said moronically.

He dipped his chin slightly. "Tell me, did you go to a university to learn shoes?"

I said, "No, I picked it up from my father and grandfather. Learned along the way."

"Self-made man," he said, patting his knee. "I respect this. This is beautiful thing about America. If you work hard enough."

"I always loved shoes," I said. "It's in my blood."

He smiled. "Everyone has their place," he said again.

This time it felt like he breathed it on the back of my neck. My skin prickled. Why didn't he just come out and say that he knew?

"I understand the importance of blood," he intoned. "Family. Understanding who you serve. My daughter doesn't like to hear this message. This is her."

Gang pointed to the closest frame in a row of photos lined up on his desk facing me. Then he leaned over to look.

"No, wait, this is not my daughter. This is Steve Jobs. This is my daughter over here."

He pointed three photos down, past the one of him and Steve Jobs posing in front of Foxconn and past whom I guessed was Gang's wife.

"But everyone must serve. You serve your father. I serve China."

He reached across the desk and refilled my cup.

"Good for conversation," he said, now refilling his own.

We threw back the liquor. But the alcohol only heightened my fear. That was it. Real fear down deep to the spaces between my bones. Like when you see an old man remove his dentures, see the sickening pink gums—and think, What part of himself is he going to take off next?

Gang gave me a slight grin that tightened my throat. He reached for a round plastic tub on his desk of paper clips, pens, thumbtacks, miscellaneous desk crap, and he drew out a long, shiny sheet-metal screw.

"A human," he said, spinning the head of the screw in his hand, "has enough iron in his blood to produce one nail. Did you know this? One strong productive nail. China is a nation of a billion nails. Someone must decide what to do with them. What would the people do with one nail?"

"Maybe hang their hats on the door with it," I said.

He shook his head. "It does not help China to make hat post. They need to build together. Each one is a nail that builds the nation strong. Of course, we must acknowledge, not every nail goes in clean. Some are crooked."

He ran his thumb over the threads of the screw. A rush of heat came swimming up my neck. I felt my heart beating against my wrist.

"We've been humiliated by the West for centuries," Gang went on. "There is a hole inside people now. A void in the spirit. Which breeds..."

His voice trailed off.

My mouth opened.

"Reactionaries, Alex. *Stinking* rebels."

He paused to let it sink in. Forgive me, I thought. I'm a dumb shit who went off the rails. I can get straight again, everything can go back to the way it was, everything will be just fine, don't worry. I fell in with the wrong girl. Ivy's the wrong girl. I can change, I swear.

"Bourgeois Western extremists," he said. "Who forgot our revolutionary roots."

He didn't take his cold gaze off me. Between the lines

he was really saying: *it is you. You're one of these crooked nails.* I remembered Ivy saying how her journalist friend talked a little shit about Gang in the paper, and the next day he was scribbling help-me notes in blood on cockroach wings up in Jiangsu labor camp. *Vacation-style therapy* was what they told the journalist's mother.

Now it was my turn. So what if Gang was friends with my father? Didn't mean shit. I betrayed Gang, I was a trouble-maker and I had to go.

Gang smoothed his hand over the desk. "Burma teak," he said. "From a protected rain forest. Six billion dollars of teak smuggled out of Burma last year. Most to China."

"If there's a market, anything can be sold," I said.

"Correct," he said. "You can't stop desire. Ask any Buddhist who ran off to Tibet to hide from it. Not us. We control it. You want something, there's a price. The good thing, Alex, is that China is mostly a country of light sleepers. The problem is that the reactionaries want to wake them up and whisper lies. My purpose is to tell you what maybe you already know. Something important to your business."

He paused again for a beat.

"I possess internal information," he said, punctuating each word with a tap of the screw, "that there are crooked nails in your factory."

He tilted his head to see if I was following.

"Radicals," he continued, "who want to undermine you. Me. Want to overthrow the Chinese government. You know anything about this sort of thing? These plotters?"

I shook my head. No. And sat in solemn terror.

Gang's face remained stoic and calm. He started cleaning under his fingernails with the point of the screw. Then he lifted his head.

"You would tell me if you had."

"Of course," I said.

"Of course you would," he intoned. "A loyal son like you. I trust people close to me. It is the others. Out there hiding."

He turned his head in the direction of a stand of willows outside the window. Squinted like he could see the stinking troublemakers roosting in the long, rich branches.

I waited. A damp chill spreading down my back.

Then he turned back from the window and leaned toward me.

"I need your help," he said.

My mouth was dry. I had to swallow a few times before getting the words out.

"With what?" I asked.

"Finding them."

"The organizers?" I asked.

"They do a good job hiding if my people fail to find them. But my people aren't inside your factory."

I nodded. Knuckled my glasses up on the bridge of my nose.

"I chose not to tell your father," Gang continued. "He is my old friend. This would embarrass him. Cause him to lose face. He would blame himself. Feel he did something to bring the radicals inside his plant. So I think of you. Soon you take over for him. You are younger. Stronger. You can help me find the bad elements. Probably a handful of rootless young people with very low IQs. Your generation causing problems again. I let it go at the Honda plant last month—a strike—to show support for the migrant class. But we can't have copy-cats. This is my purpose with you."

I stared at him. Trying to compute all of this. He was en-listing me. It was easy enough for him to make a problem dis-appear, so he must really not have the names.

His expression stayed hard and steady. Maybe that was what frightened me. He didn't seem panicked about not having the names. And this feeling—this bright gas flame of a feeling that Gang put in me with his eyes, telling me I was nothing in the big scheme, a single nail—and so was he, his look said that too—and it didn't make a bit of difference whose side I took or anybody took because the government, this colossal China machine, rolled on invulnerably and couldn't be stopped.

But he didn't have the names. I leaned back in my chair and reminded myself of this fact. The establishment didn't have everything.

"I protect public harmony. You protect your plant," he said. "These radicals operate in shadow. Lost youth. Created by Western television. False revolutionaries desiring celebrity and fame. For endangering the public, they deserve their tongues cut off."

Gang made a fist and set it on the desk. His eyes narrowed. "Find one. A ringleader. Bring me the name of a suspect."

I sat up in my chair, my breath coming fast.

"You will do this?" Gang asked in his government voice. Telling me to do it. I had to agree. It wouldn't make sense to say anything else.

"Yes," I said. "I'll put my ear to the ground and help. Best I can."

"Good," he said. "I will handle the troublemaker. A simple case of killing a chicken to scare the monkeys."

I ground my teeth. He was going to make an example out of someone. And here I was lying to the secretary's face. My shirt felt soaked. I'd sweated through the damn thing. Did he take it for anxiety over the factory? I wasn't worried about the factory. Gang didn't understand the Democratic Revolutionary Party, but maybe I didn't either. Maybe Gang knew something I didn't, something Ivy and Zhang hadn't told me, and now I didn't know who was telling the truth.

"Be delicate," Gang said. "I let things go at Honda plant

last month. But I can't let trouble happen twice. The world watches us. Beijing watches *me*. Foshan makes 90 percent of the world's computers. Sixty-four percent of the shoes. Everything is done quiet, yes? Seek truth from facts."

"Right," I said. What the fuck did that mean? Truth from facts?

"I understand completely," I said.

He rose from his chair and reached across the table. He patted me on the head.

"Be good," he said. The hand was gone. He was sitting again. "And who knows," he continued, "maybe this unfortunate event is a sign to bring us together. Our partnership. I believe I can trust you."

"Me too," I said, which didn't make any sense. I stood up and told him I was going back to the factory.

"One of my drivers will take you."

"It's not necessary," I said, but he knifed the words off my lips with a look that told me only he decided what was necessary.

"I need names."

"Names," I repeated.

Eleven

IN THE HOTEL, I WAS THROWING MY SHIT INTO my Samsonite luggage fast as I could, trying to get out before I ran into Dad downstairs and he had the chance to talk me out of it.

The zipper snagged. I tugged at it. Why was I shaking? Gang. It all went through his hands. So long as he kept logging 13.8 percent growth, Beijing was happy. They were whispering to him: keep this up and soon we'll make you mayor of Chongqing, three times the size of Foshan, and then you'll join the politburo up here with us.

Wheeling my suitcase down the hall, my computer bag slung around my shoulder, I rode the elevator down to the lobby. Dad was standing there in a bright linen jacket, under the harsh artificial lights, hard-bellied, hair combed to the side, arms like a coal shoveler.

He came right up to me with his hand out. He wanted to shake. Always first thing in the morning when we saw each other. But not this time. He looked down at my suitcase.

"What is this?" he said. "Where are you going?"

"The factory house," I said. He didn't move. I turned sideways and inched past him. Our chests brushed. He was an inch
or two taller than me—one cruel covetous inch. What a genetic
mockery to leave a son an inch short of his father. When we
were standing against a wall or it was dark out, I stood on my
tiptoes. My mother was a Russian potato—low to the ground.
What I knew about science couldn't fill a thimble, only that
a child was the median height of his parents, and then one of
them dominated you in every way that counted.

"You're kidding, right?" he asked. "Why would you do
that? This is a five-star hotel. That place is no-stars."

I kept going.

Dad was marching behind me. "Alex. Stop. Think what
you're doing. Trust me, you won't be happy living at the factory. No one washes their hands. Or they fake it. Just run
the water. It's no place for you. There's no turndown service
there! I hope you know that. There's no strudel, no Danish.
Forget cream cheese! It's a harsh cheeseless world out there.
Get back here."

I kept moving. After meeting with Gang, I didn't know
if there was much I could do to help Ivy. I needed to get to
her and tell her about Gang. I needed Zhang to get his ass
down here. The game had changed. I couldn't stay in the
hotel anymore.

Outside in the roundabout, I threw my bags into the trunk
of the taxi and Dad had caught up to me, saying, "What if I
can't get online?"

He was really reaching now.

"Restart your computer," I told him, slamming the trunk
closed.

"Restart? That's what you say to your own father? Restart
at sixty-five years old. Better to kick me in the balls than say
this."

"You realize I'll see you tomorrow, right?" I told him. "I'm not going *away*."

"Who do I eat with?" he said.

"Make friends."

"No, thank you," he said loudly. "I have you."

"Listen, you said it yourself. We need orders. One of us needs to be at the factory."

His face pinched tight, like his body was at war with his better manners. "Tomorrow," he said, and stuck out his hand. We shook.

"Sorry," I said.

He turned around and walked back into the hotel.

I felt relieved as the car zoomed along the highway to the factory. I couldn't help feeling that I'd escaped something. But then I started to think about my dad eating meals alone with the Filipino girls crooning Phil Collins—and slowly this ghost Dad all alone at dinner became more real to me than if he were actually here beside me.

The road turned past a plastics factory, a pharmaceutical plant, a porcelain factory with a pyramid of toilets out front, water cascading into a wading pool. The taxi pulled up to the sliding metal gate of Tiger Step and I got dropped off beside the manager's canteen.

I reached a little walled-off one-story house behind one of the dormitories, butting up against the abandoned brick factory. I opened the metal gate and stepped into a small front yard, a dusty plot with dragon eye trees and banyans, their roots strangling the roof as if to drag it into the earth.

A few brick steps led up to a sliding glass door. It was open, just like Yong had said. Key in an envelope on the credenza. I set my bags down and closed the door behind me and this sliced off the noise from outside.

An old cow skull sat on the dining room table, eyes hollow

and dark, large enough that it seemed to be tracking me wherever I moved in the room. I turned the corner to the living room and stopped suddenly at the sight of two men standing against the windows. Statues. Two granite warriors—seven-foot-tall mustachioed giants with swords guarding the room.

Beside them, on the wall hanging from a nail, I saw a pair of old braided straw sandals, the soles made from ancestral tablets that I knew the communists had banned when they stormed the countryside. Too superstitious.

I ran my finger over the carved characters and it came to me that this was someone's *stuff*. Strangers. It was theirs. This was the shit Yong bought up at those creepy countryside auctions after land requisitions.

Off the living room was the main bedroom with a small bed in the corner but no bureau. Just some slatted wood crates from the old Guangzhou Eagle Coin factory, and I started unpacking my clothes into the crates.

As I was carrying my toiletries to the bathroom, the cow's hollow eyes stared at me from the center table, so I took a blue towel off the rack in the bathroom and draped it over the skull. Then I went into the kitchen and checked the drawers and cabinets. There were only a few pieces of silverware in one of them. I took a spoon to my bedroom and laid it on the threshold of the door. It was an old superstition my mother used to do. When a couple moved into a new home you were supposed to step over a spoon together or else you'd have a lifetime of bad luck.

Around 9:00 p.m., as we'd planned earlier, I heard the gate creak open and Ivy appeared by the sliding glass door. It opened with a pop.

"We need to talk," I said.

She set her backpack on the floor. "Nice," she said, looking around the house.

Then she unzipped the top of her bag and took out a red
colored cutout in the shape of a woman's head. One of those
paper cuttings you saw the ladies making in the market. The
good ones did it freehand with an X-Acto knife.

"A present," she said. "I didn't want to come with empty
hands."

"Beautiful. It's you?"

She paused for a second. It was the profile of a regal-looking
woman with a tall red cowl on her head.

"If you think," she said.

I led her to the living room and, turning the corner, she
shrieked when she saw the two seven-footers, the outline of
their silhouettes.

"I thought they are real," she said, and took my hand and
put it on her chest. "Feel," she said. "So fast."

"I forgot to warn you," I said, and I could feel her heart
drumming hard through her cotton tank top.

She slipped off her sandals and folded her feet under her
butt on the couch. I sat across from her.

"I need you to know something," I said.

"I go first." She started talking fast, fingers dancing, about the
meeting she'd organized last night—small—twenty people, but
bigger than the last one and more were coming next time. The
only problem was she needed a bigger place to hold the meetings.

And then she started naming people. "Old Cao from the
molding plant, and Auntie Wei from soleing, and Sting Wang
who is very boy friendly, and Auntie Eagle—how do you
say in English? Seven mouths and eight tongues, something
like this, and Little Magnet, and Supervisor Pig Face, no one
knows his real name—"

As she listed workers, I found myself actually thinking, after each name, there was the one I could sacrifice to Gang. But I wrenched the thought from my head. What kind of monster picked? There was no choice. I wouldn't be a part of it.

In the flow of these thoughts, under the heat of Gang's orders, I didn't notice that Ivy had stopped naming people, only that she was staring at me now, lips pursed.

"Something wrong?" she asked.

"Gang called me. I met with him," I said. "He knows someone is organizing workers. But he doesn't know who. He wants me to give them up. The names of the ringleaders."

Her lips made a round O, but no sound came out.

"You need to get Zhang down here," I told her. "We need to talk. All of us. Before you take any action. I don't know how much I can really do to help you." I reached over and touched her thigh. "I'm saying it's dangerous. For everyone. Maybe you call it off."

"We can't. Did you give my name?"

"Of course not. But I'm in a real bad spot here. What do I tell Gang?"

"Tell him the rumors are false."

"You can't organize here. It's too risky."

"I will discuss with Zhang. We don't want to hurt you."

For a second I wondered if that was true, you *had* to wonder, could I even trust her at all? Or maybe I was getting paranoid. I forced the thought out of my mind.

Her gaze moved around the house. It was quiet between us. Then she cleared her throat. "Can I think of this like our house together? I know it isn't mine, but I can think this?"

"You can have a key. Come here whenever you want. It's ours."

She leaned forward and kissed me and her skin smelled like the sweet cement glue that she'd been around all day.

"He could arrest us. Send us off for 'vacation-style therapy.' Way up north. It is true. Your family never hear about you again. Never see you. I am tired. Too tired. Does he have people here?"

I shook my head. "No way to know."

"I can't think about Gang right now. I want to hear about the Peach Blossom Spring. Like my mother used to tell me."

I didn't know how her mother told it, but it didn't much matter. I thought for a second.

"The peaches are about the size of your head," I said, but I was still worrying about Gang. "And the rice leaves never curl."

"And we have a house?" she asked.

"Everyone owns their own house. And none of the seventy-year leases. Forever."

"Do I have to wear pants?" she asked, closing her eyes.

I laughed. "Whatever you want."

She grinned. "Good. I like to wear a red dress, red shoes and a tall phoenix crown like the women in operas."

"I want to match, so I'm going to have a cheongsam made. In red. For China."

"Everything for China," she said drowsily, and she was quiet and I watched her chest rise and fall, breathing deeply.

Outside, the frogs at the bottom of the water gutters belched loudly. A din of crickets and birds. All calling in different notes, their own specific frequency.

"I can get Zhang down on Friday," she said.

"I have to meet Bernie on Friday. After."

She lifted her head and kissed me slowly and then pulled back a little, still close enough for me to feel her eyelashes flickering.

I told her, "My mother believes there's letters written on every part of your body that tell your past and future, but only a tzaddik can read it."

"What's a tzaddik?"

"A smart Jew, basically."

"What do mine say?"

I reached for the hem of her tank top and lifted like I was lifting a veil, pressing my lips to her navel, a mole partly hidden by the fringe of her bra strap, the hollow of her armpits, wings of her collarbone, the scalloping shape of her lips, wide and pink.

"So what is my destiny?" she asked.

"Don't know. You need a smarter Jew."

She grinned and kissed me. Pressed me down on the couch and dragged herself over me. With one hand I reached behind her back and fumbled with the clasp of her bra.

She reached back and unclasped it, sliding the straps off her shoulders.

"There's a bed," I said.

"Those are the words on me?" she asked. "Very depressing."

She pulled my shirt over my head.

"Here is better," she said.

After, we were lying on the couch side by side, watching the threads of smoke from a candle on the coffee table. The light in the room dim and murky.

"I'm frightened of him," she said. "Gang."

"Don't worry," I said. "I'll mold a golem and send it after him."

"What is this?"

"Golem? An old Jewish monster. Made of clay. You put this invisible brand on his forehead—the Hebrew word *emet*—and then he comes to life and does whatever you want."

"Anything his master tells him?" she said.

"That's right. He obeys."

She rolled onto her side to face me and gave me this know-ing smile I couldn't read. Maybe she thought it was stupid.

"It's just one of those stories you tell kids in Sunday school," I said. "I tried to make one in art class once, molded the clay, wrote the magic word on its forehead, and ordered him to rise and kill Mike Adams who was always giving me purple nurples—that's on the nipples, it's weird—I'll explain later. It didn't work. Which is a good thing because the story always ends the same. The golem goes fucking crazy and murders its creator."

She laughed. "Why?"

"I don't know," I said. "But that's how it always ends."

We fell silent. I guess we were thinking about that. How you can only control someone so long before they turn around and bite you in the ass. I felt the cold eyes of the seven-foot warriors against the far wall steady on me, and as long as she stayed here, I could keep it away, but I knew as soon as she was gone, I couldn't fight it off—their granite eyes, their plated armor, this clawing in my chest, the dark void of the future pulling.

But I was wrong. She wasn't thinking about that at all. She touched my arm lightly.

"Please do not misunderstand this," she said. "You're some-one that I know and care about, but you are also someone I need to help me. It's something I'm uncomfortable with. Be-cause you own the factory. This should be my battle. I should be able to do this myself. I need to be Qiu Jin here. The rev-olutionary woman."

I sat up on my elbow and looked at her.

"I'm uncomfortable with it too. I'm worried you'll change things for the better around here and I'll end up getting the credit. That's how this fucked-up world works. I don't want that either. This is your battle. Sure, it's my factory, but it's

your vision. Your country. Your revolution. I want to support you. And I'm a shoe guy—no one ever needs to hear or
see me."

She smiled warmly.

"I should go," she said. "Before curfew."

She wrapped a throw blanket around her bare shoulders
and went toward the door. Grabbing the towel off the skull
head and wrapping it around my waist, I followed her outside.
Even now at night the air was thick and warm. But no moon.
Never a moon. She walked barefoot into the dirt yard lit by
floodlights mounted on the roof.

We could see the silhouette of Plant B in the night. The
high wall. But if you squinted a little you could hardly tell
what it was, or you might think it was a hill, and you were
alone here, and that sound of traffic whooshing by on the road
below us could be a fast stream.

A giant dragonfly hovered over Ivy's head like it was thinking about landing on her. Its wings a blur. It backed off only
to come forward again. Back and forth. Back and forth. Then
it darted over the fence ribboned with barbed wire.

Ivy said, "It's simple. The people must be masters of their
own country. It was one of Sun Yat-Sen's Three Great Prin-
ciples." Under her breath, she said, "Shit." Wincing, she lifted
her right foot and I saw she was bleeding. She squeezed the
wound and out came a little green shard of beer bottle glass.

"Are you okay? It's bleeding. Let me dress it for you."

"It's nothing," she said, flicking the glass over the cyclone
fence.

Twelve

ON MY WAY OUT OF THE FACTORY TO MEET Bernie on Friday, I froze outside of Yong's office. The last few Fridays, Yong and Ms. Lin and the Crazy Cat Lady from purchasing made an afternoon of going down to Li Shui market to buy lychee. They sampled from each vendor, debating quality, ripeness and price per pound, oftentimes returning with nothing.

So I had to make my move now while they were out. I put my hand on the cold handle of Yong's office door and slowly, without making a sound, pushed it open.

I slipped inside the door and sat at his desk chair.

I jiggled the mouse on his computer and the screen flashed alive and I clicked on the personnel financial spreadsheet for Plant C. The workers on the stitching line. It was sitting in a folder on his desktop. There was no reason I shouldn't have them. I was a third of the company. This wasn't wrong, I told myself as I clicked print. I needed the hard numbers, and no one was going to be honest with me unless I dug for them myself. Snatching the papers as they spit out of his laser printer,

I folded them in half, shoved them in my pocket and slipped back out the door. Down the hall I could hear Dad yelling at someone in the showroom. I felt good as I took the steps, two at a time, down the stairwell out to the courtyard.

A taxi left me on Fenjiang Middle Road in Chancheng, a little ways down from Foshan University. I headed south, squeezed along the sidewalk by a steady stream of Chinese headed into the Jinma movie theater where they play censored American movies.

I walked into a bar called Lazy Papa. Mostly expats. Bernie liked it. Only a few people inside. Midafternoon. The place was pretty dark, lit up with lamp sconces on the walls. A Union Jack flew from the rafter beams. Beat-up floral couches, ugly mint wallpaper and a dank moldy smell. Reminded me of Bernie's basement as a kid, where, lying on his stomach, he'd grind the shag carpet while we watched *Chained Heat* scrambled on Cinemax, squinting through the jittery snow in a vain search for boobs.

I grabbed a seat at a window table and waved to Chao, the bartender. He was wearing a T-shirt, clearly homemade, that said in Magic Marker, Masturbation Is Not A Crime.

Few minutes later Bernie came in wearing a ridiculous purple beret, jeans and sport coat.

"Take that off," I said after he slapped me on the back and scrubbed his hand over my hair.

"Statement piece," he said.

He ordered two Tsingtaos from the waitress, and finished his in a few big gulps before I could take my cash out to pay.

"One more," he said. "Fucking hot out there."

"Everything okay?" I asked.

"Buddy, good to see you," he said. The way he said *buddy* with that thick Boston accent reminded me of snow. Icicles.

Those huge gnarled ones hanging from the eaves of his house that we'd break off with a rake and sword fight until someone got hurt.

"How you been, Alex? You been quiet. It's a girl, isn't it?" Bernie wriggled his eyebrows. "Who's your new pound pet?"

"Bernie, you're a pig."

"Sure, sure." He lifted his head and threw his chin at the waitress. "Hey—fire? A lighter." She shook her head. "Okay, go fuck yourself," he said, under his breath. "Alex, am I the last person who smokes? I'm weak with them. Who's the girl?"

I hadn't told anyone about Ivy, and that'd been burning me up, I badly wanted to, but I stopped myself. Not Bernie. Didn't want his judgments, the little snarky asides—all adding up to the fact that I was just the same kid he grew up with and he damn sure wouldn't let me forget it. I couldn't escape so easy. A name was enough. Hell, you couldn't escape that either.

"Ivy," I said. Left it there.

"She one of these Swedish hospitality girls? They're the best. What hotel you meet her?"

"Nah. She's Chinese. It's more serious than that."

"Where she work?"

"You going to visit her? What the fuck do you care where she works. She works."

"Okay, okay. I'll drop it. Jesus, what crawled up your ass and died?"

I didn't answer him. Those two worlds shouldn't ever meet.

"What is it, Bernie? Why'd you call me here? I know it wasn't just to bullshit."

"What is it? I'll tell you what it is, okay. I got a proposition for you."

"Scrapyarding copper pipes?" I said. "From your neighbor's house, so we get grounded for six months?"

"Al, that's petty. You know not everyone's ashamed of their

past. So you never made your high school advisor proud. Big fucking deal. You rode your father for a few bucks. Who hasn't? You didn't get into Yale? Who cares? People with strong opinions at a young age about musical theater go to Yale. The rest of us have a few memories—a band, a girl, a catch. That's it."

"That's depressing—"

"Unless we do something about it," Bernie said, cutting me off. A glint in his eyes. A quiet smile. When I saw this look on his face, every bit of mischief came back. Like the time Rabbi Gelman gave us a hundred and fifty Munchkins to sell for *tzedakah*, to plant a tree in Jerusalem or some shit, and between bites Bernie kept saying, "The rabbi must be justly recompensed" until two very stoned nights later they were all gone and Bernie stumbled upon the bright idea of selling his sister's Adderall to cover the losses. It worked. I couldn't deny that.

Here I was thinking about Bernie's crazy side, and I had to remind myself that this guy actually knew what he was doing. He got Blakes's sandals division to go from plastic hangers to cardboard for only a dime extra along with a campaign for sending a matching pair to needy kids with the slogan It Ain't Small Change. And little things too. Going after independents. Making them put shoe trees in the store. Hammering them with point-of-purchase. Blakes basically gave him gas station flip-flops and he played them up with a few tricks and did a business.

He was also one of the first guys to start marketing the factory itself when everyone else was trying to hide it. Bernie built a little showroom factory: air-conditioning, floors you'd eat off, workers in white lab coats and goggles—like it was Los Alamos with real science going on, and not the abattoir of the underaged. Bernie gave tours of the new, fake factory and buyers placed big orders and left happy. So I knew Bernie had the chops. Only sometimes I caught myself underestimating him, and I had to remember.

"So what do you suggest we do about it? What's this proposition?"

"Business, Alex. A business *opportunity*. Aren't you tired of making dumb Abelson's shoes yet? Pulling your codpiece." He swigged his beer. "I know I'm tired of the Blakes routine. I swear sometimes, I get this feeling, where I stop and think, Am I still here? On this fucking earth? You ever get that?"

"Yeah, we're in Foshan. That's all I feel."

"I know you do, pal. Now look, I want to start a brand. A label. Me and you. As we always talked about. Back when we were cutting hearts out of scrap leather from Fedor's factory to give to Emily Hirsch on Valentine's. Did it work? Did we get laid? Definitely not, but our best ideas come from the girls we couldn't screw in high school. The thought was there. To start something. A brand, Alex. Me and you. Call it 'Bernard and Alex.' No good? How about 'Alex and Bernie?' Better music. We start from a fresh clean sheet of white paper like we always said. I want our faces in Who's Who of *Footwear News*. Mr. July. We don't stop until we're Mr. July. *That's* why we need to do this, Al. The only sin in the West is not being famous."

"I'm good, Bernie. Really I am. The Neptune is the magic shoe. We did a million pairs last year. Five constructions. Can't make them fast enough. And the Polar Blaze was a big seller."

I was lying to him. There was no more Polar Blaze. It was gone. Same with the Arcadia, the Skiff Aruba, the Salon Spirit.

"No one likes a gloater, Alex. It's bullshit anyway. You're doing half what you did last year. Next year it'll be a third. Abelson's in the tank, you know it, can't count on them. And Fedor—I love the man, but he's *too* loyal. It'll bite him in the ass one day. I *got* the next magic shoe. I'm throwing you a rope here."

"Give the idea to Blakes."

"I don't want to give it to Blakes."

"Why? On track for national sales manager and you want to leave?"

He rolled his eyes at that. "What's ours? Ask yourself. I'm a slave to Blakes, you to Fedor. No offense. Or fuck it, take offense. If you get mad maybe you'll do something. I want this to be *ours*. I'm talking big money. Much bigger than making cheap shit for private label. All the equity's in brands. The big bucks are in the brand."

"I got a lot of shit going on."

"What's a lot of shit?"

"I don't know," I said. "Shit."

"Don't with that. Hey, are we light-years apart? We're brothers, you and me. Not just because we both made out with your cousin Polly. Sick fuck. Does she ask about me? Of course she does. Holy Christ, Cohen, there's something in our blood. We want immortality. Every path's too straight and simple. Don't you have an ounce of aspiration left? A little of your father's balls? Some chutzpah? Are you done groping? I'm not by a long shot."

He angled his head and stared at me.

"Let me explain something," he continued. "Before your dad got me in with Blakes, I was trying to get straight. Went to this AA meeting in the South End. Basement of that Church on Boylston. Big ass circle of strung-out people. One empty chair against the wall but it was under this poster, big block letters: Strive To Be Average. That was their fucking slogan. Can you believe it? I turned around and walked right out. No self-respecting Jew sits under that sign. Maybe you could, I don't know."

I didn't answer him.

"See," he said. "You're no different than me. You aren't happy where you are right now and you know it. So what now? Now we build our own temple. Otherwise what the fuck are we doing with our lives? Even you can see that with your own eyes, beady as they may be. Let's go to war together, Cohen."

He was right about one thing. I didn't want to mess around with private label anymore. It was just giving our ideas away. Plus the designs themselves were old. Esme said it herself on the phone when she made the last cuts. The looks were stale. I couldn't bring myself to repeat that to Dad. Would've hurt him too bad.

Bernie snapped his fingers.

"Earth to Alex. You in there? What's up? I can't understand if you don't talk."

"Nothing. I was thinking about Dad. Other night, in the hotel, his room. He tried to clear this hellacious fart he'd let off by opening the window, but it only opened like an inch or two and he got pissed. Yelling that he couldn't remember the last time he lived in a place where the window opened. Imagine that. His whole life—sealed windows, artificial lights, wake-up calls from some desk clerk. Every morning woken up by someone you've never met before."

Bernie was staring at me with this puzzled expression on his face. Then he leaned in.

"So do you want to end up like that? No. Of course not. Here's your way out. What I'm saying. This brand hits and you buy any kind of window you want, yeah?"

I expected him to keep going but he stopped short. He bent at the waist and untied his Chuck Taylor and slammed it down on the table.

"This fucking shoe. Costs ten dollars to make and they do a

killing every year. One idea wins. No five-year cycles. Time-less. Hasn't changed in a hundred years."

I picked it up and turned it over in my hand. An old Con-verse. Canvas. Vulcanized. So simple. A twist on the oxford. Amazing to think that in seven thousand years we'd only come up with seven styles: moccasin, boot, pump, oxford, sandal, clog and mule. Only seven.

The rubber was ground down to the insole. Bernie had a heel-strike gait.

Had these forever. Relics. It made my palm warm like it was alive, throwing heat. Some objects had power. Meaning. Ivy's fake house in her village. Just cheap wood and weird wallpaper. But it was hers. It was her.

"Okay, Bern," I said. "I'm listening."

"So I keep asking myself, what's the next big thing? What's the next Neptune? Something we can ride ten, fifteen years. Something different. Okay, you listening? One word—*woven*. Woven uppers on a comfort bottom. Leather."

I laughed. "We'll go broke. If we use leather. Prices would be crazy."

"Al," he said, "where's your father's audacity?"

Still a hint of his Boston accent, but he never lost the Yiddish cadence, like he was tasting the words on the back of his soft palate. *Don't talk poor like grandma!* You were supposed to slide your words to the front, fire them off the tongue and lower teeth. The back was for losers. *It's good to be out in front.* We had to be winners, even in the game of phonetics. That was a lot of fucking pressure.

Bernie's hoarse voice: "Fine, fuck it. Use polyurethane."

"Won't stretch. You don't know shit about making shoes, Bernie. Who's your customer? Start there."

"Schoolteacher. Forty-to sixty-year-old woman. Urban.

Works on her feet. Remember those slip-ons our grand-mothers used to wear?"

"The 4 Give?" I said. "They still make them."

"Yeah the Aerosoles. The old farts couldn't get enough. My grandmother had them in every color. Those were leather or nubuck."

"With elastic straps," I said softly, and then this burst goes off in my head like a white klieg light. "You're a genius, Bernie."

"I am?"

"Every last makes a slightly different shoe. Right? That's the whole problem. Same shoe, same size, different fit. Feet are different. Your ten and my ten are different. So what if we go with elastic gore? Yeah? All woven upper. It'll stretch and contour to the foot."

"I'm lost," he said.

"What we're talking about is the first shoe with a 100 per-cent fit. Every time. It won't matter if our lasts are a little off. It's always comfortable. The elastic gore conforms. And a woman could hide the things she wanted to hide. Bunions. Hammertoe." I was flexing the Chuck Taylor in my hand. Stiff as a board. "We don't want to mess with rubber. EVA bottoms—lightweight, flexible."

"So you're in?"

"Well, I'm just talking," I said. "Sounds good in my head but any schmuck can have an idea. Doesn't mean it belongs on an assembly line."

"Hey, listen," he said, snapping his fingers. "Knock it off with that crap. We're not just talking. A whole shoe you just dreamed up on the spot. Not everyone can do that. Stop sell-ing yourself short."

"The timing isn't great," I said, turning my face toward the window.

"Why? Because the girl?" he asked. "Ivy. You make your own timing, Alex."

Two young Chinese women were playing badminton on the sidewalk using their bikes as a net. Both in sleeveless white dresses, their shadows thrown high up on the gray brick wall behind them.

Bernie grabbed his shoe off the table and started screwing it back on his foot, shaking the table, his beer sloshed over the rim of the pint glass and he wiped the puddle off with his hand onto the floor. He sighed.

"Let me ask you something," he said. "Why isn't there a Ralph Lauren of China?"

"Chinese won't buy shit that isn't Western."

"Not at this point," Bernie said. "You can't sell them some bullshit local brand. Information gets around the globe instantly. They want Western. They want Gucci. Steve Madden. Gimme, gimme. But what about five years from now? You're already seeing a few global China brands. Alibaba. Xiaomi. Not many. Not yet. The world doesn't trust them yet. Doesn't think the Chinese have the ideas."

"But they do."

"Of course they fucking do. I know that. You know that."

"So we're the bridge," I said. "That's how we position ourselves? A kind of Chinese brand."

"Right," he said. "The middle step. We ain't Chinese, but we ain't American. We live here, from there. In-betweeners."

I turned my head to the window. There was a blur of a delivery truck battering the road outside, making my teeth rattle, and the badminton girls were sliced off for a second.

"Okay, look," he said, "You know what? Bernie's a stupid fucking name. Let's call it—'*Alex & Ivy*.' How about that? You said yourself it's serious."

Bracketing his hands, he stretched the name out like he was writing it up on a marquee and repeated the name slow.

"Got a ring," I said. "Doesn't it?"

"*A* and *I* are nice vowels. People respond to long vowels. We run APIs for this sort of shit, believe it or not. People like long fucking vowels. Alex and Ivy. There it is."

He plucked a smoke from the pack of King's nested inside his sport coat and tapped it against the table.

But I liked that name. I really did. I could see the initials stamped on the outsole. Molded there forever. And not just the name, I liked the whole concept. I was almost sorry for how much I loved it.

Bernie was right. Why wasn't there a Ralph Lauren of China? Why couldn't it be me? The stars weren't aligned, my chi was off, aliens hadn't spelled it out in a cornfield. Always an excuse. But I could. Ten minutes ago I didn't even know I had this shoe in me.

"I sell, you make," said Bernie.

No denying it, Bernie had a genius for marketing. Something I wasn't so good at. He'd started a footwear-business newsletter on the North Shore while everyone else sat in the dark with their thumbs up their ass. Now he was doing it for Blakes. Campaigns. Facebook, Twitter—all that shit he knew well.

"You sell, I make," I repeated. "At my factory?"

"Where else? Of course your factory. Owning the factory—that's our whole competitive edge. Our best chance is to sell it wholesale to the indies and box stores at a lower price than our competitors."

"Right," I said. "Then the stores can sell it at a lower retail price point and generate more sales."

We stared at each other. Neither of us saying a word. He set his elbow on the table, forearm up, wriggling his fingers like he wanted to arm wrestle. Leaning forward. His fingers, this silence, kept stretching.

In a low voice he said, "You know what that means, don't you?"

"I know what it means."

"Why aren't you saying it?"

"I'll say it. We can't make any money on this at first."

"How long?" he asked.

"A year. Maybe two years. We got to take bubkes on this if we're going for branded."

"You see a way around this?" Bernie asked.

"Not at first," I said. "On a new brand? Why should they buy our cockamamy brand over an established one? We got to tell them clear and simple, 'Look at the value I can sell you at because we own the factory.' Make it as attractive as possible. The other guys make it for forty-five dollars, we can do forty dollars. You see? If we don't lower our price, no one will take a shot on us."

"But we *could* take a profit, Al. The safe play you know is doing it private label—"

I straightened up. That was Dad's model. "You know we can't do that," I said.

If I was putting my name on this, I wanted it to count for something. So if we had to take a loss now to make a profit later, fine. An investment. That was how you became Ralph Lauren of China. Not by pushing more cheap private label shit out the door.

"No," I said. "It's got to be our brand, or forget it."

"Okay. Then that's it."

Another silence. His eyes cut across me.

"You know what I'm thinking?" he asked.

"I know what you're thinking."

"What are you going to do about it?" he said.

"I'll talk to him." I said. "What else can I do?"

"He'll want to do it private label. You know your father. Sell it to some clowns at JCPenney who'll slap their name on it—St. John's Bay. Charter Club. Halogen. You okay with someone putting Halogen on your shoes? Giving them all the equity, all the creative control?"

"No," I said.

"No," he said. "That's fucking stupid. But that's what Fedor *wants*."

"The way he's always done," I said. "I know that."

"And you're saying you won't let him?"

"That's what we're talking about, isn't it, Bernie? We're saying that, aren't we? Now's the time to correct me if I'm fucking wrong."

"Okay, yeah, I thought so. But you never know. I wanted to make sure."

"Bernie, I don't want to be saying something we aren't saying."

"We keep saying the same fucking thing here, Al. It's Fedor you got to worry about, not me. You want me to make the pitch? He loves me."

"Hell no," I said.

"Well, you remind him a few years back when all the heels were breaking off his stripper boots, who saved him? Remind him that, okay."

"Should I remind him you pissed on his bedroom wall?"

"Al, I was seventeen, it was dark. I thought I was in the bathroom."

"His bedroom, Bernie. You pissed on his wedding portrait."

"And look what happened. They separated. I'm clairvoyant. I apologized already a hundred times. Put that much rum in a guy and he's bound to slip up. Are you going to crucify me forever? Listen, I want to meet this woman, Ivy. I do. If she means so much to you."

"Sometime maybe."

"*Maybe*. What a prick," he said, smiling. Then he tapped his index finger against the table. "When can you get me a mock-up?"

"Be patient. We start small—maybe two constructions, say a flat and a wedge, in three or four styles, four colors. Make nice clean lines."

"Just get me a prototype. I'll poach a sales team from Blakes. Comfort-driven, four-season shoe. One hundred percent fit. From work to yoga, we carry you. How do you like that? The independents will eat it up. This is the *feeling*, Al. If I could bottle it. Once you're in the shoe business, everything else's boring."

Back at the factory house, I sat at the kitchen table eating some dumplings and stir-fried pork with cabbage, and I took the financials that I'd printed off Yong's computer out of my pocket.

As I read, the chopsticks kept coming up slower to my mouth. Workers were making about eleven hundred yuan a month. A hundred and sixty bucks. No one could live on that. My face got all hot like I was standing in front of the heat setting boxes, the numbers bonding in my head, and when my cell phone suddenly rang I realized I'd been holding the same piece of pork on the end of my chopsticks for a long time.

I said hello and recognized his voice immediately.

"Alex," Gang said and all the numbers stovepiped out the top of my head. He wanted to know what I'd found out. I told him I'd just moved into the manager's house right inside the factory, next to the dorms and the production lines, so I could see and hear everything.

"Good," he said.

I let out a deep breath.

"It's important we find them," he said.

"I understand," I said, but it was quiet on the other side of the line. For a second I thought he hung up.

Then he said, firmly, "Little problem grows into big problem."

"Yes," I said. "Some more time and I'll find them."

"You call me when," he said and the line went dead.

I sat there trying to figure out a way to get rid of Gang. What if I gave him two names? Two workers I'd never met before. Wouldn't that save the rest? Sacrificing two for the greater whole. Did that make sense? Or was it sick? I was trying to rationalize the whole thing. Where was the Emperor when I needed him?

The truth was right there in my lap. The financials. Tens of thousands of yuan in unpaid social insurance. Bonuses and piece-rates that didn't make sense. It was a mess. A racket. Reminded me of what Dad had said earlier about the cost sheets. We always make it work. Why? To stay competitive. It had to be so.

It was pretty clear to me now that it was all three-card monte, a shell game. Even if Ivy started a new union, whatever they asked for, we'd just smile and nod our heads and shuffle the money around. All of that was spelled out in these pages. If we gave them a little more in social insurance with one hand, we'd just take it out of their bonuses with the other. Then we'd hold their papers as ransom. So if they chose to leave, they were now basically illegal aliens in their own country.

So how much could I really help Ivy? I sure as hell wasn't going to throw some poor bastard to Gang. No, he could run my ass out of China before that happened. And I wouldn't expose Ivy either.

I couldn't play it from both sides forever. Eventually you had to betray someone.

Thirteen

THE NEXT AFTERNOON, LED BY IVY, ZHANG stepped into my house wearing a red Polo shirt, the horse insignia upside down. He didn't even flinch when he rounded the corner and squared up against the two giant Mongolian statues. That was what worried me—he was unafraid. Even when he should've been.

He smirked at the statues before wheeling around to face me. "Comrade," he said, shaking my hand, and then reading some hesitation in my face, he added, "I call you this?"

"Alex is fine," I said. "You had a safe trip?"

"On the freeway outside the city, I am checked three times. Full arm security. Like a war zone. They check my ID and *hukou*."

"Maybe they should be afraid of you," I said, pointing to the couch. "Please."

"They feel insecurity," he said as he sat down. "Paranoid. Every citizen is the enemy."

Ivy sat on the arm of the couch beside him, her feet crossed at the ankles.

"This is a fat, juicy house," Zhang said, his eyes moving around the room. "No tea?"

"Not this time," I said. Shitty *guanxi* maybe, but I needed facts now; I needed to know his plans.

"I met with Gang," I said and paused, letting that sit with him for a second.

Zhang lifted his hand as if to button his collar and, realizing there were no buttons, his hand slid back down. The first little sign of doubt.

"I'm sure Ivy told you," I went on. "Gang knows about you, doesn't have your names, but he knows there's 'radicals' in the factory. It's not safe."

My eyes shifted to Ivy, trying to tell Zhang I meant her. It wasn't safe for her anymore. She was the one on the ground. Not him. He was up in Beijing.

Zhang's face didn't betray anything. He didn't seem fazed. "In life, always dangers, comrade," he said.

This second time with the comrade business got under my skin a little.

I leaned forward with my elbows on my knees. "I'm not sure you heard me. He tried to *enlist* me. He assumes I'm on his side."

"You are on the correct side," Zhang said.

"Listen to me," I said, realizing he was going to make me spell it out. "The way this works with Gang is simple—we answer to him, he answers to Beijing. You understand?"

"You ask if I comprehend hierarchy?"

I rolled my eyes. He was too stubborn. "Gang's money—no, forget money—his power comes straight from the Great Hall. So any change I make—any change you want me to make— cuts into his bottom line. You see? A threat to the factory is a threat to everyone's pocket all the way up."

Sharp lines appeared on Ivy's forehead.

"The law requires you pay social benefits," she said. "We only ask for the law. We are not *radical*. This goal is very moderate."

"No one follows the law," I said. "Here? In China? You told me this yourself. You're the whole reason I sound like this."

Ivy scooted to the edge of the arm of the chair and simulated sewing, back straight, upright. "See this is what my line leader calls being assertive in my performance. This is taking control of my own fate." Then she slouched. "Bad. Three hundred yuan fine."

"I'm on your side. The system is broken. But you got to be reasonable—"

Ivy cut me off. "Deduction for using bathroom twice in one hour. Even pregnant. Deduction for humming pop song." She was speaking fast now, tapping the blade of her left hand against her right palm. "Deduction for text message to sick daughter. In this factory. All of it. Empty promises. Midautumn festival bonus is half month's wage, correct? In truth, we get fifty yuan and a banana."

"A *banana*," Zhang said, parroting her, a blue vein tracking along the side of his neck. "Migrant factory workers are the shit on the shoe of China. If a million die tomorrow, nobody knows or cares. Lies too many to count. At least in America, if a boss lies, you can punch his face. That is democracy."

"Not true," I said, throwing up my hands. "You don't know what you're talking about. You can't punch anyone."

"Better to be born a pig than work here," Zhang said, rising off the couch.

"You don't even work here!" I said, standing up tall and rigid, so we were on the same level glaring at each other.

"Calm down, calm down," yelled Ivy, her voice shaky. She waved us down with both her arms. "We resolve."

Then it was quiet except for the paddle fan spinning overhead. Air muggy and thick. Zhang ground out his private thoughts with the toe of his sandal against the wood floor.

"What am I supposed to do with Gang?" I asked. "I know you think I'm the enemy. I'm not. Here's the truth, if we gave the workers back pay on social insurance, if we gave medical and housing subsidies, followed the actual law, we'd lose the whole labor cost advantage of doing business in China. The whole point of being here."

Ivy flinched when I said that.

"I'm sorry," I said, surprised a little at the way I sounded. Cynical. But realistic. I didn't mind how I sounded. "When that advantage's gone, it hits this factory, this city, hard, then it's Gang's problem, then it's Beijing's problem. All Gang cares about is saying he does 8 percent growth every quarter."

Zhang held his palm up, but it was all surging up in my chest. I wanted to say it all. "Any real change—like a 20 percent wage increase—and Gang throws my ass out of the country for hurting his bottom line, and then he brings in different owners, real assholes. You know over at Foxconn the *mingong* pay to use the bathroom. Pay for water."

"Okay," Zhang said, calmer now. "Sorry for the temper before. We want the same path. Sorry."

"Don't worry," I said.

"Moderate goals," he continued. "We both want. The *mingong* needs same rights as assembly line worker in Detroit. Baggage handler at Delta. Dockworker at General Electric. The legal right to school, social benefits, pensions, health insurance, buying power. It should be the case?"

"Yes," I said.

"GE still makes big profit," Ivy said.

"Sure," I said. "But I can't give you those things. I don't have that kind of power and collective bargaining is a sham here. You guys have this vision of American capitalism from the 1950s—but that won't work in China. It's more like 1850s America here, run by robber barons—Carnegie and Rockefeller, JP Morgan. But either way, you guys are in the wrong century."

"I see," Zhang said.

"It's a shell game," I said, and paused trying to remember the actual figures—all a blur in my mind right now, only the point was clear. "We move money around in different piles. So we could 'negotiate' by raising benefits 8 percent, great, look like heroes in the press, then turn around and make employees match contributions and that money disappears, so it's all back to even. Real wages stay the same. I've seen the damn numbers. And I'm willing to bet this is how Honda solved their strike. Or you reduce overtime bonuses. Or hours. There's a million ways to do it. I saw the figures myself. The money always evens out to maintain the advantage."

A stricken expression spread across Zhang's face. "Some of this, yes, we know," he said, shaking his head. "Maybe not in the extreme you confirm."

Ivy put her hand on Zhang's shoulder. A meaningful look passed between them. It lasted for a few seconds before he turned back to me.

"We need a different plan," Zhang said. "That is very clear. Unions do not work. Your hands tied behind your back by the government."

"Correct," I said. For some reason I found their surprise comforting.

"Impossible to change things alone," Zhang said. "According to reason. You do not possess the power."

"Not on my own," I said.

Zhang paused for a moment. "What if are not on your own?"

"Meaning?"

"Well, what if other factory owners supported you?"

"They wouldn't," I said.

"Then what is a proper course? How does change come forward?"

"You have to put pressure above me," I said. "You must go higher."

"To the top," Zhang said.

"To Gang," I said.

"Beijing," he said.

The hairs on the back of my neck stood up. Something about his burning look. I was searching his eyes but couldn't read his play here.

"How did Mao get the attention of the masses?" Zhang asked. "Before the revolution."

I shrugged.

"The Long March. You heard this? Six thousand miles. Village by village, spreading the message of liberation. Up into mountains of Yan'an. People, stick your head out of your cave and listen."

"Or Gandhi's Salt March," Ivy added, reading the doubt on my face. "Or in your own country—Martin Luther King."

"It's a different time," I said. "That won't work anymore."

"Of course," Ivy agreed. "But the goal is same. Attention of the people. Attention of the world. You have in the States the same problem. People come to pick grapes, mow lawns, cook. Outsiders. They are invisible in your country, but you need them. So here they circuit-board iPads instead of washing dishes. Live like unwanted guests here in their own country. So the world must see them. The people. Not just products they make."

Tough to argue that. They came to the cities, slaved away in the factories for their best years and maybe they stayed, but no one really wanted them. In the subway, all the handsome, well-heeled Chinese scooted over, sneaking a few pitying glances at their darker, dirtier countrymen in pith helmets, holding mattocks, covered in tunnel soot, a different species almost, exhausted, their heads rattling against a subway ad, dreaming of high-rises, and the whole thing was enraging. But what could you do about it?

"But this is China," I said. "There's nothing you can do. I mean, they locked up Ai Weiwei for flicking off Tiananmen Gate. The middle finger and he's thrown in jail. You want to start trouble with *these* people?"

Zhang inhaled sharply with a hiss. "Trouble? No trouble. No violence. We have no army. No weapons. This is not a proper course. We need visibility. Something broadcast. Over internet maybe. A platform. A forum. An instantaneous Long March, right? How do we get forum? Someone must be ready to take a stand. To step forward."

"You mean me?" I said.

"I don't mean you," said Zhang. "I mean the person who shows the willing."

"A forum," I said. "Here at the factory. You're talking about a demonstration, aren't you?"

Zhang waved his hand in front of his face. "I don't like this word."

"But you're saying it. Which means a strike."

"We want to lift the shoe and show the world," he said. "Put it this way."

I turn to Ivy. "Do you agree with this?"

She nodded. "Show the world the solidarity of Chinese workers," Ivy said. "We broadcast speeches. On the internet. YouTube. With VPNs we go around the firewalls."

"You want to rile people up," I said. "That's violent. You sound like neo-Maoists."

"No, no," Zhang said, touching his chest. "Remember what

Deng Xiaoping said after Mao, 'Doesn't matter if a cat was black or white, so long as it catches mice.' Today we need a new way to catch mice. A calico cat. This is YouTube. Think of me like Deng Xiaoping with an iPhone."

At the moment I was thinking of him as a lot of things, but none of them were Deng Xiaoping with an iPhone. Zhang was definitely talking about a strike.

"Of course you cannot stop factory operation," Zhang said, his clever habit of preemptively arguing your side of things.

"That's right," I said. "Look, I want to support you guys, but I can't stop the lines."

"But maybe for one day this is possible. To give us a forum."

So he really did mean that. I didn't know how to respond. Only I was aware that my mouth was open a little and I hadn't said anything yet. So I forced the words out. "You know that'd hurt my business. Cost money, jobs."

"We never want to lose jobs," Ivy said firmly. "We *need* you in China. Factory jobs are good jobs. *Mingong* don't want to go back to rice farming."

"I don't want to farm," Zhang added. "I have a bad back from volleyball accident."

He chuckled here, a lame little attempt at levity.

Ivy shook her head. "No, no. This isn't 'rotten capitalist go home!' The workers *are* young capitalists. They want money. Want business. Retail or trading booth in Guangzhou. The women are future iron ladies, yes? Who will provide? Not the government anymore. We help make them a path. It's only one day to spare, Alex. One day."

"This is moving ahead," said Zhang. "The real Great Leap Forward." He chuckled again at his own wordplay. "You let us have our YouTube videos, our speeches. Then everyone back to work."

"But what does it accomplish?" I asked. "That I don't un-derstand."

"Big pressure to the top in Beijing," Ivy said. "So when we ask respectfully for what we want, they are forced to give be-cause the pressure of the world is so great on them."

"Democracy," Zhang said in a tone that made it sound like he was clarifying what Ivy said, even though she wasn't talk-ing about democracy. Zhang read this confusion on my face. "Not now of course. Slowly. It should be the case."

"I think you're going to be disappointed," I told him. "I don't know if my country is all that different. A bunch of super rich people running the country."

Zhang smiled at this. "*Aiya*. So maybe we are all in the wrong century."

"Maybe so," I said.

I was staring straight at Zhang but out of the corner of my eye, I saw Ivy swallow hard. "Only a day, we ask. To achieve big goals. We have two dozen people in the factory with iPhones," she said. "And VPN connections."

"You do?" I said, my stomach sinking. The paddle fan spun overhead, but it was hot. Hard to think straight. I felt my pulse whipping in my wrists. I took a napkin out of my pocket and wiped my forehead. "From?"

"Allies in Hong Kong," Zhang said. "At the China Labour Bulletin."

I didn't look at him. I kept my eyes on Ivy.

"Be honest," I said. "Was this your plan all along?"

"We consider all possibility," she said.

That got under my skin a little. I mean, I knew they'd been inching me along this whole time. You didn't come all the way down from Beijing to brainstorm maybes. They had a plan to sell. No different from selling shoes. You didn't grab a customer and say, "Hey, buddy, buy this goddamn shoe," like a caveman. You worked up to it slowly. I would've done the same thing. Was that what pissed me off? Being on the other side of it for once?

So I was the schmuck for listening. Okay, maybe.

But you couldn't go through life on guard, in a bubble, much as I was sure Dad would love that. You had to listen. And sometimes, rarely, people said shit that made sense. That was the risk of opening the door in the morning. You could become a sucker. Like everyone else.

"What do you need from me?" I asked.

A smile just barely spread across Zhang's face, but he quickly stifled it back. "Don't call the police. Not right away. Give us a little time."

"I'll try," I said. "Buffer you as best I can, but I don't know who else is going to call the police. I can't account for my father."

"This is okay," Zhang said. "It is fine."

"If you give me a date, I can make sure no buyers or inspectors are visiting. Do you have a date set?"

"We have to act soon. If Gang is so suspicious." Zhang looked up at Ivy. "A week from now," he said.

"If we can get everyone organized in time," said Ivy.

"Soon as we decide on the date, we warn you," Zhang said. "We give you twenty-four-hour warning."

"You really think this will help?" I asked Ivy. "Tell me what you think. I'm asking you."

She looked at me. Eyes narrowing. "Yes. I do."

I turned my head to the side. Couldn't take them staring at me any longer. They wanted a commitment. The pleading looks. What was I going to do?

I could almost hear my father say, *Everyone else can act like an animal, but not you.* That's what he said when the townies spray-painted an anti-Semitic sign on the street sign by our

house and I tried to go after them with a bat. I couldn't understand why Dad stopped me. I mean, getting in Dad's car in a
wet bathing suit without a towel was some kind of mortal sin,
but when it came to something important you were supposed
to let it roll right off your shoulders. None of it made sense.

"One day," Ivy said. Cajoling. "One single day. Makes the
workers so happy they double production the next day. So
you lose nothing."

I waved the bottom of my shirt to vent some air. Too
warm in here. The breath and sweat and slickness. Too many
thoughts. They spun and drifted, one voice squashed, another
shouting. It'd be one day. I couldn't come out of this clean. It
was never going to be painless.

But at least I'd have Gang off my back. They were turning
themselves in basically. I wouldn't have to rat anyone out. A
shitty, selfish thought that I pushed out of my head.

But maybe the brand takes off and I never even feel the hit.

I nodded. "Okay. I'll look the other way. For a day."

"Thank you," Zhang said, bowing his head.

Ivy moved to the edge of her seat like she was about to get
up and touch me, reassure me—her eyes wide, telling me of
course she couldn't. She needed to stay there, on her side. Even
if it made me feel real far off. A little pinch of guilt in her
look too. Every sale carried it, because you were never quite
telling the truth. I knew that. So what were they leaving out?

"Listen," I said, looking at Ivy. "This is a dangerous gamble.
You don't know what Gang will do. You could be in deep shit."

"There is risk," Ivy said. "There is a way to make things
more effective," she said and nodded to me, and I understood
she wanted me to be a part of it.

"Absolutely not," I said.

"To give one speech," Zhang said. "Now the whole world
stops to watch."

"We need you there," Ivy said.

They were out of their minds. My support was one thing, but not my voice. If I gave a speech at this rally, then what? Goodbye to the brand with Bernie. No brand. No factory. My father would have a coronary. Gang would pull out my fingernails. The shoe-dogs would chase me out of China with pitchforks. That was why I couldn't talk.

But I wouldn't monkeywrench it either. No saying what Dad or Yong might do, but I could try to stall them long enough to give Ivy and Zhang the forum they wanted. Let them lift the shoe and show everyone the shit-smeared sole. Maybe that would do some good. I cared enough to do that. But I wouldn't put my face on it.

That's suicide. What good would it do anyway?

The workers would still suffer terribly even if I spoke. That's global capitalism. You couldn't just turn the machine off. This had been going on for hundreds of years. There was no way out of it.

No, I needed to keep my mouth shut, stay out of sight and stick to the plan with Bernie. When the demonstration happened, I'd act just as blindsided as Dad and Yong.

"You know I can't," I said. "And I don't see why it matters if I speak or not."

"If you are there," Ivy said, "the government behaves like a good son. In order to protect its image. And your partnership. Much safer for the workers involved."

"Suicide. No one in my position would even think about doing it."

"Of course," Zhang said, brushing the notion away with his hand. "This is the problem. But what if everyone in your position did this? Imagine you stand with us and your colleagues, factory owners, to our cause—what could be more? Without you. We are alone. Easy to smash. But if all the capitalist plant owners said to government, 'We're going to move elsewhere if you don't take proper care of your workers.' If you say, 'I am willing to take smaller returns for good of Chinese workers,' if every Alex takes this stance—now this is real revolution. You speak. Others speaking. They hear you up in Beijing and force a change in their policy."

That all sounded nice and lofty. And maybe Zhang was right, that to stand in solidarity with the workers and other foreign and local factory owners against the Chinese government— that sure as hell might make a difference, but who was crazy enough? You would need to have nothing to lose.

I didn't want to tell them this, but in my head I was thinking there was a quieter way. The brand. That was what it came back to. If someone turned themselves into the Ralph Lauren of China—if they weren't just here to squeeze every last dime out of these workers—well, then they'd have the wiggle room to give the workers more money, better benefits.

Because Beijing didn't *want* slave wages, that was just the way they drew business in. What Beijing wanted more than bringing in businesses was starting their own. Their own global brands. Made *by* China not just *in*. If they felt the Polos and Apples and Pradas could be based here, born here, Beijing wouldn't mind the workers getting more.

So if I could pull this off, if I could make bigger profits and compete in overseas markets, Beijing wouldn't stop me from doing better by my workers.

Of course you'd pocket less, but you could do it, if you weren't too greedy. Six percent? Five percent if the orders were big enough. No midrashic law saying you couldn't work on five percent. I'd need to sell more. Except it was going to take time. Slow. Then a little trickles down. A modest change. A start. And then maybe everyone gets paid a little more, charged a little more. The customers, the manufacturers. The market would adjust.

But not if I spoke.

"Look, I'm part of the system and it sucks, you both know that. All I can do is hope to change it from the inside. But I can't put my face on this thing at all," I said to her. "I just can't. I'm going to need every worker, every line running soon. I'll look the other way with you being here and doing your iPhone speeches, as long as it's peaceful, but I'm not talking. Do you understand? I'm a shoe guy. I don't want to be out in front of this thing."

Ivy nodded and her eyes slid away down to the floor. Like she was real disappointed. What choice did I have? If she couldn't understand this, then I was sorry.

"I see," Zhang said, but he hesitated, like he was about to say something else; the bottom of his lip twitched, or maybe he did something with his eyes—it was all too fast to register— and then he stood up and reached out his hand.

"Thank you," he said.

Weary, I lifted myself up and shook his hand, but when I went to pull away his grip tightened ever so slightly, as if he was still thinking at any moment I'll change my mind. His hand kept pumping.

"Thank you, comrade," I said, I guess as some sort of concession that even though I was not giving them exactly what they wanted, I was still on their side. Zhang showed me this odd smile that was tough to read, and it must've sounded pretty stupid, that word coming out of my mouth, though I wanted to hear how it sounded—or maybe I was embarrassed for meaning it.

Fourteen

NO SLEEP. 2:00 A.M., AWAKE IN BED WITH A SKETCH pad on my lap trying to draw a pattern for this new brand. My lead lines were getting sharper, thicker, angrier, but the design wasn't getting anywhere. Where the hell to start? I was going to pitch the idea to Dad, pitch a whole new direction for our business, but there had to be an actual shoe, a few styles to show him. It couldn't just be talk. There had to be a shoe for any of this to work.

Restless, I threw the sheets off my lap, stood up and went to my dresser. I pulled on some shorts and my old burned-out gray T-shirt from the Arlington JCC, worn so thin you could see the warp and weave, and, moving with some kind of purpose masked to me at first, I headed out into the muggy night. Outside, the faint sweet smell of formaldehyde from the shoe cement hit my lungs, and my brain caught up to my body. The sample room. That's where I was headed. I needed to be in the workshop. Needed my hands on real materials. That's the only way to start. Not doodling on a notepad in bed.

I keyed open the metal door to Plant B and took the stairs

up to the third floor. Inside it was eerily quiet and dark: just
the hulking silhouettes of the cutting machines, heat towers
and sole presses crouched in the darkness. I felt blindly on the
wall for the light switch and one aisle of chain-hung fluores-
cent bulbs shuddered and flickered to life.

Against the walls were tall metal shelves displaying our new
Western slouch boots, and unless you were a shoe-dog, you
wouldn't know which was the real Frye boot and which was
our imposter. Dad was a copycat genius. But to come up with
something fresh. Something new. Where the hell did you start?

I sat on a stool at the steel-top worktable. The table face
was scored and scratched from the tools—pegging awls, skiv-
ing knives, stitch groovers—scattered about. I picked up each
tool, felt its heft in my hand, before arranging them in a neat
row off to my right.

Dad's favorite last was sitting in the middle of the table, angled toward me. We still used this old waxy oak last that my
great-grandfather had hand-lathed, because its measurements
were perfect and Dad was a sentimental old bastard. But he
was right. Brazilian last makers always rounded the feather
line, Italian-style, but this was the old Austrian form that you
couldn't find anymore, whispering to me now to pick it up.

So I lifted it up with two hands and rubbed my thumb along
the roughed bottom, a grainy burr from all the tack nails, and
the toe box had a nice, hard-worn patina. Each whorl and
grease stain confiding a secret. Whispering that it had always
been here, right at the center, if I'd bothered to look.

The wood darkened up by the throat where Dad always held
it tight. Worn from all the times he touched it without need-
ing to touch it, just unconsciously whenever he was nearby,
like it was some kind of talisman.

I cupped the heel firmly and traced my finger lightly down
the cone and closed my fist around the toe of this phantom

foot, and it struck me how rigid it was. You could knock
someone out with this last. Heavy and dense. Way too stiff
for the shoe I wanted to make. I needed flexibility. That was
the vision, right? Mine. Zhang's vision too. A compromise.
Not too stiff and not too supple. In between. A compromise.
A way forward. A fucking calico.

I lifted my eyes to the window that overlooked the roof of
the dormitory where Ruxi had hovered a month ago, stuck
between air and land, her white dress filling like a balloon,
and I felt a surging inside my chest.

There was a way to make it work. Forget the fucking last.

I pushed my great-grandfather's last to the edge of the table.
Away. No listening to it. I didn't need it. What about stitch-
and-turn construction, I thought. But that never fit well. No,
there was a third way. I could stitch right onto the inner sole
board. Or better yet, onto Strobel board. Like the old kung
fu slippers.

I jumped out of my chair and started fumbling through
egg crates of materials on the shelves for the Strobel board.
Then I set up the three spools of woven elastic on the worktable and sat back down, my legs jittering under the table as
I poked holes around the edge of the Strobel board with the
awl, faster, then cutting off strips of elastic from the spool and
weaving it through the holes. Something was slowly forming
right under my eyes.

A new construction. It could work. I could profit and the
mingong could profit and we could advance together. In harmony. We could make this work. That wasn't crazy.

No one was crazy here. Zhang and Ivy weren't trying to
destroy the factory, just improve it. That was all. They were
all capitalists at heart in China. Zhang was for sure. They had
been doing knockoff capitalism and now they were ready for
the real thing.

I was starting to feel good about everything, but then this other voice snuck up on me and said, Who are you kidding, dummy? You can't do both.

A shiver jolted down my back. Two of me just spoke to each other here and at first I couldn't place the voices. How the fuck did I end up agreeing to both Bernie and Zhang? That was the real problem. You were either a Bernie or a Zhang. One or the other.

But I'd basically said, "Here's the key to my plant. Come in and let me help you show the whole world on fucking YouTube how my profits are too big because Beijing oligarchs and local cadres skim so much off the top and our own greed makes us nickel-and-dime workers, using the *hukou* legal system against them, and their own government encourages us."

Why risk all that?

These two voices kept grating and grinding against each other as I was weaving the upper, and one of them had to be the imposter. One of them was a fucking knockoff.

Zhang was right: the migrant workers were the shit on the shoe of China. And it was our asses that it all came out of. So this was right. If the movement spread the way Zhang envisioned then the market would adjust. Sally McGee in Topeka would pay an extra two dollars for her sandals. Everyone would. And once they did, everything would come up. Not just in China but worldwide. If my profits were a little less, then prices went up. She was going to pay another few bucks. The beauty of this vision was going to allow the market to ask for more money out of the customer. The customer would know it was fair. That was Zhang's vision. That was all he was really saying. It wasn't revolutionary. He and Ivy didn't want to kick me out.

This shoe could be the fucking solution. The compromise.

Everyone profits—the government, the workers, our own bottom line. It's something my father would never dare to do.

Gang would have less of a hard-on for catching radicals if his numbers looked better. What he cared about was getting into the central bureau, the twenty-five dudes who ran China. That's all.

In this business, sometimes if you got the right look, it caught on fire. Suddenly you were riding a goddamn hockey stick curve up. A shoe got hot. And what did that mean? Bigger margins. More to give. More to go around. See how that worked? Nice and clean. A middle ground. A way forward for us in China. Now you were paying the workers more and doing volume and everyone was fucking happy. One needed the other. And all for a day's strike. That was worth it. You almost needed to think of the strike as an investment. A way to situate yourself for the long game.

Don't think about the future, I told myself. Just focus on what's in your hands. What's in front of you. What you're doing. Snipping and weaving. A little glue pot beside me with an old toothbrush that I used to brush the bottom of the Strobel board to glue down the elastic.

And as I saw the shape of the shoe slowly emerge, the lines and contours of the upper, I couldn't help imagining the brand taking off. We were doing twenty thousand pairs the first season. Then twenty-five thousand. Then fifty thousand. A shoe got hot.

This is you, that other voice said, not some revolution. I looked up over the top of my glasses at the family last sitting across from me on the table, whispering again: *Now don't go all soft, Alex. Don't turn to mush. Pull me closer. Here's the chance to make your mark. You want to be a shitbum for the rest of your life?*

I leaned an elbow on the table and reached across to bring the old last closer.

I shouldn't have shoved it away. This thing was a part of my body. Might as well have been.

You just needed to sell the shit out of these shoes for the biggest profit, so you could buy all the Royal Doulton chinaware, so your mother could hold a crystal salad plate on Shabbat like it was the fucking Hope Diamond, and say out loud to everyone, "My son, the big *macher*."

See? Any schnook could sell shoes; you wanted a brand. You wanted immortality. No skirting it. The point was profit. Ivy didn't change that. At the end of the day you were a goat. Just like Bernie and Dad. Goats eating people's shirts right off their clotheslines. Three goats way down yonder in the pawpaw patch.

You knew this, dummy. The minute you scribbled your name on the paperwork in the hotel, you knew you weren't just joining the company, you were signing over your soul, the blood that ran deep, that treated this last like an oracle bone.

But you could also take less, I told myself. For Ivy. For the good of China. A fair and democratic China. Starting with a good factory. That was making your mark too. That was a legacy. Could those two people coexist? Or did one have to grab the other by the throat and suffocate him? That's what Dad would do. Ruthless. *Don't give me excuses.*

I could hear Dad slapping my mother hard across the face. I saw her in a rabbit fur hat loading suet into the green plastic cage in the snowy garden, the tree rustling alive with grackles swirling, their wings flapping frantically around her head. I remembered her holding a fist of snow to her cheek.

This business destroyed their marriage. But it didn't have to, did it? These were all choices, not destinies. There were no oracles.

I was sick from these voices battering. Two people tussling

in me and this pressure on my chest. Stop now. Focus. No machines. No noise.

Just snip the strands, weave them through the Strobel.

I squeezed my eyes closed and let my hands move on their own. Inside me everything was real quiet but on fire too. My hands floating over this shoe. What did I have here? What was taking shape? More than a shoe; a lifestyle brand. For the woman who was thirty-five and knew who the hell she was. The woman who had wants not needs.

Ralph Lauren made a lifestyle brand. Beautiful blonde shiksas running around the pool of a French mansion. The dream of goy. Back when he was Ralph Lifshitz. Before he changed his name to seal the deal, to become the man on the inside. He had to. Trotsky too. Every Bronstein had a Trotsky ready to burst through his chest. Every grubby little Lifshitz had a Lauren living inside them. Everyone was a mustache away from reinventing himself. One goyish name from glory.

Yes, that's where it was all moving. I was going to become the Ralph Lauren of fucking China.

I shook out my wrists. Forget what time it was; forget sleep. All this adrenaline sloshing around in my veins, my fingers moving nimbly now, tight rows, no buckling, braiding one row at a time, plaiting them, over and under, over and under, weft and warp, back and forth, and in this rhythm I almost forgot the heat, the sweat streaking down my temple, my flushed cheeks, the sweet cement hardening in my nail beds, and I almost forgot I was in a seat, no less a factory, or one in China for that matter—that was how far out I'd let myself drift.

I decided I'd put a driving bottom on one style—for this customer I was seeing in my head. Seeing her real clear now, almost like she was sitting right here whispering to me. She's got a heavy foot, I imagine, ever since that Yugo she drove fast during a semester abroad in Ravello studying art history, when some local boy carried her to the open window facing the cobblestone street, set her waist over the windowsill and made love to her with her head hanging out the window, and she could see villagers looking up at her; it was the one time in her life she didn't care, didn't mind her nakedness. She wanted the whole world to be hung out the window to see what she saw. That was thirty years ago. Her Italian boyfriend is all grown. *Where is he now?* she thinks when she hits the open highway, rolling through the dark in my driving shoes. Black-and-silver, sleek, polished, a bit dressier but still casual.

I was seeing this customer clearly now. Her hair's done up and she's driving her husband to their once-a-month dinner, and he asks, "What's wrong?"

"Nothing," she says. She can't shape other words. All she knows is that the highway is good for her. She likes riding. She raised horses growing up. She's forgotten everything she once knew about Italian art, but she knows how to put a horse down. She presses hard on the gas pedal.

And she was more than willing to pay an extra two bucks for her shoes because it was fair. That was the beauty of the vision. Everyone would have to compromise a little.

The patterns scribbled down my arms and I was weaving faster: a simple chessboard design. A herringbone. All for different customers I saw as clearly as the first.

Then I brushed all the elastic scraps, tools and coffee cups aside to clear room on the table and I lined up the three shoes in their lasts, side by side, making sure the toe lines were flush with the edge of the table. I lined them up just right, and then I squatted down with my hands on my knees like a football coach, legs staked wide, my nose only inches from the toes, and the room seemed to fall away, no Bernies, no Zhangs. I was not hearing them anymore. I could picture only the cushiony footbed silk-screened with the name *Alex & Ivy*.

That was what the foot rested on. Her sole nestled against the footbed, this delicate part of her pressed to my name, as though part of me was in the shoe bought by some woman in Des Moines, in Dothan, in Methuen. Who, upon stepping into the store, saw the display tree and saw herself, saw me, and we were one, her and me, my name right up against her skin, this secret part of a woman, and if she went to Ravello, Italy, I'd go too, wherever she went, I'd see the places she saw, and the fact that I'd never meet the woman or know her name made it that much better.

I stared at the shoes with my head cocked to the side like I was listening to them, like we were having a private conversation, and then, without warning, I suddenly switched the order of the shoes, so the all-gray was on the right and the checkered in the middle and the herringbone on the left, and then I backed up five feet to take in the collection. Three or four times I rearranged the order until it was right. I could see these were something special.

These were the damn Cohain of shoes.

And now staring at all three styles on the table, I understood what my father and grandfather and great-grandfather already knew: that making shoes was not just practical or stylish. The right shoes gave you a coherence, a purpose. The secret hand moving inside a puppet. They animated *you*, not the other way around. I got that now.

If I sold only a single pair of these, it'd be enough.

Which was why it was okay for me to take nothing on them because it wasn't about profit, it was about me. My name silk-screened on the insole, embossed on the footbed, pressed right up against the arch of a woman as she slipped over me. No longer subsumed by one of Abelson's private labels—Halogen, St. John's Bay. No, I am remade each time the iron mold opens, the heat plate lifts and the ink cures with a swizzle of smoke, and I'm burned into the suede, the shammy footbed, I'm in every elastic fiber and rubber molecule. My real *b'rit milah* ceremony on the eighth day. When Alex became not just some name I had to bear, but who I am.

The sun was rising pink through the window. The shoes on the table simmering like mirages over asphalt. Everything looked odd. Slowly coming back. The way a subway car suddenly rattled aboveground with a fading horn blast and the sun was too bright, as if you forgot what real light and sky looked like. That was how I felt now. Like I'd just come up out of the ground.

I still needed to get Dad on board. If Dad was willing to cut out his own profit on this line for the first few seasons, we could make these shoes for maybe four dollars cheaper than normal. Much more competitive. Then it would retail for a better price. And it would grow. Slowly. We'd start building in a profit after a few successful seasons. But we couldn't keep making Dad's cheapies. We were drowning. The brand had to drive the business going forward.

Of course Dad was going to tell me I was wrong and we should stick with private label and take our normal profits. But what was right was owning this thing. For me at least. Dad was happy behind the curtain. Not me. No future in that for me. It had to be branded. For my name to be on it. Which meant we had to make it for no profit. Dad wasn't going to like that, but there was no other way.

Of course I needed his expertise too and I'd better make that clear. I needed him. Puff him up a little first. That always worked on him. Then I'd say, I'm doing a mitzvah by bringing you this brand. Present it like that. I'm doing *you* a favor.

And now at 6:00 a.m., delirious from an all-nighter, I heard music from outside. I went to the window and the workers were doing jumping jacks in the yard. Chinese music piped

into the courtyard through loudspeakers. Mandatory morning calisthenics. Production manager Shen led them from an
elevated platform, barking orders into a microphone. Tight
rows and columns. But this music was different. Different from
anything they'd played before. I heard the high strings and
brass. I was swaying a little in the window, the tune moving
back and forth inside me. This was a marching tune. Maybe
an old Mao song. Maybe Shen was one of Zhang's secret two
dozen and he was playing this as some coded message for the
demonstrators. I bent to the glass, listening—the sun warm
on my face, the movement rising now—and I was aching to
know what it meant.

Then I tried to picture myself standing in the yard with a
microphone speaking to the demonstrators, but I didn't know
what I'd say. No. It couldn't work. But then I closed my eyes to
the sound of cheering, and I got this other vision of the future
where I was living in a dusty hot village with the old fish-scale
roofs. Ivy was beside me in a beautiful red silk *qipao*, wearing my sandals. I pictured myself at peace, in a place where I
stood out so goddamn bad that I finally fit in.

Fifteen

NO WORD THAT AFTERNOON FROM IVY OR
Zhang about the demonstration date, but plenty of bad news
from the Abelson's headquarters. Esme called to tell me they
were dropping our winter boot program. The third program
they'd cut in the last two years. A big hit for us. Before hanging up, Esme said she'd tried Dad's office first but no one
answered. She was lying. That was sort of chickenshit and
understandable of her. To put it all on me to tell him.

I knocked on his office door and there was no answer,
even though I could hear the hunt-and-peck typing and the
phlegmy—*Ach!*—as he bungled some email. He obviously
didn't want to be bothered. I turned to leave, but then I caught
myself in those little lies. I was afraid to tell him. Scared to
pitch the brand idea too. Well, tough, I told myself. Get in
there and say it.

So I turned the handle, pushed the door open and found
him at his desk two-finger typing on his laptop.

"I need a minute," I said.

He didn't answer. I've always envied people who can

stonewall a person like that. I guess that was Dad's genius, blocking out the obvious things right in front of him.

"Abelson's cut our winter program," I blurted out, and the typing stopped.

His head came up slow from behind the screen. Mouth pursed tight, face ashen.

"The Snow Lite?" he asked.

"Got a call from Esme an hour ago," I said.

His face slackened.

"I've been here all day," he said.

He meant, *Why the hell did she call you?*

I didn't answer.

"This is bad," he said, rubbing the back of his wrist over his lips in overdrive. "They're pulling the fucking plug?"

"They want a new feeling," I told him. "They don't want Snow—"

"Oh, fuck them," he said, sitting up in his chair. "With this new feeling." He slammed his laptop closed. "We did 1.8 million the second year of Snow Lite and the minute we hit a slump, they get a new feeling. See, there's no loyalty. Only scum in this business. Who got our orders? Gold Valley I bet you. There's a crook. That owner. Loves to screw people."

Dad picked up a leather sample swatch and slapped it against the corner of the table.

"Know what? I bet it's a kickback to Esme," he continued. "I bet they're buddies—she and the liar."

"Well," I said, "they got some fancy state-of-the-art tech over there and—"

"Bullshit. Their shoes are made with a hacksaw. All action leather. Corrected leather—oh, hoho, you got that look on your face. Don't tell me not to yell, 'cause I yell, okay? When you own the factory outright everyone can whisper, or pass around a goddamn Speak and Spell. Now, tell me as she said exactly."

"She needs fresh direction."

"She needs her fucking head examined. From handbags. You know that? Esme came from handbags. *She's* going to tell me about direction in footwear."

"Everything's changing," I said.

He flung the leather swatch behind his shoulder and it slid down the wall. "Don't start. I've suffered enough, haven't I?"

He waited for the correct answer I never seemed to give. By now you'd think I knew the script. What was I supposed to say? You're dried up, your styles are outdated and plain. Midwest America wasn't going to stay in the '90s forever. In so many words, that was what Esme said. Why she called me and not him.

"Dad, I think we need to find a new angle. We're almost dead. We're on life support here."

Up came his pointer finger, but no words. For once, silence. Now was the time. I took a deep breath.

"I want to show you something," I said.

Nothing. His face was TV snow.

"You heard me?" I asked. "If she wants fresh, I've been working on something. Me and Bernie. I want to show you. I'd like to. In my office. If you think it's any good, maybe we pitch it to the buyers. I don't know. I want you to keep an open mind. You do that?"

He slowly brought his eyes down level with mine. "I'm always open."

"When Yong bought us double-layer milk curd off a food cart you were not *open*. You sang your 'It's not for me' song."

"Off the *street*, Alex. I said open, not crazy. I should stand on death's doorstep for milk curd?"

He followed me into my office where I'd arranged the styles on a sample table in the order I had them the previous night.

Dad walked over to the table and looked down. I couldn't read the expression on his face. He didn't touch anything yet. After a few moments, he reached down and picked the first one up—this picnic-basket weave of light gray and black. He felt the shape of the shoe with his fingers. Then along the insole and back seams like he was a blind man reading a face and the only way to know it was to touch every part.

"You and Bernie cooked this up?" he asked.

I nodded, watching him closely, having seen him handle thousands of shoes and knowing that he'd already made up his mind about the design and style, but his hands had to feel it for a while to understand the construction. A lot of high-minded designs never could translate to an assembly line. I was bouncing on my toes waiting for his answer.

"Can we talk about something important?" he said finally. Off came his glasses. "What's for lunch?"

My heels sank. I wanted to grab him by the throat and choke him. I shouldn't let it get to me, but this jolted me. I stared straight through him.

"Oh, you're serious about this?" he said, putting on his glasses again and picking the shoe back up.

"Well?" I said.

"I'm looking."

"At quality," I said.

"Why didn't you do an all-over black?"

"I wanted younger, peppier. I don't think we offer enough color. I believe in color blocking."

"Oh, that's a good name for your autobiography," he said. "*I Believe in Color Blocking: How I Became Such an Authority* by Alex Von Dickweed."

When he saw I wasn't biting, he leaned against the table.

"Okay, okay. It's not nothing. The Strobel, molded bottom, elastic upper—clever."

"That's it?" I said, squeezing my fists. "All you got for me?"

"You're no Saul Katz," he said and that really got under my skin too, but I also noticed he hadn't put the shoe down this whole time, in fact he was cradling the shoe like a bunny and petting it. So I couldn't let his stupid little jabs get to me. Had to stay calm.

"These are special," I said. "You see that, don't you, and you're just putting me on. Right? You see the quality. How different they are. These are the Cohains of shoes."

I said that just for him, and he couldn't resist a smile.

"Ha," he said, still holding the shoe. If he hated it, he'd have put it down by now. I'd seen him turn his seat around at meetings so as not to offend his eyes with bad styles on the table. It meant I had a little opening here.

"Listen," I said, "sit down, will you? You want coffee? Let me make you some."

"I'll have yours."

I set my coffee on a proper coaster just so he knew I understood the value of things. I asked if he was comfy, if he wanted a pillow for his back.

"Why do I have to sit?" he asked. "Nothing good comes from sitting. Only bad news. You're going to put me in a home? Is that it? Or you're marrying that Chinese farmer girl?"

"She's not a farmer for the millionth time. Just listen please. Okay? I want to start a brand."

His face pinched. "A brand?"

"Yes. A brand. That's where the equity is. It's my long-term plan, I guess you'd call it—for the factory. Let the brand drive the business."

Dad sat forward in his chair and rubbed his hand over his cheek, thinking.

He knew the subtext of course: to be competitive with a brand, we couldn't take a profit the first few years. But sometimes you needed to have two years of nothing to become Ralph Lauren—no, not just him, but to meld the two, Bernie and Zhang. To be both. The two could exist together. I could have it both ways and wouldn't even have to change my name.

"Have you lost your damn mind?" he said, sticking his hand down into the toe box and flexing it back and forth. "It takes years for a brand to turn a profit. Do you know how much capital we'd need? How about logos, marketing, sales. You got a website?"

"Bernie's at Blakes six years now, thanks to you. He *knows* sales. He'll pull a team."

"For free they work? I know you think you got this all figured out, but there's a lot of shit. You got a trademark? Vendors? No, you got bubkes. Lawyers for regulations, taxes? For *compliance*. Something you know *nothing* about. Let's start small. Did you get those new chinos hemmed like I asked? No. You can't even do that. And they are *great* pants. So how can you start a brand? Huh?"

He was baiting me. The old infant gambit. Stale but still lethal.

I gulped. Told myself to stay calm.

"Dad," I said. "I need your support. Got to have it."

"You *need* my factory. I'm chopped liver in this deal."

"I need *you*. Your ideas. Advice. No one hand-antiqued polyurethane until you. Who hand-antiques plastic? And then, I don't know, you're electrostatically flocking the shit out of polyurethane to look like nubuck—genius. I know that. So help me. Right now you're thinking with your head. Forget your head for a second. What's your gut say?"

"Go to lunch. Strangle son."

"This is a way forward. New direction."

Right now it was all economies of scale. Better was more and that's why it was all shit. Cheap labor and mass market. But it didn't have to be. You could slow down. Make quality.

"What's our biggest asset?" I asked. "The factory. We control the manufacturing, right? That's why a brand makes so much business sense. All I'm proposing is leveraging our experience and our factory."

"We just lost Snow Lite," he said. "A brand, if we were flush. If we were on a hot streak. But not now. Already tight on cash flow. The risk is too high. And just these few styles you've done."

"Of course more styles," I said. "This was just to give you an idea. A taste. You're right it's work, but I'm prepared to do it. I think it will hit. You got to learn to trust me. Look at me. Put that down."

He leaned away from me and wouldn't set the shoe down. Like a petulant child. *Mine.* Maybe it was a good sign if he didn't want to part with it, but then again, he wasn't looking at me.

"This is how you get big," I said. "It's entirely doable."

I placed my hand on his shoulder, and he startled a little and looked up with this strained face.

"What's going on here?" he said.

"What's what?" I asked, but I got a bad feeling in the pit of my stomach.

"We do casuals at my factory," he said. "We do leather and polyurethane. That's our niche. That's what *I* do. What I've always done. *My* expertise. You want to change the factory?"

"I never said that."

"You did worse. You made." He shook his head like he was tossing off a bad dream, and he started to rise out of his chair slowly, his chest all puffed out. "Threw it right in my face. All this done behind my back. You and Bernie. The kid who pissed on my wedding photo. This is who you trust? I think the two of you are pissing on *me*."

"Are you being funny?" I asked, less a question than a wish.

"No one's laughing. We have a reputation. We have a look. We make a certain kind of a shoe and we make them private label."

"We could make better. Am I wrong? Instead of playing up cheap shoes as more money, we could make better."

He took a step toward me, and I tried not to lean back but my hips opened.

"My shoes are crap?" he asked. "I'm learning a lot today from you. A real education."

"They're not crap, I didn't say crap," I stammered.

"We fill a need not a want," he said through a tight jaw. "Casuals for the masses. Mr. Heart Bleeds should appreciate this, but instead you want to change the factory's image. Our customer base. Something that took me *decades* to build. And, look, when I came up, I wanted to start my own brand. Eons ago. Every *nebbish* wants the same thing. You aren't the first. Got it? Nor are you the first guy to get a blow job from a Chinese farmer."

"How did you get like this?" I asked. "So awful."

"Because I tell the truth? Or because you don't like it? Sorry, Pollyanna. You think I'm stupid, but I know you. She put these ideas in your head. How do you like that? What you think you want is what *she* wants. She's playing you, you dip."

"I think you're jealous. That's what I think."

"Of you? Of her? The shoes? Don't start. I'm going to say this once. I know you're sensitive. This factory has a *feel*. Got it? A recognizable style. I run a respectable goddamn business. Don't show me novelty footwear again."

"These aren't fucking moon boots," I shouted. "They're casuals."

"How do I make it clear?" he said, slamming the shoe down on the desk to accentuate each word. "We do leather and polyurethane."

"It's a different direction," I said, trying to push back. "We're expanding. I thought you'd like that. You're losing sight—" But he cut me off.

"This?" he said, rattling the shoe over his head like a saber. "This is woven elastic gore. For a comfort shoe? Leather or polyurethane—that's my whole fucking business. In Tržič, we made *pearls*. Full aniline. Calfskins cut to the spine. Tight as a fucking drum to the last. That's what I brought here. Leather. The beautiful hand and grain. Pearls."

"You don't scare me yelling," I said, but I didn't believe that and he didn't either.

"Tiger Step is my *brand*," he shouted.

He picked up a measuring tape off the table and, pulling the tang out, poked me in the chest with it, saying, "Before me, the Chinese couldn't draw a hand turkey much less make a decent shoe."

"Uh-huh. The Messiah returns! Do you ever hear yourself?"

"Joke it up but it's true. Not Yong, not anyone. I taught them. And you know what they call me?"

"Who can forget?"

"Tell me." He poked me again in the chest. "I want to hear it." The tape suddenly slurped back into its sheath. "Jack Hong. Merry Xian. Alena Fan. These are *names* in the business. They'll tell you. Yong'll tell you."

Suddenly he reached across me, over my desk, and stamped his thumb down on the phone's intercom button. His smell wafted over me and I was having a hard time thinking straight. What was his smell? Schmaltz and cordovan. Old Jew. It made me nauseous and at the same time I wanted to bury my head in his neck and sleep.

A staticky *"Wei?"* came over the intercom.

"Yong, what did Jack and Merry call me? Back in Tai-chung."

Yong said, "The Emperor."

"Thank you," Dad said and slammed the button again.

"Got that? *Emperor.* Pick any department store in the States, and I had the window display. You understand? Not some shitty wall in the back, I got windows. *My* shoes. Snow fuck-ing Lite."

"It's in the past, Pops," I said, and that stopped him dead in his tracks.

His shoulders tensed.

"What the hell are you talking about, Alex?" he yelled. "The past? The past?"

"It means behind you. Face it, Dad. All of that's history. You're stuck back there. I mean, you even ride in the van backward. And you're going to bury us if you don't trust me to lead us forward."

"Where do you get the nerve? You know how long it took me to build this factory? For you to piss it away—no, I can't have it."

"Look, it's the same factory," I said. "I'm not asking to de-vote the whole fucking factory to this thing. Just a line or two. Relax. The plant will still make money. Leather and polyure-thane. Casuals. Our core business. All that stays. So I don't know why you're so upset."

"Why I am upset?" he stammered. "I got a *nayfish* son, a business in the tank and I haven't crapped in three days. Is that enough?"

"This is visionary, Dad," I said, holding my hand out flat

close to my chest, palm down, like that would somehow force my voice to stay calm and even.

"No," he said. "This is death. We just lost a big program, we can't afford to lose more. I won't be pushed. Not by you. Not by—" And he started coughing and pointed at my water bottle on the desk. In a thin, hoarse voice, asking, "You mind?"

I handed him the bottle. He took a sip.

"Thank you," he said, all polite and civilized, before going right back to yelling, "Forget it. Ain't happening. No way, *bubelah*. Not on my watch. Do you even have vendors for this elastic gore?"

"Where do you think I got it? Of course. But I'm thinking we can make our own, here. More vertical integration, more hours for workers, more business—"

"You want to make this crap? Elastic? That's even worse. Did I wrong you? Do you not love me? I know we're in a slump, but you don't just leap for the throat the minute someone's weak. I mean, you do, you should, but not *my* throat. Them. Out there."

He pointed to the window.

"Who the fuck is *them*?" I said. "We're not against a *them*. Look, no one likes change. I wish everything could stay, but it can't. It's not uncommon when you get older—"

"Oh, blow it out your ass," he said. "Not uncommon. You sound like a snob. Whose voice is that? You went to college. Am I supposed to be intimidated?"

"I need your blessing," I said.

"*Baruch atah*, it won't sell."

"You don't know that."

"This is for a different factory. Here, I call the shots," he said, taking one last step toward me so I could feel his belly against mine. His lip quivered. That big nose like an old crooked stovepipe, saying he was all soot and rust inside. A hardness to the man you didn't fuck with. What could I do? It was a ruthless world. That's why Dad was good. Because he was ruthless right back with it. Maybe I just didn't have it.

I took a long step back away from him and leaned against the desk.

He glared at me for a second. "I win," he rasped, stabbing his thumb on his sternum. "I always win."

"Mazel tov," I said.

Dad dragged himself over to the window behind my desk and leaned toward the glass, stretching his neck toward the upper-hinged sash of the window as I'd often seen him do in the hotel. Nose in the air. Trying to get fresh air.

I heard him sigh. "What did I do wrong," he said under his breath, looking out over the dirty-gray city.

"Okay," he said, spinning around to face me. "Let me see the fucking shoes again."

I rushed over with the strongest style, the wedge, and waited silently with my hands behind my back.

"Lose these dimples," he muttered, like he was talking to himself. "Crepe sole. Too much busy stuff. A little more extension, little more framing. Maybe cork sidewalls."

"I like sandblasted," I said.

He arched an eyebrow. "Your brain's blasted."

"This is my—" But my voice trailed off and I was thinking, Don't push him away. He's about to bite.

"It's good," he said. "You said you wanted my help?"

I nodded. He was quiet for a moment, thinking, and I tried reading his face, what was in his head. He was interested. No question.

"You told anyone else about this?" he asked.

"No."

"Bernie told anyone?"

I shook my head.

"He's got a big fucking mouth. You sure?"

"No. Yeah. Bernie didn't say shit. Why would he?"

"I'm asking. So we don't get ripped off. It happens when you run your mouth. I floated the Ecco shoes idea to Ben Kaplan in the *schvitz* once—then I blinked my fucking eyes and he was buying his father a hundred-twenty-foot yacht and house on the Cape. It happens."

Now was the time to speak up. Say to him: To really give this brand a chance, you know we got to do it no-profit for a time. I know you like private label. It's safe and easy. But this is a different thing. My thing. When you passed the plant to me, when I signed with my clothes stinking of the river we poison, eating all the Chinese food you don't understand, when I signed my name—this was why. I was signing my name to this perfect fucking shoe.

I felt these words gathering in me. Ready to speak. Spit it out now. As soon as I opened my mouth to speak, Dad cut me off.

"Good design," he said. "But this is no brand, you know that."

My legs went rubbery. Until the very last second he waited.

"We can't take profits for maybe two years—you know that's impossible. Tell you what, I'm going to take this thing and make money on it the way I know how, my normal lines of distribution, but listen to me, I want to tell you how proud I am."

"You mean private label," I said, a numbness running over my skin. "Not branded."

"Of course. It's the smart option. Abelson's puts up the line of credit. They pay freight and first cost. They're the importer of record. It's *their* ass on the line. Not ours. We have security. Your way, if the whole thing flops, *we* eat it."

"I understand that," I said, gritting my teeth. But we were

giving away our designs. Everything we made was owned by someone else.

"Okay, well, it sounds like you don't understand. I can only go off how you sound. And you sound confused."

"I'm not confused."

"Then what are you?" he asked, scrunching up his face.

"I don't know. Everything's fuzzy."

"Well, unfuzz. Listen, Alex, you're getting bent out of shape over nothing. This isn't personal. It's business. You've done a beautiful job, now leave it to me. Okay? We're going to make your line. That's the point, isn't it? That's what you wanted, right?"

"Sure," I said. I was just staring straight ahead. No. That wasn't what I wanted. It was taking a lot of energy to stand there.

"Alex," he said, smiling. "This I like." He pointed to the first shoe lined up on the table. "Reminds me of a Stuart Weitzman. Nice lines here at the low point, and this one, you got textures, good detailing. I'm very content."

"You like them?" I asked, but as soon as it was out of my mouth I wished I could take it back. Groveling again. Just what he wanted.

"You kidding? You did great. I don't think I've said that enough. Couldn't be more proud of you." His chin lowered. Looking at me over the top of his glasses. "Hey, I'd say that even if you weren't my son. That you're my son makes it all the better. You're way ahead of where I was at your age."

I felt myself straightening up. It felt good to hear even if I didn't want it to. It really did.

"You're not bullshitting?" Someone would probably say if you had to ask, you already knew the answer. So what? I knew he'd cut my balls off the minute I tried to grow some, anticipating the very moment and snip—I got that, but this other thing felt real good. A little pat on the head. For once. How long had you been after it? How far? All your frantic dog-paddling halfway around the world just to hear your father say you weren't a turd. To pry one fucking ruby of kindness out of his throat. That was all I really wanted, right? So we were equals now, he said as much, and there was nothing to feel ashamed about anymore.

"What I think doesn't matter anyhow," he said. "Forget a hundred-twenty-foot yachts—*this* is the dream. Family business." He rubbed my shoulder, a big smile on his face. "So we got a deal?"

"Okay," I said, backing down.

Maybe to an outsider I sounded chickenshit, but it was honestly stupid to try to get everything in one shot. Let him get attached to the design first. Then I could chip away at him. Make him see it was the perfect stand-alone brand. A shoe-dog adjusted on the fly, midpitch, and that was all I was doing. Adjusting my plan. I hadn't given up, hell no; I was taking the long way around.

When learning to become an old shoe-dog, these were the things you did. All of us, we were charred inside from the same fire—I don't know from where—maybe some Podunk shtetl pine-fire, maybe a place much darker. But it was the same. You couldn't scour it out of us.

Dad was gushing now. "The sandal, the Mary Jane, peep-toe wedge—beautiful stuff. You were playing music last night, boy. All different notes. But I want *you* to be proud. Don't do shit for me. Will you remember?"

Before I could answer, I heard that noise again. Coming from outside. Music piped in over loudspeakers in the yard.

We both turned our heads toward the window.

A Chinese military marching song. A song that made you think about Red Guard youth with their arms around each others' shoulders. Chins up. Boots polished. What you'd listen to if you didn't care if you lived or died.

My phone trilled. Ivy's name flashed across the top of the screen—and my skin went cold. Warning me maybe about the demonstration. Tomorrow? I fumbled for the silence button and dropped it on the rug.

"What's wrong with you?" Dad said.

"I stayed up all night making these," I said.

"Take the rest of the day off, will you? You're a man, not an elf. You're no good to me like this. Rest up."

He started pushing me in the small of the back toward the door, saying goodbye, but I was leaning back, dragging my feet, making my body go heavy.

"Everything's an ordeal with you," he said, edging me toward the door. "I thought you have children and the children love you. Simple."

"There's way too much going on," I said.

He stopped pushing for a second. "Interesting," he said.

Then he gave one last hard shove and slammed the door behind me.

So I was in the corridor, outside my own office, staring at the wood door and wondering what the fuck just happened. And it slowly started dawning on me that he did it. Exactly what Bernie and I had feared.

I rode the elevator down to the ground floor trying to understand how it had happened, how I could undo it. I stepped out into the yard. In the humidity, it felt like I was swimming toward my house and I patted my pockets for my wallet and stopped, remembering that I'd left it upstairs. So I did a quick about-face and went back to my office, relieved to see that Dad was gone. I scooped up my wallet, and right before I left I stopped short. The table was empty. All my samples were missing.

For a moment the floor seemed to slant, my knees buckled—everything in me, on the table, vanished. He'd taken them. Dad. Taken what I made and scurried off.

My hands were trembling.

The motherfucker ripped me off. After that whole speech about Ben Kaplan, the hypocrite still took them. Buttered me up and swiped them from under my nose.

I paused, trying to be logical—maybe he just brought them to his office. Which didn't mean anything necessarily—that he took them. Not on the face of it.

But it did. It meant everything.

He slid me right into the Fedor machine and spit me out. It shouldn't matter that he took them out of my office without asking or giving a reason, but I felt fucking gutted. I couldn't put anything of myself into this factory. It was Fedor's show. His factory. His vision. The shoes were gone. I was gone. My stake in this plant. Standing here like a dumbshit *gweilo* who just crawled out of the Pearl River. It wasn't my factory. I understood. There was no use pushing for the brand later. I'd give the designs to Bernie to take to Magotan or Gold Valley. Why should Dad make a penny off it?

My whole I'm-just-a-shoe-dog-adjusting-on-the-fly rationale I'd told myself—man, what a load of horseshit. Stop lying to yourself, Alex. You wimped out. Wake up and face it, he'll always run you over.

I walked out of my office without even closing the door behind me and rode the elevator down and stepped out into the yard.

Across the way, from under the arcade of the canteen, the workers were swarming into the courtyard to punch the shift clocks. Hundreds of them returning to work, a sea of people between me and my house and nowhere else for me to go but into them.

I walked straight into the crowd, the current thickening around me. All of them straining, jostling to punch their time cards, every second costing money. I felt their closeness and smelled their sweat. Dad hadn't said no to my ideas, he'd devoured them. What were my choices now? Submit or get lost. Nothing would change—that was what I realized—squeezing through the current, catching flashes of a few faces: a boy's lips moving silently like he was still counting dwell time on the sole press machine; a young girl with plastic shavings garlanding her hair. I knocked shoulders with an old aunty in a floral smock and a wobbly head, the rictus of a benzene smile, she was in there, somewhere, thrashing. Time for their drowsy eyes to widen briefly—nothing more—before I was past them.

These were the people I cared about. The workers. This flow of bodies pressed tight around me. The ones suffering because of me. So if I was going to bitch and moan about the system we profited from, then I'd better be willing to do something about it. If I wasn't a hypocrite, I had to pick up the microphone. Make a moderate speech. Go public with it all. Every wrong against the Chinese workers. Nothing to lose now. I'd call on all the factory owners in Foshan and in Guangzhou, the whole Pearl Delta, to get it right. And if that ruined Dad, if it fucked the whole business, I couldn't say I cared anymore. What was the business to me now? This black emptiness I was hurtling toward. Why play nice anymore? Why be the good Jewish boy? For what? To carry Dad's legacy? So I could be some walking urn. His musty hope chest, smelling of pine and old tea, aromas of the old country. No way. This man treated me just like he treated the workers. He could be a shithead—*was* a shithead. Shocking how long it'd taken me to realize. It was nothing personal, Dad. I'd tell him that too. Tell him to hurry up and get into grapefruit spoons before the market closed.

I spilled out of the crowd and jogged to the corner of the canteen on a sunny quarter-triangle of pavement facing the sky—a little clearing, a crisp triangle of light. I took my phone out of my pocket, scrolling down, and I pressed my thumb over Zhang's name, and while it rang I lifted my face to the sky. It wasn't going to rain today. That was a real stupid thing to think in a moment like this, with the phone ringing, so I looked down at the pavement and made a quick spin, but I couldn't see my shadow. Nobody threw a shadow in Foshan— I'd been here long enough to know that, not with all the grit and smog—but it only registered now as a conscious thought that chilled my skin. And I heard Zhang saying my name. Saying hello? Is this you? My tongue was dry, pressed hard against the back of my teeth, and Zhang was saying my name, how many times, thumping in my ear, and before he could hang up, I said, "I'll talk." Then I said it again, louder. "I want to talk."

Sixteen

IN THE MORNING, I WAS EXPECTING TO HEAR it: a crowd, music, megaphones but it was quiet. I moved down the cool blue brick alley between dorms and stepped out into the courtyard. No Zhang or Ivy, no demonstrators. Just some stray dogs licking ropy cow guts out of the storm water drains, a cook carrying a basket of watercress to the canteen. When I'd called Zhang he told me only to be ready, but he hadn't given me a day. It wasn't today. I was relieved by that. There was still time to get to Ivy, tell her what I'd decided.

Up on the third floor of Plant C, I toed the cyclone fence, put my nose right in one of the diamonds, searching the workers on the production line but I didn't see Ivy inside the cage—that's what it was, it struck me, a cage. I nodded to the manager at his desk. He opened the hinged wire door, and I walked down the line to the stitchers at the far end of the floor.

The workers were sitting on either side of a long metal table and I spotted Ivy from the back wearing my old JCC basketball T-shirt, our names in flaky white plastisol on the back: Goldstein, Jablonski, Cohen—the "Lynn All-Schnoz" my mother liked to tease.

Sensing me beside her stool, Ivy's hands froze on her Golden Wheel sewing machine and then she went back to stitching zippers into boots. I was looking down at the white centerline of her scalp and the tip of her ear glowing red, poking up through her hair tied back in a ponytail, and I felt a great love for her, our closeness, even if she wouldn't look up at me, or maybe it was for that very reason.

The muscles in my neck relaxed. She was here and safe. Of course why wouldn't she be, but she was, that's all, and this must have been the reason I came up here, not to ask her about the demonstration. Just to stand by her. To keep everything the way it was for a little longer, even if it couldn't stay that way forever. I knew that. And I knew I couldn't talk to her here in front of the other workers, so I picked up one of her finished pieces and pretended to inspect her work, but then, because I couldn't help it, I found myself actually looking at the boot in my hands.

Fat marks on the leather. Streaking. The vamp and shaft almost two different colors. Cheap split leather. From the cow's neck. Bound to buckle.

This was what I'd tried to move Dad, move *us*, away from. But Dad wouldn't listen. He devoured. So, right. It was the other path now.

I tossed the shitty boot into the plastic basket on the table. I didn't need to notice anymore. Not shoes at least.

The boy across from Ivy sensed me reading his name tag— Liu Jianbin—and he lifted his head, our eyes met just for a beat before he looked away. He had spikey hair, real sharp cheekbones, denim shirt with the sleeves cut off and a gristly nub on his left hand where his index finger ought to have been. Splitting machine, maybe. Embossing plate.

His white jade bracelet clinked against the glass cutting board as he skived the leather with a flat razor.

I started walking down the line when a cell phone rang.

My eyes snapped up and the only one on the line who met them was Jianbin. The razor frozen in his hand.

The phone trilled again and Jianbin reached into his pocket for his phone, fumbled with it, hands shaky, and groped for the silence button, and set the phone on the table. It was an iPhone. Thin. Brand-new.

He was one of Ivy and Zhang's twenty-four. The secret group.

Jianbin looked down at the flashing number. Then up at me, straightening, like someone had pressed a cold stethoscope to his back. The silence between us stretched out. We held our looks. Not even a breath. A moment longer. Then longer.

I nodded at the phone sitting on the table. To tell Jianbin I knew what I was seeing. To say: It's okay, I support you. Jianbin gave me a halting smile. His four-fingered hand slowly covered his phone and slid it off the table back into his pocket.

But Production Manager Shen was already beside me, shaking his stopwatch, red in the face. "No phone! In factory, no phone. Understand?"

Shen turned and looked at me. "So lazy it break my heart."

I told him it was okay. Don't worry.

"This last chance," Shen said to Jianbin. "You want money with success? Last chance."

But Jianbin ignored his production manager and started humming into the popped collar of his jean vest, that same marching tune I kept hearing, swaying a little in his chair.

Shen's mouth swung open, quivering for a second. "Deduction!" he yelled, pointing at Jianbin. "No singing!"

Down the line, a girl snickered.

"Deduction," Shen shouted again, pointing in her general direction. More giggles. "All you. Deduction trouble. Must be strong."

Ivy leaned away from her machine. The bobbin unwound, the rubber belt fluttered to a stop. I saw the tips of her fingers pressed white against the table.

"That's enough," I said to Shen. "Calm down."

So he started yelling at the workers in Chinese, as he would normally if I wasn't here for him to show off.

Right then I heard the scrape of the stool against the cement floor and Ivy stood up. She slowly untied the apron knot behind her back and lifted the loop over her head.

"Where is restroom permit?" said Shen.

Ivy folded her apron neatly in half and placed it down on the table. The machines fell silent as she walked the length of the whole production line, past me and Shen, past the inspectors, past the manager by the gate, whose pen slowly slipped out of his mouth and rolled onto the floor. She opened the fence and walked out.

So, I was right. It was today.

And I had to resist an urge to smile. Maybe even I set it in motion by calling Zhang. That was fine. It was what I wanted. Still something was gnawing at me; if Zhang wanted me involved so badly, you'd think he'd give me an exact date—but that thought broke off when Jianbin stood up.

He pulled the hand-sewn finger guards off and cut Manager Shen a look of complete contempt, and walked for the door.

"Where you go?" Shen asked him, pulling self-consciously at the front of his shirt to get it to sit up on his shoulders. "You go back here. Hey! Hey, you like McMuffin? Then you go back!" The tips of his hair were wet with sweat. "Hey! You like green tea Frappuccino? You want good future. Sit work!"

Jianbin briefly looked back, not at Shen but at a girl. Another stitcher. Tinted tortoise-rim glasses, very thin. She nervously touched the silver cross necklace on her neck, and slowly stood up.

"Sit down!" Shen shouted.

She looked at Shen, then me, then back at Shen. Sweat pooling in the pockets below her eyes. Her shoulders turned toward the door, as if every few degrees she was measuring

Shen's reaction and, realizing there was nothing he could do to stop her, she went toward the exit.

"Stop!" Shen yelled, fumbling for the whistle tucked inside his shirt, and blowing it, shrill and loud, he stormed after them.

I glanced down at Ivy's empty stool. The seat paint stripped from the hundreds of workers who'd sat here and I couldn't help touching it. A shallow scoop, smooth as river rock. I didn't know why, but I sat down. On Ivy's stool. Right in front of her Golden Wheel, and around me I saw the stares of the kids, the shovel-faced rage scraping them up inside.

They were on the move now.

The line managers yelled at the shuffle of heavy feet. Maybe half of the workers stood up and walked. The whole building seemed to sway as they headed down the stairs.

Hongjin, my friend from purchasing with the scar on his chest that my father touched—he was over by the manager's desk rocking back and forth on his heels. He looked over at me—a Yancheng drooping from his corner lip and his left eye squinting even though the cigarette was unlit—and I gave him a quick nod. Barely anything. It's okay. It's fine.

A beat of hesitation, but then he gave me a flick of his chin and fell in behind the queue of workers headed for the door.

I turned to the window facing Plant A. They were coming down too.

A few stools down from me, one girl was left. The only one from Ivy's line who stayed. Very dark skin. Cheeks sunken. She was looking at me, but I didn't have any sense of what was on my face. She cranked the flywheel and the Golden Wheel shuddered to life, the pedal squeaking—letting me know she'd keep working no matter what happened.

I lifted myself off the stool and started to the stairs and I had to remind myself why I was going out there. I was done here. Sorry, Dad, but these aren't the faces of people who give a shit if Andrew Carnegie started in a textile factory—buck fifty a week shoveling coal—saving every penny. No one believes you anymore when you say their time will come. It's either now or it ain't coming.

So, it's now, I reminded myself as I slipped through the cyclone fence and down into the stairwell, when I heard someone shout my name. I looked up.

One flight up, Dad was leaning over the railing.

"Hey, you're going the wrong way," he said. "Get the hell up here. You see what's happening? A strike. Honest to God. Where the hell you going?"

"Out there," I said.

"What the hell for?" he squealed. "To apologize? Are you crazy? We don't beg. Not to people like that. Get up here and let the police handle it."

"Don't call the police."

"Are you nuts?"

"Let's hear them first."

"Alex. Please."

I took a step down. "I'm not chasing you," he said, stretching a little farther over the railing to keep me in sight.

I took another step down. "I can't," I said, midstep. The diagonal slice of the stairwell severed his neck, then his face vanished, and I started hurrying down the stairs two at a time. Maybe Dad had already called the police? Or he was about to? Either way I had to find Zhang and Ivy and warn them.

Outside, a tumult of cheering, shouting. If Zhang was anywhere he'd be up there, near the front. I forced my way through the crowd. Red tongues. Yellow armbands. Workers with wood placards strung around their necks. Words in scab-red paint, English and Chinese, 我要作人 *I will be a person.* I turned for a second and coming straight at me, head level, was a wide white bedsheet, red paint: 围观 *Surround and Watch,* and I ducked as the bottom of the banner slipped over my head, brushing my hair.

I was wheeled along by the workers' marching toward the front gate. Everyone pushing in that direction. Where the fuck were Zhang and Ivy in all this?

I looked up. Fourth floor of my building and Dad was in the window looking down on me. His hands pressed against the glass. No body. Just his white face and hands. A bedsheet banner dropped from the roof opposite him and in the window I could read the paint backward across his chest: 合鞋 *#FittingShoe*.

Up in the fire escapes and squatting along the ledge of the roof, workers were filming live on their iPhones. A girl climbed up on a company van and aimed the red phone light at me, then a thump on my side: a woman's right shoulder—a green butterfly beneath the strap of her overalls—slipping past. A crunch under my foot—broken sunglasses.

Another surge and I was spun right into the face of Die Jo, our former foot model turned Poker Committee Chair.

"Oh, Mr. Younger Cohen," she said. "Where you hide that gorgeous face?" The words came out slowly, like she was remembering them from a film.

"*Sunset Boulevard,*" she added, bringing a cigarette to her mouth and, over her shoulder, for a second, I saw *Goldstein* in white plastisol. My T-shirt. Ivy.

"Got to go," I said, trying to step around Die Jo, but I was cut off by demonstrators on both sides and Ivy vanished in the flick of Die Jo's lighter.

"Fuck," I said.

"Don't be a wet blanket, dollface," Die Jo said, blowing menthol in my face.

The crowd roared. I snapped my head to the sound.

Zhang sailed out on the bow pulpit of one of our rolling ladders, wearing a green cape coat and a cloth cap, gripping the handrails, like some shit you'd see in the National Museum, Mao crossing the Yellow River, and my legs wobbled. I had to reach him fast.

I dipped my shoulder and wedged my way through the crowd, prying open seams with my hands, squeezing through, zigzagging, and up near the front I saw the four boys pushing the rolling ladder like it was a royal palanquin carrying Emperor Zhang. Trailing them were another few boys pushing two wheelbarrows full of shoe lasts and cement glue cans. Suddenly I heard the feedback squeal of a PA system and Zhang's deep voice saying *Ni hao* into the microphone.

All the hairs on my arm stood up. The crowd constricted around me.

I was too late.

"Comrades," he said, "we are not shit youth. We are true Chinese."

He spoke first in Chinese and then translated himself into English for the YouTube audience.

Everyone cheered and stamped their feet.

"Democracy lives in our hearts," he said. "Remember the poet's word, comrades, 'I am no hero. In an age without heroes, I want to be a man.' Bei Dao wrote this on the fateful date we don't have the freedom to say out loud or type into a computer. Forced to say May 35. But it was June 4. Just because our voice is small, how can we not speak it? I was there as a boy. Twenty-five years later what changed? Some very few people are very rich. Not migrant workers. Not you. You built the path—where is your reward?"

The crowd cheered.

Ivy made her way to the platform, wearing a red armband, and she took the microphone. She said, first in Chinese, then translating herself into English, "Workers of Tiger Step, today we write a new of China history. We are starving of basic human rights, social insurance, citizenship, and we demand change. We deserve equal treatment to workers in America or Japan. We ask workers all over world to support us and join us."

There was a low rumble and everyone turned to the side

alley. Out came this faux marble pillar, fifteen feet tall, like those columns around the Forbidden City with some kind of griffin on top except as it drew closer, this one had a toad's body and a human face. Chinese face. Gang's face it looked like to me. My stomach dropped. When it drew closer, I saw that it was shaped like a boot, slogans written down the shaft.

Ivy waited for the cheering to settle and said, "In the old days we used these *huábiǎo* to criticize government. Ordinary people like us. Writing on the statue to speak against injustice. Few years ago, in speech on national development, President Xi Jinping says, 'Only the wearer knows if the shoe fits.' Every Chinese remembers this. This is the meaning of the Fitting Shoe Movement. We say to our government and our factory bosses and the world—bad fit. The future only we can choose. We must have say in the fit of our country. In our path. What is our historical fate? This is what we must decide for ourselves today and tomorrow. We are here with peaceful hearts. We are in love with the future of China. This is why we are here."

She quieted the crowd with her arms.

"Today is special unique because we have the support of our factory."

I felt my throat clench.

"Let us hear from Mr. Younger Cohen," Ivy said.

The crowd murmured as I pushed my way to the front, past the boot *huábiǎo*. I staked my foot on the first step of the ladder and the railing wobbled. Zhang and Ivy were on the platform above.

I took another step up. And there was Zhang beside her, gold buttons down his cape, a red star on his cap. Ivy reached out the microphone to me, smiling. In her red armband and my ridiculous JCC shirt. Why would she wear that today? For me. The same way I was here for her. What we talked about the other night after sex. What we understood about each other. My factory, her vision. Equals.

The ladder swayed.

I felt this invisible thread from the fourth floor window tugging on my chin. Couldn't bring myself to look. My resolve could slip. No, I was doing what was right. Supporting the workers. The shoe didn't fit. So you had to speak. Couldn't be afraid of fathers four stories tall.

Don't look, I told myself, but my eyes skipped to the window. He was there. I turned away immediately. Kept climbing.

On top of the platform I took the microphone from Ivy, covered it with my palm and leaned in toward Zhang.

"Fedor called the police," I said.

Ivy took a sharp breath but there was a half grin on Zhang's face, like an ax stuck in a trunk.

"No problem," Zhang said. "Peaceful hearts." He nodded his head. "Is true," he said. "This is normal. Police come."

I looked at Ivy.

She nodded. "We go on."

A few moments passed between the three of us and then I felt the weight of the workers' eyes on my back.

"Go ahead," said Ivy, nodding to the crowd. "I translate."

I took a deep breath and turned into a rustle of warm air. All that wide air between me and the demonstrators and the iPhones filming. My ankles turned out. Shins sweating. The workers pushed forward to listen, their faces upturned, banners bobbing on stakes. The microphone heavy in my hand.

"These two people," I shouted, and hearing myself through the PA speakers, how strange and loud I sounded, I dropped the line. The echo still clanging in my chest. I stood there, feet wide apart and the only words in my brain were *these two people* like they were the only words one can say and they'd rush up and roll back into my lungs forever. Ivy and Zhang. What the fuck did it even mean? Where was I going with it?

But then Ivy took the microphone out of my hand and translated it into Chinese, which was worse.

Dead silence. My throat went dry. Their faces gaping at me. The crowd. My father. Out of my periphery. His lips moving. I could imagine him saying: *Son of some other man. The factory put you through college and this is how you repay me?*

Forget him. Be honest.

I felt the microphone in my hand again.

"We need to do better," I said. I leaned forward against the guardrail. "The management. The government. Me."

Ivy repeated what I said in Chinese.

Dad was banging on the glass. I wasn't imagining it.

"We need to see you as full citizens of Foshan," I continued. "Not just migrant workers, but a big part of what makes this city run and grow. That starts with us returning all your IDs and paying back your social insurance." Then I paused because I hadn't expected to say anything like that and in my head I wasn't even sure if it was possible, but I wanted it to be. This would be my last act before I left. I had to leave. I'd give the workers their IDs back, and then they could leave too. If that ruined the business for Dad, too bad. He should've listened to me.

"If we don't do better, you'll leave. Find other work." I was almost planting the idea in their heads. Walk out. "But then all these jobs will move to India or Vietnam and that's bad for the future of China."

As Ivy was translating, I felt my throat tighten. I thought, No, wait. Wait a minute. This isn't right. I have a chance here. A real chance to do the thing Dad never could. Walking out doesn't solve anything. It's the same shit down the street, same at every factory. You made the choice to be here. No one forced you. You signed the papers. How long are you going to fight with him like a little kid?

The brand was the solution. It's what would please the workers, please the Chinese government, please the bottom line.

I was doing this for all of us, wasn't I? No, I wasn't doing it. We were.

My factory, her vision. I was up here to show them we could work together. The idea that an American businessman could do right wasn't just quixotic. We could move forward together. That's why I was up here. To make things right. Or if not right, better.

Ivy handed the microphone back to me.

I said, "You're the ones sticking your necks out. This is a huge chance you're taking by being here. Standing here. It's incredibly brave. You're putting your lives on the line. Your livelihoods too. But I can do things at this plant that can help us."

On reflex, my eyes ticked up to the fourth floor. "What goes out the door doesn't have to be shit," I said, and I realized I was talking to him too. "There's no reason for it. Everyone knows, you give Chinese engineers a product to copy and no problem—it's perfect. But that's the problem. We're letting knockoffs hold us back."

There were a few heads nodding in the crowd. Mostly tight, worried faces.

I took a deep breath.

"We need our own ideas. We need our own brand. We need to want to think for ourselves."

It was true for our business, I thought, waiting for a smattering of claps to die down. True for China. And me. Certainly me. I glanced up to the window. Dad shaking his arms over his head, dragging his finger across his throat.

And suddenly I recognized what was going on. My throat went dry.

I turned back to the crowd.

"No, I'm sorry, I said that wrong. Let me rephrase it. When I said *we* I meant me and that guy in that window up there. I don't mean that now. I don't mean that anymore. I mean we. You and I. We need a brand. We need to make this together but it's going to be a recognizable Chinese brand. So I designed a new style. But it's just as much yours. And the next shoe, I want you to be part of the design process. We can do this with the right training. Elevate everyone."

Then I stopped abruptly because I knew the next words out of my mouth were going to be about shoes and developing our own commodities—but that's not what they needed. They needed Ivy.

I turned to her.

"I've said enough. I'm here with you as a partner."

She looked me in the eyes as I passed her the microphone. She nodded. Her eyes firm and clear. "Thank you," she said under her breath. "You understand."

She turned to face the crowd and I stepped back, off to her side, as she began translating what I'd said into Chinese. The crowd cheered and clapped.

I stopped looking over at Dad altogether. Fedor. He treated the world like his own piñata: club at it blindfolded, and when the candy falls, grab what you can. Because we were Cohains. Because divine election was always there like a thick pane of glass to hide behind. So swing away, boychick. But it wasn't about that. It wasn't about becoming Ralph fucking Lauren. I was wrong about that. Because what did we, me, my ancestors—what did we make all these fucking shoes for? To lift the boot off our own neck only to slam it down on someone else's? No. I couldn't believe that. I refused.

Then I heard Ivy speaking in English for the videos: "If we make it work here, other factories in China will follow our example however they can. But we don't want trouble. We don't want to clash with the government. This is why we must work together. Shared prosperity. We can move forward in harmony. Not bullshit harmony but something closer to what you deserve."

I took it all in as she translated herself into Chinese: the clapping and stomping, the workers sawing their banners up and down, the bedsheets rippling, trembling like they were going to leap out of the workers' hands.

"The way we think about ourselves," Ivy continued. "This must change. It is not up to the foreigners or the government. This must come from us. We spent centuries in a class of people on the margins of society, of wealth. Outsiders. Ghosts. We have to change how we see ourselves. This plant can be an example to China of how democracy can look. The Fitting Shoe Movement is not only about extra yuan or health care or benefits. It is who we are. Our strength. Chairman Mao dreamed of the endless creative power of the masses, but we have never lived up to those high ideals. Equal opportunity. China as one people. As harmony—"

Ivy stopped suddenly. She was right of course, about everything, but something had tripped her up. Her face tensed as if she hadn't said quite the right thing. She looked down for a moment. Her thoughts seemed to shift. Pondering. Then she glanced over at me and I felt something unfolding in her and between us, some deep unspoken thing, and then she turned back to the crowd.

"Wait," she said, "I say these things and they are true. But this is how politicians talk. Same in Beijing or Washington, DC, or Moscow. These are not my words and they are not yours. Here is what you and I understand—tonight, very tired, each of us goes back to the same dormitories. We hear each other sleeping and dreaming. We live together. Then in the morning we all put our feet on the floor and into our shoes and at that moment they are our shoes. Not only theirs. And we are this plant. What we put into the world from this plant carries part of us. This is the Fitting Shoe Movement. When I was a little girl, Grandfather first told me the story of the Peach Blossom Spring. Everyone know this myth. A land beyond this world. Food and water for everyone and peace.

Where ghosts and the living are equal. People say it is a dream. It sound insane, people say. But, workers, listen to me, is it insane to hold an acorn in your hand and say, 'This is the beginning of a great peach tree.' Is that insane? No great tree ever shoots to life full grown. This is our plant. All we have control of. This is what utopia looks like for us. Where we have enough to live. Enough to go home and see family. The work we do here is who we are and we can be proud. We can create. Let us be here in a way that carries in it the roots of this great thing that could be. That is not crazy. Is it? This is the way it happens. Why we video record it. To give other plants and managers and investors and workers in China our vision. Every tree must know what it is."

The moment she finished translating this into Chinese the crowd roared so loud I could feel it rattling in the back of my neck.

She turned to me and smiled.

Then I watched as Ivy lifted her arm and made a fist. I faced the crowd. Their fists were high too, stained indigo, black, violet, green—dyes from the pigment spray-guns—and with their arms held high, Ivy started singing "Internationale," the workers joining in, all their voices swelling up, rising as one, their eyes fixed on me to see what I'd do, so I raised my fist too and I opened my mouth and sang. Even though I didn't know the words. Even though my voice is for shit. I sang it loud. What slipped into my head was the old synagogue where I used to fake-sing Hebrew songs all the time to make my dad and grandmother happy. Right now I strained my throat and mimicked the shape of Ivy's mouth, humming the tune—same way I used to do it back in synagogue—convincingly, selling the damn thing to the point where I almost believed I was really singing "Internationale" in Chinese with the Democratic Revolutionary Party—but suddenly the chorus was sheared off by the hammering of engines behind me.

I snapped my head around. Beyond the gate I saw them coming and all my certainty dissolved.

Policemen in black helmets and gas masks, batons and clear shields, fifty men maybe, marching up the road leading to our gate, a hundred yards off. Splitting now into two platoons, off to either side of the scrub along the road, and a green Humvee driving up between them.

My throat clutched and I reached for Ivy's hand but only grazed air. She was scrambling down the ladder to join the demonstrators who were retreating into the yard in panic.

Suddenly Zhang snatched the microphone out of my hand and shouted in both languages to keep filming. "Stay your ground!" he said. "Document greatness!"

He was signaling up to the roofs and I followed his finger. Bodies, dark forms, moved along the tops of the roofs, crouching, smartphones poised to shoot video, another sliding on her knees to the edge of the roof to get into position. Climbing up onto the hoods of the company vans, leaning out of the factory windows with their smartphones. Every angle.

The sound of the engine grew louder.

"We need to close the gate," I yelled to Zhang.

He stared at me for a moment, his face jutting forward like he was peering into the darkness. Then he turned back to the crowd and shouted, "Look up! See the sky glow red. A good omen. Don't be afraid. This is the Will of Heaven."

"Zhang," I said, grabbing his shoulder. "You hear me? We got to keep them apart."

"My friend," he said, taking my hand off him. "You knew the risk. They are coming into the factory."

He was standing straight and still, face blank, like there was nothing left to say and nothing to hide now anyway.

I balled my fists on reflex—he *wanted* the police to come in. Of course he did. And he'd lied to me, but there was no time for it now. Nothing was holding the two sides back. I needed to close the gate.

I ran down the rolling ladder, fast as I could without tumbling over, and sprinted the twenty yards past the wide-open slatted gate and threw my shoulder into the door of the security hut, but I stumbled backward. Locked. The button to close the gate was just inside. I shook the handle. Banged on it. But the door wouldn't give.

The gate was already open. No way to get to the controls.

I could hear the engine snarling, the grind of the Humvee's gears as it clawed closer, and I heard the steady scuff of those heavy Goodyear welt army boots. I turned around, my back flat against the door, right as the Humvee, flanked by police, came to a stop fifteen yards from the mouth of the gate across from the bloc of demonstrators. Maybe only thirty yards between the two groups now.

The Humvee door opened, it was quiet now, no one so much as breathing, and it was Gang himself who stepped onto the running board so he stood higher than the truck roof. He was wearing a green military cap, cotton jacket with gold epaulets and a green tie.

I crouched down, knees apart, flat on my heels, like that was going to do something, making myself small, but that was what I was thinking: get down, maybe he hadn't seen me already. Just stay out of his sight.

Gang's elbow rested on the hood of the cab. His face blank. Uncomprehending. These things didn't happen at his factories, in his town.

I looked up and Dad wasn't at the window. I felt this instinct to slip the red armband off and slink away, belly crawl down the canteen alley and back to the house. Why put your father through more pain? I felt the clammy air weighing against me, my knees shaking. No, that's deserting, I told myself. You can't desert an army you joined ten minutes ago. You aren't a deserter. You're scared—that's all.

I inched away from the door. A short distance back from the gate, Gang lifted the receiver to his mouth. The speaker mounted on top of the Humvee crackled and his voice boomed around us in Chinese.

The crowd stirred. Ivy was facing the demonstrators. A dark oval of sweat on the back of her cotton shirt. She shouted into a bullhorn, first in Chinese then in English, all for YouTube, for the outside world watching, which didn't even seem possible to me right now—that there was an outside, that it wasn't just us here alone.

"How are we trespassing?" Ivy said. "We invite you to listen. But you order us to leave immediately."

Gang spoke again. Louder, angrier. Only in Chinese.

There was a stirring on both sides. Everyone seemed to take two steps forward.

"He calls us traitors to the country," Zhang said from up on top of the rolling ladder. "Enemy of the people. Terrorists. Threatens us to go back to work *or else*. They built a fortune off our backs and now they want to teach us another lesson. For speaking up, we deserve a beating?"

The demonstrators' voices grew louder, a rolling slur of confusion and anger. Hisses and boos.

I turned back to Gang. He barked an order and the officers lowered the shields over their faces. The black canisters of tear gas hooked to their rigger belts shimmered in the heat. They patted the magazines jutting out of their rifles. I heard the clatter of boots and vests. Gang was losing patience.

Ivy was yelling into the bullhorn at the demonstrators, "Stay peaceful. Stay back from the gate. This is a peaceful strike. Stay back. Forward is trouble. Don't provoke. We stick together."

A noise came up from the crowd. They were pushing toward the gate, tightly clotted. Faces blurred by me. Sweat glistened. Sinewy, sunken cheeks. Angry. Who were these people? Were they really ready to die now?

Across from them, the police came forward in slow vine steps, strafing toward the gate.

Ivy looked over at me.

I froze.

She nodded my attention toward the policemen. A desperate look on her face.

I shook my head no.

She put the bullhorn down on the ground.

I shook my head again. "Get out of there," I shouted, waving her away.

Ivy turned slowly to face Gang and took a step forward, then another, and suddenly there were two other girls beside her and all three girls linked arms and walked several more steps forward, shoulder to shoulder, and they lay down on the ground in the middle of the gate blocking Gang's way.

My throat tightened. It couldn't be the plan. She hadn't meant this. She was panicking. She thought it was all going to shit and the only way to save the workers now was to sacrifice herself.

I looked beyond the girls to the Humvee. Gang, balanced on the running board, braced against the half-open door, slammed his fist against the roof of the truck and shouted orders in both languages now: *fēn-sàn,* disperse; *fàng-qì,* give up. Again and again, his voice rolled over me.

"I am the Secretary of Foshan Municipal Party Committee," he shouted, using his full title, his voice tense and strained.

But why wasn't he throwing the tear gas already? Or sending in his officers? He was grandstanding almost. Maybe Gang didn't want this to get out of hand. Didn't want to lose control of the situation.

I looked straight ahead to Zhang and I pointed to Ivy lying in the road. I shouted, even if he couldn't hear me, "What is she doing? What the fuck is she doing?"

Zhang scrambled down the ladder. To get the girls up I was sure. To stop this. But when he reached the ground he didn't go for Ivy or the two women. Instead he stood in front of the wheelbarrows of shoe lasts and cement glue at the foot of the rolling ladder—and he grabbed one of the shoe lasts from the pyramid, lifted it over his head and shouted to the workers, to the smartphones still rolling video, "Don't give them your neck to chop. They won't hesitate to shoot us. Don't act surprised. Come on. Self-defense. Grab a shoe and charge them. Throw hard as you can."

My mind wobbled.

The shoe lasts and cans of flammable cement glue—these aren't props for the strike, you fool, they're ammunition. This was his plan all along.

The crowd came forward a few more steps, blocking my view of Zhang.

All right. You're running out of time. First things first. Stop Zhang. He wasn't far off. Twenty yards. The width of the courtyard. Across the road. Only a short distance off but I needed to fight through the crowd to reach him.

I started clawing my way through. I could knock Zhang on his ass but that would only start a riot. He wanted that. I needed the workers on my side. I needed a translator.

I stopped. I scanned the crowd, searching their faces. Suddenly there was the wide-open shirt, the chest scar shaped like a rampike.

"Hongjin," I shouted, but he sailed past. Didn't hear. I took two quick steps and reached for his shoulder.

"Lǎobǎn," he said. Boss.

I leaned close to his ear. "Zhang wants a massacre," I told him. "I need you to translate."

Working our way back through the crowd, we quickly reached Zhang, whose eyes widened when he saw me.

He cocked his arm back, ready to hurl the shoe.

I froze.

Zhang had a breakaway group surrounding him. Twenty workers—some armed with lasts, others dousing the *huábiǎo* statue with flammable cement glue. They were going to light it on fire.

I started shouting to them, "Stop," over and over, while Hongjin repeated it in Chinese, *Tíngzhǐ*, loud, like metal scraping metal in my head.

The breakaway group turned to look at us; their faces puzzled.

"Put the shoes down," I said to the workers in the breakaway group. Hongjin beside me translating. "Don't throw. Put them down. Get back. This isn't the way. This won't change anything."

Zhang was yelling, "He's one of them. A government puppet."

Their heads shifted back and forth between me and Zhang.

"Listen to me, please," I yelled. "If you provoke them," I said, pointing toward the gate, "everything I told you during the rally that we can do will disappear forever."

Zhang, standing in the middle of their group, reached into his pocket, took out a lighter and started toward the *huábiǎo* statue standing ten feet away.

"Hold him!" I shouted to the workers, pointing at Zhang. "Stop him! Or everything I said, everything Ivy said, the whole vision, will burn up with it."

Hongjin repeated it and suddenly the two men closest to Zhang grabbed his arms, twisted him away, heels skidding, carried back away from the *huábiǎo*.

Zhang looked at me hard but then his gaze shifted over my shoulder.

I turned.

Beyond the gate, Gang took his hat off slowly and flung it into the cab. Then he dipped his shoulder and sank behind the wheel, pulling the door closed behind him.

Zhang's voice behind me, "It takes blood, Alex. Sacrifice."

He gave me this sly closed-mouth smile. No joy to it though. A certitude maybe that he was saying what deep down I'd always known.

I heard the growl of the Humvee engine.

Before me, a few yards ahead, lay the girls in the road.

I was moving forward. Fists doubled.

Gang revved the engine now.

It was a short distance to the mouth of the gate, maybe twenty-five quick strides on a sharp angle. I pressed.

Suddenly the Humvee rolled forward, headed straight for Ivy, but slowly, still giving them a chance to stand up and surrender, but I knew they wouldn't. And he wouldn't either.

A few more steps and I passed the girls on my right without looking down, I was just enough past them and I had to stop Gang and he was still coming and now I was in that empty no-man's land between the girls on the ground and the Humvee and I stopped. I stood between the workers lying on the ground and the oncoming truck, my feet planted shoulder width apart.

The Humvee was twenty yards away and rolling and I squared myself in front of the radiator and Gang was coming, the gleaming fender pointing at my chest, the truck crawling forward, a terrible stretching slowness. The engine gurgled, pattered, and I smelled exhaust and cow shit. I saw the outline of Gang's face through the tinted windshield, ten yards off, and I wavered, a faint voice saying to run, to get the fuck out, but I forced my knees to lock.

I could try to stop him with a flip of my palm, but that seemed absurd, somehow, to do that with everyone watching, but what else was there? All it takes is standing here, I told myself. You must stand here with your arms heavy by your side, the world dissolving in the flared headlamps.

Here I am.

I brace myself. Squint my eyes.

The squeal of brakes, the chrome brush guard stops an

inch from my belt buckle, the fluted hood of the truck pant-
ing, the radiator hissing, a plume of road dirt cast into the
air, rises, sinks.

Then the window on the driver's side slid down.

The sun hammered down on my neck, but I didn't bother
to wipe the sweat away. I stood still. Hearing my own breathing. I didn't want to face him.

I took a deep breath and walked to the open car window.
His eyes stayed fixed ahead.

"You ready to confess?" he asked after a long moment.

A spike in my throat. I looked into the cab. On the seat
beside him sat a snub-nosed revolver.

"What do you mean?" I said, trying to buy time.

His neck stiffened. He turned his head.

"You are liar," he said. Deep folds in his brow. "This going
to be big trouble for you."

I had to speak. Had to cop to something. Any second he
could reach for that revolver.

"You betrayed me," he said. "China. Your father. No more
home now."

I put my hands on the sill of his window. "Sometimes," I
said. This made no sense. Neither the gesture, nor the word.
My heart thumped. I sometimes lie? Was that better?

"You have come here to overthrow the government. This
is your plan, true?"

This picture rippled through me: Gang leading them out
to a field, making them kneel, hands tied behind their backs,
facing a freshly dug ditch, the cold snub-nose pressed to Ivy's
temple, and Gang flipping his chin, saying, *Shoot them all.
Then burn the bodies.*

There was that side of Gang too. Not just the pragmatist.

He revved the engine and I felt it in my legs. The moment
stretched. He wasn't going to shoot me, I realized. He was

going to kill. Ivy. Hongjin. Die Jo. I'd failed. I couldn't even get myself killed right.

I had to speak fast. But calm.

"Okay, yes," I said. "I lied to you."

Gang stared at me. His dead milky left eye somehow more alive than the good one. I couldn't read his face.

"Gang," I said, softening my voice. "I want you to just look over on the balcony of the dorms. Fifth floor."

I pointed to the left and Gang's line of sight followed my finger. He peered forward, a shadow falling over his face.

"See her with the iPhone? Now look to the roof. You see the iPhone up there, Gang? It's pointing right at you now. It's pointing at us. Look at the girl with glasses up on the corner of the roof. See her? And see over there," I said, pointing right, to Plant B. "You see those girls filming, leaning out of the windows? Plant C. Closer to us. And kneeling there on the ground down by the gate, see them? And crouching on top of the vans with the red bandanas, see them?"

I watched his eyes tack back and forth even when I'd stopped talking. I let it sit with him for a moment, all those iPhones.

"Have you heard about YouTube, Gang?" I asked. "I think you got VPN, you've seen YouTube, haven't you? Of course. Here's what they're going to see, Gang, they're going to see you in this Humvee and three beautiful girls lying in front of you and you're running over them and killing them. Fifty million people are going to see that around the world. You're going to embarrass Beijing. You're going to make them look like murderers, just as you want more foreign companies to come in here. Jobs are way down, stocks way down, everything down—now you go and do this and you'll be remembered as the guy who lost China."

His jaw twitched. Grinding his teeth. His mind grinding too as his eyes jumped from one iPhone to the next. All angles covered. All the spots that Zhang had meticulously planned—I used them, used Zhang's own plan against him, drawing Gang's attention to every position.

"What are they going to think in Beijing when they see you drive over these women?" I asked. My tone was almost kind, cloying. "To you they're expendable, interchangeable people, but what are they going to think around the world? What are businesspeople going to think? You know. I know you know. And now what is Beijing going to think about you when the businesspeople are all thinking that?"

I let that sit with him for a moment.

"We don't have much time, Gang," I said. "You got to decide. You decide what happens next. Imagine what's going to be the next scene streamed live. In that little movie they're filming. Let's say you send your officers in to clear the yard. The workers—they're ready to fight. What are the soldiers going to do? Throw tear gas. Hit kids, half of these are kids and old ladies, you know, hit them with nightsticks, and then, I'm going to tell you something, they have weapons too, Molotovs, homemade. So your officers lift their rifles. Even if it's just rubber bullets. Still there's a bloodbath all over the internet."

Here I paused again and let those images sink in. His hands restless on the wheel. He kept shifting his gaze back and forth between all those iPhones. Not saying anything. Which meant he was listening, didn't it? He was choosing.

"You're the enemy in that movie, Gang," I said, still in that cordial voice. "You'll make Beijing the enemy. You probably want a different ending. So listen, because we don't have much time. Imagine, in this next ending, you're going to step out of the cab, Gang, you're going to walk over there, you're going to help pick those girls up off the ground and you're going to shake hands. You put your arm around them and say, 'Calm down and go back in. We can work out a solution.' Just because you say that doesn't mean you've changed policies or that your profits go down. It's already done. I mean, this is already streaming. Going out to the world. If you want to keep your 8 percent growth, they got to understand that a thing like this can be defused peacefully. Beijing and the business world need to believe you got things under control."

His hands dropped from the wheel.

Finally he turned to face me. He nodded slowly.

He understood.

A flick of his wrist shooed me away from the door. The cab door opened and he stepped onto the running board in his shiny black boots. He took off his right glove, tucked it under his armpit and walked out in front of the truck.

Then he reached out his arm, barely bent at the waist, and extended his hand to Ivy.

From the ground, Ivy glanced at me briefly, then back to Gang. Her arm came up slowly and she reached out her hand to his and the crowd of workers drew close, so they were standing right behind the girls on the ground and the iPhone shooters pushed their way to the front to film it as Gang helped her up off the ground.

There was the noise of the crowd clapping and I saw Zhang come forward, glaring at me, but he shook Gang's hand and soon they were all fake-smiling and posing for photographs.

Someone thrust the microphone into Gang's hand and he waved the police officers forward so they were shoulder to shoulder with the demonstrators, still wearing their riot helmets, and Gang spoke about the big truce.

The Chinese Dream—that's what Gang kept talking about. President Xi Jinping had been drilling that doctrine into everyone's head for years. No one believed it anymore. There was a lot of talk about gestures of friendship, which was how you knew it was all bullshit probably. That Gang was talking about gestures of friendship, not real friendship, and I looked up to the fourth-floor window.

I had to find him. Though it wasn't all clear in my head what I intended to say to Dad.

But I didn't need to stay around for the photo-op, the fake smiles and handshakes, the crowd all pushing in, trying to get their picture taken with this man they'd wanted to hack apart a moment ago.

Right before I could pull away, I heard Gang's voice.

"No one was hurt." He stared at me coldly, and glanced at the workers holding iPhones close to us. Filming us talking. "I hope," he added.

"Lucky," I said.

He forced a fake smile and gave a sharp nod. "Tomorrow," he said sternly, "we discuss the future."

Then he leaned in close to my ear and whispered, "Everything is going to go back to normal and you know it."

"Tomorrow," I said.

"You have no idea how little you have done."

"Tomorrow," I said.

He flashed a smile to the girl holding the iPhone right beside his shoulder and then he turned around.

I snuck out of the circle and walked back into the factory yard.

I was headed for the glass doors of the admin building, but then I stopped myself. I didn't go up there. I didn't know what I wanted to say. To him. To Ivy. So I stood there like a schmuck, my world in two pieces, and I went straight back to my house and it was much later when Ivy came back, after I heard the Humvee pulling away and the loud cheers rise up from the yard.

It was evening. No human sound, just the cicadas fiddling, frogs lowing in the rain gutters, and Ivy and I sat in my little kitchen eating frozen durian, chopped in half, and we dug into the smooth and sweet and funky meat with a spoon. She had one half, I had the other.

We were silent for a while. Looking at each other. The spikes of the rind pressed into my palm. The adrenaline only now starting to settle. But I still felt my skin tingle and my legs were all rubbery.

I put my durian back in the freezer and I stood for a long time in front of the open door, feeling the cold on my face. Then I went and sat back down beside Ivy, who kept taking one more spoonful and saying, "No more," and she licked the back of the spoon and pushed the frozen fruit away, but then taking one last bite, and sighing, and pushing it again, farther each time, until finally it was out of arm's reach. When she couldn't push it away any farther, she drew her feet up onto the seat of the chair, knees to her chest.

"The others told me," she said, pausing. "Zhang wanted violence."

"He would've gotten you run over."

"I trusted him," she said. "And he betrayed me."

"I know," I said.

"It was his plan all along."

"You won't work with Zhang," I said. "Right?"

She laughed. "No. Never. He only wants a military coup. This is not a good answer to our problems."

"I'm sorry," I said.

"Thank you," she said. And I could tell she wanted to say more or clarify what she was thanking me for. Instead, she said, "The speech you made. You mean all this? A real Chinese national product here. At this plant. Do you really believe this can work?"

"I think so," I said.

She looked off for a moment. A crease of worry on her forehead.

"What about the rest of China?" she said. "What you suggest works for *this* plant only."

"I don't know. I can't do anything about the rest of China. Isn't it enough to start here?"

She nodded.

"Your way means China depends on outsiders. Outsiders to invent product to make the plant profitable. This won't work. Do you see? We need this for ourselves."

"The brand is for them, the workers, as much as for me." I was irritated. She'd called me an outsider twice. Drawing some sort of line. "But it has to be from the top down. At first." I shook my head. "What's going on here?"

"Zhang failed me and your vision is more outsiders coming in. Between that, no place for me."

Her eyes strained, but her voice was flat, calm.

I sensed what she meant, but I didn't dare say it. Or ask.

And we said no more.

She went off to bed.

Seventeen

BUT I DON'T SLEEP. IT'S ALMOST OVER. ALL OF IT.
I go to the window to look outside and the whole night nearly passes. I rode that houseboat on the Pearl River all the way here, and now it is very late and the air is thick and tight, and I'm looking at the tattered banners swinging from the factory windows, and what people will see on YouTube tomorrow will maybe lead to the next protest, and the next one. And one of these times the Chinese won't lower their guns. They'll shoot. Rubber bullets the first time; real ones the second. This started way before me.

And us?

I love her. But I keep hearing Ivy's words, *You're not home in the revolution. You're not home here. You're still an outsider.*

But she hadn't said that. No, she never said that. I'm saying it. Of course I don't belong there.

What's so bad about being a Jew?

Once we were so powerful we had to be expelled, imprisoned, burned to ash. Marked for murder because we were too big to live.

But in America I was just another white person. Born into bland nothingness. We all were. Look, act the same as the rest.

Incinerated by sameness.

So maybe I came to China to be hated. Important enough to be loathed again. To make a name. A brand. In his own way, a shoe man can stand out.

I turn around and Ivy is sitting up in bed watching me. Her face is in the shadow but the rest of her I can see, the outline of her body under the white sheet and her one leg twisted outside of it.

"Come to bed," she says.

"How long have you been up?"

She doesn't answer.

I get into bed under the cool sheets. She hooks her leg between mine. Her feet are cold. She stares at me. Our heads on the pillow and the smell of the clean linens and with the blue light from the moon behind me, her face in shadow, I can't tell if she's smiling or not, even though we're inches away. Our noses almost touching.

"You will talk to him?" she asks. "Your father."

"I have to. In the morning."

She kisses me slow and sweet. She draws me near. The ceiling fan thumps softly overhead. No, she is smiling for sure. Running her hand through my hair.

Then I feel a shift in her.

She gently places her palm flat against my chest.

"You are going to tell him?" she says.

"Tell what?"

"Tell him you're the Emperor. This is the silly name he calls himself, right?"

I shake my head. "No more empires."

She smiles. "You must speak to him."

"You'd make a much better Emperor anyhow."

"Maybe," she says. "But not here. This is your place."

I feel my heart sink.

"I need you here," I say.

"The goal is much bigger."

"Why are you saying this?"

"Because it is true." A sadness in her tone. "Here is not enough."

Her eyes widen. It takes me a moment to understand.

Then it's quiet and we both are realizing that we are in bed for the last time together.

I lift my hand to her cheek and my palm is burning.

She smiles. "It's okay. You know your job is here. If you want to help, this is your small corner of the revolution. This is how it starts. Small. What other way is there? A coup? Another dictator?"

I knew she was right. I didn't want to know it. I wanted to unknow the whole thing and make her stay.

"I'll tell him," I say. It catches in my throat.

I ache for her. To make this last. But it starts to sink in. No more. She senses it too. She's pinching me tighter with her legs.

When the sun rises, I'll have to put one foot in front of the other for the rest of my life.

And I'm already crying.

She swipes at her eyes with the back of her wrist. "I wanted your father to like me."

"Impossible," I say. "I don't think he even likes me."

She laughs. Shaking a few tears loose. She wipes them off.

I'm aching for her even as she's an inch away. I'm nearly blind from it. From looking so hard into the shadow of her face. And she knows me, which is why she can say these things. And I know her. I do. In this moment I am sure of it. Sure that this is the closest I've ever felt to another human being. Complete.

"What if something happens to you?" I say.

"I explained before. Everything for China."

"I'm no Emperor," I say.

"You are the rabbi, yes? The rabbi of shoes."

"Ha. No, not that either. Something different."

"You will think of it. I am confident."

"You won't sleep, will you?" I ask. "Tonight." It's a teenage thing to say. Like falling asleep with the phones against our ears.

"No. Will you?"

"No."

But we do. Both of us. Our eyes get heavy and we try to fight it but that makes us fall asleep even faster.

When I wake in the morning, I open my eyes and she's not here. What is here? She's put a mint from the Intercontinental Hotel on the crisp white pillow where her head had lain.

I smile. I sit up and say her name. Ivy. I say it again. I listen for the shower. I say it again. Louder. In Chinese this time. Even though I know. And then I stop. She's gone.

That is it. She's vanished into the plant. Into me. And she's gone on to do bigger work.

I cross the yard and head inside the admin building, a quick scent of incense from the altar table in the lobby, and I decide I want to run up the stairs. I pull open the door to the stair-well, and take the stairs two at a time, this tightness growing in my chest as I push forward against the thick heavy air, and then I'm jogging over the terrazzo floor in the corridor and there's Dad's office up ahead and I grab the doorjamb with my hand and swing myself square in the center of the frame, breathless. Dad's facing the window, hands folded behind his back, like he's still listening to the crowd cheer, and the noise quiets and my breathing with it.

Without turning around, Dad says, "You ruined us. I hope you're happy. No one will touch us now. We're dead."

"We're not dead," I say. "We're changing. They're telling us what they want."

Then he turns around slowly and holds the back of his chair.

"Help me understand what kind of moron stands in front of a truck," he says.

When I don't answer he sighs and starts walking toward me and we meet at the center of his office.

"All these years I put into you—for you to throw spite, throw shit at me, after I made you. Trained. Invested. What did I tell you after you signed? The one rule. In the van. One rule."

"Don't fuck your own family."

"That's right. And what did you do?"

"You know you lied to me the whole time," I say. "You could've told me. Any of it."

He pushes me away. "Lied? I protected you. When it's time to tell, I tell. Oh, wipe that look off your face. You're going to judge me? Because I got my hands dirty. This is the world. We do things we don't like. You think I liked going to shul every Friday with the hardest seats in the world, so my *tuchus* hurt three days after. No. But I went. You do what it takes."

"That's what I'm doing," I say.

His eyes widen.

"Let me say something," I say. "And I want you to listen. Really try and listen."

"Look what you did," he says, pointing out the window to the courtyard.

"Look at me when I say this, please. You won't like it. But let me talk. I'm going to make this brand. I won't do it private label. We're going to make it here as a brand at no profit for the first few seasons."

"Are you fucking nuts? You'll ruin us."

"It's for them," I say. "They risked everything to be out there."

"Who gives a fuck?" he says. "This isn't about them."

"But it is."

His face goes slack. Uncomprehending. What can I say to him to make it clear? Gang's path is profit by any means; Zhang's is bloody revolution, but this is the third way, and I was doing it for all of us.

It's something Dad will never understand. That's why he tried to steal it. It was the very thing separating me from my father, so of course he had to steal it. Possess it. All that was between us.

"You're going to make the brand?" Dad asks.

"That's right. I'm going to make *Alex & Ivy*—" and that just slips out. I'd meant to finesse it. Wait for the right time, pick my spot, but it's out now.

"What is—" he asks, slow and strained. "Is that the name of the brand? What kind of *farshtunken* name is that? For her? You did all this for the farmer?"

I stare at him cold.

"Jesus fucking Christ, Alex." He takes a breath and speaks in a low, confiding voice. "Alex, tell me, am I supposed to give all my money away to beggars and we live homeless so everyone can be happy? This you want? I should give it away. Out of the kindness of my heart. You want me to give Ivy money?"

"I never said that."

"I can't understand," he stammers. "The name. Not Bernie? Not Fedor and Alex? Which would fucking make sense by the way. Since I am your father. You and me. Not even *us*? Listen, honey—" he actually says *honey*, like I'm five. "Alex, honey, we've got to understand each other to make this thing work. We *have* to be on the same page."

"Maybe we don't," I say.

He shakes his head like I slapped him. "What does that mean?"

"I'm going to do this my way."

"Your way—" he says. His lip trembles.

"I want my name on this. You're happy to sit here and fuck Karri and ignore everything that's happening right under your nose in China and have other people's labels on your work. So, fine. But that's not the future for me or for this factory."

"What's going on here?"

I look at him hard. "Maybe we don't need you."

He straightens up. His face bloodless, drained.

"What?" he asks. Louder.

I swallow hard. Feels like there's a spike in my throat. "I said maybe we just don't need you."

"Gonif!" he yells, pointing at me with a shaky finger. "Luftmensch! Shitbum!"

Before I can make sense of anything, he's driving me backward with his finger and big barrel chest, yelling, "You want to take it. Then take it. Really take it. You're gonna have to take it. Punch me."

I stop backing up. There's a burn in my chest where he keeps poking me.

"Do it," he says, steeling his voice. "You want it that bad. Hit me. Take it from me."

I hold my fists down by my hips. My breaths coming hard. His bushy white eyebrows all buckled up.

"Either you hit me or I hit you. Got it? You choose."

I cock my arm. I tighten my grip. I watch his shoulder muscles move beneath his shirt, a heat in my wrists and at my throat and temples. This ripple across my shoulders ferreting its way down to my fingers. Just swing. Cuff him in the temple. Put your weight into it. Step in and swing.

"See," he says, "this is why I can't leave you in charge. You're a coward. Come on. Hit me. Take it from me."

"You're pathetic," I say, unclenching my fists.

He wavers a little. Swaying on his feet.

"Who are you?" he says in a wobbly thin voice. He takes a step back, chest heaving. "I don't know you," he says under his breath.

Then he turns and walks around the corner of his desk and slumps into his chair. His shoulders pinch forward. Elbows on the desk. Hands up by his ears like he's about to cover them.

Then he makes a sound. A sob in the back of his throat that makes the hair on my neck stand up. A *krechtz*.

He does it again and I wince.

This *krechtz*—my grandfather explained—it's a type of Yiddish klezmer note played on a violin. Sounds like warbling heartache. A real sorrow. One of them lurches out of Dad's throat. It grabs me cold from behind and I shiver.

His fists are balled up by his head and he sniffs hard and looks down at the desk.

"I'm fine," he says, trying to maintain his normally dignified stare. He looks straight at me. "I'm fine."

I don't say anything. A long beat of silence.

"I'm going now, Dad," I say. "I have meetings."

No answer. I hold the door handle tight. I should say something to ease the awkwardness. Or the sadness.

"You going to be all right?" I ask.

No answer.

I wait a moment. Then I turn and step into the hallway.

Eighteen

IN THE BRIGHT LOBBY OF THE INTERCONTINEN-
tal Foshan, Dad stops with his bags in his hand and turns to
face me.

Hong Kong, he said earlier at breakfast. A little R & R.
There's an Interconti with a hot tub on the roof looking out
over the ships in the harbor. But I know it's really because
we're starting production on my line this morning. Four link
lines. Three hundred yards of conveyor belt. The perfect ge-
ometry of it. That's where I'm headed once he's gone. Straight
to the factory.

"You got your passport?" I say, meaning please stay.

Of course, he says, but he pats the breast pocket of his new
safari shirt anyway just to make sure. Then he holds out his
sleeve.

"*Expedition* grade," he says. "One hundred thirty percent
UV protection Australian bush shirt. Feel."

I reach out and rub it gently between my fingers—for a
moment too long probably. I figure I ought to let him decide
when it's enough.

"Soft," I say, firm and clear, meaning I love you.

"Durable," Dad says low, meaning screw that but me too.

"Quality," I say, pitching my voice low like Dad's, the two of us basically grunting like apes, somehow communicating perfectly.

First me bush shirt, now you bush shirt.

He pulls his arm away.

He says, "You sure you don't want to share the van?"

"It's the opposite direction," I say. "I'll catch a cab."

His face draws down. "Well," he says. "Goodbye."

I have to fight off the old impulse to crumble. To give him what he wants. Smooth everything over.

We stare at each other for a moment.

"Goodbye," I say to Dad.

I hug him and he gets one clumsy forearm across my back and squeezes, a quick pulse, it lasts only a second and then I step back.

He chews his lower lip for a second, like he's got more to say. His hand comes up and pats my shoulder, then he turns and walks out of the lobby, avoiding the revolving doors as always, out into the pool of sunlight into the roundabout where Jianguo carries Dad's bags to the van and helps him into the back seat facing backward as always.

I watch the van disappear into the traffic and my shoulder's tingling, like he's some sawed-off phantom limb my brain keeps sending signals to. I shouldn't have let him go. A man like that isn't safe in the wild. A man who'll never remember that beets turn his pee red. *I'm dying, Alex, come see—you'll want to see this.*

I bet he isn't staying in Hong Kong. You can't trust a man like that. So where then? Home? And where's that? The States, maybe. He isn't crying, is he? In the van. God, I hope not. No, he wouldn't. He's fine.

But this image flips through my head of him standing alone in one of those outlet malls in Freeport, Maine, staring at the additional 40% off sign on a rack of his own shoes, telling a pimply sales associate, "I made those," and the kid giving him this look like, "Sure you did," and then Dad, in a trance, shuffles out into the bright atrium, hands in his pockets like some old ghost of the shtetl, and in every direction there's discount stores and chain restaurants. He'd rather starve. It's not home. It's hell. *His* hell. His Pale of Settlement. This shitty outlet mall dumping his designs. A cemetery of last looks. The overstocked, the seconds, the blemished, the unwanted—Jesus, I bet he's sobbing in the van. He knows. There's nowhere to go.

The room seems to wobble and this dark, terrible vision crystalizing: nothing will change.

But then I feel heat rising up my collar and I'm thinking, Nah, that's not it, not by a long shot.

Forget Dad. Everyone's gone. It's only me here. I tell myself that. Here's me.

All I have to do is focus on what's in front of me: a strip of red carpet tressed with gold vines and leaves between me and the revolving doors leading outside.

I fall in with the stream of suits trailing cool aftershave and wheeling their monographed briefcases, always dragging their names behind them. See. That's all it is. A name. Cohen. Not some invisible brand on your forehead.

The lobby's loud with cell phone chatter, but as I'm walking, this feeling slowly gathers in me, something still and quiet, like when I first stepped into Ivy's fake house in her village and there was French cottage wallpaper, but you knew it was holy, more holy than an ancient temple—that's the feeling I have suddenly here in the lobby of the Intercontinental Foshan with the light pouring in from the windows. This is where I belong. It's like being inside an old shul during the Days of

Awe when the Cohains cover their heads, slip off their shoes and chant for the next world, and all the while you're sitting up with the women in the balcony behind a curtain and it all sounds like gibberish because that's not the holy part; what's holy is sitting between your mother's legs on the floor and her toes are red as blood and her hair's not her own, it's sewn from others whose lives you can only imagine, and your father is already halfway around the world.

The air pops as I step into the revolving doors and I push the glass with my hand and then spill out into the bright morning sun. Warm on my arms.

A taxi waiting on the curb.

One of the doormen rushes forward and opens the taxi door for me.

"Mr. Younger Cohen?" he asks.

I look at his face. He's new. Trying to learn everyone's name. Nervous. Eyes darting. The faintest growth, more longing than mustache, above his lip. A boy.

"Alex," I correct him. Feels like I say it too fast.

He apologizes.

I smile at him. "It's fine," I say. I reach into my pocket and palm him about ten bucks. A good tip. Start off right.

He closes his fist around the money and gives me a quick head bow.

"You'll be seeing a lot of me," I say and duck into the cab.

★ ★ ★ ★ ★

Acknowledgments

MY LOVE AND DEEPEST RESPECT TO MY DAD, who's done everything in his life with dignity and integrity, putting his family first. Dad, thank you for encouraging me to find my own way.

I want to thank my mom for always taking me to the Andover Public Library and passing along her passion for reading and literature. I love you dearly.

And to my brilliant sister, Laura, thank you for being my first reader, my biggest supporter, and for making me read *The Master and Margarita*.

A huge, undying debt of gratitude to my mentor, my Cus D'Amato, my dear friend Bob Butler. What a ride. I can't begin to express my admiration for you.

Taylor, my true love and best friend—thank you for your wisdom and kindness, and for keeping me afloat. I look up to you in so many ways.

I also want to extend my thanks to my incredible agent, Duvall Osteen, for her humor and patience, and to my editor,

John Glynn, for recognizing something in this book and being its brilliant champion.

I offer my most sincere appreciation to the following people for their friendship, guidance and generosity: Karri Liu, EJ Liu, Fred Huang, Vega Leung and Bob Infantino. And of course, thanks for the love and support of Marni Wise and Eric Wilner. This book couldn't exist without all your help.

THE EMPEROR OF SHOES

SPENCER WISE

Reader's Guide

HANOVER
SQUARE
PRESS

INTRODUCTION

The Emperor of Shoes *is a timely, urgent novel about a son, his father and their family's legacy shoe factory in southern China. It's also about Ivy, a seamstress and embedded political organizer who has infiltrated the shoe factory in hopes of organizing its workers. Debut novelist Spencer Wise draws on his own experiences living and working in a shoe factory in southern China to bring this dramatic milieu to life. As the story barrels toward an explosive climax, every character must form their notions of morality, weighing the costs of loyalty within the realities of today's complex globalized world.*

QUESTIONS FOR DISCUSSION

1. Discuss the evolution of Alex's relationship with his father. In what ways does Alex defiantly forge his own path and in what ways is he hemmed in by his father's expectations? Where does the end of the novel leave this father-son relationship?

2. Ghosts, or *gweilos*, appear throughout the book. How does the figure of the phantom function within the context of Foshan and its factories? What or who are the novel's ghosts haunting? What truths do these specters reveal?

3. Bernie identifies Alex and himself as "Inbetweeners"— the "middle step" between America and China. How does Alex embody this intermediary role? Where do you see his sense of identity shifting and redefining itself? Is there a kind of freedom that comes from his in-between state and unstable identity?

4. What part does Alex and Ivy's romance play in the factory workers' revolution? Does one exist without the other, or are they inseparably tied together?

5. Who is the emperor of shoes? Do multiple characters share this title? Does the label shift from one person to another as the story goes on? What is the significance of "emperor" as a title—why not be the king, tsar or president of shoes?

6. What makes Ivy a revolutionary? Where do we see her fighting for change or challenging societal norms? How does she reconcile her respect for cultural tradition with the realities of her contemporary moment?

7. The southern China of *The Emperor of Shoes* is in many ways built upon divisions—distinctions between the Americans and the Chinese, between foreign capitalists and factory workers, between father and son, between the countryside and the city and so on. However, how does the novel go about breaking down these divisions in a setting in which they seem so apparent? What happens when these lines are blurred?

8. Discuss the role of faith in this novel. In what ways does it shape certain characters' identities? How does it intersect with notions of history and ancestry?

9. A variety of languages are used in this book, such as English, Cantonese and Yiddish. How does language operate as a barrier and a bridge? Do the characters always need a shared tongue to communicate? Are there any moments in which information or meaning gets lost in translation?

10. What does it mean to find peace "in a place where I stood out so goddamn bad that I finally fit in?" Where is this place for Alex? Where is this place for Ivy or Fedor? Where is this place for you?

11. What does the novel suggest about personal responsibility in a world in which it's easier than ever to pass the buck?

12. Ivy and Alex's connection is partly based on a mutual sense of loss. For instance, there's a parallel between the loss of Chinese traditions and the attenuating role of religion in Jewish American life. What does the book suggest happens when we shed these defining traditions and customs? How do we know what is worth ceding or preserving?